# COLD
# FEET

## Patricia
## Weaver
## Francisco

**SIMON AND SCHUSTER**
New York London Toronto Sydney Tokyo

**SIMON AND SCHUSTER**
SIMON & SCHUSTER BUILDING
ROCKEFELLER CENTER
1230 AVENUE OF THE AMERICAS
NEW YORK, NEW YORK 10020

DESIGNED BY NINA D'AMARIO/LEVAVI & LEVAVI
MANUFACTURED IN THE UNITED STATES OF AMERICA

1   3   5   7   9   10   8   6   4   2

LIBRARY OF CONGRESS CATALOGING IN PUBLICATION DATA

FRANCISCO, PATRICIA WEAVER.
COLD FEET.
I. TITLE.
PS3556.R3315C65      1988   813'.54      88-18305
ISBN 0-671-63165-9

Chapters from this novel have appeared previously, in slightly different form, in
*Great River Review*, and the anthology *Believing Everything* (Holy Cow! Press).

FOR TIMOTHY, WITH LOVE.
MY PARENTS, HARRIET AND JOSEPH, WITH THANKS
AND THE FOREST STREET IRREGULARS.

I would like to express my gratitude to the Bush Foundation and to the Minnesota State Arts Board for providing financial support for the writing of this book, and to the Ragdale Foundation for its invaluable support.

# COLD
# FEET

1

THE FIRST THING he noticed was the women. They strode past him, looking more than ever like a different species. Since he'd been away they'd closed up like morning glories at dusk. Their arms were full, clutching briefcases; shopping bags with the names of stores he'd never heard of spelled out in pink and mauve; and babies, bundled against the cold in soft quilted sacks. Six years before, he'd left them flowing through the streets of Ann Arbor in loose skirts, colors drifting across the grass, their hair wild, eyes naked. At least that was what Yoder remembered. It had seemed then as if the world were a street dance on a summer day.

He'd arrived the night before. Unable to hitch a ride across the border, he'd bought a bus ticket at the Windsor station with his new American dollars. The bus crossed the Detroit River by way of an underwater tunnel. Yoder remembered it from the trip in '70—dim, the tile walls lit with bare yellow bulbs. Every hundred yards a small door appeared in the wall and Yoder imagined the black river on the other side, pressing to get in. The walls seemed to curve under the pressure. How long could mortar hold underwater? His fantasy

had been to return across the high expanse of the Ambassa-
dor Bridge, preferably on a hot summer day when the river
would glisten beneath him, Detroit's humble skyline dissolving into buildings and dirt and stoplights as he became absorbed in the city and began to turn with it. But on this 22nd
day of February, the city looked unceremoniously bleak.

As the bus plunged into the tunnel, a sensation of speed—
of barreling toward a beginning as if over the falls at Niag-
ara—had pinned him to his seat. *Ah, but I was so much older
then....* No one on the bus offered any clue as to what might
await him on the other side. His fellow passengers were
American tourists, clutching maple-leaf souvenirs, thinking
nothing of a day-trip to a foreign country.

In grade school he'd read about "The Man Without A Country," who spent a lifetime criss-crossing the Atlantic, longing
for two countries that would not have him. He had thought
the man ridiculous. But crossing the river, Yoder hoped he
wouldn't be forced to spy on his country from behind the
green windows of a tourist bus. Despite everything that was
wrong with America, he wanted it. America had invented
baseball. It held the Grand Canyon with ease. You could get
hot there. He had learned to fish in America, pulling carp,
sometimes swollen with poison, from the Hudson River. The
hook was still in him, the bleeding down to just a trickle.

At least there was no essay test required for re-entry—no
25 words or less. Yoder imagined what he might say. The
concrete and steel, the fat hands, the discount catalogs and
roadside attractions would have to be suppressed. He would
say: "I'm hoping for the best. I miss my friends. I want to see
the Hudson River, the Blue Ridge Mountains and Crazy
Woman Creek again. I'm giving you bastards another chance.
If you'll all just move over a notch, I'll try to fit right in."
Sorry, too many words—six months hard labor in New
Brunswick.

A sign posted near the windshield cautioned the passengers not to speak to the driver. Yoder studied the sagging
jowls of the black man behind the wheel. The perfect job: So
many people want to talk to you that it's guaranteed no one
will. How to get an arrangement like that with the world?

Yoder leaned out into the aisle. Behind him lay one

hundred doors stretching back to the country of his exile. Six winters. Six years of banishment. The Bad King had been deposed and the minstrel was coming home for the hand of the Princess. Facing forward, he turned toward the ground rushing away beneath him. Toward hot dogs and money, the Mets, McDonalds, and the woman he loved.

He'd give America six months.

The bus slid into the station. Yoder closed his eyes, leaned back into the seat. Safe, at home, he whispered, like an umpire deciding a close call. A baby who had squirmed on his mother's lap throughout the trip let loose a scream whose intensity won Yoder's admiration. In the tunnel, Yoder watched them struggle—the infant grappling at his mother's breast while she bounced him on her knee, trying to distract him. Feed him! Yoder wanted to say, but he couldn't risk making any kind of trouble. He followed them off the bus into customs, relieved to see a female agent on duty. She'd be easier to charm if charming became necessary. It wouldn't have surprised him if amnesty was a code word for entrapment, the way Vietnamization had meant defeat.

The agent's lips were lollipop-red; her hair was cut in shaggy layers like a waterfall down her back. While she cooed over the baby, Yoder smoothed his hair off his forehead, wet his lips, tried to keep from compulsively rocking back and forth on his heels. He fingered the change in his pocket, as nervous as if he were a mule with a load of cocaine drifting in the bottom of his suitcase. The agent's eyes flickered over his body, her hand closed around the leather straps of his knapsack. She rifled through the dirty clothes, glanced at the books lining the bottom, lifted his carved sandalwood box to her ear and shook it.

"It's mostly paper," he said dryly, watching her carefully, desperate with an unjustifiable panic. "Photographs and letters," he added weakly. Finally, she asked him the simple questions, the same ones she had posed to Ms. America before him. He answered in the calm voice he reserved for responding to seemingly simple questions. Destination: Ann Arbor, Michigan. Length of stay: Indefinite. Purpose of travel: He hesitated, then answered: Going home.

Passing into the crowded station, Yoder waited for some

sensation to overtake him, then chided himself for expecting one. For a few seconds he thought: American air, American concrete, American litter, but even that momentary sense of significance quickly dissolved. A bus station like any other— cold and grey and overlit. The orange plastic chairs linked together at the base forced strangers to sit too close to strangers. The green metal newsracks displayed the Detroit Funny Papers—the *News* and the *Free Press*—but he did not buy one. He had no business here. No desire to dart through the huddles of people to seek the falling light on the streets of Detroit. From the first it had been clear that it would not be here, nor to New Jersey that he would return, but to the city he left behind that simple summer midnight.

Approaching the Greyhound ticket counter, Yoder spoke without looking the cashier in the eye. "One ticket. One way. To Ann Arbor," he said, still on guard, too old to completely trust a piece of paper signed by the President. The man selling tickets reminded him of someone—the high waxy forehead, the wire-rimmed glasses flashing in the light over his counter like semaphores. "Bus leaves in five minutes," he said, holding Yoder's eye for what seemed an unnecessary moment. His Forestry Practices professor? Shepard? Was that his name? Would it be like this with everyone?

Nearly alone on the bus, Yoder pressed his forehead to the glass as Detroit flashed by: Auto Parts. Body Shop. Bob's Car Wash. Abandoned cars, flattened wrecks, yards full of cars. No Parking. No gas. Nowhere to turn. A playground of tires, capped in snow. In the middle of the block—a mountain of dirt, a plain white cross planted on top. *Hello,* he whispered. *Hello all you fuckers, I'm back.*

When he'd left six years before, Detroit had been humbled with grief. The '67 riots left forty people—and a city—dead. He'd read about its renaissance—wondered if the reflective tower he glimpsed out the green window was the building meant to save Detroit. Perhaps the city should no longer just be bombed—leveled—and built again from scratch, as he'd once thought. But it looked as if the streets were still speckled with litter, storefront windows X'd with tape and the statues in Grand Circus Park lonely at night. Was this a renaissance? He understood why American flags decorated rich people's lawns but why were they displayed in the windows of the poor?

At the Ann Arbor station, Yoder collected his knapsack and the box of things Julie had packed for him, smiling at the neat string bow and the words "We'll Miss You" written in red magic marker on top. Faded cardboard wolverines decorated the walls, punctuated by signs advising passengers that the management was not responsible. He hummed "Hail To The Victors" without irony and left the station.

Under the cover of night at least, it looked like everything had waited. The Dunkin' Donuts shop glowed pink and gaudy on the corner of Main and Washington. Yoder ducked inside, jingling the new dimes and quarters in his pocket, feeling like he had real money for the first time in years. It was close and warm in the shop, the windows fogged with breath. Two cops sat at the counter and a black woman wearing a pink uniform wiped down the glass cases. Yoder bought a cherry-filled doughnut and two crullers, and sat apart, slowly dipping, scattering crumbs on the surface of his coffee. The woman watched him and he avoided her eyes, afraid she knew that he didn't have an apartment or a telephone number, didn't have a driver's license or a credit card or a dentist he could call in an emergency. He wanted her to know that he'd sat right here at this counter a million times, watching the pink formica crack, spider webs of black grease creeping across its surface. He searched for some way to tell her this. Does Willy Lee still come around here? Say, I remember when doughnuts were a quarter. Instead, he left too big a tip and set out across the dark campus.

The streetlights flared in the cold air, halos around each lamppost. Shrouded in snow, Ann Arbor had always looked provincial, sweet, a Christmas card. He could almost see Sal and Josh and Goldie, like carolers from some fabled era, heaving snowballs into the carved cherry doors of the president's house. WE WANT IT. AND WE WANT IT NOW! Yoder felt a rush of generosity toward every building, each solitary walker. He knew these streets. Somewhere beneath the snow, his footprints marked the sidewalks. One summer he'd dipped his bare feet into a bucket of blue paint and traced a path between three downtown bars. The advertising stunt earned him a week of free burgers at the Del Camino. Surely six winters had not worn those cold blue feet away.

Yoder cut across the grassy Diag to reach the Chemistry Building on central campus, a granite monstrosity whose outer doors were, for some reason, always open. He gave himself five points for remembering, and the town five points for not letting him down. He headed for a bench in the main lobby where he'd slept a few times in the old days. A bronze plaque above the bench quoted some long-dead professor: "When you can't stand up—stand up!" it read. Always a pleasure to stretch out beneath that sign. Yoder tucked his knapsack under his head and let his arms drop to the floor. He was not cold and the hum of the fluorescent lights provided enough company for the moment. From somewhere he heard a train whistle give three long salutes—a sound so American it touched him with a strength unrelated to memory. He was back. Such a simple thing, almost too easy to be trusted. He tried to concentrate on what he wanted. Everything the same? Everything changed? He wanted a blanket, a wool blanket to curl up under and the sound of the train again, moaning through America while he lay safe and warm inside it.

In the morning he would marry Sally. Not right away of course; it would take some doing. A funny word, *marry*. Like the word *sunrise* it meant nothing unless you stood in some clear high spot and paid attention. In the morning he would eat at Pizza Jim's, buy a white rose from the flower woman. If nothing else, he would see Sal and she would see the difference in him—what had changed and what had stayed the same.

In those six years, it had been places more than people that he'd missed in a hard way. Right now...right now, I'd like to be sitting in Pizza Jim's finishing off a double cheese and onion, he would think. A whistle would call up wintry evenings when he'd wait in the shadow of the library and listen to footfalls muffled in snow, someone's high note coming to him clear in the cold air. He'd longed to walk the Arboretum where trees flowered on top of one another in every color— fuchsia and lilac and yellow, and the white dense dogwoods behind them all, where the intensity of their flowering was the only visual match he'd ever found for the way his heart burst in spring.

But out on the streets the next morning, Yoder recognized only himself, reflected in the cold glass of shop windows: back slightly hunched against the wind; mouth hanging open, his lips too large and too red; black hair curling toward his shoulders. There were three moles on his left cheek, arranged in a triangular pattern that he fingered like beads. He saw the dark gypsy brows, his father's full lips, and skin so pale it seemed made of rice paper. Women found him attractive, for some reason he thanked the gods for but did not understand. Something in his eyes made them think him a wise man—ending any hope he'd ever had of finding wise men. He had never been told that he resembled someone else. He had never spotted a twin.

The Harlequinade Bookshop, the Del Camino bar and the all-night restaurant where he'd cooked in exchange for meals were gone. In their places: "athletic footware"; a McDonald's done up in fake stained-glass; a disco whose neon flashed against the daylight. But crossing State Street, watching the women, Yoder smelled chicken broth—the salty, greasy, slightly comforting smell of institutional cooking—and he knew exactly where he stood. On the north side of the Student Union it had always smelled of soup.

The carillon bells in Burton Tower chimed the hour with one stroke, then rang haphazardly in a kind of happy shout before settling down to a version of the Beatles' "Yesterday." Wherever he was—in Port Hope, or Toronto or Quebec City —when he heard bells he wanted to be scurrying across this town in deep October. It pleased him that the memory of the bells satisfied him as fully as the cold clanging they made now. Yoder scanned the streets, peering under hoods and stocking caps for the people who, in his absence, had passed out of childhood. He knew to expect changes, but held in his memory only a flash of hair spilling across an embroidered shirt, a beer can lifted in a toast on the back porch of The House, a smile meant for him across a chanting crowd. WE WANT IT. AND WE WANT IT NOW.

At one time nearly every face on these streets had looked

familiar. It wasn't that he had a lot of connections, but he was on the streets all the time. He'd count how many faces he could recognize in an hour and try to locate them in the line-up of his life: a friend once removed, an enemy by reputation, a lover's lover's lover—like the baseball cards he shuffled as a kid, quizzing himself on the hometown and batting average of each player. Who would he see first? Not Sally—that meeting had to take place in private. Eliot, Goldie, Trucker, Squanto? How many were missing? How many dead? How many living blissfully in Kansas City?

Had he stayed, would he have been forced into the premature stuffiness he glimpsed in tweedy men his age bustling by on the street? Forced into a gravity of spirit to distinguish himself from the young? The whole damn town wore blue jeans now, whether 13 or 30, born-again or still atoning for some past life in Calcutta.

A block ahead, by the music building, Yoder spotted a fall of black hair, a tall woman moving head and shoulders above the crowd, a stiff-armed marching stride reminiscent of C.V. In Canada, he'd learned to disavow a familiar walk, but this, he realized, could actually *be* C.V. Yoder ran, weaving around big coats and women. The head thrown back, the arms swinging as precisely as a metronome. He figured she'd be in L.A. by now. Calling her name out, Yoder brushed his hand against her arm with more force than he intended.

She spun and hair flew into her open mouth. Her forehead wrinkled up as if to scold him. "How do you know that name?"

Yoder wanted to hug her but was stopped by the abruptness in her voice. Tipping his hat so she could see him, he said his name, then repeated it when she showed no recognition. "I used to back you once in awhile at the Del Camino. I was playing bass then."

"Oh, sure," she said, cocking her head to the side then looking back at him. "Sure, I remember. You played with The Rangers, didn't you?"

"That was Goldie, but you're close."

She tugged on a floppy red felt hat and her lips were red. "Well, it was a hell of a long time ago anyway." He studied her face for signs of change. She was leaner, her sharp features no longer softened by smooth curves of skin. Three earrings dangled down from each earlobe. "So what are you up to?"

"I've been in Canada. Just got back last night."

"How fun! Some friends of mine live in Vancouver." Her voice was deep and rutted with feeling. C.V. was the best bar singer he'd ever heard. "I hear it's gorgeous. Flowers everywhere, of course not at this time of year."

"It's a tourist town," he said. "I couldn't afford to stay."

"These people have gobs of money. They own a club." C.V. kept looking over his shoulder at the people on the other side of the street.

"Still singing?" he asked, shifting his weight and looking down the street himself.

"God, no. I've got my own business now. I do color readings. I know, I know, what's that, right?" C.V. was always on stage. He used to fantasize about knocking on her door at 4 A.M. just to see what she looked like without make-up. "I advise women—and men," she gave him a wink, "on what colors they need to look and feel their best. For example, you need bright colors to perk up that skin of yours. Here, let me give you my card."

Each letter a different shade of pink: "Carol Valient—Color Therapist."

"No thanks," he said, keeping his hands in his pockets.

"Suit yourself." She ran her pink tongue over her red lips without altering their color in the slightest. "God, nobody's called me C.V. in a hundred years. Well, take it easy, Yoder." She wiggled her leather-gloved fingers at him and he decided to pretend he had not seen her.

The town seemed to be in the throes of a tribute to the Beatles whether it liked it or not. The melody of "Norwegian Wood," obscured by lots of ringing ornamentation, rose above the cars slushing through the blackened snow. Yoder's fingers plucked the chords out of the air. It was one of the first songs he'd learned to play on the guitar—a simple song and a silly one, though he'd thought it deep at the time. Color readings—now that was deep. He scooped a handful of snow from the edge of the street and aimed at the Bell Tower, then shifted direction, heaving the snowball at a parked car like a commando caught in cross fire.

*Hey, I've been havin' the same old dreams./But mine was a little different you see./I dreamt the only person left after the war was me.* Bob Dylan was doing his thinking for him again. He'd listened to Dylan's lyrics so many times they'd become homilies, rising unbidden to inform his life. When he'd heard Dylan for the first time—a cheerless October afternoon in 1963—he'd felt the solace of a sympathetic mind. The strange proud voice, at home in its own roaming, had claimed the gloom of the bedroom he shared with his brother, altering the day forever. Yoder had turned the old radio—whose tubes glowed in the dark—up as loud as it would go. It didn't get any better.

Years before, in elementary school, he'd felt at home in the same way when he'd seen the bird in the shadow cage. By the stairs leading down to the cafeteria in his school, an ornate light fixture cast a shadow that reminded Yoder of a bird-cage. One day, swinging down the stairs on the way to lunch, he saw that someone had painted a yellow parrot on the wall inside the shadow cage: Proof that at least one other person saw the world the way he did. Yoder ran to show his friend Benish, but Benish had not been impressed. With the bird in place, it was obvious that the shadow looked like a birdcage. Any fool could see it.

He felt empty and spent, like when he took too many drugs or ate too much sugar. He didn't have the heart to find out whether Pizza Jim's had turned into a tofu joint. He longed to disappear into another time, to clamor up the stairs at the back of Drake's Sandwich Shop, wearing a muskrat coat and waving a pennant that said: "Go Blue," to meet the guys for a burger in the Martian Room. He spun in circles in the slush. Then, like snow clearing from a T.V. set, he remembered the hospital.

The front doors swished open at the first touch of his boot. Yoder stood aside to let a woman in a wheelchair, balancing two potted plants and a small suitcase, pass by. The air in the lobby was clouded with bluish smoke. A man wearing a seed cap and a white starched shirt that strained around each button, glared in his direction and Yoder tucked in his own shirt and smoothed back his hair. The clock behind the information desk told him he'd come just in time.

On the elevator a nurse, and an elderly woman carrying flowers so stiffly arranged they looked like plastic, stared solemnly at the blinking yellow numbers. The nurse tapped a pencil on a clipboard and the woman cleared her throat three times. Yoder leaned against the back wall and tried to imagine the three of them trapped in the elevator for a few hours. The women would play cards, he decided. He'd make them a deck from the papers on the clipboard—and he would play solitaire with their discards. They'd sleep all rolled up together and the old woman would amaze them with stories about her days in vaudeville. Once rescued they'd never see one another again—except perhaps in the grocery store—where it would seem best to simply turn away.

He got off on Six West. His skin prickled along his shoulders and down his back—the old body song his blood sang when the game was in progress. Betting that the routine had not changed, Yoder strode past the nurse's station, taking care to hesitate and stare as if he'd never been there before. The nurses lounged behind the counter like waitresses on a coffee break. Still, he stopped to check the posted room numbers as if looking for his father's room. The trick in fooling others was to believe in the deception himself.

Yoder eased past open doors, glimpses of pink robes and thin slippers, television sets droning and the heavy smell of roses. From one room came the sound of a child crying and from another, someone talking to an adult as if he were a child. And above the smell of alcohol and dead skin rose the friendly, greasy smell of lunch. Around the corner, a deserted hallway was lined with silver lunch carts begging to be ransacked. Scattered among the empty trays and dirty dishes were a half-dozen untouched leftover lunches. Yoder preferred to think they belonged to patients who had miraculously recovered, checking out before lunch. More likely, he knew, they had checked out for good.

He darted for oranges, stuffed bread and chicken parts into

his knapsack, dipped an elbow in butterscotch pudding, tipped over a water glass. Swoop, grab, wrap, stuff. He squatted to snatch a brownie from a low tray, stood on tiptoe for a skinny chicken leg. It was all in the rhythm. When he heard the rattle of an I.V. approaching, he dropped a chicken wing in a pool of gravy and walked calmly to the back stairs, feeling guilty despite a lifetime of practice.

He let his feet fly out underneath him, circling down the stairs like a kid caught stealing. "Quiet! People Are Getting Well Here," said the smiling face painted on each landing. At the V.A. in Jersey, where his father had eye surgery, the sentiment had been less cheerful. "THE PRICE OF FREEDOM IS VISIBLE HERE." His father had pointed out the sign chiseled in bronze at the entrance, as if he could read Yoder's mind, as if he'd known that his son was about to disgrace the men closeted there in long, silent wards. Yoder remembered the smell of the place, and the sound made by old men in slippers shuffling down hallways gleaming in the waxy light.

Leaping off the last three steps with his legs held high, Yoder barrelled through the exit door into the blinding winter light. Brilliantly executed! He hurried up the street to Mosher Hall, the dormitory where he'd lived as a freshman. The furniture in the expansive sunken lounge—more like a drawing room than any place he'd ever been—stood exactly as he'd left it. Stiff chairs covered in a satiny fabric with a tiny vertical print, and formal couches with arched wooden backs. The sun threw an impression of the leaded glass windows onto the pale blue carpet. The grandfather clock had chimed—Christ, how many times since he'd left? About 87,000 maybe? He ate breakfast off china for the first time in his life in the cafeteria here. Heavy white plates with a blue ring of birds and flowers on the rim. The place setting for two that he'd stolen at the end of his freshman year had been his moving-in-together present to Sal.

He'd first seen her here, in the cafeteria, standing by herself, staring off as if she'd stopped talking in mid-sentence. He'd watched her glide through the line, taking nothing but three dishes of chocolate pudding, and pegged her as a woman who knew what she wanted. It had taken him just long enough to fall in love with her to discover how wrong he'd been about that.

Yoder ran his fingers along the scratched mahogany of the grand piano, then let them creep from Middle C to the last note—a high C that still gave out a silly plink. A note used only by tinkerers; its enamel shell smooth and clean. He saw that the dignity of this room lay in its resistance to change. Hushed tones, company manners, phony harmony—that was what had put him off about the whole stuffy set-up when he lived here. Now, it seemed he could hear the room breathe. It was the only place he'd felt welcome all day.

In a window seat at the back of the room, Yoder unpacked his meal, pleased he'd remembered to grab napkins and butter. He peeled an orange, stacking the skins in a neat little pile. He had a special liking for oranges; their skin was so strong he could carry one around in his knapsack for days. He ate quickly, the congealed gravy and cold butter leaving his tongue slightly furry. Food tasted better when you were half-starved, very cold, or depressed—and best when it was free.

When he finished, he stood to pull The List—folded into a fat square like a junior-high love note—out of his back pocket. The writing was faint in places where the snow had melted the ink away. The names and addresses on the back of the envelope had been revised several times since he'd decided to come home. Sal was Number 1, but their reunion had to be in person—had to be a surprise. She would appreciate the drama. Josh was next, and Yoder realized that by the time he'd written this list, sitting up in bed in the high attic room of the Toronto Farmhouse, the U.S. had blurred into a single entity. Josh lived unimaginably far away, in some tiny town in northern Maine. That left a handful of people whose whereabouts he could only guess. It didn't matter which one of them was home, as long as someone still lived here. What were the odds? Could Goldie be the father of twins with a house on Whitmore Lake? Eliot a professor in the J. school, teaching gonzo journalism to kids who believed what they read in the newspaper?

At the very bottom of the envelope he'd written "Sam" and

then "My parents." Both back home in New Jersey. He was struck by how cramped his handwriting became as the list progressed, and by the formality of the last entry. Too bad he didn't think of them as Mom and Dad, but he didn't. And brother Sam—so different from himself that Yoder had once taken it as evidence of his own adoption, something he still held onto with a thread of belief.

Frenetic letter writing had kept him in touch with Josh and Goldie, his mother and Sal. He had kept all their letters until he got sick of re-reading them when new ones didn't arrive. More than a year had passed since he'd received a letter of substance. He knew something was wrong when a Christmas card—a stiff golden angel, her hair entwined with doves—had arrived in January. The card was signed "Sal"— no love, no note. Sal had sent him a Christmas card. It was unbelievable. He stuffed The List back into his pocket. General principle: Don't supply the ending until you've lived the whole story. It was time to walk the old neighborhood. See The House. Find Sal.

He knew the route well: under the overpass to the corner store where Lila once cashiered; past the parking structure —check for old Mac sitting on the bus bench wearing his homemade "Dump Nixon" sign; cross the boulevard to the frat house where Temptations music blasted out a window on the top floor and it's always 1965; head down the residential street whose huge elms join in a perfect arch over the pavement in summertime.

A flower shop had opened next to the corner store where the bagel place used to be, its plate-glass window now shameless with neon hearts left over from Valentine's Day. Neon. He thought of Harriet, the flower woman, pushing her paisley flower cart up South University to the Arch and back. She wore kimonos. He always stopped to talk; she knew everything about flowers—which ones meant "I love you" and which meant "Adios." When he'd first fallen in love with the shape of Sal's face, he'd asked Harriet which flower meant forever and she had given him a white rose. No point looking for Harriet. Mother of two? Working for the phone company? A backyard full of daisies? Surely, by now, heartbreak.

Yoder pushed open the door and jumped at the jangling of the bell. The shop appeared to be unattended. He walked among the potted Island Pines, fingering jade trees, ferns and azaleas, toying with ways he might steal one or two.

"May I help you, sir?" The man wore a white shirt and a thin black silk tie. His face was soft but his eyes regarded Yoder with a familiar suspicion.

"I need a white rose," Yoder muttered, moving toward the glass case of flowers in plastic buckets.

"May I suggest the rainbow carnations? Half dozen for only a dollar."

"I said I wanted a white rose." Yoder pulled two bills from his wallet and tossed them on the counter. Just because he looked like he didn't have any money didn't mean he wanted to be treated like he didn't have the money he didn't have. Not here.

Yoder cradled the rose in his arms and headed down Grove Street, past the parking structure—no Mac, past the fraternity—no music. But six blocks down, The House still anchored the middle of the block like a New Yorker's idea of a barn, icicles ringing the misshapen eaves, red paint peeling. The shrubs lining the driveway had doubled in size.

Yoder saw with mild surprise that The House was ordinary. One of dozens just like it with wide front porches; rooms chopped into apartments; windows loosened by bass notes; carpets ruined by neglected pets, and wallpaper faded around patches where posters of Jimi Hendrix or Tolkein's Hobbit Kingdom had kept the colors true. But these houses were the town in a way their transient tenants could never be. All of his friends had lived in houses just like this one—two blocks over or six blocks down. At some point everyone he cared about had passed through this house. Struggled with the way the bathroom door didn't latch, heard leaves scratching at the upstairs window. In the morning, the living room floor would be littered with blankets and bodies. Lila and Josh and Miles and Goldie had slept there for a day—or a year. It had seemed like the beginning of a family—a neighborhood that could only grow: We'll buy some land and you'll be the doctor and you'll be the cook and you'll play the music and you'll read the tarot. The family had disintegrated and he hadn't even been around to prevent it. As far as he knew, only Sal still lived in the neighborhood.

It was hard to recall the urgency of those last months before his draft board date when idle talk about drugs and revolution had been replaced by the need for facts. Facts about draft lawyers, urine specimens, eczema, high blood pressure and how to act insane. It had been a small thing then to turn his back on this house. The wind blew down the street, playing with a wind chime on someone else's front porch. From inside he heard the drone of a hair dryer or an electric mixer —a private sound a stranger should not be able to hear.

A lanky boy bounded out the front door. Yoder hurried on a few steps, startled, watching over his shoulder as the boy climbed onto a Honda 750 and roared off across the hard snow, jumping the small knob in the middle of the yard to land in the street. He did it perfectly and it didn't matter that Sal used to sunbathe on that spot where his wheels had burned the grass away, or that one pitch-black January night it was here that Yoder decided God was in the moon.

No one was home at 520 Island, six short blocks away, but the screened front porch stood open. Yoder pulled a cord and the overhead light lit up blue and icy. The rocker he and Sal had used in the living room sat by the door, a gash torn in its red leather seat. Clay pots and an open bag of potting soil cluttered a corner. Yoder lay down on a plaid couch he didn't recognize, pulled off his boots and wrapped a blanket tightly around his body. The cold bit his face but he closed his eyes to it.

He would never have guessed he could love a woman named Sally as much as he did. Not that names meant anything, but if you were going to be with someone and say her name 59 times a day, you wanted it to roll off your tongue or capture your imagination. Sally was Charlie Brown's sister and his own mother's best friend. Sally was a girl's name. He almost always called her Sal.

She was taller than he and skinny. Yoder liked her best in cutoffs and a deerskin halter top that showed her belly and back. Her face had a flatness to it that made her less than beautiful but the fact that she loved him made up for a lot.

They'd been together two years when he left for Canada. Her decision to move out of The House and live on her own was one reason he decided to go. The other was that his number was up.

It came up early on the evening of December 1, 1969. He and the others watched the draft lottery on television as if it were a game show, watched some congressman pull the little blue capsules out of the fishbowl like senior citizen's bingo. Heard his birthdate assigned number 34, the highest in their group. It was the year of the moon landing, the year of My Lai. The days of rage. Nixon about to bomb Cambodia, and a deserter shot while trying to sneak back across the Canadian border. Yoder didn't pay for a single drink that night. At the Del Camino they mangled chorus after chorus of "Happy Birthday" and he finally stumbled home alone.

Six months later he'd gone to the mailbox and found the letter. "Greetings," it said. Report for a physical. Prepare to die. His student deferment was still in place, but he didn't want his life to depend on a Botany final. He ripped the letter up right there on the sidewalk and stood a long time watching the wind play with its remains. It was all a matter of form.

In May of that year, four students had been killed by National Guardsmen at a Kent State anti-war demonstration. The nation had made a great show of mourning their deaths and it worried him. He wanted to know about the 10,000 who had been killed in the jungle. What kind of a country would refuse to mourn those men? The war began to look to him like a giant machine manufactured in America with an appetite for young men. He became obsessed with the image of his body splayed out cold in a hot, green place. His mind ran the footage over and over but his feet wanted to move. He made connections, asked questions, but he didn't know he was going to run until the week he left.

Sal did.

She visited him only once, during the first year, bringing an arsenal of stories about people who'd beaten the draft without leaving the country. Starvation, fudging the eye test, faked x-rays from expensive doctors, faked psychosis, stolen urine, no sleep, temporary obesity, and even a man who had chopped off the tip of his finger with a hatchet. That was the only scheme Yoder envied. There was enough pain in it— enough blood and sacrifice—to still the brutish voice of doubt. Sal saw it all differently. Though she couldn't parallel park or tell you at any given time how much money she had in the bank, she claimed to know why he'd gone to Canada. Why he'd never bought a draft lawyer or pulled off the insanity act he rehearsed for his physical. Sal made it clear that he'd only done in a big way what she'd accused him of many times before: He'd walked out on her.

The screen door rattled and he sat straight up on the couch. Sal let out a small scream. "It's only me," he shouted so she would hear his voice clearly.

"Oh. My. God."

"I'm back, Sal. It's only me."

"It's only who?" She peered at him in the weak light. "Yoder? Jesus Christ."

Her blond hair lay tangled over a ratty fur coat. She wore a shapeless pink hat and her lips were sticky and red. Lipstick? Yoder moved toward her. "Did I scare you?"

"Jesus, yes. This is too much. My god, Yoder." When she pulled her hat off, her hair stood up in a tangle at the crown of her head and shone in the light. She kept her head down as if there was something about her face she didn't want him to see. "You must be freezing out here," she said, rummaging through her purse for her keys, letting checkbook, brush and papers drift into a pile at her feet.

Sal didn't speak again until she'd paced the living room, turning on all the lights. "Let me see you," she said at last and took him by the shoulders. Yoder expected her to be laughing in her old way but she only shook her head. "You look just the same. I can't even tell you've been gone. God." She put her arms around his neck and he could smell her hair, like the cucumbers and vinegar his mother made for summer picnics. She held him and he let her do the holding, wanting just this: This warm sweater, yellow lamplight, radiator hiss. They stood in the middle of the room, holding tight, until she pulled away.

"I should know better than to say good-bye to you." Her laugh was weak. She kept pushing her hair off her forehead with the heel of her hand—a new compulsive habit, he wondered?

"Where have you been?" He tried to keep the whine out of his voice.

"At work, Yoder. I'm head teller now. I always work this late."

Sal worked for a bank. The irony of the fact that this woman who could not remember her own birthdate, now managed other people's money, was so great that he never remembered that this was what she did with her days. She liked having her hands on all that money, she'd said, liked knowing how much space a million bucks took up. Once he'd stood beside her in a chanting crowd as she lofted a rock into the two-story window of the bank where she now worked. Shatterproof glass. The next day Lila set up her easel outside the bank to sketch the pattern of its breakage. Tonight Sal was wearing a brown tweed suit and cowboy boots.

"When you stopped writing, I thought you'd stopped thinking about coming home. I was glad, you know. It wasn't healthy for you to be thinking about coming back. When I heard about this amnesty business, I wondered." Sal flopped down into a fat blue chair that he remembered dragging up the steps of two other apartments. "You look good, Yoder. How do I look? Older, right?"

"You're beautiful, Sal."

"Listen to me fishing for compliments. You hungry? Well, you'll have to help yourself." She threw her arm out in the direction of the kitchen. "I'm beat. I'm just beat tonight."

He peered at her face in the light. "What's wrong, Sal?"

"Yoder, I don't know how to say this, but you picked a bad night to come here. That must sound awful but you just did, that's all."

Her embrace had been genuine, he felt certain. He would listen even if it took all night. Help her with whatever was bothering her, just like he'd always done. Or maybe they would go to sleep and start over in the morning. "We can talk in the morning if you want."

Sal stared into her suit jacket, picking off little brown fuzz balls as if it was the most important thing she had on her mind. An orange cat appeared in her lap and as she stroked it, Yoder noticed a fullness in her face that was attractive in a new way.

"You want to stay here tonight, right?" she asked without looking up.

"Anything wrong with that? I mean, just say the word, Sal."

"I don't live here alone, Yoder. See those boots in the corner? They belong to a man named Jerry. But *he* won't be sleeping here tonight, I'm afraid."

"I thought you got this place because you wanted to live alone."

"That was six years ago."

In geology they called it plate tectonics: Africa pulling away from North America—an ocean coming between them. Love was not the question, though he hadn't understood that until just this moment. "I can sleep on your goddamn porch if you want me to, but Sal I need a place to stay."

"Do you know how many people have passed through my life since I last saw you? What if they all started showing up here, needing a place to stay?" She stood, throwing the cat from her lap. "Oh, never mind that, of course you can stay. It's just a bad night for me. I'm sick to death of this town and I don't know how to leave. I'm in love and it's not working out. I'm getting wrinkles—here—under my eyes, just like my mother. Yoder, the toilet overflows all the time and I *know* how to fix it. I don't listen to Bob Dylan any more ever. I've had an abortion, Yoder. Lila's dead for christsake."

Yoder grabbed her by the shoulders, afraid.

"Let go." Alarm toughened her voice and he dropped his hands. "I'm sorry." Her arms hung at her sides, her head bent toward the floor. "I shouldn't have told you like that."

Lila was beautiful, so beautiful he had never gotten beyond it to any real closeness. What he remembered most was her traveling garden. She planted things, snuck into yards and slipped sunflower seeds into a sunny spot by a friend's run-down apartment. Others found mint creeping along the side of a garage or sweet peas on a fence. That last summer she'd planted strawberries in the backyard of The House, hoping to make him stay for the fruit, which would not appear for another year.

"Did you ever get any strawberries?"

"Every year. Yoder, I'm sorry. She died in a car accident near Portland last year. She lived out there. She was happy, I think. I'm not trying to say that things haven't happened to you but I can't help you now. You can sleep here tonight but you can't stay. Six years is a long time."

"I can see that."

"In a couple of days when I'm not feeling so crazy, we'll have dinner or something. I do want to know how you are. I am glad you're back. Really, I am." Sal reached her hand out to him but did not take a step forward. It was a gesture, and an awkward one, her fingers hanging in the air between them.

"Dinner? You want to have *dinner?*"

"Yoder, don't be so hard on me."

"I can't promise you I'll even be around in a couple days, Sal. I just thought you might like to see me. I've got other places I can go. I know it's been a long time."

"Why didn't you call first?"

"Good question."

"You could have called collect."

"Really?"

"Yoder!"

"Sal, it's been said. Let's not say it again." He pushed open the door and ran down the steps, remembering the rose wilting in his knapsack. Abortions, schedules, wrinkles—it was ridiculous that he had to compete with them. Lila. If he could have told Sal what his day had been like, how tired he was, how beautiful Detroit had looked with the snow flashing by its streetlights and the man on the corner shouting about redemption and the brittle Christmas wreathes with their dusty bows on wooden doors swollen with the cold.

Yoder watched the snowflakes scurry toward the ground without melting, like bubbles that last an unbearably long time in the bathtub. Sal didn't listen to Bob Dylan anymore. What was that supposed to mean? His feet burned with the cold and he saw that he was not wearing shoes. His boots lay slumped against one another on Sal's porch. It was one thing to be without a place to sleep in a snowstorm and it was another to be without shoes.

Turning back up the driveway, he saw his own footprints going past him in the opposite direction. Yoder crept up onto the porch, pleading with the steps not to creak. Through the gauze curtains he could see Sal at the dining room table, her head buried in her hands, her hair covering her face like a sheet of yellow cloth. He laid the rose on the couch and pulled the blanket over it. Sitting down on the porch steps to lace his boots, he looked up at the sky. Snow fell into his open mouth. There was so much of it.

———————

*All I could think at the time was: I don't want you here. Just: No. He wasn't supposed to come back. Somehow, knowing that, I could go ahead and be myself. Though I was actually a better person with him around, if you know what I mean. I had to everything. We spent half our time looking at our motives for the few things we got done the rest of the day. It was exhausting. I guess it made me feel important. Like I was taking myself seriously for a change instead of just looking in the mirror and thinking: Ugh, your face is too flat. What should I wear? Who's playing at the Grande this weekend?*

*But it doesn't get you anywhere. It isn't me, is what I'm saying. With Yoder around there's this pressure to be better than yourself. I couldn't tell him I was pregnant. I couldn't tell him I was going to keep this one. How could I tell him that? He was acting like no time had passed. He looked like hell that night. He ran off like a jackrabbit the minute I got slightly, slightly hostile. How far could he have come in six years if he's still doing that shit?*

*I felt bad about him the minute he left. But I didn't run after him. That's the way he is. He makes you feel so shallow and at the same time like you're the only human being even worth mentioning. Like you've got potential. I'm too old for potential. Potential went out when they shot Martin Luther King.*

———————

RED LIGHTS FLASHED SCHLITZ, throwing pink shadows on the mound of dirty snow outside Izzie's, a town bar he'd passed by a hundred times without ever going inside. The rumble of the jukebox carried out into the street. Yoder stood on his toes to peer through squares of glass, thick as block ice. Beer bottles, softball trophies and a failing philodendron in a yellow pot cluttered the window sill. He faced the street, clasping his arms tightly across his chest, watching his breath materialize and disperse.

The energy of a real storm was building, the sky dark as a thunderstorm. Cars moved in a funeral procession through the empty streets, their headlights muffled in snow. The walk from Sal's had taken everything out of him; the snow pitting his skin like sparks from a bonfire. Alone on the streets, the sight of smoke streaming from chimneys nearly broke him. Friends had gathered around oak tables; couples tossed together under white blankets; someone sat curled up in the kind of fat armchair he knew he'd never own, reading of Russian winters and women whose eyes burned brightly. He had nearly turned back. Sal would take him in, but she did not love him. Worse, he did not love her in that way he'd hoped would be his homecoming.

Yoder leaned into the door with all his weight, as if it might be locked. Inside, the noise closed around him like a blanket. He stationed himself way down at the end of the curved wooden bar, hoping to avoid bar talk, though his genuine interest in baseball and the weather made it come easily. A single row of booths stood empty, but for a couple who had wandered in from the campus. The man snapped his fingers to the jukebox music—"Ramblin', Gamblin' Man"—ignoring a woman whose face Yoder could not quite see.

The beer tasted harsh against the back of his throat—too cold. Yoder focused his attention on a group of men around the pool table, having learned that if you appear to be watching something intently, people will not disturb you. There were other watchers: Two men in leather jackets hovered over the game, whispering now and then to the players. Yoder noticed with only mild surprise that one of them was The Crocodile. Before he could think, Yoder was out of his chair, shouting over the music. The Crocodile turned his head toward the bar and a slow smile spread across his face like syrup on hotcakes. "Yoder? Am I seein' a ghost? Hey, man."

Yoder deliberately shook Crock's cool hand, ignoring his outstretched palm. He hated that phony black power stuff. Crock was a WASP from Detroit, as white as anyone in this Midwestern bar. Though balding, Crock's hair still hung to the middle of his back. Everything about him was too thin; his body drooping from his shoulders like a heavy sweater on a hanger. It was after midnight and it was February, but Crock was wearing mirrored sunglasses. Crock reached into a leather shoulder pouch and pulled a bill. "I'm drinking Red Label," he said. "Buy us both one and come on over."

He was called The Crocodile but when Yoder looked at him, he thought: snake. The campus dealer of last resort, you could count on Crock to score quickly, but you had to pay the price. He took a twenty percent cut and you had to listen to his stories—long, confused complaints made amusing by his investment in the telling, tedious by their glorification of the teller. The ice clinked against the glasses as Yoder made his way toward the pool table, wondering whether Crock would notice or care that he'd pocketed the change.

"That's my boy there," Crock said, setting his glass down without taking a sip and pointing to one of the players. "Come on, Frankie. Finish him off and we can all go home happy." Frankie's vacant face assumed the dignity of concentration when he bent to take a shot, his chin resting lightly on the cue. "You want in on this?" Crock asked. "Odds on Frank there are five to one."

What he wanted was to lean into the mellow wood paneling and drink. The Scotch slid down honied and warm. If he could keep it up, Sal's face might blur into the white globe light over the pool table and disappear, along with the snowstorm and the smoke from chimneys.

"So what's happening?" Crock asked, his question slipping out of the corner of his mouth. "Aren't you supposed to be in Canada? The FBI never forgets, boy."

"Amnesty," Yoder said, realizing that he needed a Presidential proclamation to be stranded in this two-bit bar.

"I think I heard about that," Crock said, drawing hard on his cigarette. "It's a good deal for you guys, isn't it? Would you look at that?" Crock led him by the shoulder to the table where the nine ball veered neatly for the corner pocket. "Sinker," Crock cheered. "You got him now, Frankie." Crock called the play-by-play like a baseball announcer, shifting his weight, smoking, jamming his fists into the pockets of his leather jacket and directing jibes at his opponent in the other corner. Yoder stopped responding, drinking the scotches as quickly as Crock could provide them. Frankie had the moves, all right. General principle: If you expect to score, you have to play. But you had to pick your bets and Crock had never seemed like a good one.

An image from years before: Crock in the food co-op, standing before a box of pineapples. Unnoticed, Yoder watched him weigh one against another, turning each to inspect the dimpled surfaces. Halfway to the cashier, Crock had turned on his heel and walked back to the pineapples to make yet another choice. After that Yoder had been more careful around Crock, aware of what lay behind the easy laughter. His obsessive attention to detail made him a perfectionist and that made him dangerous.

"What time is it?" Yoder asked.

"Late. Why? You want another drink?"

"I just got into town. I could use a place for the night."

Yoder felt Crock's hesitation in the way he pulled the last smoke from his cigarette and walked across the room to find an ashtray, despite the butts which littered the linoleum just beneath their feet. "My floor's your floor. Hey, it's my patriotic duty," Crock said finally, slapping him on the shoulder. "But I can only do you for one night."

"Sure. I understand. Besides I'll be seeing Sal in the morning." A lie to which, once stated, he felt suddenly loyal. Of course he would see Sal in the morning. Wasn't that why he'd come home?

"Sally? No shit. Hey, would you look at that!" Frankie took the game with an impossible shot—commanding two balls to form a broad V and nestle softly into the corner pockets. Crock huddled with his opponents, emerging with his Crocodile smirk intact, crisp bills between his fingers.

"A round—on me," Crock swiveled to gesture toward the mostly empty bar. A guy in a suit trying to sweet-talk a woman half his age looked up with interest. The bartender rolled his eyes. It was nearly last call and with so few people left in the bar, hardly worth the trouble to indulge Crock's gesture. "A toast," Crock insisted, hopping up on a chair to address the desultory crowd, "to my man. A guy who stands on his principles if not always on his two feet."

Yoder studied his fingernails, searched for exits, room to move. Crock pulled him up to the bar. Don't do this, asshole, he thought. Do not do this.

"Been sittin' up there in Canada eight years now, waitin' out the war," Crock announced to no one in particular.

"Six," Yoder hissed.

"Didn't the war end a long time ago?" Frankie asked, his hands shoved deep into his back pockets, his eyes avid.

The room blurred and heaved. Yoder stood before a group of strange-smelling adults, reciting the silly words he'd learned in French class. They cooed and clucked. "Imagine," his mother said, "and only ten years old." He wanted to tell them about the explosives he made in the basement, the Tootsie Roll Pops stolen from the corner store; wanted to confess that he loved one grandmother better than another. Yoder raised his glass. "To Frankie," he said weakly, "One hell of a pool player."

"Don't give the kid a big head." Crock slammed his glass to the bar like a B-movie gangster.

All down the block, people bundled in heavy coats drifted out of bars, huddled and blurred in the snow falling steady and slow. Yoder could barely walk from scotch and exhaustion. Crock put a key into a new Mercedes so white it made the fresh snow on its roof look dirty. "Business must be good," Yoder said.

"Definitely." Crock's easy laugh did not match the leather and the slouch. He looked ridiculous propped up in the plush red seat. Yoder had a sudden impression of Crock as a child: Too tall, too thin, too smart to have many friends. Too foolish not to care. "I've diversified, see. Hooked up with some people—Detroit people—about a year ago. They're heavy into concert promotion. Needed a connection to keep their performers happy. Money doesn't mean a thing to these people." Crock leaned over, whispering as if they were still in a crowd. "They're looking at Dylan in the spring." For a long time Yoder had been certain that he and Dylan would meet one day. He still held Dylan responsible for his own failure to write songs. It was like trying to box with Ali in the world. The idea of Crock and Dylan having anything to do with one another made him sad.

The car glided into the driveway of a stone house with crumbling steps not three blocks from Sal's apartment. "How come you still live over here?"

"Low profile." Crock unlocked both their doors with the push of a button. "Besides, moving is a hassle. Pretty soon I'm gonna buy this sucker, take a trip to Jamaica and pay somebody to rebuild it from the inside out. That way, I'll never have to move, see?"

The living room was nearly empty. A worn leather couch and a stained-glass lamp hanging over a card table were the only things that looked permanent. No chairs. Nothing on the walls. *Rolling Stone* magazines in a pile on the floor. It could have been 1968.

Crock reached behind the couch and produced an army blanket with bits of popcorn scattered across it. "I guess I should say welcome back." He shook the blanket and the popcorn fell like snowflakes on the carpet. "It's a new world out there, buddy boy. Kids actually go to class. No more conga music on the Diag." Crock closed his eyes, moving head and hands in syncopation with imaginary drums. "I should warn you, they've started cracking down around here —small timers even. I don't know what your plans are, but I intend to make my bundle and cut out—for Jamaica or someplace. Maybe buy myself one of those big fucking sailboats—you know, the kind that sail themselves while you entertain the ladies below deck.

"I imagine you'll be appreciating this system." Crock put his palm flat on the smoky grey of the turntable cover, like a salesman. "State of the art. Made in Holland or Sweden or someplace. Listen up." The Crusaders came on strong, horns bleating: Badadada bada dadada. Ba dadada....Crock closed his eyes, moved his head, up and down, up and down to the beat, and they were both better people for an instant. When he killed the music the silence left them stranded. "So, what are your plans?" Crock asked.

"No plans," Yoder said, throwing his wet jacket to the floor and stretching out on the couch.

"You've been back, what, a day? That's fair. But you can't walk around like the unwashed wonder forever. Especially a man in your situation. You've got to assess, right?"

"I just want to sleep." Yoder unlaced his boots and took his frozen feet in his hands. His socks were still damp from his run up Sal's driveway.

"We're about the same age—the big 3–0?" Crock leaned against the door frame and crossed his arms over his chest. His posture and the way he sucked in his breath, as if about to deliver a speech, reminded Yoder of his own brother.

"You're older."

"You want to quibble over a year or two? Go ahead. The point is that sooner or later you look around and think: What am I doing? Right? I mean, here I was making money hand

over fist but where was the future in it? That's when I started
connecting with these Detroit people. I thought, where's the
future in peddling grass to freshmen? I've done that. I tell
you—those are babies walking around out there. Anyway, so
I figured rock 'n' roll—that's where the big money is. It's
working out too. You like the car?"

"Sure, it's a great car." Yoder fought the remarkable weight
of his eyelids.

"Did you notice the glide? Man, that baby slips through the
streets so smooth. Sometimes I just drive it around. I'm not
even going anywhere. Watch the ladies check me out." Crock
sunk his knuckles into his eyes and seemed to disappear for a
few seconds. "I was with the same woman for two years. You
ever been with anyone that long?"

"In a sense." He wanted to close his eyes but there was a
certain etiquette involved in crashing on someone's couch.
With Crock, that meant listening to him talk.

"Then you know what bitches they can be. See how empty
this place is? She took it all with her. The goddamn moving
van pulled right up. She's loading furniture and won't even
look at me. We're in bed one morning and she won't let me
touch her. She says: 'If we met today, would you still want to
be with me?' I said sure. I was half-asleep, man. And she
says: 'I'm not so sure.' That was it."

A black cat prowled the edges of the room, turning amber
eyes toward their conversation. Crock whistled and the cat
bounded across the room to perch on his knee. He stroked the
cat with long slender fingers, massaging its belly, digging his
fingers into the fur beneath its chin and behind its sharp little ears. Crock's face turned soft with the effort. Yoder felt
slightly embarrassed, as if he'd interrupted a private moment between intimates.

"Like I said, you need some kind of plan," Crock continued.
"If you're interested we can talk. Now that I've got the music
connections, I'm looking to swing my own action. Looking at
a system I heard about that could put me in the import business. You think you might be interested?"

"Depends. Any idea if Josh is still out East?"

"No fucking idea. He and I didn't get on, if you remember."

"He might have a band together by now."

"A band?" Crock looked as if he'd just announced a plan to sell insurance. "Yoder, it's 1977. You want to play little jive-ass joints the rest of your life? You got to have backing—connections. There's money to be made writing tunes but you won't get anywhere in some little band with old Josh boy. You gotta get yourself some clothes."

"Money's not really a problem. I came into some cash a while back—family money. I couldn't get my hands on it until I got back to the States but I can pretty much do what I want from now on." These fictions came so easily that he adopted them without blinking.

"How much?"

"Enough. Plenty."

"Listen, we should talk. We might be able to help each other out if you see my point."

"I'm not really interested." Idiotic to let Crock think he had money. "I don't even have it yet. I mean, I'm broke at the moment."

"Don't jump, my man. We're talking down the road—two, three months. You ain't heard the facts yet."

Get him off this. "So, you ever see Sal?"

Crock rolled his eyes. "She lives a couple blocks over. I don't know. She's—I don't know—weird."

"What do you mean?" Yoder sat up and pulled the blanket around his shoulders.

"You seen her yet?"

"No."

"Let me give you some advice. If you're thinking of checking her out again you should know that she hasn't been alone more than a couple of minutes since you left. We spent some time together a while back. I wouldn't be looking to her for anything if I were you."

"Spent some time together?"

"You know, we hung out. I saw it coming a long time ago. She always had the itch."

"Do me a favor—shut up about her."

"Hey, look, like you said, you've been a long time gone. She doesn't look so good anymore, either." Crock raised his hand like a preacher giving benediction. "Listen, I'm wasted. So, sleep tight or whatever, and just pull the door shut if you leave before I get up. Like I said, if you ever want to talk business."

Yoder pulled the moth-eaten army blanket over his head. His body shook like a cottonwood in a breeze. How could she have even looked at Crock? How many others had there been? He kicked out against the darkness where there was no resistance. Sal had never mentioned Crock nor any lover in her letters. They'd both lied out of love, though the truth had lodged like a dark stone in his heart. There had been signs, but if you paid attention to a woman's signs, you'd spend your life alone.

"Home is where the heart is," his mother always said when discussions turned to his errant uncle, the brother she'd been defending for years. He was aware of the muscle on the left side of his chest. His heart was in his chest. His heart was doled out in pieces to women who called it a jewel, then left it sitting in a box, dusting it off to show visitors. His heart animated the woods, and the slick New Jersey streets when headlights surfaced in puddles and a car radio blared the right song for an instant. It was in his mother's face a long time ago when he'd thought that life was only a matter of waiting for her to tell him the secret. He heard it in Dylan's low notes, in the wizardry he worked with his face, howling under stage lights. Home was not a piece of earth—not the country you were born to, nor the one that took you in. It was not in what he did or thought but in unpredictable flashes of himself showing up somewhere else. He'd hoped the whole town would flash for him—a parade, a dinner attended by people he didn't know, but with whom he shared something important. And his mother would be there, stepping up to the podium to whisper into his ear exactly what he should do next.

When he woke each morning, he tried to pay attention. It was something he believed in, the way other people believed in God. If a woman lay beside him, he pulled her close and paid attention to her breathing, the shine on her eyelids, how she clutched at the pillow or abandoned her body. He tried to identify individual sounds: A dozen birdcalls colliding or the monotonous screech of a single sparrow, cars idling, the whine of a saw, the oddly comforting drone of a lawnmower, the clock ticking, his own heart. He saw the sun painting the sheets, the wind folded in the curtains, fuzz balls on the blanket growing into boulders when he closed one eye, waterspots like sunfish caught in the plaster.

He lay still and grabbed at fragments of dreams. A clear dream image plucked from the unconscious allowed him to enter the day with armor on. This day he woke seeing Crock's clammy hands on Sal's thigh, his mouth—the head of a snake—suckling her breast, his low hiss in her ear. She had said something about an abortion. He should never have left her. The fat pears and round-bodied birds on the stained-glass lampshade caught a bit of the early light, and he thought of smashing it. Yoder crossed the room to the turntable and spun the Crusaders album a few times with his finger. He pulled out his hunting knife and scratched a long thin Z—for Zorro—into the perfect black ribs on its surface. Sal was beautiful. He wouldn't have people talking about her that way.

Taking the apples and bananas languishing in Crock's refrigerator, Yoder slammed the door hard behind him. The darkness was benign, the grey wash of night's dissolving lifting into dawn. It put a spring in his step. Yoder jogged through the streets, his boots slapping against a thin coating of melted snow. The taillights of a car braking at a stoplight a block ahead threw red streaks in his path. He ran behind the car to the freeway.

WINTER WAS NOT the best time for trees, but with every twig outlined against the sky Yoder could get a clear look at how they were made. Most were unbalanced, branching off more heavily to one side. Only mature trees had that nice rounded curve that kids drew in their pictures. As Yoder reached the top of a hill, one of those perfected elms rose up across the highway. The snow etched the inner web of branches with whitewash, like the painter had taken a coffee break, leaving the job half-done. Plan. You didn't get a tree like that by following any plan. His plan worked like jazz: You didn't care where it was going as long as it made you move.

Yoder held out his hand and the huge snowflakes began to collect on his outstretched thumb. Though he knew better, he'd accepted the first ride he was offered—from a smiling, talkative couple on their way to the Farmer's Market. Did he realize the benefits of organically grown vegetables? Had he ever seen a winter like this one? Wasn't he cold in that thin jacket? He kept his answers to himself but there was no discouraging some people. They left him stranded on a little-traveled stretch off the freeway between Ann Arbor and Detroit.

Yoder bit down hard to quiet his chattering teeth. If he'd stayed in Ann Arbor a day longer, he might have found a wool coat and some gloves at the Salvation Army. He always thought of such practicalities just slightly too late. Still he felt relieved to be on his way to somewhere else, where no one was supposed to be waiting for him. If he didn't get a ride in the next hour going east, he'd cross the road and head west—to the desert, maybe, toward red rocks and strange trees.

He turned to face the road and the full expanse of wind rocketing along the ground until it reached him, when it swept up and hit him from below. His hair blew straight back, exposing the almost bloated outline of his face. Yoder tried to hold his hair in place with his favorite shapeless old denim hat, but the wind whipped the hat off each time. He was better looking when his thick hair framed his face. Maybe that explained why he wasn't getting any rides.

So far, nothing had hit as hard as the clear fact that he could no longer stand on the side of the road with a knapsack on his back and expect to be picked up before he could get through an a cappella version of the Beatles' "White Album." What had happened to America? Cars flashed past, windshield wipers racing. Yoder managed occasional eye-contact with women in flannel shirts driving pick-up trucks or blowing cigarette smoke in his direction; once in a while a shrug that said: Sorry, you guys blew it a long time ago. But mostly he waited alone in the acoustically perfect winter silence. The crows flew too high to be heard and the wind found nothing to rustle. Yoder put his hands over his ears to stop the burning, and the silence became complete.

When he closed his eyes to the silence, he could hear the sound of cranky violins—a soundtrack for the inevitable bleak days in a lifetime when nothing was really wrong but his mouth would be dry, his eyes might sting. Music for a featureless sky broken by low clouds like thumb smudges on clean paper. Sunday afternoon, 1957. On the blue diamond-patterned sofa, he shuffled baseball cards while his mother and father sat stiffly by the radio, chins raised slightly. The yellow sodden light reflected off his father's glasses as he listened with a faint smile to the violins.

Yoder jumped as three cars roared around the curve, blasting him with their tailwind. The last, a blue and white Chevrolet, careened by going way too fast and braked hard, pulling onto the shoulder about a hundred yards ahead. Yoder sprinted toward the car, waving his hands in the gesture of all stranded parties about to be rescued. When he was close enough to touch the mud spatters on the tailpipe, he heard the tires spin, spit gravel and roll. Jacket flying open, hat in hand, he shouted after the Chevy, pleading for what had obviously happened not to happen. The car pulled back onto the road and sped away. Yoder threw his knapsack to the ground. Asshole. Adolescent in a Chevy. Someday he'd buy an old Yellow cab and travel Route 66 one end to the other, paying back all the rides he'd been given in the past fifteen years. Doing it right.

Yoder retrieved his knapsack and continued up the sloping roadside, watching slush squirt out a hole in his boot. He loved his boots, leather Sorels with laces that took a full ten minutes to do right. They'd suffered through seven Canadian winters and he didn't expect them to last until barefoot weather, when all he'd need were foam rubber shower clogs. There was something superfluous about shoes—a societal decision like neckties. Shower clogs, on the other hand, were one of the most sensible inventions of all time—as long as you didn't wear them in the shower.

A whining sound from over the next hill took his eyes off his feet. He looked up to see the blue-and-white rushing back toward him in reverse, someone in the front seat hanging out the window, waving his arms and shouting directions to the driver as the car fishtailed on and off the road. Yoder started up the hillside at the edge of the highway, leaving the maniac at the wheel plenty of room as he struggled to stop the car. The rear tire sunk in the mud and the passenger window rolled down. The driver leaned over. "Looking for a ride, buddy?"

College kids. Four of them. "How far are you going?"

A toothy guy in the front seat let out a hoot. "New York City!"

Incredible. A two-ride trip—a new record. "I'm headed east myself—New Jersey," he said, as if he'd known it for weeks.

From the back seat came a moan. Two guys whose shoulders rose above the seat backs stared out at him: a young Marlon Brando in a black leather jacket that creaked and strained at the seams when he moved; and an Andy-of-Mayberry type who had the vacant look of boredom Yoder associated with gas stations. "Come on, Jake. There's no room back here," Marlon Brando complained to the driver in a voice that was almost a whine. "He's a big boy. He can get another ride."

The driver sighed; they had been through it all before. "Listen Evans, this is my car, my sister who has an apartment in New York City, and my line of bullshit that saved your ass with Carbury so you could even come on this trip. So don't tell me who's riding and who's not."

"Right, Jake. Real easy for you to say, sitting up there in your bucket seat with your feet stretched out. You know damn well if he's riding with us, he's gonna end up back here." Evans struggled to cross his arms over his meaty chest.

Jake twisted around to face the back seat. "It's a blizzard out there. Can you see that, Evans?"

Yoder thrust his head inside the crowded car. "Listen, I need to get to New Jersey fast, to see my father. He's in the hospital and I could sure use a ride if you think you've got room." He watched their faces as they absorbed the lie.

The driver waved him in. "We'll get you there by sunrise. Evans, throw that beer up here and move over."

Evans did not move over. He and his friend in the back spread out toward the windows. Evans pointed at the middle seat with the hump on the floor. "You can sit here," he said. Yoder slid his knapsack onto the back ledge and climbed over their legs to his seat. Evans watched his every move.

"I'm Jake," the driver announced. He looked like a young politician, handsome and shifty-eyed. "This is Buck and that's Evans and Willie back there with you. Don't mind them. What's your name, friend?"

"Yoder."

"What did you say?"

"It's Yoder," he said, stressing the first syllable.

"That your first name or what?" Buck snickered through his widely spaced teeth.

"It's just my name, OK?" Yoder looked the driver hard in the eye, hoping to end the conversation.

"OK, Yoder." Jake pulled the car back onto the road and continued to shout back at him, moving the wheel playfully with two fingers. "You from around here? Go to the U., or what?"

"Nah, I don't go to the U. Look, you mind if I take off my boots? They're soaked through."

"Go ahead. Get comfortable. 'Cause New York City here we come. Hey, Yoder, you hungry, thirsty? We got plenty of beer, doughnuts. Help yourself."

Willie and Evans opened beers, spreading out around him as if he were a piece of luggage. The thick odor of Cheetos clogged the air. Evans kept jamming his hand into the bag, tossing a handful into the air and catching them in his cheesy mouth. Willie chain-smoked Marlboros in short, angry puffs.

Willie rolled down his window and tossed a beer can out onto the highway, cheering as he picked off a pile of snow from the top of a fence post. "Beat that, Evans," he shouted. Evans got a mileage sign square in the middle and Buck scared off a group of crows sitting on an overturned tree. Evans hung out the window, attempting to hit a post on the opposite side of the road, lobbing the can over the roof and back as the car sped past. Each time one of them missed a target, he would chug another beer, emptying it for the next one to throw. No one asked Yoder if he wanted to try. Evans had already asked him a couple of times if they were boring him. Yoder crushed his beer can in his fist and dropped it to the floor of the car.

Pulling his denim hat down over his eyes, he pretended to sleep. He had learned the technique long ago, relaxing his muscles one by one, regulating his breathing to approximate sleep. As a child, bored by long nights out with his parents, he would curl up, avoiding the cousins he was expected to like simply because they were the same age. The habit had caused him to be branded a "delicate" child. He could still hear his mother telling relatives with the presumption of a parent: "Yoder needs a lot of sleep. Gets it from me, I suppose. I have always liked my sleep."

It was the closest he ever came to invisibility and it hadn't made him any fonder of people in general. Without the distractions of gossip, greed and sex, most people were as hopeless as the dog he'd had as a boy. When let out on his own, Salty wandered aimlessly about the backyard, nosing here and there at a stick or a pile of leaves, utterly at a loss about what to do with himself. Luckily there were exceptions. Occasionally someone whistled or sang to themselves. A farmer who drove him across Ontario tuned in the country stations and sang all the drum solos: TADADADADUM TADADADA-DUM BUM TADADUM TADADA! All the way down the road.

Girls, wrestling, passing out, crashing cars—their talk floated by in the darkness beneath his hat. Apparently all four belonged to the same fraternity. A few times Yoder strained to catch the end of an episode, but they knew the stories too well, one eclipsed another, their voices became one voice. He had a moment of envy, wondering how it would feel to find a group of people who could take one look and say: "You're one of us."

They reminded him of the farm boys whose trucks had taken him across Canada those first four years. In British Columbia, teenagers cruised their territories in pick-ups the way street gangs had roamed the neighborhoods in Jersey. And they had picked him up for the same reasons: To have someone to show off for, someone who might gasp as they pushed the gas pedal to the floor, whipping by miles of fields, plunging into valleys and taking hills with yelping speed.

At least in Canada his status as a draft evader had given him certain privileges. Canadians never hesitated to offer food, transportation, even money. All they expected in return were platitudes about peace, and Yoder had learned to mouth them convincingly. He had a flash of anger at Sal— she'd been less generous than some Canadians with whom he had nothing in common. Just days ago, he'd left a woman who cared for him. He could feel Julie's calloused hands on his back, kneading his muscles with a rhythm steady as music. The weekly massage had developed from a casual lie about a bad back that he'd let build into a medical reality. At the end of this ride he would actually need a massage and there would be no Julie. She would be at the resister's center in Toronto, patiently processing the others who wanted to come home. Few would have their possessions packed in a box with a red bow, but she would have words for them. Her eyes would glisten with real tears. Yoder hadn't been able to get beyond what seemed her nearly genuine sentimentality and in the end, it kept them from having any sort of real relationship.

The farmhouse outside Toronto where he'd lived with Julie and ten others could have been any one of the houses they were speeding by on the Ohio Turnpike—white frame boxes with side porches and black cows crouching in the snow. When the war ended in '73, Georgia had kept her house open to Americans like himself who couldn't "get landed" and so could not work. Some, especially Walter, the cheerful, dull-witted kid who had deserted during the last months of war, could not have found work anywhere.

Buck, who read signs out loud for some reason, announced Ashtabula. Six more hours. Yoder felt a poke in his side. "Looks like our passenger here is mighty bored. Yo—da, hey Yo—da." In grade school the other kids made fun of his name, yodeling when they saw him coming across the playground—Yoder—le—he—hoo! His friend Benish always took the bait: "His name is Y-O-D-E-R, ya stupid," he would say. Benish was the stupid one. He only made things worse.

Yoder braced himself, strangely excited to hear what they would say about him. They'd been scuffling on the playground in '70 when he'd walked away without a second look. He'd bet silver they wouldn't stand him a round of drinks. The Vietnam War had the sticky dust of collective guilt all over it—like the Depression, the Holocaust. Boring, troublesome, a war without heroes. A draft resister was some hippie who didn't love America.

"Hey, you awake in there? Wonder if the little guy is alive." Yoder felt Evans lift the rim of his hat away from his face. "He's been sleeping here for a hell of a long time. Willie, check his pulse. Maybe he died on us."

Jake's voice, loose and drunken. "Yeah, pick up a hitchhiker and he croaks. Who'd ever believe it?"

"Geez, the way his feet stink," Willie said, "maybe he's starting to rot."

"You know he started stinking up the car the minute he got in here. We're choking on it back here," Evans whined. "I told you we shouldn'ta picked him up, Jake."

His body had a strong natural odor that soap and water couldn't touch. A drawback with women, it guaranteed him a seat to himself on buses. When Willie started trying to force Yoder's wet boots back on his feet, Yoder broke. "Keep your hands off me," he said, shoving Willie toward the door.

Willie shoved back. "Your feet stink and this is a small car. Remember, you're riding free."

The car swerved slightly as Jake eyed the back seat. "Look, Evans, his father's in the goddamn hospital, so lay off. Yoder, you want to put your boots back on and relax? We've got another 300 miles to travel and you're not making it any easier. We're doing you a favor here, OK? Drink a beer or something. Willie, pass the man a beer."

"Forget the beer. I'm trying to sleep." Startled at the reminder of his earlier lie, Yoder sank back into his seat. His father *could* be in the hospital for all he knew. He wasn't going to sweat it. Jake was taking the whole thing surprisingly seriously. Maybe Jake's father had died, some long illness, maybe. It was just as well—the lie. Jake would probably feel good about the whole thing for days.

His stories didn't feel like lies. They were an edge he had on the world, like some people had money and some had skin smooth as nectarines. The lies tumbled out full-formed and gorgeous. They were the best of him and they were not the kind of lie that hurt. The world outright lied all the time. And the biggest lie was its beauty—the yellow milk of the sun, pink apples in the grass. In Canada, when the prairie broke there were towns like Hope where the Cascades loomed like black shadows circling the sun and puffs of fog got caught in the pine trees in early morning. He went for it every time.

Yoder had first understood how the world could lie while on an airplane when he was six years old. Sitting next to his mother, his head resting against the scratchy wool of her funeral suit, he had stared out the window for most of the flight to Florida. His grandmother had died. That meant a shocking flood of tears from his mother, his first airplane ride, and, he supposed, no more sacks of grapefruit delivered to their door each winter.

Leaning over him that morning to fasten his black bow tie, his mother had told him that he did not have to look in the casket. Yoder wondered what point there was in going all the way to Florida if not to at least get a look at a dead person. He intended to look. He intended to touch her if he could. The person he could not stand to look at was his mother— the rims of her eyes bloody red, her black hair braided and coiled around the back of her head and her skin very white against all the black. She stared straight ahead, holding a magazine on her lap but never opening it. Something was wrong with her, so he looked out the window all the way to Florida.

He caught onto the lie in the first ten minutes. He watched as the cars and buildings got small. That did not surprise him; cars and buildings were small when Superman flew over them on T.V. But soon, the clouds were *below* him, drifting by like icebergs on the sea that had been his sky. He strained against his seatbelt. No one had told him that there were two skies. The blue that he stared up into was not a protective bowl stretching over the earth and giving it limits. For the first time he understood that he could not trust his eyes. "How many skies are there?" he had asked his mother and she had looked at him and blown her nose.

For the rest of the trip he was lost in the landscape of the clouds—the way they rolled and curled like mountain ranges, stretching into geometric prairies until they were as transparent as the sea. He knew that clouds were an illusion too. In science class he had learned that clouds were made of water but really were smoke. You could not get your hands on them. You could not sleep on them like the angels in church. But up there he could not believe that the mountains and caves and rivers of the sky had no substance.

He decided he would not be an astronaut after all. The world made of clouds looked just like the one below it, except everything was white. The way New Jersey would look if all the color was drained out of it, the way his mother's face looked. The way dead people look. He was in heaven. Ghosts lived here. The only thing that kept him from losing his substance too was the seatbelt around his waist. He had started to cry but couldn't make his mother understand why.

After discovering that first lie, he devoted himself to staying alert. He stopped taking anyone's word for anything. His grades dropped as he started writing: "I don't know for sure," in answer to questions on history tests. Science appealed to him for a while because it could be proven, but science never answered the questions he most cared about.

When he first saw the pictures of the Hiroshima mushroom cloud, he knew its purpose immediately. It looked exactly like the cloud kingdom in the second sky and it would turn everyone into ghosts and there would be no sky at all. Was it his duty to die for the way of life that produced that cloud? He didn't know for sure. If the bombers had droned overhead and turned New Jersey into scrap metal and bone, necessity might have commanded him to fight. That kind of thinking kept him on his own in Canada the first four years and made the last two at the Farmhouse a struggle. Only one kind of exile got food and shelter in Canada and that was a noble one. His kind learned to keep their mouths shut.

**4**

CENTRAL CANADA LOOKED remarkably like his memory of America. The rocky plains, the big sky, could fool him on a bad morning. Ragged lines of Norway pine, an empty highway, now and then a gas station with the old curve-top pumps he loved so well, a yellow frame house, cows, quiet, crows. From the front porch at the Farmhouse north of Toronto, he'd call the view Wisconsin, Nebraska, Michigan. Then he'd hear Georgia yelling at Steven and remember.

Tonight there would be twelve for supper. Twelve carrots, twelve potatoes, 24 onions for the stew. Third Sunday in January and no snow. A mild wind in the wheat fields; everyone home. Yoder stood in the Farmhouse kitchen peeling carrots, cutting potatoes into "bite-size pieces" according to Georgia's instructions. Bite-size was a precise measure, it seemed. Georgia kept coming into the kitchen, stealing a handful of carrot slices, pointing to the potatoes and saying: "Bite-size, Yoder. Cut them smaller."

The kitchen was his favorite place, cooking his favorite job. It was solitary; he was good at it. Everyone murmured gratefully to him at least once a day. Why the rest of them weren't out walking or playing touch football in the field, he didn't know. All afternoon they'd been camped out in the living room—on the pink pillows, on the sofa covered in an Indian print bedspread—drinking homemade beer and arguing about the amnesty. The war had ended in every house but this one. In Georgia's living room, you'd think dazed American boys still fled across the border into her arms. From what he'd heard, Georgia had been something of a celebrity in the old days. The press had called her the "Madonna of the Dodgers." He'd taken to calling her Donna.

Yoder had helped himself to too much beer and his aim with the knife was off. No potato peeler or tongs or spatula to be found in this enormous kitchen. Two years without a spatula—his eggs swam in butter or never left the pan at all. To cut the rotten parts away, Yoder used his buck knife with the black grip handle that clenched his fist. With each stroke, the knife came to rest against the bulb of his thumb. One potato for the dodgers, two potato for the Canucks.

Jamie appeared at his side and Yoder gave the boy a carrot. Not yet eight years old, Jamie spoke of God whispering stories to him at night. Already a vegetarian, he sometimes refused food entirely. The crunch and mash of chewing hurt his ears, he said. Jamie had blue eyes like his mother's. "Show me the trick again, Yo," Jamie pleaded. "I forgot the middle part."

Yoder fought a moment of exasperation; they'd practiced the card trick a dozen times. Jamie had trouble focusing on the fine points of deception. His imagination got in the way, inventing stories about the battle between the Jack of Hearts and the King of Diamonds. "Not now, Jamie," he said, hearing the impatience in his voice.

"Please." The boy was fidgeting, opening and shutting a cupboard door.

"After dinner. Go ask your mother if she wants to get out of here and take a walk." Yoder propelled Jamie by the shoulders through the doorway.

In the next room, Steven's voice rose above the others. They lived on talk. Like fish, they opened their mouths to get air and it turned into words. Yoder cooked to keep quiet, ran in the wheat fields to keep from talking, hid away in his attic room—reading anything—to keep from shouting. Like his father, he scorned gatherings of the clan. He didn't believe in mass movements, and he didn't want to be found out. The first winter in Toronto, he'd joined the beer and pizza debates, grateful for community after four years on his own. But he heard a chauvinism he distrusted, sanctifying everything Canadian, rejecting anything that smelled of their own country. That kind of blind belonging was as dangerous here as it was at home.

As he dropped the vegetables into the roiling water, Yoder heard the argument escalate. He hoped Julie would come away and walk the fields with him. The others would be up all night, picking Carter's motives apart until they found a way to stay in Canada and congratulate themselves for the rest of their lives. For the dodgers, going home meant giving up a crown of thorns. And the deserters, as usual, were being bullied. Most wanted to go back, but they needed the dodgers' permission. There was something almost Catholic about the dodgers' ethic: Only one right choice—but you can make it at any time and still be saved.

Yoder watched them through the kitchen doorway, blocking out their voices to see if he could make them into fish, into big pale flounder. Talking all at once, hands stroking the air, it looked like a discussion but he heard the words "war machine"; he heard "moral duty"; he heard "legacy of resistance"; he heard, for the hundredth time, how much Bobby missed his horses back home, his ridiculous goddamn horses back home.

Steven jumped to his feet to shout at Walter, who was too pliant to give him any real argument. "I'll never go back," Steven said. "And I've got no respect for anyone who does." Steven paused, almost daring someone to contradict him. Georgia sat knitting a sweater, maintaining her resolve to stay out of this messy American discussion. A black caftan embroidered with elephants and tigers hid the girth of her body. Yoder kept imagining how nice the same shirt would look on Julie.

"I'm thinking maybe I'll just go visit my sister in Wyoming," Bobby was saying. "She's got my horses. Then maybe come back here. I don't know. What do you all think, eh?"

Bobby looked as confused as he had the day he arrived, limping up the driveway, claiming he'd been told the Farmhouse was a place he could get a chocolate bar and a bed.

"That's letting them win, Bobby. Don't you see? And what about Walter here? He can't go back for a visit. Deserters need a case by case review." Steven spat the words out, punctuating them with jabs of his finger. The sun coated the grimy picture window, turning it opaque. Steven's huge shoulders were outlined against the glowing glass.

"I like it right here," Walter said. "Beats the hell out of East Texas." Walter had enlisted after hearing Barry Sadler sing "The Ballad of the Green Beret" in concert. He still had not recovered from the betrayal.

"And West Orange." Smoke from Randy's pipe lingered in the air. The household's other deserter, he'd grown up so close to Yoder's hometown that they knew some of the same people.

"The point is, we don't need a pardon. We didn't do anything wrong," Bobby said.

"Now you're talking," said Steven. "I'm not moving until they admit that we're the real heroes of this fucking war."

"Amen," someone said.

"Give it up!" Yoder barked, stepping into the room, holding the knife before him like a spear. "How long are you going to sit around and talk about this?" They snapped their mouths shut, turned in slow motion to stare at him. He could feel the waters part. "You just didn't want to get your asses shot off. Why can't you admit it! The war went *on*. We didn't save anybody but ourselves." An echo of his voice returned to him. Instead of a room full of talk, it seemed he'd disturbed a great silence. He heard the slap of Jamie's cards on the bare wood floor. Outside a crow wheeled and screamed. "There have always been cowards and I'm sick of hearing about how this time we're heroes."

"Speak for yourself, Yoder." He knew it would be Steven who would stop him. Steven became Georgia's lover shortly after moving in and his position in the household was secure. "We all know there's cowards among us," he drawled. "But I didn't think there were any in this house."

"This house reeks with cowards."

"It only takes one." Steven took a step toward him, his flannel shirt tight across his belly.

"Yoder, you don't really mean that." Julie broke in, as she did whenever there was tension, leaning forward from the low orange chair with the broken spring. "You've said yourself there was no other choice to be made." Yoder flinched at the mention of their earlier conversation. He'd said things he didn't quite believe because he was attracted to her. "It's a brave thing you've all done. Leaving your families and your country behind."

"It's not my country," Yoder whispered. "It's not my country any more than this is. Being born in a split-level in New Jersey does not make it my country." Among them now, his knife flashed in the weak sunlight. "I've got no desire to kill anyone, but believe me I'd take on any one of you if it meant I'd be here to see the next morning." He saw the horror in their pale faces, saw Steven reach into his pocket for his own knife, heard someone whisper: "Yoder, put it away." His time in the house was over and the sooner he buried the knife, the easier it would be for all of them to dismiss the afternoon as theater. But something moved in him like water before a dam. He thrust the knife into the air and felt a strength in his stance that had not been there before. It was power, and he held on to it to see how long he could balance on the edge between what was real, and what was wrong with everything.

Betting on the truth to keep them in their seats, Yoder turned to locate a rustling noise from over by the kitchen door. "Stop it!" Jamie hissed, leaping into the circle. Yoder dropped to his knees, sheathing the knife seconds before Jamie's small body hurled against him, knocking over beer bottles, the foam running in waves across the scarred wooden floor. "Stop it! Stop it! Stop it!" Jamie's smooth fingers tightened around his neck. "Hey, kid, it's me. It was only a game," Yoder said as lightly as he could. Jamie's eyes surfaced, cleared of their determination. He rolled off Yoder onto his back, stopping still with his legs in the air, staring down at his fingers. Yoder remained on his knees, rubbing his palms back and forth against the grain of his blue jeans, dimly aware of Julie leading Jamie away. Beer ran between his toes.

"Everybody in this house drinks too much." It was Bobby.

"You're a lucky asshole, Yoder."

"I saw you go for your knife, Steven," Yoder said, leaping to his feet.

"Those knives are for baling hay!" Georgia screamed from the corner where she'd retreated during the fight. "I don't want this in my house. Get out of here. Both of you."

Yoder wanted to put his arms around her but instead he went outside where the sun was warm, though it was just after Christmas. *The sun's not yellow it's chicken.* The war was wrong. He believed that. But more important, it was convenient. He had chosen exile, in the way that a hungry man must learn to love his stomach's gnaw. He'd traded Sal and the Mets for a cold country where he did not have to pretend to belong. Since he'd been old enough to sense the difference between himself and others, he'd wanted nothing more than to feel at home. At home. Having already arrived. Hold out your hand and we'll give you a stamp that won't ever wash off. A tune to hum, clothes, a job, T.V. shows that won't fail you, something to strive for, something to buy. In grade school he invented Thor, a planet of twins that he claimed as his true homeland. He and his twin had been tragically separated, the fantasy went, but would be reunited some day, some Christmas, some quiet August morning.

During the next few days Yoder found himself spending most of his time with Jamie. Jamie had not yet separated from the birds, the trees, the river. He began to perch on the steps outside Yoder's door in the morning, waiting to sit with him over breakfast, hardly speaking, acceding to the bond he believed had formed between them.

He called him "Yo" in a voice that squeezed out of his throat, high and questioning. "Do you know God, Yo?" he would ask and there was no point in lying. Yoder tried to explain about the moon—that the closest God had ever come to him was in moonlight one cold January in Michigan. He explained how he felt about trees—that they were holy like a church, and Jamie listened. But since Jamie knew God like a brother he seemed only to feel a bit sorry for him, to sit a little closer on the steps while Yoder worked on Georgia's car or cleaned fish.

When Tundra, Georgia's sweet blue-eyed husky, was found dead in the road, brought to the Farmhouse by a truck driver who told them that he kept his own dog tied up to prevent this very thing, Jamie accepted comfort from no one but Yoder. Georgia's screams could be heard throughout the house, while Yoder helped Jamie dig a grave in the back by the lilac bushes. Yoder did not believe in decent burials for animals. He'd let pet turtles, snakes and rabbits decompose in their natural way. But he hadn't known what else to do with the energy of his grief. When he saw the dog who'd walked so many miles by his side blotched red with blood, Yoder spat in the face of the driver's horror, taking the dog roughly from his arms. Though he'd hoped to show Jamie how to face the truth without flinching, his tears had mixed with the dirt on his face as he dug out the heavy black soil and laid the white, white body in the frozen ground.

That night the accusations began to surface. Jamie and Julie had spent the morning in town. The others had been working at the resister's center in Toronto. It was obvious to everyone who had left the gate open. Yoder couldn't completely deny it, even to himself, though he had a vague memory of latching the white iron gate behind him and seeing Tundra's pink tongue hanging out as he turned away toward the shed.

It was not enough.

Julie drove him to the highway and they were quiet together. Three years of continually falling toward one another, continually breaking the other's heart, had made them friends. Without the pressure of commitment, they could talk and walk the wheat fields when everyone else said it was too cold.

They stood by the highway intersection for a long time. Julie kicked the gravel into little piles with the toe of her boot. In composure her plain face took on a dignity, like a pioneer woman looking into an approaching storm. "I've always wanted to get a letter from you," she said. "Watching you hunched over that blue pad of yours, I've envied the people you hold so close."

"I'll write," he said. He reached to put his arm around her shoulder but dropped it quickly, remembering how awkward it was that she was taller than he.

"We'll all miss you, you know that. The others just can't say it."

Yoder wanted to kiss her on the mouth but hesitated and hit her cheek instead, instantly regretting the lost opportunity. "Nothing stopping you and Jamie from coming down for a visit someday."

"I've been thinking we might do that." She said "bean"— he'd miss the way the Canadians stretched their vowels. "Jamie wants to see the Houston Space Center."

"Just let me know. I'll show you around." He knew they would never leave this flat country and so did she and that was why he had to leave right away so that nothing more would be said that wasn't meant. "I'm glad I know you," he said, trying to make it come out in the plain way he felt it. "And don't worry about Jamie." He had touched her arm then and picked up his knapsack and the box tied with red string, and walked down the road, staring at the gravel. He remembered thinking how much it resembled the gravel that lay alongside every road where he'd ever said goodbye.

Yoder woke in the dark car with a series of small jerks, like a spasm, the kind that Sal had when falling to sleep. Once, he'd asked her if she noticed that uneasy passing in him but she hadn't understood. He could catch it only upon waking, some resistance to returning, physical proof of the distance he traveled in sleep. His dreams had been of Tundra, of his warm body slit open and stuffed with weeds, and of his own arms pulling hard on the dog's flesh to close the wound.

Yoder stared out at the darkness, still caught in the dream, remembering the way Tundra's whole body would twist when he wanted a walk in the field. He returned to the gate, the white paint chipped along its curve; the expectant bark; the yellow hay poking through the snow; bits of saliva shiny in Tundra's fur. He'd closed the gate—but firmly? Decisively? There was no getting around it. Some part of him had said goodbye in that last look over his shoulder. In his life-time he'd been accused of not being responsible by just about everyone in a position to accuse. Responsible to whom? Everyone? Everyone at once? It made him feel tight and cloudy. As a kid he could relieve that feeling by slipping a Tootsie Roll Pop in his pocket at the store. Later he'd learned to slip away to a space inside where he was responsible only to himself. Was he responsible for Tundra? For the 51,000 dead? For the boat people? His father's shame, Jamie's love? His chest closed, his eyes opened, shutting out the memory of the white fur embroidered with blood.

Up front Jake drove with both hands clenching the wheel, elbows bent, nose to the windshield like he was having trou-ble seeing the road. Buck had his arm slung over the seat back, his beer dangling near Yoder's face. Headlights of pass-ing cars lit droplets of condensation on the can. Shifting slightly in his seat, Yoder noticed a sickening wetness in the crotch of his pants. Had he somehow pissed in his sleep? Was that even possible? Had they noticed? Yoder pulled his hat back down over his eyes and wrapped his arms across his chest, jumping slightly at the sound of Jake's laughter.

"You, Ratner? You used to be an altar boy?" Jake said. "Hell, so was I. Our priest, Father Peterson, he was a drunk. My job was to check the chalice to make sure he hadn't downed the wine before the service. Everybody knew. He ended up in some home for alkie priests. A retreat they called it."

"Right," said Buck. "So, didn't you hate it? Having to fold your hands and bow all the time like some kind of Jap house-boy?"

Assholes, he thought. Did they know? Evans would annihi-late him for this one. They'd leave him by the side of the road. He'd demand a gas station, he'd make them drop him off at a gas station. Why couldn't he control his own body? He wondered about the seat. Had it spread?

"So, did you think that nuns never went to the bathroom?" Buck asked.

"Or that they were bald?"

"Hey, Jake, they are bald. Don't you know?"

Opening one eye, Yoder looked out from beneath his hat to

the left and then to the right. Evans was slumped against the door, head thrown back, his rubbery mouth wide open. Passed out. They were both passed out, Willie still holding a beer can tipped across Yoder's leg. Beer. The asshole had soaked him in beer like a Wisconsin knockwurst. It was perfect. He was a fool but they didn't know it.

"So you were an altar boy. I'll be damned, Buck."

"We'll probably both be damned."

Yoder laughed in the dark car.

"Don't tell me *you* were an altar boy," Jake said, turning slightly at the wheel.

"Where are we, anyway?" he asked, resting his arms on the front seat back.

"A couple hours outside Newark."

"You want me to drive?"

"No way," Jake said. "Hitchhikers don't drive my car." Jake turned back and began to talk to Buck about someone named E.J. who had eaten a beer glass in a bar in Detroit.

Yoder put his hat over his crotch and stared at the pinpricks in the plastic on the roof of the car. He couldn't tell them how good it was to hear that kind of talk—the late night idle insults between friends. When he had hitchhiked with Josh for the first time, they'd gotten stranded about 50 miles outside of Ann Arbor in an incredible rainstorm. The sky had been clear all day but one nasty cloud had moved in on the sun. He remembered the raindrops, big as jellybeans, and how the water came down like it was poured from a bucket. Josh had worn two sweatshirts; he was always prepared, as if he had special information. Josh had just thrown him the gray hooded one when the storm broke. He thought it was the funniest thing in the world—them getting soaked and nothing to be done about it.

The sweatshirts quickly became useless and Yoder peeled off his shirt. Josh did the same and they ran down the empty road barechested and yelping in the October rain. They ran like they were in some movie shot in Wyoming, expecting to be on the road for miles, but the road curved and just ahead was a town with a restaurant called The Coffee Cup where they used all the paper towels in the bathroom to dry themselves off, then sat at the counter and Yoder had coffee with cream for the first time in his life. Coffee in a white china mug with real cream because coffee was the restaurant's specialty. It had tasted like rescue, smooth and rich, and he had two cups—like the heat of a campfire or someone catching your eye in a crowd and smiling.

When he thought of Josh he saw him striding slightly ahead with his Labrador retriever, Blue, at his side, and his blond hair pulled into a curly mass at his neck. Josh both believed that Blue was a higher being *and* loved baseball. His family had money and you could see it in the way he held himself upright in the world as if surveying from an elevated spot on the property. Josh's presence in his life was the closest thing to approval Yoder had ever had. He remembered with embarrassment the hours Josh had spent teaching him to sing. They'd play their guitars while Josh sang in his ear, over and over, until Yoder had his own part recorded in his brain. Then they would sing together, Josh's whining voice sounding like Neil Young and his voice underneath, softer and deeper.

More than a year ago Josh had written of his plan to live alone on thirty acres of land he'd bought in the mountains of Maine. He'd sent along a sketch of the house he hoped to build. But Josh was a dreamer. Josh might still be living in Rydertown, wherever the hell that was—near the coast, he'd said. Yoder decided to go there. He needed some time with Josh, just the two of them. He sat up to speak but was stopped by the sight of Buck, his head thrown back over the seat, snoring slightly, and Jake, tight at the wheel again, talking to himself. Talking loudly.

"Carol's gonna be pissed that it's so late." Jake talked right into the windshield. "We're gonna wake her up and she'll be pissed. I'm going to see the Statue of Liberty. Evans and Will won't want to go. They'll be checking out the action in Times Square by tomorrow noon. Carol will go with me. No, damn, she'll probably have to work. I want to ride past it in that boat."

And see her rising in green. See her face as big as a canyon, never faltering. And love her. And wish it were true. A lady in the harbor to welcome us all.

He wrote only once—just a week after he left Toronto. Every-thing was fine, he said; his friends in Michigan were taking care of him. I was a little jealous of how happy he sounded to be with them. I wonder if he married the woman he spoke of when he arrived at the Farmhouse. Her letters had stopped coming that last year. I know because she always covered the outside of the envelope with these fantastic drawings.

I missed him with a kind of aching for a good long time. He needed me, and it's embarrassing to admit how much I liked that. He talked to me. He listened to Jamie. Sometimes I'd pre-tend we were a family. That was the one thing I could never tell him.

He's the only one who went back. Some of the guys are still at the Farmhouse, though Jamie and I left more than a year ago. Steven and Walter applied for citizenship; Bobby moved to Brit-ish Columbia with a woman he met a short time after Yoder left. They're going to raise horses out there, I guess. At the Center, we still get a few every day coming in to find out about amnesty, or just to talk through their confusion. Most of them decide to stay in Canada. They miss their families, but now they can visit. I'm glad they like our country, but it makes me wonder what's wrong down there to make so many good men leave a whole country behind. They're going to build a memorial in Washing-ton, I hear. For some reason it means a lot to me that it was designed by a woman.

I wonder if he ever thinks of me. I'm simpler than the other people he knows, but he seemed interested in what I thought and felt—like he was looking for something. When he was lis-tening, he was yours. He never took his eyes off you. Nothing distracted him. I've never known anyone—except Jamie, per-haps—who could get as happy about something simple like the sun on the wheat fields and a bird swooping by at just the right moment, crying once. Of course, he'd say there was nothing sim-ple about it.

There was always a little tension between us. I think he would *have liked us to be lovers. But when I told him that I wasn't in love with him—I just loved him—it seemed to be all right and he was there for me in the same way. It was perfect really. For me, I guess. Not for him.*

———————————————————

Evans AND WILLIE remained unconscious, waking only
to applaud his leaving on the steps of Penn Station in downtown Newark. The stone steps, worn to a curve in their
center, looking soft and broken in the moonlight, cheered
him. He'd begun many trips from here in the days when he
still believed he would be missed. He loved this old station,
its shopworn elegance teetering on the edge of decay.

It was just after midnight and the building echoed his
progress across the deserted waiting room. Young black men
lounged in corners, watching him pass, sometimes nodding
in his direction. Yoder wondered what they saw in him—
what solidarity they imagined. On the wooden benches lay
the others: Old men with faces like cottage cheese, retching
in corners; women curled under cloth coats. He moved
among them, counting. Fifteen. Fifteen with no place to go.
Each marked a territory with shopping bag or purse, a pil-
lowcase tied with rope, a dented suitcase. He too carried his
home in a sack. But that was because he wanted to travel
light; he'd look silly with a Naugahyde suitcase.

When he discovered that the train for Boston wouldn't

leave until morning, Yoder reluctantly took his place on the benches, locking his arms around his knapsack, resting his head on his cardboard box. He did not strike up a conversation as was his custom when among those with special knowledge. He didn't want to know them.

His eyes were opened by newspapers rustling, the sound of high heels and the smell of aftershave. Monday morning— the world in a big fat hurry. While he slept, the crowd in the station had replicated itself, like amoeba on speed. Men and women struggled with luggage, with time. He watched the flow of their dance across the lobby, in time to the litany of possibilities called over the loudspeaker. For once these tightly bound people, pinched inside their shoes, had one up on him. They knew where they were headed, their destinations spelled out in fuzzy carboned letters on tickets they clutched in their hands. To Boston—to Maine—then what? What if Josh had already moved out to his land in the mountains? What if he were dead? Or working?

Yoder washed his face and rinsed his mouth in the bathroom sink, then wandered past food stands, the smells nauseating him and awakening his hunger at the same time. Everywhere people were eating, standing at counters wolfing down doughnuts, munching out of paper bags on the benches. His seatmates had vanished—to curl up in a corner somewhere—or take their chances outdoors in the weak sunlight.

Lightheaded from a hunger so familiar he barely recognized it, Yoder stood in line for a Sabrett. His father had taught him to love the spicy steamed dogs buried in chili and onion. To eat three and four at a sitting, looking out over the track at the Meadowlands, watching the horses beat the dust. He'd missed the hot grease, the doughy bun. He reached into his knapsack to pay for two dogs and a Coke, and saw that his wallet was gone.

"Help," he muttered helplessly, and everyone shuffled away, leaving him on his knees, emptying his knapsack onto the floor while suits filed around him for coffee and Danish. Toothbrush, buck knife, harmonica, the essays of John Muir, blue writing tablet, wool socks and shirt, two oranges. No wallet. Which one of the bastards had done it? Evans, he guessed. Why? The length of his hair, his smelly feet? Had Evans overheard his conversation with Jake about Vietnam? He'd underestimated Evans, figured him for a harmless jerk who didn't know the depth of his own immaturity. In all of Yoder's 15 years on the road no one had ever violated the code: You didn't steal from hitchhikers. But they were too young to know that.

Once it seemed a mark of success not to need money. But the constant tallying of his dwindling cash had turned money into an obsession. With nothing but lint in his pockets, he couldn't take the train to Boston or the bus to Maine. He considered calling his brother but the thought just made him hungrier. He stood up, forcing people to break stride around him. He knew to expect the worst. Expect it. And expect it and expect it. Then stand up and walk. He took a deep breath, drawing on the exhaled sighs of travelers. The only thing he believed in was movement. Shielding his eyes from the assault of winter sunlight, Yoder walked out of the station, stepped off the curb crusted over in dirt, snow and garbage, and stuck out his thumb, turning his back toward the road north to Maine.

The Maine of his imagination was laughably romantic and wrong. It looked more like British Columbia than he would ever have guessed. A desolate rocky country broken now and then by beat-up towns whose citizens seemed to retire early and hide in dark houses. Where were the lobstermen in yellow slickers and where were the artists painting lighthouses, and where were the lighthouses? "Ten bucks says I'll see you by the side of the road on my way back down." A trucker about his own age had taken him all the way up Highway 1 to the Rydertown turnoff. Twenty says you won't ever see me again, Yoder thought, slamming the heavy door. The inside of the truck smelled of gasoline; Yoder felt soaked in it.

Alone on the road, the silence nibbled at his confidence. He hugged himself and glanced about, expecting wolves or highway robbers. Snow blew across the pitted asphalt like cocaine on a mirror. He walked what he thought to be a mile without seeing a light, the forest of jackpine muffling the

sounds of the receding highway. Even the moon's light
seemed to bounce off the frozen ground and dissipate in the
air. He hadn't imagined that it would be this remote. Josh's
last letter had assailed him with paranoid ravings about
cities. "Armies of blank faces" was a line that stuck in his
memory. At the time he'd thought Josh had simply come to
his senses. Now his words seemed more ominous.

A muddy sign around a turn in the road announced the
town. There were 32 houses in Rydertown, Josh had written,
and the one he'd rented could be found just across "an old
covered bridge, hacked-up with 60 years of graffiti." The
town offered little to the stranger, less, Yoder thought, to the
resident. Not much more than a field, scattered with misshapen houses, their windows covered in heavy plastic. The
buildings looked half-repaired as if work had continued until
the last minute when winter blew in, freezing the paint in the
can, the ladder to the side of the house.

Once across the bridge he let out a little yelp at the sight of
Josh's old red pickup truck parked in the yard of a frame
house that sagged comically to one side. He ran like a child
toward the lights of home. Josh would open the door and
slap his hand to his forehead in amazement. They would
drink a beer and dissolve the darkness. Yoder would never let
Josh know how needy he felt standing on the bridge at the
threshold of his little town, a supplicant. Yoder knocked non-
stop, staccato, on the door whose green paint curled away
from the wood like apple peelings. A five-pointed wrought-
iron star swung from a nail. Years ago he'd given the star to
Josh, an embodiment of what he saw as the great difference
between them. Josh's life evolved in perfect harmony with
his dreams; he got what he wanted, always. But it seemed
not so much his own doing as the unfolding of some cosmic
scheme—some lucky star on the other side of the universe
from Yoder's own burning comet. He smiled to see it hanging
here now.

An impatient voice: "Hang in, I'm coming," reached him
just as the door opened and Josh's face emerged from the
darkness. Something different. The beard? No, Josh had
always kept a beard to stroke with his long fingers, while

doing the thinking out loud that was his idea of conversation. Then he saw that Josh's curly blond hair was cut short and tucked behind his ears.

"Yoder! What the hell?"

"I'm not sure. I was headed for New Jersey."

"Good Lord in heaven. How'd you find us?" Josh's face broke into a huge confused smile. The ability of his black eyes to soften, as they did now, made women trust Josh in a way Yoder had always distrusted. "We're not exactly on the map."

"No problem. I looked for the pickup."

"Are you—Is it OK? I mean, are you in trouble? What'd you do—just split?"

The greatest threat to democracy is an uninformed public. Someone very perceptive had said that. For the first time, it seemed that the years he'd spent in Canada had been stolen from him.

"Amnesty, Josh. You ever hear of it? Carter—he's the President. You ever hear of him? He granted amnesty a few weeks ago. I'm not asking you to hide a criminal. I just wanted to see you. Besides, I've never been to Maine."

Josh scratched his head, looking up from under his thick eyebrows as if trying to decide whether he believed him. "Come on in. Jesus, come on in and meet Ruthie," he said finally, stepping aside.

Ruthie. The name made him think of patent leather shoes and candy bars. He had hoped to find Josh alone here. Yoder ran his hand through his hair and kept his eyes low, as if meeting some girl's parents for the first time with dark thoughts on his mind.

Sea shells circled plants the size of saplings in the small front room. Rosy-colored braided rugs lay scattered across the badly scratched wooden floor, and from the walls hung weavings sprouting furry streams of yarn, feathers, leather, sticks and bone. The air smelled of wood smoke and saddle-soap. Sand candles in various stages of meltdown lined the windowsills and a sewing machine in the corner was jammed with yards of yellow fabric that hung to the floor. This was not Josh's kind of room. In a rocking chair, bent over a hand loom, sat a woman whose hair was pulled into thick braids. Yoder was struck by the strength in her face—like textbook photographs of the women of Appalachia. Josh's hand on his back urged him forward.

"Ruthie, meet Yoder. From back in Michigan. I've told you about him, remember?"

Ruth nodded, her face registering nothing.

"He's the one who went to Canada while I sat out the war in a rock 'n' roll band. He's been up there, what, five years now?"

"Six."

"He tells me Carter decided to grant amnesty. We don't pay much attention to the news, Yoder. What's the deal? Is it like a pardon?"

"Welcome back." Ruth's polite smile seemed an excuse to stare. Her mouth hung slightly open.

"It's complicated," Yoder said, turning to Josh. "Not everybody gets to come back."

"You should have let us know your plans," Josh said. "We're only a couple hours from the border. We could have met you."

"Actually, I came in through Windsor."

Ruth set down the loom and tipped her head toward him, puzzled. "You don't mean you drove all the way up here just to see us?"

"I hitched."

Her eyes dropped to his feet. "Impressive. You must be tired." When she stood, stretching her back with her hands at her waist, he saw that she was a little thick around the middle, like most women who wore flannel shirts over their sweaters. But he could also see why Josh might think her attractive. She had oatmeal-colored skin and clear eyes—the morning beauty of a twelve-year-old. And her voice—low, with a beery rasp to it, promised a sense of humor. "We're not real prepared for company," she said. "Let's see, why don't you just take off your boots—they look awfully muddy—then we'll figure out where we can put you for the night."

Yoder tried to pull off his boots without sending mud flying all over the rug. He wanted to sit down but his pants were

dirtier than his boots. Ruth watched him, glancing over now
and then at Josh who rubbed the top of his head vigorously
as if he'd just woken up.

"You know, Josh," Ruth said, "we should check our box
more often for mail."

"I didn't write," he countered a little too abruptly. "It was a
spur of the moment thing—coming here, I mean."

Ruth seemed not to hear him. She scraped a footstool
along the floor to a closet and rummaged around on the top
shelf. "We should have kept those blankets and pillows we
gave away to Beth and Jack," she said.

"Don't worry, Yoder can make himself comfortable on any
floor, isn't that right, Yoder?" Josh had a way of building an
answer into every question he asked.

He'd opened the wrong door, stepped on stage, and now
the actors were trying to cover for his unexplainable presence in their play. *Because something is happening here/But
you don't know what it is/Do you, Mister Jones?* The wind rattled the shutters; it was cold here. "Sure," Yoder said, pulling
words from somewhere despite his exhaustion. "In fact, remember the time, Josh, when we got so drunk we spent the
night in the john at the Flame?" He waited for Josh to join in,
feeling ridiculous standing in the middle of the room with his
boots balanced in his hand and his knapsack still on his back.
Josh stared at the floor, the tips of his fingers tucked into his
jeans. He wore a ring. Had he married this woman?

"Sure, I remember."

"And remember how the guy couldn't believe it when he
opened up the next morning. The look on his face. And you
told him—what did you say?—that it was simply a case of
constipation. That was a great line. That was great."

Ruth swept the boots out of his hand and disappeared
through a swinging door into the next room. Suddenly he felt
certain that he'd interrupted a fight. Josh gestured toward
the rocking chair. "Sit down, Yoder. Ruthie's about ready to
go to sleep. We try to be in bed by 10:00, so we can be up by
6:00 for the cows and chickens. We've got cows and chickens
out back. Did you see? I'm trying my luck with them here
before I have to depend upon them on the mountain. If you
stick to their schedule they'll give you all the eggs and milk

you could want." This was the old Josh, his eyes lit up, words rushing against one another. "Can I get you something? You must be starved."

"You got a beer?"

"Ah, no. We don't drink, but let's see, we've got apple juice, tea, roastaroma."

"You don't drink? What do you mean? You mean beer? Since when?"

Josh perched on the edge of a straight-backed chair and extended his legs out in front of him. It wasn't the same Josh without his long hair framing his face. "Yoder, I've got to tell you, I've learned a lot in the past few years. Ruthie's taught me a lot." He'd seen that look before; Josh on a roll. "I don't need alcohol, nobody does. Think about it, man. It makes you sick, right? Dizzy, stupid, and sick. Your body tells you every time you drink that it's wrong. Robs the body of vitamin C. Speaking of that, I want you to try a couple of these." An impressive wall of bookshelves made from split logs and tree stumps held a whole row of what looked like vitamin bottles. Josh flashed a label at him.

Yoder waved it away. "No thanks. I don't like vitamins. They stick in my throat for hours."

"Do you more good than a beer. Go ahead, pop a couple."

"It's a rip-off, Josh. You're going to die anyway. You really into this stuff or what?"

"I've never felt better in my life."

"You used to feel pretty damn good when you were loaded, too." Yoder rocked back in the chair, betting that it would hold his full weight. "I suppose you're going to tell me that you don't eat regular food anymore either. I suppose you eat sprouts or some goddamn thing. I suppose you're going to tell me you don't have an Oreo cookie in the house. What are you, some kind of born-again hippie?"

"That's right. No Oreos." Ruth stood erect and still in the doorway, a white flannel nightgown moving in waves about her ankles. "We don't eat anything made with white sugar. And yes, we believe in God." She turned to Josh. "I'm going upstairs. Here's some blankets and Yoder's boots. I've cleaned them up a little. See you both in the morning."

She blew in and out of the room like some kind of kamikaze priestess. Was he supposed to kiss her feet? "You let her speak for you like that all the time?" Yoder said when she seemed safely out of earshot.

"What she said is true for both of us."

"White sugar—OK. But God? What's going on here, Josh?"

"What's going on? It's 10 o'clock at night. I answer the door and you're standing there expecting I don't know what from me, and Ruthie is a little pissed off. As far as God goes, it's no big deal. I can't explain it and I don't care whether you understand it or not. I don't go to church, I just go to the woods. And when Ruthie's sick, sometimes I pray."

"OK, OK." He felt so tired. "I do know what you mean about the woods." It shamed him that he couldn't tell Josh about the moon, the way he spoke to it sometimes, the way it shone hot or cold in rhythm with his feelings, and how once a sliver of a moon had appeared to him in a sky so blue it had looked like the white light of heaven shining through a slice in a creamy blue drape.

"Let's just put it this way: The less said about the old days the better. Ruthie wasn't there and I think she feels left out. Besides, she doesn't find the details of my past very interesting. I was pretty crazy back then."

"Crazy? *This* is crazy. I thought you came out here to build your own house, not to purify yourself, for christsake."

"Ruthie's shown me that I was wrong about some things."

Josh had never been wrong. He was the single rightest person on earth. "Look I'm history, OK? I'll be out of here first thing in the morning."

"Yoder, don't be stupid. You're staying. Tomorrow we'll go see my land."

"Forget it, Josh. You don't owe me anything."

They held each other's eyes, dueling, until Josh moved over to the woodstove. He bent and selected a few pieces from the woodpile, placing them with agonizing deliberateness on the bed of ashes. "I've missed you. Don't be a jerk."

Josh always said the right thing. You couldn't trust him.

"In the morning, then," Josh said, leaving with a wave of his hand. "Sleep near the stove tonight. It gets cold down here."

When he heard a door close upstairs, Yoder kicked the pile

of blankets across the floor. They made no sound. The streetlight by the bridge projected shadows on the wall. He
watched his huge hunched form prowl the living room, opening closets and drawers. He wanted an explanation. The
shelves held books on organic gardening, solar energy, reflex-
ology, homeopathic medicine, and a tattered book with a
Betty Crocker mom on the cover titled *Sew Your Own*. The
name Ruth Kassa was written on the flyleaves. In her clear,
perfect hand she'd inscribed a book of e.e. cummings poems:
"To Josh: We're all we've got—never, never stop." It sounded
a lot like a Moody Blues song. He hated the Moody Blues. He
was thirsty and angry all over again that he'd come this far
and there wasn't a beer. Homelessness, it seemed, wasn't
simply a matter of borders.

He awoke the next morning to an incredibly annoying sound
that he later decided was a rooster crowing. Above the morning noises of pans rattling and water running, he heard
voices. He heard his name. Pulling a blanket over his
shoulders, he crawled across the room and crouched by the
door, holding his ear an inch away so the door would not
swing inward, exposing his naked body. His chest had become gooseflesh, ugly white and riddled. They seemed to be
talking about breakfast, about having enough eggs but not
enough bread.

   Josh spoke deliberately, as if to a small child. "He's a friend
of mine."

   "I thought you didn't have any friends. It was one of the
things I liked most about you."

   "Ruthie, the guy's been in Canada for five years." A cupboard door slammed. "The least we can do is give him a
place to stay for a few days."

   "Six."

   "What?"

   "He said he was there six years."

   "Whatever. You might learn to like him."

   "He's got the smell of the city all over him."

   "So did we."

   "We need to be alone, Josh."

Eavesdropping was its own punishment, like reading a

lover's diary. Yoder pulled on his clothes and darted out the front door. He sprinted to the bushes at the side of the house and unzipped his pants. The air felt dangerously cold and he finished quickly. The countryside looked fully as forbidding as it had the night before, only in the morning light its scrappy poverty was more evident. Fields of brown grass rose above the snow; trucks and shells of automobiles lay scattered in all directions; property lines seemed vague, marked off sometimes by wooden fences, sometimes only by the barking of dogs. From behind him came the sound of machinery turning.

His hair had grown stiff from three days on the road. Yoder drew it back, shaping a ponytail, then let it down flat against his neck. He walked around the house to the backyard. A pair of dusty red sheds leaned comfortably against one another at the end of the long skinny property and off to the right stood two beautifully constructed chicken coops. Through a window in the back door, he could see them moving about the kitchen in an easy rhythm, Josh breaking eggs into a big blue bowl, Ruth slicing a thick loaf of dark bread, talking while they worked. There was something awesome about the simple kitchen and the early light on their faces, as if men and women had always known this dance, circling one another in morning light. This murmur of words and movement was intimacy, and he wanted it.

When he entered the kitchen, Ruth looked up, drew in a breath and turned to the stove. Josh managed a tight smile. "Morning," he said. "Slept well, I hope. Were you warm enough?"

"No, but that's all right. Morning, Ruth."

She glanced back over her shoulder and spoke with her eyes focused on his feet. "I'm fixing eggs here and there's juice. You're welcome to have some."

"No thanks. I don't eat breakfast." Yoder realized he was putting Josh in the middle of the silence that fell between them but he didn't care.

"Were you out with the cows?" Josh asked finally.

"Nope, I was out taking a piss."

"We do have a bathroom," Ruth said. The eggs she stirred

with a wooden spoon were a soft creamy yellow. The way
they looked next to the sleeve of her blue chambray shirt
made him slightly hungry. "It's upstairs. Please use it. Take a
bath or...something." Yoder caught Ruth rolling her eyes at
Josh and remembered he hadn't washed in three days.

Josh grabbed a pail sitting on the floor next to the back
door. "Come on out with me while I milk the cows."

Yoder wanted to watch the sun on the shiny white surface
of the stove and the eggs thickening in the pan but he didn't
feel up to being alone with Ruth. He followed Josh out, taking care to close the door behind him. Brittle blades broke
beneath their feet as they walked to the back of the property.
Josh stooped to enter a shed that held two cows and a bull in
stalls piled high with hay. Yoder hung back, studying the animals, moving gradually closer until he stood face to face with
an enormous pale brown cow. As always, something made
his blood move when he looked an animal in the eye.

"This one's Lucy—she's pregnant." Josh moved his hand
down her back in long, even strokes. "This lady is Quick—
when you milk her she comes on like a horny adolescent.
That big old bull, he's called Roar."

"You named your cows?"

"Are you kidding? Ruthie named the *chickens*. We've got
Scratch, Salad, Pot Pie, Heart. We ate Little last week."

Yoder stood to the side while Josh milked Lucy and Quick
routinely, murmuring encouragement the way one coaxes a
car to start. He couldn't take his eyes off Josh's bare hands on
the mottled flesh. He noticed the ring again, a heavy band of
carved silver.

"Go ahead—try it," Josh said, pushing his stool back, a
familiar glint in his eye.

"No thanks. It's making me kind of sick just watching you.
So are you two married?"

"Us?" Josh laughed, gesturing toward Quick's ample flank,
"Nah." The skin had gone soft around his eyes; daylight exposed deep lines in his forehead. "Actually, I'd like to be," he
said, lifting the pails of yellow milk, "but Ruthie, well, we'll
talk about it later. Let's head out before she thinks of something for us to do."

. . .

The pickup truck took them up an empty highway into a brittle sky scalloped by pines—more color than Yoder had seen in months. Norways and balsams and birches roamed thick and wild, interrupted now and again by the straight rows of a commercial forest. These massive, uniform plantings never failed to impress him, though Yoder knew they appealed to the fascist part of the soul that likes marching bands and drill teams.

"Paper companies own just about half of Maine," Josh said, pointing one out. "OK by me; keeps it wild."

"That's not wild," Yoder countered, but Josh seemed not to hear him. He never took his eyes off the road and talked with urgency, as if they had but a few hours and much vital business. His talk was all about his house: the man who'd taught him to build a windmill; the R factor of his insulation; how he would have passive solar heating using barrels of water; how his house would be efficient, tight, perfect. Yoder found himself not quite listening. He wondered if Josh was even aware of who sat beside him.

"Wait till you see it," Josh said. "I've been looking for a piece of land like this my whole life."

"What are you going to do with it? Farm?"

"Some, though it's not especially good land for that. Mostly I bought as much as I could because I wanted to put a lot..." he looked at Yoder for emphasis, "a lot of distance between myself and the rest of the world."

"We haven't passed a car in half an hour."

"That's how I like it."

Yoder wanted to shake him, to say: "Remember me?" but he tried never to ask a question unless he was prepared for the answer. So instead, he betrayed the memory of a strange and lovely girl. "Did you hear about Lila?" he asked, ashamed immediately.

"No. Is she out here too?"

"She's dead, Josh. Last year. A car accident in Portland."

The truck lost speed, the gears groaning as if speaking for him. "Oh, man, that's terrible. That's horrible. How did you find out?" Josh looked as if he'd bitten into something sour.

"Sal."

"You saw Sally?"

"For a few minutes."

"And is she all right?"

"I couldn't tell. She's living with some guy and they'd had a fight so I didn't stick around."

"Lila? God. I was in love with her for years. She's beautiful."

"I know."

"Why'd you tell me this, Yoder?"

"I thought you'd want to know."

"I wish you hadn't. And if you've got any more news about those people, I don't want to hear it. I never think about those people. Jesus, and now you tell me Lila's dead."

"I saw Crock too, and C.V."

"Crock—that piece of slime. Is he still hanging around there? Still dealing, I imagine."

"He's into big money. Coke, I think."

"Don't tell me about those people, Yoder. I don't want to know."

The sun burned through the windshield, lighting up the cluttered dash, making it almost hot in the cab. Josh pushed the old truck to its limit, accelerating on all the curves. Every few minutes he ran his fingers through his hair, giving the strands a slight tug at the end of each stroke. It was Josh's only nervous gesture. Over the years, Yoder had come to picture actual bugs—in neon orange—that would nip away at Josh until he dispelled them with this motion.

"You're going to love it for the trees," Josh said finally. "You can't believe how many we have. There's nothing but trees for miles. Miles."

"In Alberta, I met a guy who had a Christmas tree farm. That's what he called it."

"Maybe we'll do that—the J & R Tree Farm—get your baby pines here."

"Have you got balsams?" Yoder asked.

"I don't know," Josh said. "Are they good?"

"The best—they smell like Christmas."

The hand again, rousting demons out of the thicket of his white-blond curls. "How was Canada, anyway? You haven't said anything about it."

"You haven't asked."

"So I'm asking. How was Canada?"

Yoder opened his mouth but had no response. The whole morning felt like a nightmare high school reunion. Impossible to account for so much lost time. It hadn't seemed lost until he'd gotten back. Was it lost for Josh? "It was great," he said, twisting away toward the muddy window.

"Really? Why'd you come back then?"

"It wasn't all great."

"You mean—it wasn't great at all?" Josh laughed.

"Yeah, that's pretty much what I mean."

"So tell me what it was like."

Should he tell about jerking off in the small bed of his attic room at the Farmhouse and looking out the cloverleaf window at birds on the powerline? Or the winter he worked at the gas station in Alberta when his hands got so cold he couldn't open the gas locks on the cars and the women in fur coats turned in their seats to see what was taking him so long? The summer in Vancouver with all the flowers would make a good story, but self-pity was useful only as long as you kept it to yourself. "Later, all right?" Yoder said. "So tell me—what's with Ruth? Doesn't she like me?"

"You've just got to get to know her."

"Help me."

"Let's see," Josh said, pushing back into his seat, "She's stubborn, smart. Beautiful, I think. She wants what I want."

"Which is?"

"To make a home for ourselves. Live on very little money. Fuck our brains out in the grass. I want to marry that woman. Trouble is, she don't want to marry me." Josh shrugged, an edge to his voice that warned Yoder into humor.

"Your smelly old body ain't good enough for her?"

Josh gave him an even look. "Something like that."

"You wrote me about a band. Did it happen?"

"What, like a year ago? That sort of fell through. I've mostly been working on people's houses. Ruthie takes in sewing. But, check this out. There's a new band that plays around here—does gigs once in a while in Boston. Cheap Blooze. They've got an outrageous horn player they call Mountain John. Anyway, they need a singer. They've asked me to play with them a few times this winter, so maybe I'll take them up on it."

"Maybe?"

"If I can talk Ruthie into it."

"Any idea what happened to the Rangers? Where's Goldie?"

"No idea. We went out big, did I tell you? Our last gig we backed the Turtles at the Grande Ballroom."

"That's too bad." He hated the Turtles for massacring one of his favorite Dylan songs.

"So they weren't the Grateful Dead. The best part was playing the Grande. I mean, Eric Clapton played the Grande. We're hanging out backstage like it's everyday stuff—drinking Southern Comfort with their drummer while the crowd's filing in. It got louder and louder. Goldie, he's so nervous he's standing on his head like he always did before a gig and their drummer starts banging away on his feet. Goldie is freaking out. By the time we went on, it was chaos out there. A roar— a wall almost—you could almost touch the energy coming at us. I was scared shitless. If I could have chosen, it's what I would have done forever."

Yoder smiled with him but kept silent. He'd heard the Rangers a hundred times and hadn't thought them particularly good, certainly nothing special. "You better take the gig with that band, Josh."

"Ruthie's afraid she won't be able to handle things on the mountain if I'm traveling with a band. But she's strong enough."

"Says who?"

"Says me."

"I can see you haven't changed."

"What's that supposed to mean?"

"You're still deciding for everybody else how they should feel. How do you know what it's like for her? Maybe she's not so much afraid, as in love with you."

"You don't even know her, Yoder."

"I'm just saying that maybe you should take her at her word."

"We'll work something out. Ruthie and I are pretty tight. Look sharp, now, this is it." Josh pulled onto the shoulder and stopped the truck, throwing open his door and jumping to the ground. "We have to walk from here."

They set out following a barely visible trail through bare-limbed birches and Scotch pine. Not a balsam in sight. There was little snow on the ground and in patches the grass was dry and brown. Josh broke into a run. Without warning, the trees parted for a clearing set right on the crest of the mountain. Yoder was not prepared for its beauty. Across a narrow valley, the shadowy peaks of mountains were silhouetted against the sky, alternately snow-streaked and green, fading to violet. The ragged fringe on the furthest peaks indicated that much of the forest had been logged. But those directly across the valley had the smooth curve of undisturbed forest that told him they were completely alone. He let out a low whistle. "It's fucking gorgeous," he said quietly. He was oddly irritated; it didn't have to be this beautiful. In all directions, trees dipped and swayed like dancers. Yoder became gradually aware that the silence was made of sound—wind passing through the trees, water dripping, bird calls fading overhead and a humming sound like hundreds of insects that seemed to intensify as he listened. "What's that sound?" he whispered when he could no longer ignore it.

"I knew you'd hear it. Sometimes it gets so loud I have to talk to myself or sing to keep it from driving me crazy. It's the sound of life. That's all I can figure. And buddy, you're the only person who's ever mentioned it." Josh slapped him on the shoulder and Yoder felt that, without realizing it, he'd earned his way back. "Come on, I'll show you where the house is going to be."

Through a narrow stand of trees, they entered a larger clearing ringed in birches, which also faced out onto the valley. In the center was a muddy space on which a rough floor plan was plotted out with sticks and string, like the work of children marking rooms for a pretend house. Stepping from one patch of ground to another, Josh painted pictures of each room with his hands and the voice that could talk you into anything.

"The living room—all windows out to the valley—a fireplace here, bank of skylights. Over here, the kitchen—room for two rocking chairs next to the stove. We'll generate electricity with a windmill that goes out there." Josh pointed past what materialized suddenly as a window, hung in tie-dyed muslin curtains, overlooking the woodpile and the windmill. "There'll be lofts running across the whole back section of the house and here in the center, an atrium for Ruthie's plants and a passive solar collection system." Josh could have been a preacher, a medicine man, an astrologer, a stockbroker, his eyes crazed with the vision his words made corporal.

"And on the front here, overlooking the valley, a full porch open to the air where I can tip back my chair on summer mornings and play my guitar." They had often talked of having such a place where one could play and sing loudly, where no one could hear. "Check this out," Josh led him to a hole in the ground where a rusted-out freezer sat covered over with branches and wet leaves. Inside were jugs of water, hammers and other supplies as well as Josh's old Harmony guitar and a scratched-up Martin he'd never seen before.

They moved a log over into the imaginary porch and brushed the leaves off the guitars. Josh plucked his strings one at a time, cocking his ear with the attention, as private as worship, that Yoder loved in all musicians. They ran up and down the scales together, matching sound for sound, Josh lost in the tuning until he lifted his head, looking straight at Yoder, his eyes holding memories of all the times they'd sat this way, preparing.

"What should we sing?" Josh asked. Yoder opened his mouth and shut it, waiting a moment for Josh to answer his own question. "How about that Bromberg song—the Rip Van Winkle thing?" Josh coaxed a melody out of the guitar and sang the old words in a clear quavering voice.

Yoder let him sing a while—the key was way too high. He leaned back and listened, and when he felt sure, he joined in. Their voices blended as they always had, according to the tapes in Yoder's memory. They sat on the log, legs crossed over knees in the same way, sending the music down into the valley and sometimes waiting, listening for it to come back to them.

*W*HEN RUTHIE SAYS *come see her/In her honky-tonk la-goon.* Dylan lyrics had pursued him all morning. *Where I can watch her waltz for free/'Neath her Panamanian moon.* A huge moon, swollen and golden, quivering in a plum-blue sky. It was warm in the honky-tonk lagoon. *Ruthie says come see her* . . . The snow drifted past him and down into the valley. Heart-attack snow they called it in Canada. Snow so wet and heavy it buckled a man's knees—and sent him home. Yoder's shoulders ached and his toes had stiffened and he couldn't get the damn song out of his mind.

That morning they'd framed in the main section of the house and at lunch Josh was ebullient, gesturing with his sandwich in his big gloved hand, all carried away about how the sun would rise in the bedroom window and set in the dining room and how he and Ruthie could walk naked in the grass. No one would walk naked out here in wintertime— ever. Summer, and anything even faintly resembling a dining room, was a long way off. But Josh seemed able to hold a vision of his home clearly in mind. When he looked at the stud nails he saw the oak-framed blueprints he planned to hang on the atrium walls. As far as Yoder could tell, Josh was never bored by the steps it would take to get there.

When Josh had asked Yoder to stay, he made it sound less like charity than some kind of enormous favor. "I could use your help," he'd said as they stood beside the little river running through town. With the toe of his boot Josh poked at sheaves of ice clinging to the riverbank.

"I nailed my father right into the wall when we finished off the basement. That the kind of help you're looking for?"

"Help me figure out who the hell you are these days," Josh barked. Emotion in any form seemed to irritate him now—a change from the man who'd once freely proclaimed his love of dogs, Motown, women drivers. "I can't pay much. Room and board—maybe fifty bucks a week. I mean it would be slave labor. It would be a favor. If you don't have other plans..." Josh had trailed off tactfully.

"I'm dead broke, buddy."

"And there's that."

After nearly a month of six-day weeks and ten-hour days, Yoder had begun to question his decision. It was cold, stupid work. Splinters, purple thumbs, fingernails that yellowed and died. His boots ruined by concrete and mud, his nose always running like the faucet in the cold-water bathroom. Clumsy with a hammer, sometimes barely able to follow instructions, he could only take Josh's word that the pile of boards would become a house where Josh could live out his dream.

Each morning, Ruth prepared an elaborate breakfast before they left for the mountain, claiming: "It's important to start the day knowing you've been fed." She had a way of saying things that implied a coherently ordered philosophy about the most routine matters of life. While Ruth cooked breakfast—cheesy, sticky scrambled eggs or Whole Wheat Blues, the berry pancakes he was quietly crazy about—he and Josh milked the cows. The rhythm quickly became musical; he worked the teats in his hands like a set of bells. The milkstreams foaming into the bucket, the smell of hay, Lucy's sweet steamy breath on his neck—a strangely satisfying way to start the day. The direct connections he noticed here appealed to him: The way eggs came from the chickens in the back yard, milk from cows he called by name, and bread from a concoction of flour and yeast. It reminded him of the first time he'd seen grapefruit, ridiculous and obscene, drooping from the trees behind his grandmother's house in Florida. He'd appreciated grapefruits as minor miracles ever since.

With the hour barely decent, they'd drive to the mountain, the trip broken most days by a stop at McDonald's where Josh indulged an obsession with special sauce. Sworn to secrecy, Yoder liked to make him sweat every burger—predicting Ruth's discovery that Josh was not the perfect vegetarian man.

Yoder looked up from his work on the underlayment. Josh straddled the roof joists, hammering. Yoder swore quietly. Lifting his eyes to take in the whole picture was a mistake: The sky immovable; the wind carrying the dampness of the ocean; common wet snow. March going out like a lion. They were crazy. Worse, Josh hadn't noticed. The sound of his hammer never faltered. Dressed in a red and black plaid shirt and a down vest, he looked graceful, his body in constant motion against the sky. Yoder sat back on his heels to watch the swift accurate strokes that drove a nail home in half the time it took him to do it. As always, he felt no desire to compete with Josh, content to watch, as one might observe a gymnast at close range. And what's more, he knew Josh would be out here, working with this same ease and enthusiasm, whether or not Yoder stood by watching.

"Indigo buntings," Yoder shouted, "have no blue pigment in their feathers." He waited to see if Josh would remember their old game.

"No kidding." Josh was measuring and Yoder couldn't see his face.

"Black. The feathers are black. The blue is a trick of the light. Your turn."

Josh looked puzzled. Yoder waited, pleased to see his face bloom with sudden understanding. "Oh, right. Sure. Hey, it's been a long time. I'm out of practice. Let me think. OK—listen to this: The ink the Treasury uses to print up money is poisonous. How's that?"

"Beautiful. You win. So, you think we'll have the roof up soon?"

"If we work like hell. Hand me that rafter square."

The cold steel penetrated his gloves. "Did you notice the snow, Josh? The wet white stuff that soaks through to your fucking bones? Did you notice how it's coming down by the bucketful?"

Josh gave the valley a cursory glance. "Pretty," he said.

"Pretty damn wet."

"Couple more hours, Yoder. Just till dark."

"I thought being your own boss meant treating yourself better than somebody else would."

Josh wiggled the two nails he held between his teeth to indicate that he had something to say but couldn't answer. When he'd removed the last nail he spoke, punctuating his words with firm strokes of the hammer. "I'm in a hurry. When this house is built, when my windmill is turning a generator, when the garden is harvested and a well dug, when Ruth and I can look at this beauty every day, I'll be my own man." Yoder opened his mouth to object but Josh rushed on, leaning over the ladder to look down at him. "The last time I was in Boston, man, I was shaking. Subways, forget it. The city makes me sweat. I don't want to live with that anymore. I want a home for my family and this is the only way I'm going to get one." On his knees on top of his slowly growing dream, Josh did look at home, framed by the dark pines and the snow falling like paper stars.

"Now that I see it," Josh said, pointing down at Yoder's morning's work, "that section should be laid on the diagonal. Better pull it up and start again. If it really starts comin' down we'll quit, I swear."

"Right," Yoder mumbled, turning back to the crippling work. Josh was no architect. In college, he'd deluded himself into social work, then drifted into music and poverty. He was designing his house by instinct, by reading and sketching, bothering his neighbors for advice. He made mistakes, and on days like today when they had to backtrack, it took a force of will to keep Yoder from lofting his hammer into the snow of the valley below.

After dinner almost every night, Josh and Ruth huddled

over the blueprints, talking about the house as if it were a child. Yoder caught some of their spirit, working those first weeks to drive his nails straight, then pushing into the deep snow of the woods, standing among the pines to gather strength and breath for another hour of work. He understood why there were draft resisters in the forests of British Columbia and pockets of vets deep in the Washington woods. Trees repaired the breach. Walking Josh's land was doing that for him. Each day the hammer grew lighter in his hand, the heavy boards rested more easily on his shoulder. He began to think that parts of the house belonged to him, said "my floor" and "my bedroom" and had to explain that he wasn't planning to move in but was simply proud of his work.

Best of all were the hours he and Josh spent in the shanty they'd built, warming their feet on the oil drum stove, drinking the bitter herb tea Ruth fixed for them each morning. The communion of work between men was one thing, but Yoder desperately needed talk. He preferred to do both at the same time, but work for Josh was almost a sacred thing. Yoder's father had been that way—serious and silent about storm windows, as if the work was a form of atonement.

Talk was what Yoder valued most about his women friends. The kind of talk that left you feeling as if you'd been turned inside out and shaken, all your coins and keys and secrets rattling to the floor. Long talks that bridged the night, connected by a quirky logic, where you learned more about yourself from listening than from exposure. Quick, fluid, full of presumption, the kind of talk Kerouac worshiped, talk that covered the cosmos from God to excrement and specialized in fantasies, perversions, pitiful dreams, and admissions —always—of love. At their best, he and Josh had talked that talk. As the afternoons passed into early darkness and they huddled in the shanty at day's end, Yoder sensed Josh shaking loose, remembering how.

After the first week, Yoder felt confident enough to bring beer up to the mountain, sinking it in the snow, sometimes losing a six-pack under the weight of a night storm. Josh never objected though Yoder caught him eyeing it a few times. One dark, impossibly windy day, Yoder urged Josh to

drink a toast to their days in Ann Arbor when they'd down a
12-pack, their legs stretched out long from the sofa, rock 'n'
roll on high; days when they'd mined one another for secrets
in the belief that the other knew something about truth. Josh
refused, but they passed the day waiting for the weather to
break, trying to determine which time, out of all the times,
they had been the most out of their minds and what drug
they had used to achieve it. The sky darkened as their stories
rolled one into the next. Yoder remembered thinking that if
he could just keep Josh talking, the six years between them
might dissolve.

"Remember that time on MDA when we thought we were
in Chicago?" Yoder leaned forward, trying to catch the memory and flesh it out, but it remained shadowy and uncertain.

"I do. Why'd we think that?"

"Nothing looked familiar, remember? We heard saxo-
phones. I don't know."

"That was the night I decided to burn all my blue jeans."
Josh leaned back, laughing with the force of men physically
much bigger than he. "I almost did it, too—you stopped me.
You always kept your head—I remember thinking you were
more on top of it stoned than cold sober. Cold sober is not
your strong point."

"What about the Man Who Walked Slow. Remember him?"

"Like a piece of pie dough rolling down the sidewalk," Josh
said. "Sal was there that time, wasn't she?"

"And Eliot." And Lila, Yoder thought. Lila and Eliot—
lovers at the time. Spring in the Arboretum. Lila running
from tree to tree, touching their trunks with urgency, like a
doctor with a stethoscope. They'd been afraid for her, made
her sit quietly on a bench while Josh told her that the trees
were still breathing and ground was solid and Eliot was
alright. "We're all alright," he said, and she believed him.
Everyone believed him.

The ultimate on which they could agree was the time
they'd taken blotter acid and spent the early morning hours
in a half-panic running through the cavernous steam tunnels
that ran underground, connecting most buildings on campus.
Their mistake had been to plan this activity just as they were
beginning to get off, when the color variations that painters

see were glaringly obvious in everything. The idea had
seemed pure genius. Yoder knew how to jimmy the lock on
the trap door to the tunnels, though neither could remember
whether the job took two minutes or two hours. The bushes
by the undergraduate library had been snoring, on that they
both agreed, and Josh remembered that the white lights that
lined the campus walks each contained a brilliant colored
gas, swirling inside the globes.

They had a list of things to accomplish inside the tunnels:
Sneak into the stadium and run midnight touchdown passes;
raid the fabled West Quad kitchens; and infiltrate the hospital, where, they reasoned, everyone would be asleep and
stealing drugs would be as easy as lifting a loaf of bread from
the kitchen. But in their fascination watching water drops
explode and the mossy growth on the walls evolve into a
tropical kingdom, they had become hopelessly lost—convinced for a time that they were inside an umbilical cord.
They eventually stumbled out into the morning air at the
north end of campus, a curiosity to students rushing toward
8 o'clock classes.

*An' here I sit so patiently/ Waiting to find out what price/ You
have to pay to get out of/ Going through all these things twice.*
The vowels belonged to Dylan, all of them, and he sung them
as if they were part of a secret language he wanted to learn.
*Girl*—Dylan pulled the *i* out long—*burn, you, pain, your
world.*

"What do you say we quit for the day?" Yoder called up to
Josh. "I'm burnt out on this flooring."

Josh did not stop hammering or even look up. "You go
ahead. I want to get this thing roofed in."

Yoder let his hammer rattle to the ground and shuffled
over to the shanty. The enormity of the job made him want to
quit. Had he been responsible for the railroads or the inter-
state freeway system, they'd still be a concept. Too hard, he'd
have said. Too impossible to comprehend. Each day Josh
outlined their work, going over details in detail, explaining
projects that would be done weeks later to give him a feeling
for what Josh kept calling "the big picture." As he listened,
Yoder could feel his shoulders droop into a slouch, just as
they had on chilly fall afternoons when he'd been bound to

his father for endless house and yard work. Yoder recalled especially the physical discomfort: The dry eyes and throat, his long hair hanging in his face, his clothes stiff with paint and sweat. His mind would be clouded with song lyrics, stuck as this one was stuck until, like a powerful dream, they revealed their message. That glimpse of the adult world—the secrets of furnace maintenance and lawn trimming—had frightened him and he could only trail behind his father, suffocating on silence.

Inside the shanty, Yoder threw logs into the oil drum stove and pulled a chair up close, resting his feet on the edge. He felt immediately comforted. After a few moments, he sat tentatively on the top of the drum, letting the heat burn through his clothing to see how long he could endure the contact. Yoder stared at the crooked nails in the shanty roof—his first—pleased to see how much he'd improved. Outside the snow swirled like memory, altering the landscape to its own shape.

Those Saturday mornings always began in the same way. His father would appear at Yoder's bedroom door dressed in full uniform—white painter's overalls and a brimmed white cap. "We've got work to do," he'd say. Sensing that his father did not want to see his naked body, Yoder made a great commotion with the covers until his father pulled the door shut and turned away, his back curving with the hunch of a handyman as it did only on Saturdays. Work would stop precisely at noon. His father drank a beer and ate a bologna sandwich on bakery pumpernickel, his tall stick of a body leaning against the stove. Yoder poured down an Orange Crush and read baseball scores at the kitchen table.

All day they would battle in silence. Yoder worked toward an explosion. But his father would only turn away, retreating to the basement to clean his brushes, scraping the sticky paint from the bristles with his fingernails, lost sometimes for half an hour in the rushing water. One Father's Day, Yoder gave him a dozen new brushes so he'd never again have to see his father bent over the grey iron sink with the long, skinny rust stain. His father examined each brush as if it were a work of rare craftsmanship and then, placing each carefully back in the box, closed the top. It had never been opened again, remaining on a shelf in the garage, the red cardboard fading to pink.

The door swung open. Josh stepped in, knocking his boots against the door jam to loosen the snow. "What happened at the Pentagon on October—like 20th—1967?"

"Melvin Laird was created—and God went back to school."

Josh poured himself a cup of steaming tea. Yoder took a cup, willing to tolerate the bitterness in order to feel the warmth against his chin.

"50,000 idiots—including me, though I can hardly believe it—tried to levitate the Pentagon. Remember that?"

"No, nor do I believe you."

"I was there. Although it's possible I made the whole thing up. Your turn."

"Pass."

"You sure?" Josh pulled a crate up to the stove and set to work removing a splinter from his thumb. "Anything wrong?" Josh said finally.

"Just tired. I had no idea this was going to be such a monotonous job."

"Sorry about the mix-up. Think of it this way: When we're all done you can make your fortune building houses."

"No thanks. I don't ever want to do this again." Yoder's hands and feet began to burn, thawing. He had to let his mother know he was back in the country. How to do that without tangling with his father?

"You have any idea what you are going to do?"

"How come everybody's always asking me that? 'What are you going to do with your life?' As if you could spend it like cash. For what? A great time? Go ahead and try."

"You're going to have to get involved in something," Josh said quietly.

"I'm pretty fucking involved in your goddamn house right now, I'd say."

"Hey, I appreciate your help but you obviously can't work on this house forever."

"Something will come up."

"Wrong," Josh said, pointing a finger in his direction. "We're too old to just let things happen. That's what I like about the mountain. I'm in control of our food, our electricity, our water, heat."

"Control is a word like Santa Claus, Josh." The wind rattled the tin roof. He closed his eyes, smelled heat. His father had said never. Never meant never. "Aren't you just a little afraid of getting bored when you're sitting alone out here a year from now and you've already cut the wood for the next month?"

"Not at all. Survival is a full-time job."

"Tell me about it. What if you don't like it?"

"Yoder, you don't necessarily like everything you do."

"Is it my imagination Josh, or has everyone lost their nerve?"

"It's your lack of imagination, my friend. Remember when we used to pick out people at random on the street and try to figure out their dreams? This is mine. It was finding the land that really sealed it and that seemed almost like fate."

"Don't you think it's always almost like fate?"

"Maybe. I'm too tired for big concepts today."

He'd write her a letter. Maybe they could meet somewhere. "It's pretty simple, Josh. There are things inside you which set you on a course against your will. Fate. For example, you'll never be a great scientist."

"Not necessarily. I could go back to school. It's a long life."

"No kidding. But not a long life full of possibility."

"Yoder, I said it seemed like fate because I stumbled on the land, could afford it, and knew what to do with it all at the same time. I wasn't really looking but I was ready."

"Your whole life has been like that, Josh."

"Yeah, I stumble around a lot."

"No. Everything has always fallen into place for you."

"I don't think you can really say that. You haven't lived my life, Yoder."

"I've known you a long time and as far as I can see, you've just kept on going strong since the last time I saw you." There, it had been said.

"Hey, you had a tough break."

He let the silence speak.

Josh appeared to be staring at his thumb, but one hand was running through his hair. "Remember that night right before you left, when you showed up at my place—you and Sally had had that fight—and you asked me to come with you to Canada?"

"I wasn't serious."

"I know, but the point is, I couldn't have gone. I remember thinking: Here's this pretty screwed-up guy—you have to admit you were doing weird things back then. Anyway, I thought—look what he's doing! I saw myself as a pretty ethical person; I mean, I thought we were kind of even until that night when I realized I couldn't go."

"There wasn't anything ethical about it, Josh. I didn't want to get killed."

"But you did something about it. I just got lucky."

Fate, Yoder thought, just like I said.

"I've always liked you because you tell me the truth, Yoder. So tell me the truth now. Did you—do you—think less of me because I didn't come with you?"

For all their talk about truth, back then they hadn't realized that truth was relative and meant to be useful. "Hey, I never thought that much of you in the first place."

Josh let out a truncated laugh but was able to look him in the eye.

"There's no difference between you and me on this one," Yoder continued, pleased he'd found a way to release Josh from the grip of cowardice without denying his own.

"What if I hadn't happened to read in the paper, on the day, the very morning of my physical, that my draft office had been torched," Josh said, amazement still evident in his voice. "I would have gone in like all the other suckers and tried my little tricks and probably gotten drafted and killed a couple dozen poor jerks in a rice paddy or more likely gotten killed myself. What horrifies me is that leaving the country seemed much harder than that."

"Leaving wasn't hard at all."

Like always, it was dark when they pulled into the yard. A single yellow light shone in the front window. Inside, the house smelled of tomatoes and garlic. Yoder wondered if Ruth had cooked the spinach lasagna that Josh kept urging her to make, as if to impress him. Since Yoder rarely spoke to

Ruth, it made little difference to him what she cooked.

Never had a woman he was not in love with caused him to go to such lengths to please her. Ruth seemed to read a lot and for a while that had given him hope. But the few times he'd asked what she was reading, she'd looked offended. When he learned that she'd made the weavings on the living room wall, he commented on their sense of design. "Tell him I like people who are honest," she'd stage-whispered to Josh. Though Ruth hadn't worn her hair in braids since that first night, he still thought of her that way—pulled back and all tucked in. Loose, her hair fell in waves.

Most evenings, Yoder ate quickly and left them alone, retreating upstairs to stare at the peeling grey wallpaper dotted with tight pink roses in his tiny room. They'd cleared a spot for him but it was still basically a storage room—boxes of burnt-out amplifiers, envelopes labeled Taxes-74, Taxes-75, Taxes-76 rising in piles around him. Over his cot hung an ancient hand-colored photograph of a dog—a setter striking a noble pose—framed in mahogany and beveled glass. He would miss that dog when he left. It wasn't the only thing about their lives he wanted to steal.

It was never easy to understand another's intimate relationship, particularly when you observed it at close range. The daily compromises and cruelties were small nuisances compared to the dead weight at the center of what so many couples called commitment. But Josh and Ruth seemed remarkably solid. They caught one another's eye, touched, listened critically. Read aloud only when unable to contain themselves, fought privately and well. Still, he heard too much silence from Ruth. She did not seem to share Josh's excitement about the house. She flirted with the man who delivered chicken feed, a man whose nose bloomed purple and whose eyes focused on Ruth's breasts when he spoke. What Yoder heard was a quiet disengagement and it puzzled him. Perhaps it was only his imagination fueled by jealousy. He was thankful that he begrudged them their closeness only on his worst days.

Each night Yoder read until he fell asleep, usually with the light still on, the collection of Norse fairy tales he'd found downstairs lying limp in his hands. Sometimes he could hear them playing cards or Scrabble, and always there was music. A few times he suspected that they were dancing and he pictured them swaying in the tiny front room, Ruth's cheek pressed flat against Josh's sweaty chest, or hands joined, rocking back on their heels. On nights when Josh played his guitar and Ruth sang, her voice thin and hesitant with an unexpected laugh in it, Yoder longed to join them. He'd listen at the head of the stairs, then creep down the narrow hallway back to his room, the floorboards cold on his feet, and ease the door shut. Sometimes he heard them making love in the next room and twice he had woken to hear Ruth running water in the bathroom sink to hide her sobs.

Dinner *was* spinach lasagna and it was a little bland for his taste. He preferred meat but there didn't seem to be much of it left in the world. He'd eaten so many carrots and so much zucchini at the Farmhouse in Toronto that all vegetables had begun to taste alike—nothing but texture anymore. He'd snuck into town a few times to eat dry hamburgers at Rydertown's only bar where there was a waitress whose looks he liked. She had red hair but he was fairly certain she was married.

They ate at little spots cleared of the books, magazines, bills and papers which seemed like fixtures on the oak table. Every night the mess got shoved to one side and every day it spread its way back across the full length of the table. It was things like this—habits to which people were absolutely blind—that made it so hard to live with them. Ruthie never answered the phone; Josh never washed anything but the dishes.

"Do you cook, Yoder?" Ruth wiped her mouth with the tip of her napkin over and over as if there was some permanent stain. The most personal thing she'd said to him in a week. "Any time you want to impress us with one of your recipes, I'll be happy to sit out a shift in the kitchen. I don't know if you realize it, Josh," she had turned away from him, addressing Josh again, "but you two come back from working on the house and sit out there in the living room and talk like you haven't seen each other all day. I miss you, babe." She reached over and rubbed Josh's forearm.

Josh pushed a bite of lasagna into his mouth and gestured with his fork. "You got it," he said. "Tomorrow night Yoder and I will make you the best pizza you ever tasted."

"I'll do the cooking tomorrow," Yoder said, shaking his head. Josh could be in such a rush to solve a problem that he sometimes solved the wrong one.

"Thanks, Yoder." Ruth smiled at him—a pretty nice smile, one that included her whole face, one that included him. "So, Yoder, does your family know that you're back?"

"Nope."

"Don't you think you should tell them?"

"What do you think?"

"Well, I can't imagine what mother wouldn't want to know that her son has come home."

"Ruthie, stay out of this." Josh said. "You don't know what you're talking about."

"I suppose I can't presume to understand a mother's feelings, is that it? I think I can."

"Ruthie, drop it," Josh insisted.

"All right, Josh. All right." She glared at Josh with an impressive malevolence. "I didn't mean to intrude on your personal life, Yoder. There's enough of that going on around here already. By the way," she said. "I had to go into your room to get some thread and I noticed that you had a lot of dirty dishes under your bed."

"Sometimes I get hungry in the middle of the night."

"It's no big deal, but if you could bring them down the next morning, it would help. We run out of dishes pretty fast around here."

"I can do that," he said, pushing away from the table and carrying his plate to the sink. What was with her? First the smile, then the inquisition. He scooped the last bite of tomato sauce from the pan with two fingers. How much longer before she made him leave? When he came back in the room they were standing facing the door, arms around one another.

"Feel like staying and playing a game tonight?" Ruth asked, rising up slightly on her toes—reaching for perky.

"How about it, buddy?"

"We could play Dictionary," Ruth suggested.

"No, Yoder's a terrific liar," Josh said. "We wouldn't stand a chance. How about Categories?"

"We could use ourselves instead of letters—like we did last Christmas at Jack's. Have you ever played Categories, Yoder?"

"I don't like games very much." He began heading toward the stairs. It felt like a set-up. "You two go ahead."

"Come on, Yoder, this is a good game for getting to know people. And I already know Josh so we need you to play. Don't go upstairs to your room and mope. Sit down. Stay." Ruth indicated a place beside her at the table, and held his eyes a long moment. Some ancient voice warned him not to trust sudden kindness from women. "What you do is make up categories like animals, famous people, furniture—you know," Ruth continued. "Then you have five minutes to write down what the other two people would be in that category. For example, Josh would be a polar bear if I were doing animals because he's big and clean and friendly and lopes around with his arms open a lot. You don't have to have a good reason—just write down the first thing that comes to mind. Get it?"

"Sounds like Psych 101."

"It is—sort of. I mean, it's interesting what people come up with. You should have seen Josh the last time we played this game. He was brilliant with Insects. Weren't you, babe?" Ruth's eyes were shining. "I'll get some paper," she said. Obviously, in this game the players agreed to be nice to one another. Black widow spider, crab tree and killer bee were out.

"Anyone want something to drink before we start?" Ruth shouted from the kitchen, her voice reckless and animated. A beer, he thought, but kept quiet. Ruth passed out paper and crayons like a kindergarten teacher. "Now, everybody has to name a category. You start, Yoder."

"Diseases."

"Great," Josh roared. "You always reminded me of malaria."

"Be serious," Ruth commanded.

"I thought this was supposed to be a game," Yoder said. "OK. Musical instruments."

"Good. Josh?"

"I pick flowers and trees."

"And I say, let's see—desserts. Now, I've set the timer in the kitchen so go to it."

Yoder wrote "Ruth" at the top of his paper and drew a blank. She had given him a red crayon and he smeared it across the page. Crayons did not invite precise thinking. He didn't know the names of many flowers. Trees were his specialty. Yoder stared at the ceiling, trying to call back the hundreds of varieties he'd memorized in forestry school, searching for something esoteric and impressive. Linden, banyan, hemlock. Hemlock was out of bounds. He settled on loblolly pine, solitary and fragrant. She could also be a jumping cholla, the desert cactus that shot spiky thorns into your leg if you so much as brushed against it. She was a set of bells, he thought, and carrot cake—healthy and crunchy and brown. If they were doing colors, she would definitely be brown, her eyes like weak coffee, her hair the soft beige of Lucy, the pregnant cow.

Josh presented less of a challenge. A guitar with deep resonance and an elaborate inlaid mother-of-pearl bridge; a fine classical instrument that was never out of tune. And a sycamore tree—with leaves the size of your palm, and seed balls like hailstones that hit you on the head when they dropped but never meant to. For dessert Josh was a fortune cookie that always read: Good luck.

When the buzzer went off Ruth kept writing, staring off, then sneaking looks at the two of them and scratching furiously. She'd written whole paragraphs. Josh looked immensely pleased with himself and volunteered to go first, leaning back from the table with his thumbs hooked in the top of his jeans. He hadn't written anything on his piece of paper.

"Ruthie, you're my little chocolate soufflé," Josh said in a poor imitation of W.C. Fields.

"Come on," she laughed, slapping his shoulder.

"All right, then you're a hot fudge sundae."

"A what?"

"Sometimes sweet, sometimes cold."

"Very funny." The smile had slipped from her face.

"And you're a harp."

"Thank you."

"And a ginkgo tree."

"Ah, yes. The tree that bears no fruit," she interrupted.

"No, the tree with the fan-shaped leaves—my favorite tree," Josh said firmly.

Yoder reminded himself never to play games with these two in the future. He read his list quickly, keeping his eyes on the page, hoping the list revealed more about them than it did about him. Josh loved that he had identified Ruth as carrot cake but told him he lacked imagination for calling him a guitar, and preferred Ruthie's French horn. Yoder had a hard time listening to their descriptions of him. He knew he was in danger of taking the game too seriously, but when it was over he put on his coat and went for a walk in the clear air so he could remember it all.

When Ruth looked at him she saw a tuberous begonia, a flower, she said, that grew inward and hid its bright colors under furry leaves. Josh had called him, of all things, the twisted mysterious Joshua tree, which grows in the Arizona desert. Though Josh claimed not to know this, the Joshua was one of his favorite trees. Its limbs snaked around themselves in wide sweeps as if they had been formed in a gale wind. Josh called him vanilla pudding with red hots, and Ruth thought he was a Tootsie Roll Pop. "Josh tells me you have a gooey center," she explained with a shrug and a smile he'd have called flirtatious if he didn't know better. Gooey and angry and mysterious and not so hidden after all, it appeared. They had both pegged him as the crashing cymbal because, they said, there's only one in every orchestra.

When he returned to the dark house, he eased the door closed so as not to wake them. Leaving his boots at the door, he tiptoed toward the kitchen for a piece of the banana bread he'd baked the night before. As he slid the foil off the pan, Ruth's voice from the front room sent his heart to his feet. "Cut me a piece, too," she said and the house fell silent again.

Returning to the front room, he saw that it remained in

darkness but he could make out the white glow of Ruth's nightgown in the rocking chair by the woodstove. As she reached for the bread, her hand covered his for a long moment. Hot. As if she'd fired it in the stove. He backed away toward the stairs. The game had left him feeling self-conscious and he didn't want to know why she sat in the dark, why she wasn't in bed with Josh where she belonged. "Great bread," she said. "Who taught you to cook?"

He paused with a foot on the stair. "Every woman I've ever loved," he said and when this caused her to go silent again, he hurried toward a joke. "Leaves me with about two recipes. I'll make the other one tomorrow."

"I've got just one question before you run away," she said. "Why a set of bells?"

It took him a moment. "Your voice," he said finally. "There were carillon bells in Ann Arbor and whenever I heard them I'd stop what I was doing and listen. You have a voice like that, I guess."

"That's nice," she said. "Good night, Yoder. Good dreams."

He left her sitting in the dark, the heat from her hand still marking his.

S OMETIME THAT SPRING, Ruth began making dolls.
Weekends while Josh worked on the blueprints, Ruth
stitched wide eyes and stiff orange smiles onto the ragdolls
with yarn; sewed dresses and bonnets and pantaloons from
scrap material. She lined the completed dolls up along the
window sills, tucked them into the crooks of armchairs, until
the front room seemed full of stares. One Sunday Josh slew
the entire fleet, knocking them to the ground with a grand
sweep. "Get these things out of here," Yoder heard him shout.
Yoder hustled down the stairs, hoping for a fight, a clue to
Ruth's strange new preoccupation.

Ignoring Josh, Ruth turned to Yoder on the staircase.
"What do you think of this one?" she said, raising a doll for
his inspection. Lately she'd been asking his opinion on a
whole range of things, from music to why their black hen had
stopped laying eggs.

"Lifelike," he mumbled.

"I don't know why I bother to ask either one of you," she
said abruptly, gathering up an armload of dolls from the
floor—mostly girls with downturned lips and others who

looked like Hendrix. "Boys don't know about dolls."

"Well, are you going to sell them, babe?" Josh sighed, digging into his hair, "or just clutter the front room with them?"

"I'm practicing," she said, and though she continued to make the dolls they were no longer on display. The only time Yoder saw one again was the rag doll he found in his bed, tucked between the sheets, face down like a dead thing.

By April Fool's Day the house on the mountain had a shape. The steep slanted roof and front porch silhouetted against the horizon startled them each morning; they were no longer alone. Yoder began to accept what Josh had known all along—the birds would come back, the trees fill out and they could walk naked in the grass. In a matter of weeks they would complete everything but the finish work. He wished he were a master woodworker, or decent with drywall— wished he knew something that would make him useful just a little longer.

He'd considered no future—wanted to stay until summer, when the sun returned and women with golden skin walked the world. He lay awake late into the night, wondering what he would do next. He would never be a rock 'n' roll star, never write out his soul like Dylan. He could wash dishes, short-order cook, pick lettuce, counsel drug addicts, repair cars, classify trees into herbaceous and woody, milk a cow. But he couldn't do any of them for long.

He took to drinking a cheap Chianti that he bought by the gallon at the Rydertown bar, hiding the bottles somewhat pointlessly in various places in his room. He maintained the illusion of privacy though he was certain that Ruth snooped about his room regularly. The doll in his bed was a response, he'd decided, to the note he'd planted for her under his pillow. "Boo," it said, "I'm watching you." In the mornings he woke groggy and irritable, snapping at Ruth over breakfast, sullen on the ride to the mountain.

The sound of a choking, racking cry woke him from a nap on a Sunday he'd elected to spend in bed with a red wine headache. Yoder pulled on his pants and clamored down the stairs toward the door and the animal in distress. Seconds before he saw the baby in Ruth's arms he realized that the cry was human.

"Something wrong?" She held the baby stiffly, almost posing, as if she wanted him to remember her this way.

"Apparently not. I thought. . . ."

"This is Elijah Steven. Eli."

He pressed his palm hard against his temple. "What's going on?"

"Isn't he a beauty?"

It sounded like she was describing a racehorse. "You hatch one overnight or something?"

"Oh, go back to bed. I'm looking after him for a friend—you might know her—Marla from the bar in town."

"Red hair?" That settled that. His imagination mourned the affair that might have been.

"This is her daughter's new baby—six weeks old. Look at his little feet."

He was fighting to keep up. Surely Marla could not be a grandmother.

"A grandmother at 35. She's a little freaked out. Could you hold him a minute while I fix his bottle?"

The sun was cruelly bright. He needed coffee. A massage. He landed on the couch just in time to catch the bundle Ruth thrust into his arms. It weighed nothing.

"Have you ever smelled a newborn?" she asked as she left the room.

Immediately the baby's face reddened and the creases around its mouth flamed white. It howled right in his face, loud as an air raid siren, regular as a drumbeat. Afraid to move, he began to sing the first song that came in mind. The baby paused briefly to stare at the shadow of Ruth's plants on the white wall. He sang louder as the baby revved up again.

"What did you do to him?" she asked, snatching the baby back.

"I sang the first two verses of 'Blackbird.'"

"He's a baby, Yoder. He's too young for the Beatles. Try 'Rockabye Baby.'" Tiny hands came up to clasp the bottle. "There," she said, beaming over at Yoder with satisfaction. "Isn't he the most beautiful thing?"

"I don't know, Ruth. I don't think so." He liked the hands, the way the knuckles sunk in, a little dimpled line like the raisin buttons on the gingerbread man Yoder's mother made every Christmas. "Not *the most* beautiful. Baby German shepherds are cuter. A waterfall is more beautiful to me."

"Go away, Yoder. I won't have this afternoon ruined by your depressing opinions."

"Come on, Ruth. Take a close look at that kid. You think that's beautiful?"

"Smell him."

"I did. He smells great—white—like soap and milk. Where's Josh?"

"Cleaning out the animal sheds. Lucy's close, so he's putting down fresh hay. We'll have another baby around here soon." She directed her words at the oblivious Eli, as if she literally could not take her eyes off him.

"I guess I'll go out."

"Sit down, Yoder. Keep me company a minute."

"Seriously? What's up?"

"Nothing. I just . . . ." She pulled the baby to her chest, her hand covering his entire back, and closed her eyes, her body rocking him slowly. "Tell me about Canada," she said, forcing her attention away from the child. "You didn't like it there, did you?"

"Canada?" He took a long breath; already he was tired of talking about it. "Canada was full of all the people without the money or brains to get out another way. Plus a bunch of people who really considered themselves heroes."

"And you don't."

The baby was guzzling the milk, eyes closed, *becoming* contentment. "You'd watch their girlfriends stop visiting, their big anti-war buddies stop writing. They ended up hating America more than I ever did because they expected so much more out of it." What was the point, here? Ruth afraid to be alone with the baby? "Want me to call Josh?"

"No. Why should you? You know, he thinks you did a very brave thing."

"Josh is thinking about himself when he says that."

"It's *hard* to admit that your country has blown it. I remember trying to like Nixon, some part of me hoping he was just a good, stupid man. It's like finding out your parents are racists or embezzlers or something. You'd rather not know."

The sun had slipped over the house and away. He rubbed his face with his hands, groaning, wanting a hot shower.

"Hush, sweetie."

Yoder looked up, startled.

"I was talking to Eli," Ruth explained in a rush. "Well, I think you should be proud of yourself and stop acting like somebody's going to kick you if you don't keep your head hung low. That's what I think."

"Delighted to hear it," he said.

Josh and Ruth sat up most of the following night with Lucy, the pregnant cow. Drunk on wine, Yoder remained inside, picking out tunes on his harmonica until late into the night. Josh woke him at 5 A.M., shouting up the stairs, "Get your ass out here!" Yoder pulled the covers back over his head, then gave in as he always did.

The hard snow squeaked with each step as he crossed the hundred yards between the house and animal sheds, wrapped in Josh's wool coat that gathered ice trailing on the ground behind him. Though the days had warmed to sweater weather, the nights still dropped below freezing. Clouds of breath gathered around his face, softening the yard lights and the starlight that decorated the empty sky. Lucy had been moved to the largest shed, cleared now of the other animals. The bull lay in a dark heap on the frozen ground, steam pouring from his nostrils. Yoder shrugged his shoulders in sympathy as he passed.

Inside, Ruth stood over a small heater, warming her hands. Shadows danced near the ceiling, the light from kerosene lamps giving the shed a ritual glow. She nodded solemnly, whispered: "It'll be a while," and turned back to the heater. Josh leaned against the back wall, circles of fatigue darkening the skin under his eyes. He lifted a hand in greeting but otherwise his eyes never left Lucy's dark belly. She stood in the center of the shed, her back the soft color of sandstone. She took a few careful steps in what looked like impatience, but mostly she stood still, her legs planted firmly in the straw.

Yoder settled into a pile of hay bales in the corner and tried to stay out of the way. His mouth tasted of stale wine; Ripple and champagne were one and the same the morning after. For a long time nothing happened, though the contractions shuddered along the tight skin of Lucy's belly. He wondered if there would be blood. His only image of birth was animal —and tragic—the panicked, bloody scene from *The Red Pony.*

"When does the show start?" he asked to break the silence that threatened to put them all back to sleep. Ruth glared at him and began to sing, rocking herself, arms crossed over her chest. Josh bent to check Lucy's progress, ran a hand along her distended belly. Yoder blew a few quiet riffs on the harp, branching off into a low-down blues whine that seemed to give a rhythm to their waiting. Even Lucy rolled her head with the beat.

Without warning, an opaque bubble of heavily veined membrane appeared, inflating like a thick pink balloon, and receded, emerging and expanding with each contraction until it was forced out onto the ground. "The water sac," Ruth said, catching sight of the shock he knew had registered on his face. The rest of the calf came slowly, taking nearly an hour to inch its way out. Ruth dozed in Josh's arms. Josh talked aimlessly, keeping them both awake by detailing his schedule—Bangor in the morning; a possible gig in Portland with the band that weekend; no work on the house until next week—and his shopping list: sheetrock and finishing nails and a new barrel for the stove in the shanty. Soon a hoof poked through, dangling down from the mother like a fifth appendage, shiny black, and hard. Lucy remained standing, maintaining an unnecessary dignity, as if she understood how closely she was being watched.

When the forelegs finally cleared, Josh called Yoder to come around behind Lucy in case she needed help. Dutifully, Yoder moved in behind her, raising up on his toes in readiness, his hands cupped like a quarterback. The calf's legs stayed crossed, one hoof placed demurely on top and slightly above the other—a comical mutation: Lucy on all fours, two dwarfed legs hanging from her swollen middle. Freeze the process right at this point and Lucy would be a star attraction at a carnival midway. Yoder tried to make a joke about this but no one laughed. Lucy held their silent and complete attention.

The end took them all by surprise. The calf's shoulders broke free; its body, suddenly slippery, dropped to the ground with a thud. Josh gave a low cheer and hugged Ruthie, burying his head in her neck. Then his hand landed flat between Yoder's shoulders. "Girl," Josh announced, as if he'd had something to do with it.

"That's a good name for her," Ruth said. "Let's call her Girl."

"We'll see. Just look at her."

Yoder couldn't look at anything else. She was born. She had not been there a moment before. At first just a bloody bundle in the hay, she raised her head, sweeping her black eyes around the room. Perfectly at ease, trusting them all to make the next move. Josh checked her for signs of trouble, whispering "That 'a girl, back away now, that 'a girl," to the mother. Lucy repeated his actions, shifting her great weight to begin removing the mucus that clung to the calf's body in strings. The air turned hot, filled with the sound of Lucy's tongue slapping against the wet skin. No one spoke above a whisper.

"Don't you dare," Josh commanded as the calf rolled onto her side and poked blindly at her mother's belly. "Give me a hand, Yoder."

"What do you want me to do?"

"Grab Lucy's back legs—pull hard."

"Why?" Reluctant to touch either of them, he shoved his hands deeper into his pockets. The cow and calf were sticky and dazed and, it seemed, appropriately in charge.

"Just do it." Josh planted his feet wide apart like a catcher and leaned into Lucy's flank. She fought them, holding her ground by tensing her huge body, refusing to be led away. "Hurry," Ruth said, and knelt to stroke the calf's neck, singing under her breath as they pushed and tugged on the cow's powerful body until she was forced into her stall, her head craning back toward her calf. Yoder backed away, his hands drenched in Lucy's sweat, hating what they'd just done.

Josh milked her and transferred the milk to a glass bottle

capped with a metal nipple. The calf drank quietly from the bottle, her head tilted back on Josh's lap, staring directly into his eyes.

"What was that all about?"

"If they bond at the first feeding," Josh said, his eyes on the calf, "it's impossible to separate them."

"So?"

"So it's nothing but trouble after that. With our first calf we didn't know they were bonding. It looked sweet—the calf nosing around trying to nurse. But from then on they wanted to be together all the time. The mother became aggressive. When I tried to separate her from her calf, she put her foot down right here," he said, pointing to his instep. "Wouldn't budge. And—get this—when we finally sold the mother, both Ruthie and I saw the calf cry."

"What?"

"I swear. You've got to separate them before the attachment is made. That way, neither one will ever know the difference."

"You sound real sure about that."

"I am," Josh said, pulling the bottle from the calf's mouth. "Enough."

The three of them emerged from the shed to a clear pink dawn. The fields of snow undulated like a spill of fireflies. Yoder had forgotten about the world. Reality had narrowed down to the darkness, the lamplight, smells of birth. He'd been conscious of the routine at the core of the drama—a predictable unfolding of the miraculous. This larger world with its horizons and roads seemed uncertain and threatening compared to the events, rehearsed for an eternity, that had just taken place in the shed.

Exhaustion came over him like a drug. Josh and Ruth meandered back to the house ahead of him, arms slung around each other's waist. "Comin' in for breakfast?" Josh shouted back to him. "Ruthie's making her Birthday Special —feta cheese omelet." Yoder waved them on. He felt no hunger nor any desire to eat. Clearly they wanted to be alone.

Collapsing onto the back steps, he closed his eyes to the morning sun. He saw the calf, her head a small copy of her mother's, hanging out below the cow's tail, waiting for the rest of her body to be freed. Didn't believe Josh's claim that calf and mother would feel no connection following the morning's ordeal. Wondered if his own birth had been as bizarre and as mechanical. He knew none of the details, not the time, nor how much he had weighed, nor the number of hours his mother had labored. She never spoke of it and he had never been able to ask.

He still clung to a childhood belief that he had not been born in any ordinary way. At nine, he knew the mechanical facts of life and began watching his parents, trying to imagine their coupling. He thought it sneaky that his life had begun without his knowledge or consent. As he grew more distant from his parents, he became convinced that, at the very least, he was an orphan. To his friends he told an elaborate story of life in the orphanage, leaving his true origin open to speculation. Privately, he preferred to believe he had been born in another galaxy and dropped mistakenly onto this alien planet. It comforted him to think he had no ancestral connection to the species with whom he had been forced to live.

The door banged shut. Yoder looked up to see Ruth balancing a plate full of eggs topped with a mound of the sticky homemade jam that only she seemed able to eat. She sat next to him on the steps under the slatted wooden roof. Yoder pretended not to notice but kept a watch on her from behind his fluttering eyelids.

"So, Yoder, what did you think of it?"

"It was all right." He wished she would eat somewhere else. The smell of the food made him nauseous.

"It was all right," she mimicked. "Come on. If you didn't feel something stronger, I've been giving you too much credit. Didn't you find it disturbing?"

Opening one eye, Yoder turned slightly to look at her. He had expected a lecture on the wonders of birth. "Did you?"

"At first." She gave him the beatific smile he always took as a challenge. "It seemed empty—the production of another milking machine. Neither seemed aware of the other, nor that something extraordinary had happened. Later I learned to appreciate just watching something extraordinary happen. Maybe it's because I never had animals as a kid—it just knocks me out every time. It always makes me wonder how I would feel." Yoder nodded absently. "I think I should have been a midwife." Ruth tapped his shoulder. "Hey, come on. Tell me. What did you think?"

"Mostly how shitty it was that Josh separated them."

"Oh, that. Well, you have to."

"Josh told me the reasons. I don't know much about animals, but that calf knew its mother. You could see it."

"Believe me, Yoder, it's for the best. It's easier if there's no bond."

"For who? If the birth seemed empty, you're the ones who made it that way." Ruth's fork scraped against the plate.

"You ever thought about having kids, Yoder?"

"I don't think that's the question here. You ever thought about having a kid, Ruth?"

She drew back, sinking into herself as if trying to remember a name. "Yoder, Josh is sterile."

Yoder opened his eyes.

She met his gaze, but he glimpsed the answer to all her puzzling behavior in her quivering lip. "Didn't he tell you? He had a vasectomy about two years ago, just before I met him."

"I didn't know."

"Oh, he had reasons, you know, good reasons. 'The world's no place for a child,' he said." Ruth grabbed air with her fists and drew them to her chest in a remarkable imitation of Josh's speech-making. "'Too many of us already,' he said. And now he's changed his mind. And now it's too late. Isn't it women who are supposed to be fickle?" When she smirked she looked coarse and spoiled.

"How do you feel about it?"

"He wants to name the calf Baby. Don't you think that's weird?" Ruth flopped back against the side of the house, holding her plate limply in her hand. The fork clattered down the steps to the ground. "Part of me hates him. He had no right to deprive us of children."

"At least he was thinking, Ruth. You're making a very important decision for another human being here."

"He's already *made* the decision."

"No, I mean for the kid. Give someone life, and you throw

in loneliness, boredom, pain. It's a package deal."

"Oh, please, Yoder."

"Maybe you're doing some potential somebody a favor—saving him the trouble so to speak."

"What do you mean?"

"You really don't know, do you? Look at me. Would you want my life?"

"Well, nobody ever . . . ."

"Right."

"Yoder, I want a baby. I want it more than I've ever wanted anything. I get almost sick with longing." She looked around as if for the words to explain it to him. "It's like being horny all the time," she said.

"Has Josh been to a doctor?"

"Yes, yes. But you know Josh—when he has something done, it's done right." She swept her hair back off her forehead. The sun lit the fine lines in her skin. "Josh loves me because I can split a log and cook lentil soup, but we don't talk like we used to. It's become this *thing* between us. We both want a child but if we stay together, neither of us will ever have one." She seemed momentarily embarrassed, as if she'd broken a confidence. "I don't know why I'm talking to you about this. Except that it was probably you who gave him the idea in the first place."

"Stop right there. I didn't know about this until just now."

"It's not your problem, anyway." She looked at him with a hint of amusement. "See, you're not the only one with problems."

"Who ever said I was?"

She rubbed her eyes in exaggerated circles. "Look, it's just that I'm tired of hearing about how you've been misunderstood all your life. Like you're the only one who ever felt that way."

"Listen, Ruth, you understand why I'm here and so do I, but that doesn't answer the real question: How long am I staying? You could get stuck with me forever. Isn't that what you're saying?"

"No one asked you to leave." She said the words flatly, but in her eyes he saw a hint of alarm.

"No? It's been too wet to work on the house for three days

now. I'm lousy with the animals. You talk to me only when you have to, and Josh treats me like some wounded war hero."

"Josh likes having you here and that's that."

They were shouting, both disrespectful of the country silence. He held her eyes until she looked away. "Look, this isn't the place for me. I know that. But I honestly don't physically know where to go from here." He sprang off the porch and scratched a handful of small stones from the ground, throwing them with force at the chicken coop, rattling the wire mesh. The flurry of squawks pleased him and he threw another handful. "I'd just like to know what I'm supposed to do now. I don't even recognize this country anymore. Everybody's jumping into a slot as fast as they can—I'm ready to jump—no slot." He swung his leg around, stiff as a two by four, and kicked the porch post full force, absorbing the pain until it exploded in his ankle. He fell to the porch and buried his head. He swore until the pain receded, rocking his body hard to distract himself. Ruth put her arm tentatively around his shoulders.

Memories surfaced in no order, fragmented like the songs set loose when his mind was at rest: Vision of Marla streaming by, red hair flying; the wine, had he remembered to hide it?; the calf looking up at Josh with the blind trust of a child; Tundra's eyes skimmed over with death. He could feel the wind on his neck and noticed that Ruth's arm tightened in rhythm with his heaving breath. He wanted her gone. He wanted them all gone.

"Where's Josh?" he asked, his head still buried.

"Bangor—remember? Are you all right? He said to tell you he'd be back tonight. He ought to be here," she said to herself. "We have a new calf."

At least Josh was not inside listening. But he would be told—no doubt about that. Yoder sat up, aware that he had just a little time to make her understand. "Do you ever feel like you and Josh are—I don't know—almost like twins?"

"Twins?" Clearly a word she disliked. "No. In fact I made him promise we'd never ever dress alike."

"No, I mean, do you feel related?"

"He's a man, Yoder. We don't talk even like I just talked to you, if you want to know the truth. I love him but we aren't at all the same."

"That's all I really want. I'd like to feel related. Is it so much to ask that out of two billion other human beings there be one twin?"

Ruth lowered her eyes and pulled away. Brushing off her jeans, she mumbled: "I don't know, Yoder. I don't know," and crossed in front of him to reach a bucket of chicken feed hanging from a nail on the porch. She ran her hands through the grains and seeds. "The only way I know to do that is to have a child. Maybe you'll have more luck at that than I." She narrowed her eyes at him, then hurried inside, letting the door slam.

"I only told you because it came to mind," he shouted. The echo of the door banging shut. The echo of his voice. Yoder closed his eyes to the sun. Strange how Allie's features had faded. He could not quite bring her back, though she was the closest he'd ever come to spotting a twin.

He'd met her the summer after high school when he'd worked the carnival circuit up and down the coast. His first job had been to drive a jeep across the ground separating the midway from the rides. Hose it down, then tear it up with the jeep's wheels, creating a muddy path so the customers would be forced to walk right next to the midway, right past the barkers. A lowly job, but the sneakiness of it appealed to him. By the end of the summer, promoted to ride man, he ran the merry-go-round ten hours a day, lusting after young mothers in shorts and halter tops, feeling dirty and old with his first scruffy beard as he watched the peach-skinned babies squeal.

Allie ran the mallet machine. He first noticed her walking away toward the main trailer in tight blue jeans and a baseball cap and had no idea she was female. The next day he'd passed by her machine and was stunned by her looks. She had curly brown hair that sprouted from beneath a Cubs cap, and a body stretched tight as a slingshot. A fullness around her mouth and nose made her look as if she were perpetually about to speak. When they'd finally made love it had been like learning to love himself. As long as he knew her, he never saw her do a weak thing. Except disappear without saying goodbye.

Shaking back his hair, Yoder stood and looked around at the landscape of chicken coops, dead cars and patchy hills rising and falling toward the ocean. The morning deserved to be over, though by the sun he knew it could be no more than 10 o'clock. The calf was four hours old.

The sun had melted the top layer of icy snow and the ground gave slightly under his feet. Yoder bent his head to enter the shed where the new calf and her mother stood, separated by a stall wall. It took a few minutes for his eyes to adjust. The calf lay on the ground, her head resting against a pile of hay. Her eyes stared patiently into the darkness. Yoder approached apprehensively and, since she seemed not to mind his presence, sat down beside her. He stroked the calf's head in long slow motions, as the mother, bending her head around the partition, watched.

$\diamond$ 8 $\diamond$

H E HEARD HIS name before he knew why and woke with a start. Darkness. The smell of milk and manure. Night. Was there danger? Lying under Josh's coat on a stack of hay bales four feet off the ground, Yoder could see only the roof sloping close to his head. He reached up and ran his hand over the old wood. Soaked with weather and age, it gave him comfort, like a dock that absorbs so much sun it warms your feet. A hand on his arm—Ruth—her voice the voice calling his name, a little more insistently each time. "What?" he said, shaking the slur from his voice, "What?"

"You want some dinner?" She had the kindness to whisper.

"Dinner? What time is it?"

"Dinner time. You've been asleep in here all day. Come into the house, Yoder."

He squirmed away from her in the hay bed. "Is Josh back yet?"

"No, not for hours."

"I think I'll stay here."

"Aren't you cold?"

"Not under this coat." Yoder shut his eyes, smelling straw.

When the world got this small, contentment seemed possible. Just one body under wool and enough cold nipping at your face to let you know the warmth wouldn't last forever.

"Well, I am very cold and I'd like to talk to you," Ruth said. "I'm sorry about this morning."

"Forget it."

"No, I can't really. It doesn't have to be now."

"What doesn't?" Yoder surfaced to catch her words then sunk under their nonsense.

"You needed someone to talk to this morning. If you feel like talking now, I could make some tea."

The calf and the shouting. He had collapsed in her arms. The woman was incredibly insensitive.

"I was thinking that it makes sense that you feel lost. You were gone for so long, everything so uncertain."

"I've felt this way all my life."

"Oh." Ruth pulled her knobby white sweater tighter around her body. It hung to her knees. Did everyone wear Josh's clothes? "I brought you a quilt," she said, laying it gingerly across his legs.

"Thanks. It's nice of you to come out here, but I don't need your sympathy." He pulled the quilt of blue stars up under his chin.

"You know, Yoder, at a certain point you either decide to throw yourself off a bridge or you just stop complaining."

"You think it's so easy to jump? Obviously you've never tried."

Ruth drew in a sharp breath. "I didn't mean it like that," she said. "I didn't mean actually jump."

"I know, but I did. I used to be very lucky. I didn't realize it at the time."

"I'm sorry." She put her hand to her mouth and took a step toward him.

"I was a kid. I'm glad it happened. Because, believe me, things got worse and I've never been tempted again."

"Yoder, life just doesn't have to be this hard."

"'To be too conscious is an illness,' says my man Dostoevsky."

"Please don't start quoting great miserable geniuses. Is that what you think you are?"

"Unfortunately, that's one of the last hopes to leave."

Her laughter *was* like a set of bells. "So, what's the cure?"

"Love," he said, and fell back on the prickly hay. The slats in the roof were covered with spider webs swaying in the wind. If he lay still long enough he might get to see one spinning.

"Men," she said, laughing again. "What makes love the cure?"

"It appeals to me. Us selfish, childish types like love. It's good for us; we're good at it."

"So, you look. Do you ever find?"

"Sure, but I tend to scare people away. I go at it like a demon."

She put her hand on her chin and got comfortable, the way women did when they talked to one another. "Tell me about some of the women in your life. I'm curious."

"About what kind of woman would fall for me?"

"Yes."

"Well, when I was in high school, I almost got married?"

"You, Yoder? Married?"

Just enough of a laugh in her voice to warn him. "Don't make it sound cute. It wasn't cute. I loved her. She was one of those rare girls who wasn't afraid of trouble. We started getting into trouble together, setting off firecrackers in mailboxes, spray-painting stuff on the cop house. Susan's real talent was shoplifting. She stole a pair of skis right off the floor of our biggest store. I mean, she looked so innocent, no one even thought to stop her."

"So what happened?"

"Don't know. Nothing had gone wrong between us. I've always thought maybe she was pregnant. I wonder sometimes: Did she have the kid? She just disappeared. That's actually happened to me a lot with women. And here's the thing—since then I've been in love fifty times and it's always the same."

"You romantic, you."

"No, I mean the end is always the same—like a winter day here when the sun goes behind a cloud. You just start to shiver and then it comes on again, stronger and stronger. Changes everything, makes it all more intense—the trees, water, cars, grass, your blue jeans. Then just when you're warm, it disappears, sucking the heat away until you're colder than you've ever been."

Ruth seemed to be appraising him, like a cantaloupe at the market. "I know exactly what you mean."

She was watching him and he couldn't take his eyes off her. Their words were threads and the air had filled up with lace. "You don't find me very attractive, do you?" he said.

"I'm sure you don't see me that way either, Yoder."

"Don't be so sure. You want to know what I see?" He looked at her face in the dim light. She had freckles across her nose and forehead, like Lila. They had the same oatmeal-colored skin. He was glad to be a man because of the beauty of women's skin. Like any truth, it was worth losing your head over. "I see hands that are strong and graceful. They speak for you. You remind me of a deer. That's what I would have said in that game if we'd done animals. I imagine your stomach is slightly rounded and golden." He stopped, aware of how intensely he'd been looking at her. "Someday, if you really want to hear, I'll tell you what bothers me about you."

"Tell me now."

He wanted to laugh. People were dying to know what was wrong with them. But telling them was as dangerous as looking in the mirror when you were on acid. "Nope. The sun is setting and when it goes down, I'd like there to be some warmth left between us."

Whatever was happening seemed to be playing itself out on her face. "Can I come under that quilt with you?" she asked finally. "I'm getting cold."

"Maybe we should go inside now."

"No, I like it out here." Ruth boosted herself up onto the hay bale. "Do you mind if I just crawl in here and lay down a while?"

He threw part of the quilt out to her and moved over against the wall.

"This is cozy." Ruth lay her head back on the straw. Their feet were nearly touching. He felt himself go rigid. "Look at how green your eyes are," she said, turning her face to meet his.

"Pop bottle green," he said, almost whispering.

"Yoder?"

"What?"

"I don't know how to say this. Maybe I'll just say it. I want you to make love to me." She turned and propped herself up on one elbow and her hair fell into her face. Waves like a river. She brushed the back of her hand across his cheek. "Would you please?"

A hundred voices screaming. Nearly two months since he'd touched a woman. Grab her. This isn't just any woman. Run. Vision of her legs beaded with water drops. Bathroom door ajar; sun in a patch on the cracked tile. Peach towel wrapped around her body. He stared at the roof, praying for a spider to distract him. "Come on, Ruth. You're just lonely for Josh."

"Can't you consider this on its own merits, Mr. Clear Thinker?"

"I have."

"And?" She traced circles on the quilt over his chest.

"I thought you found me sloppy, childish, selfish."

"Haven't you changed your mind about me?" Their bodies were touching, legs to waist. Ruth slid one leg over his, arousing him with the movement. "Yoder," she whispered. He could hear the wind rustling in the pines outside. On the other side of the partition, the cows shuffled in their stalls. Her hand stroked his forehead, smoothing back his hair, maternal and sensual and it broke him. He found her mouth, lips dry and slightly chapped. He'd noticed them peeling yesterday. When he ran his tongue over her lips, she relaxed in his arms as if released from some lingering modesty. Yoder began to feel for the shape of her body under the layers of sweaters. "Here, let me," she said.

The room was still, the wind circling outside. The sweater and the blue turtleneck came off in one motion. He remembered watching her breasts for the first several days, trying to make out their shape beneath her clothes. Now they hung before him, globular as rain drops, her flat brown nipples the color of the calf. She yanked his shirt back over his shoulder blades and he was glad for the labor of the past months that had made them hard. "Nice," she murmured, rubbing her hands across them. Could it be that Josh was not satisfying her? Was she as lonely as he? How sweet this was—how sad for Josh. Her eyes were closed and she spoke his name in that trance-like voice of women on the edge, but something told him to keep his eyes open.

"Are you sure you want to do this, Ruth?"

"Don't worry, he'll be glad."

"Who? Josh?"

"Don't analyze this, Yoder, for once."

"Ruth...."

"Quiet!" She sat up, alert, her hand at her chest. "Hear that?"

Faintly, he heard a car door slam. Ruth pulled on her clothes, cursing as she gathered her hair in her hand and pulled it out from underneath her sweater. Yoder heard Josh's voice calling her name. Then his own.

"Yoder," she said, her voice firm, "Don't say anything."

"What's going on here?" Josh stepped into the barn, his eyes hollows. He hadn't changed clothes since morning and now his black pants were covered with sawdust. "Something wrong with the calf?"

Yoder took a long moment to think the question through. A good explanation, but too hard to pull off. Tempted to embarrass them all, he fought an impulse to check his fly. "I fell asleep out here," he said, running his hands through his hair to shape the strands into a ponytail. "Ruth came out to wake me for dinner."

"Well, if there's dinner, I didn't see any signs of it," Josh said, pointing back toward the house. "And Yoder, with that cold of yours it's stupid to sleep so close to a new-born calf. Ruthie, you should know better than to let that happen. You been asleep, too?"

"I took a long nap. We were up all night, Josh."

"And I was up all day. I haven't slept a minute. Quick is obviously in pain out there from not being milked. The fire's out in the stove and the house is freezing. I thought maybe you two had run off or something."

Yoder stared at the pile of hay where they'd lain together moments before. Josh's coat had fallen to the ground "I'm

freezing," he said, bending to pick it up and they all filed out
of the barn with Josh in the lead. Dark, its sagging roof silhouetted against the horizon, the house seemed a hollow
shell, like when they worked late on the mountain and the
night air blew through walls invisible to everyone except
Josh.

"Why'd you sleep in the barn?" He was like a goddamn dog
sniffing out what was rotten.

"I didn't know where else to go. Ruth had a crybaby on her
hands," Yoder said.

"What the hell are you talking about? Ruthie, what is he
talking about?"

"It's nothing. Yoder got it into his head that I wanted him
to leave. He wouldn't listen to reason. That's all. Oh, look."
Her breakfast plate lay face down in the mud. The apricot
jam had frozen, trapping small pebbles on its surface. "Food
art," she said. "I'm going inside to make some tea."

Yoder stared at Josh in the darkness, feeling guilty for
someone else's crime. Why had he yielded to her? Josh was
his oldest friend. Josh put his hands behind his back, and
bounced impatiently against the house. "So, what's going on,
Yoder?"

Suddenly he didn't know who was lying and who was not.
"Later, Josh, OK?"

"Fair enough." Josh cupped his hands to yell, "Ruthie! Forget the tea. Quick has got to be milked." He turned toward
the wood pile, slapping Yoder on the shoulder. "Give me a
hand."

Under the canvas tarp lay a month's supply of split logs,
Yoder's main contribution during his time at the house. He
glanced with embarrassment at the jagged pieces, some
hacked to slivers, others too big to be carried comfortably or
fit into the stove. He was miserable with an ax, not strong,
not coordinated, and afraid of the power in the swinging
blade—how much damage it could do just slightly out of
control. He did not trust his unconscious.

Yoder piled on more logs than he could comfortably carry,
struggling to position them and pausing frequently on the
walk back to hike them up with his leg and shuffle them in

his arms. The edge of the logs pricked his forearms and he felt sweat running down his sides in the cold air. He thought he heard an exasperated sigh as Josh turned to hold the door open and watched him coming slowly, ten feet behind. "We can make more than one trip," Josh said, shaking his head.

As they started out for the second load, Josh's walk regained its swagger. "You should see the truck," he said as if describing one of the wonders of the modern world. "It's full to the top with wood from a house a friend of mine is tearing down. Mostly studs and one by eight's but it's old mill cut, full-dimensional. There's a ton of nails we'll have to pull before we can use it, but you and I can do that in a day. There's some oak trim, too." Josh's long frame bent smoothly and straightened again, bringing up a heavy load.

Yoder searched the pile for short pieces. "The first National League baseball game," he shouted to Josh's receding back, "was played on the day of Custer's Last Stand."

When they finished stacking the wood in the deep firebox, they sat in the living room watching the logs burn, turning to glow in the ashy bed of the stove. They ate bowls of the brown rice and mushrooms that Ruth made by the gallon and which always gave him gas. No one spoke. Yoder wondered if he was the only one unsure of what could and could not be said. Ruth avoided his eyes or looked blankly past him as if at a wall. He needed to talk to her alone but she stayed close to Josh, curled up under a blanket on the couch. He felt a strange jealousy. What were their hands doing beneath the blanket?

"Stopped in town and ran into Will," Josh said, speaking to Ruth's head, which was tucked into his chest. "Date's been confirmed."

She sat up. "When?"

"This weekend. I leave tomorrow, play tomorrow night and Saturday, come back Sunday afternoon. I want to go, Ruthie. I need to play. But I told him not to count on me in the future."

"I think you should go," she said.

"You do?"

"Yes. I'll be fine. Yoder's here so I won't be alone."

"What changed your mind?"

"I just changed it, that's all."

Josh rubbed his hands over his eyes. "Hell, that was easy. I've been worried about telling you this all day." He kissed the top of Ruth's head. "Thanks, babe. Yoder, I promise I'll take you along if there's a next time."

Yoder saw Ruth's eyes glowing at him from across the room. "We'll be just fine," she said.

All the next morning Ruth circled them, pretending to water the plants, but mostly she seemed determined to keep Yoder and Josh from being alone. They played a few songs before Josh left, and as they played, Ruth sat with her arm around Josh and stared at Yoder, raising her eyebrows in his direction now and then. What was he to make of this woman who ignored him for weeks and now flirted with him in front of her lover, his best friend? He decided to walk into town and leave them alone to say their goodbyes. "You're a real friend," Josh said out of nowhere, as Yoder headed out the door. Everything seemed to be in code. "You two have fun, now," Josh added, his arm around Ruthie. He didn't know what he was saying.

Yoder spent the afternoon staring at the tractors and combines littering the grass at the implement dealer by the highway, their enamel skins shiny as new leaves. He spooked around the hardware store, thinking that someday he might want to own one. Put nails in little brown sacks for people. Talk rivets and elbow joints, the smell of fertilizer always in the air. He caught sight of himself in a window, his shoulders stooped and his head tipped as if warding off a blow. It was going to come up again between them. Nothing else could explain the predatory gleam in Ruth's eye that morning. Josh hadn't seemed to notice, but those who were blind were easy to fool. That was the problem with love—whole universes could change before you noticed, so drugged were you with dull-witted bliss.

Sitting on the steps of the grocery store, plowing his way through a package of Oreos so mindlessly he didn't bother to separate the halves, Yoder returned to the barn, to the sight of Ruth's body in the smoky darkness, to the way his body quickened and his mind raged against it. When he thought about women's bodies, a procession of buttocks, breasts and bellies floated in random configurations before his eyes: belly buttons that curved inward or popped out like a third eye; moles and freckles; nipples pale and pink like a child's or wide and flat and dark; hip bones that seemed to push their way through the skin; huge dimpled thighs.

After learning Susan's child body so well, he'd gone through a stage when he simply needed to look at women's bodies, as many as possible. He and Susan had used one another to learn, spending more time stroking and turning to see how the other was made than in clumsy love-making. Each thought the other a perfect specimen. They were so close in body size that they could cup their hands around each other's buttocks and roll together. He was disappointed when, with Allie—she long-waisted, he short in the arm— this feat was impossible. It was his first clue that all women were different and that sex with different women would be an endless surprise. With Sal he'd discovered that sex with the same woman could be endlessly surprising.

Someone desired him—that feeling reached beyond the loyalties that kept all of them tangled together. Could Ruth see something in him that he could not? Or were they twins? There was a sad victory in winning something that belonged to Josh. His heart sickened at what men did to women—how they set them out like prizes to be stolen from one another. He didn't want any part of that and yet there had been a warmth like good scotch between him and Ruth in the barn last night. An unexpected oasis of pleasure had been set in his path. He forced his imagination to leave the barn, envision the pain this might inflict on Josh, flash back to their talks in the shanty. He crumpled the Oreo package into a tight wad and aimed for the stop sign across the street.

He crossed the bridge at dusk, certain that Ruth was lying in wait. The house trembled—her face reflected in every window. He'd decided to head straight for his room, skip dinner, write letters to Sal and Julie, stay in bed until Sunday.

Ruth sat in the living room—fully clothed he was glad to

see—working on the loom. "Yoder," she called as he headed for the stairs. "Let's quit hiding from one another."

"I haven't been hiding. I've been in town. I bought you a new plug for the bathtub."

"Whatever. Look, I scared you last night and I'm sorry. I want to make it up to you."

"Let's get one thing straight: You didn't scare me. There's nothing to apologize for. I've forgotten about the whole thing already."

"Well, I haven't. Come into the kitchen. I've got a treat for you—one of life's greatest pleasures." She paused long enough for him to think: Acid? Chocolate? "It's not what you're thinking," she teased, spinning out of her chair. She'd done something to her hair, or to her eyes. "I'm going to wash your hair."

"Ruth, thanks, but I can wash my own hair."

"It's a favor, Yoder. I'm doing you a favor. When we're all done, I may even throw in a foot massage."

"No. No foot massage."

"Why not? All your nerves end in your feet, Yoder. You need to take good care of your feet."

"If it's so important to you, I'll let you wash my hair. It needs it, believe me. But no foot massage. I've got things to do later."

"What could be more important than getting a massage from me?" A singsong in her voice. Ruth spread her arms as if she were on stage.

A kitchen chair had been pulled up to the sink and stacked with pillows. On the counter: a fat blue towel, bottles filled with apricot and creamy rose-colored liquids, and a kerosene lamp. "We'll do this by lamplight," she said, "More relaxing."

"Now look, Ruth. Last night was a mistake."

"Hush," she said. He almost left when she asked him to take off his shirt. They compromised by wrapping a blue towel around his shoulders.

As soon as he sunk into the pillows and dropped his head back into the sink, he went rigid with fear. Ruth took his hair into her hands and he sunk beneath the steady roar of the water, broken now and then as she tested the temperature with her fingers. "Still too cold," she said, oblivious to the way his body had become a plane stretched across the chair as if there were no chair. Yoder tried to draw air to inflate his body but it got trapped behind his Adam's apple, which pulsated in the lamplight.

"Let go of my hair." He managed to get the words out without any breath to support them.

"OK. Water's ready now."

"Let go of my hair." He yanked his head forward and his body sank into the chair, pliable again.

"Yoder?" Ruth came around to look him directly in the face.

"I need a minute—alone."

"I'll put some music on," she said with the discretion of a saint.

Something about her hand clutching his hair, his Adam's apple exposed—something from a dream? A deja vu? Dylan's voice wailed into the room and he sat straight up, rubbing his throat as if he'd been grazed. What was going on? Ruth hated Dylan's voice, thought he sounded like "a whiny little brat." But before he could question her, he was singing the words, riding the hills and gullies of the music, tangled up in blue. Yoder laid his head docilely on the edge of the sink, saw cracked white plaster, a bit of fern at the kitchen window and Ruthie's hand again on his forehead, cool.

"Now, relax," she said, easing his head into the stream of water.

The water breaking over his head had a healing warmth and the smell of apricot made him close his eyes and walk through the music. An orchard in August, the peaches dropping into the grass, a waterfall nearby and someone's hands on his head and someone's nails in his scalp, her fingers circling toward his temples and the peaches too ripe, too sweet, and a moan from him.

"Feels good, doesn't it?" Ruth purred, her voice in the orchard, her thumbs on his temples. His body left him. There was only pleasure, the water and the peaches sweet as summer.

"Yoder," she called through the lather, "I want to tell you something." Her words lapped over him in disconnected phrases as he rose in and out of the garden. Life, she said, is a gift from God and the gift is nature. Cities are a mistake we made without realizing it. We're here on earth to applaud— that's the true meaning of worship. She had it all worked out. Human creativity was a misunderstanding, too. Music nothing but a poor imitation of birds. "Birds are enough," she said, "Just walk out in the morning and listen sometime." He had to agree. The other morning he'd spotted a cardinal. Heard its sentimental song: *what-cheer, cheer, sweet-sweet-sweet.* There weren't many of them in the world; perhaps because their red feathers made them an easy target and predators didn't know that sparrows tasted equally as good. She needed a child, she said, because as she got older it was harder to worship. Only a child could bring the beauty of the world back to her. She was desperate. She needed him. They both needed him.

"Wait a minute." Yoder sat up and soapy water ran in streams down his face. "Wait just a minute. Is that why you came on to me last night?"

"Yoder, if you'll just hear me out. You can help us. You're like one of us; Josh loves you very much."

"Are you out of your mind? Didn't you listen to anything I said the other day? I am *not* like one of you. And I can't do this." The possibility of things being simple between him and a woman suddenly seemed astronomically small.

"I knew I should have just seduced you."

"Ruth, would you listen to yourself? You know how I feel about bringing another human being onto this sinking ship. If you could go ahead, knowing that!"

"Yoder, I don't see what difference it makes."

"How I feel?"

"No, I don't understand what you feel."

"So you figured you'd just skip over it? How about if you let me explain it to you."

"Fine. But you have to lean back now, I've got to put in the conditioner." Yoder smelled cloves and roses as the liquid oozed onto his scalp. "Just give me one good reason why you won't help us. I'll listen, I promise."

The garden was gone. He felt like a child, forced to wait as his mother cleaned his ears in the bathtub. "To start with," he said, "you're admitting that there's a bit more to the world than owls and irises."

"Of course. I'm not blind."

"But you'd like to be."

"Well, yes. It's part of the reason I want to live on the mountain with Josh. You can't see any of the crap from there."

"Right. You hide out here without any idea what's going on in the world. You should watch T.V. sometime, Ruth. Read a newspaper. You might think twice about this little project."

"Look, I only said all that because I thought you'd go for it. None of that really matters. 'I want' is what it comes down to. If I can't have a child with Josh, which I can't, I may have to leave him. Do you understand? I'm 34, Yoder. I don't have much time."

"What about ugliness?"

"What about it?" Her voice was full of irritation but he knew she'd talk about this all day if it would get her what she wanted.

"Cruelty, loneliness, pain. Your child gets in on those numbers too."

"Oh, for God's sake, Yoder. Maybe my childhood was different from yours but I couldn't get over how green and musical the world was. You—Jesus—you'd think you'd never spent a sunny day flat on your back in the grass. You are so depressing, Yoder, it makes me want to scream." She dropped his hair into the sink with a slap and wrapped the towel around his head.

"Maybe I am," he said, sitting up, startled by how dark the room had become. "I honestly don't understand why people are so sad when a child dies. To me, they've gotten the best of it." They were like old friends, these memories: Watching seagulls at the Shore and flapping his arms in unison with their wings. His mother's arms around his waist on the sofa, reading *Twenty Thousand Leagues Under the Sea*. Knowing his legs were strong and could carry him down the alley and around the back where a peanut butter sandwich and tomato soup would be waiting.

"Yoder, we're getting off the track here. I've helped you and so has Josh. I think you're taking yourself and your semen a little too seriously. Why did you go to Canada if you don't value life?"

Why indeed? Because the memory of his own blood on his hands was still too close. But cowardice was easier to live with than even that much of a commitment to this life of his. "I was a lot younger then," he said.

"Maybe you need a child yourself. Although," she dropped her eyes, "I must admit I asked you to do this because I figured you wouldn't have too many parental feelings."

"How'd you figure that?"

Ruth studied his face for a clue. He tried hard not to give her one. "I don't know you well enough to say that, do I?"

"Well enough to sleep with me behind Josh's back."

"Yoder, I told Josh last night. He thinks we should all talk about it when he gets back. Legally and things."

"You told him! And he wants to talk it over when he gets back?" Yoder stood, throwing the towel across the room. His wet tangled hair fell in his eyes. "I suppose he'll want to watch. Make sure we'd doing it exactly right. Probably go over a general outline of it with me first."

"Let's think of this clinically, OK? It will be easier on all of us."

"There's nothing clinical about it."

"Yoder, don't get angry. Just think about it. Think of it as the greatest favor one human being could do for another."

"I don't have much choice, Ruth. I don't think I'll be able to stop thinking about it."

Life kept him hooked because he could never predict it. He knew he would leave Josh and the mountain before he was ready but he could never have guessed it would happen this way. He simply could not do this. It violated too many personal rules. He was not, as Kerouac had said, about to "multiply corpses of himself." Heredity was a fact. Yoder let himself think about what he would pass on if he were allowed to choose: Not his looks nor his digestive system. His voice perhaps, his love of music. Half his critical abilities, twice his tolerance. Less ego, less greed, less intensity, more joy, more blindness. A strange and useless game, this modeling of a child to avoid all the bumps and duplicate the high points.

No matter what, he would be taking responsibility for the very deep moment when his child would know death as something palpable hovering over his shoulder. How could he do that to another human being? He had to admit that something about children called to him. Oblivious, running with their bare legs and blindness, children seemed as beautiful as the forests. But mostly he knew they were doomed, pitiful in their small pleasures, exhausting in their struggle to learn what was not known by anyone. There was no hope in children and to believe otherwise was to give the merry-go-round one more push, to keep everyone spinning though we feel we might be sick.

---

*The first time I saw him, he was coming across the bridge to the dorm at sunset, lit up from behind by a huge orange Midwestern sun. He looked like a little ape, his jeans cut off at the knees, this ridiculous hat on his head. I was standing there with my and he comes right up to Blue, takes his head in his hands and talks to him—directly. Blue's loving it, licking his hands and panting. This goes on for about five minutes and he walks away. Never even gave me a look.*

*I won't say anything bad about him. He let me down, it's true. We needed him—and he split. Didn't even stick around to say goodbye. I know it was asking a lot, but back then I'd see Ruthie's face going sour on me and I'd ask anything. I didn't want to lose her; I didn't want to end up alone like him. The fact is, I've always helped him out, and still I feel like I owe him. You've got to remember: He's an orphan. That does something to a person. And then gone for so long in Canada. In a letter once he said: "It's sad, but some things you have to abandon for your own good and maybe what you abandon is your country." I remember thinking: Jesus, he's a stranger there.*

*He's that jumpy guy at the back of the bus—that guy by the side of the road. You don't pick him up. You watch him in the rearview mirror and you think about him, alone on the highway, the streetlights coming on and Thanksgiving just a few days away and your car loaded down with cranberries and oranges and firewood. There's no way you could possibly understand him and that makes him dangerous, and you've got wood to chop. He's that guy. And when you've known him and he's been kind enough to listen to your vaguest nightmares and still you pass him by—then he's like all the hungry people in the world you can't feed. It's him or you, and you cut him out. You can't blame yourself.*

9

JUST BEFORE DAWN, after the night birds had stilled and while roosters slept with heads tucked into feathered wings, Rydertown was quiet. Like all underexplored hours of the day, at the moment, this seemed the best one. Yoder paused at the bottom of the stairs, listening to the luminous silence, happy about the shapes of the furniture in the dark, and the shine of the floodlight on the floorboards. He would have liked to stretch out as he'd done that first night and cast his eyes around the room until the sounds of day began to accumulate: first the rooster, then the dogs, the birds, the tractors, the cars, the bath water. He would have liked to stay one more day.

With slow, deliberate movements, so as not to wake Ruth, Yoder collected his things. For the first time, he felt thankful that Ruth was compulsive about keeping his belongings separate from theirs. He loaded a half-loaf of rye bread, cheese, apples and a green pepper into his knapsack. He would leave no note. Leaving this way delivered its own message. He did not want to turn back at the end of the driveway to see Josh with his arm around Ruth, the two of them lit by shafts of pink light diffused around the edges of the house. He did not want to do something he would always regret. His hand brushed across the oak table, gave the rocking chair a push. When you grew to love things, they stole a bit of you away. He'd left himself behind in so many rooms that he felt whittled down into something he never intended to be.

The iron star knocked against the wood as Yoder shut the front door behind him. He reached up and snatched it away. He'd lain awake long into the night, listening for the sound of a door closing, considering his next move. He'd watched the clutter of his little room take on life: shadows wavering across the floor—the ghosts of childhood; boxes stacked in crazy angles like falling bodies caught in mid-air; a basket full of rag dolls. He imagined the baby whose fate he held in his hands hovering over the house, its breath caught in the frosted window, its voice a low, howling no.

The covered bridge that led to the highway gave shape to the darkness. How different it had looked that first night when it was only a landmark. He hadn't seen the stream rushing below, so close to the ocean its power was great enough to run through the winter. Hadn't seen Rydertown that night, looking past its foreign landscape for Josh's red truck. Tonight the landscape no longer seemed foreign, but lost to him.

By the time he reached Portland, rain had crowded out the day. Black clouds moved across the sky like funeral boats, thunder drummed his bones. The water raining off the brim of his hat soaked his tennis shoes, half-buried in the mud seeping up out of the gravel. He hated rain. On the road it was the enemy. Blurry headlights, like smudges of warmth on the slippery roadway, swept past so fast he could not keep count. A roar and a plash, another car gone by; he felt as weak as if he'd let himself cry. Seen from a car, a heavy rain like this could actually improve the world. The water gliding down the curve of the windshield, thick as honey, gave everything outside the softness of a reflecting pool. But out on the highway, it was just mud and slush and blindness. He kept remembering a Ray Bradbury story about a planet where it never stopped raining and there was no refuge and the people went mad.

A woman in a green Datsun finally stopped for him, but he was too wet and grumpy to indulge in his usual fantasy: Woman gives me a ride. We talk. We keep right on driving until we hit the Pacific. This woman appeared to be an unlikely candidate in any case. On her way to work, she looked locked-up in a plain blue suit with a little plaid bow tie at her neck. He couldn't get over the change in women—how cool and distant they'd become, with a seriousness that confused him. This woman was definitely a sympathy ride, a "no-one-should-have-to-stand-out-in-the-rain-like-this" ride. So he lied to her, said he worked as a forest ranger and his truck had broken down. Because this seemed to please her, he described in detail the job he'd spent three years preparing for, the only job except writing songs that made sense to him.

"Let me get this straight," the woman said, envy giving life to her voice, "Your job is to babysit a mountain?"

"It's a little more complex than that."

"Do you have a family or, I mean, don't you get lonely?"

"No," he said, turning to watch the rain sliding down the window.

When he hit Newark two rides later, the sky had cleared. The sun trembled in the chrome, rattled the tinfoil in the streets. His body snapped to attention, stirred by the noise, the sewer smell. In cities his habit was to keep his head down, never let anyone catch him looking, never look anyone in the eye. But he found himself reaching into strangers' faces, wanting to shove them up against a wall and ask how it was with them. Everyone looked familiar, names teased at his tongue.

Winter was hard on a city, and with the first softening toward spring, the damage was apparent everywhere. Dripping at the edges, Newark seemed held together with tape, and boards nailed in crazy crosses before doorways. Slush on the sidewalks. Grime in the corners. Spittle running in the gutter. Sloshing through the loud commercial streets, past failing repair shops and the littered sidewalks of fast-food joints,

Yoder felt dislocated. He expected this city to exist exactly as he remembered—or to have disappeared altogether. It seemed entirely possible that the candy stores and firehouses and poolhalls of his memory were as illusory as his childhood self.

Yet here and there buildings and personal landmarks confirmed the memories that told him he'd loved this city: The glass boxes cutting the sky into steel and blue; the newspaper where his father worked—presses roaring like the ocean, and man after man greeting his father by name; Saturday afternoons at the symphony when he'd squirm in his seat and stare at the man who sat beside him. Newark *was* his father. To walk these streets was to wonder how he'd allowed himself to lose the man who had introduced him to the rough and musical world.

Before long, Yoder noticed lines of trees forced to march the border between street and sidewalk. Ginkgos. Concrete rose out of concrete, like sky meeting water, an arbitrary perspective line the only separation. In the country the buildings had been soft. Yoder squinted into columns of glass, unaccustomed to the straightness of the lines. Here people walked with purpose and obeyed the traffic signals. He was headed straight into the center of the city. Lunch hour, and warm enough for women to walk with fur coats unbuttoned to the wind. On the corner, a grey-haired black man blew a raunchy saxophone for the lunch-time crowds. Yoder stopped to listen, forcing walkers to break around him. He tossed a dollar into the man's open sax case. Street festivals were gone, mimes and painted faces the province of children's birthday parties. Music had faded from the air. It was all recorded now—locked away in discos and synthesized to guarantee that even those who'd lost heart would move.

Yoder found a phone booth and scanned the book for the name of his brother's company. No doubt Sam still middle-managed somewhere in the vicinity—giving pep talks to fleets of software salesmen. Yoder pictured lines of doughy men, their shoulders drooping toward rounded hips, being punched and kneaded into the kind of real men needed to sell soft wares. Sam wasn't "in," as the voice on the phone put it. No telling when he might be "in" again. Was he out, then?

Out on the streets, about to pass by at any moment? Was there a message? Never call a middle manager at lunch time. Yoder slammed the phone down, irritated that Sam had a secretary, and that his own clothes smelled swampy. He was out of energy for the only game he knew how to play.

Yoder crouched on the sidewalk before a bank of revolving doors that spun like windmills catching the sunlight, longing for something trivial and urgent to fill up his mind. Others murdered their hours with papers to be filed, mail to be sorted, memos, appointments no one wanted to keep. Some paid to make lunch last all afternoon. Some drank from bottles on the street. He wanted something—a newspaper full of basketball scores, stock reports and anything at all from an Assistant Secretary. They had named the new calf Baby. Either that was sick or he was. He could not carry this weight. He would have to find a way to leave it on someone else's doorstep.

When he spotted the shoe store with platforms of shoes layered like wedding cakes rotating noiselessly in the window, he put his head down and pulled on the heavy glass door. This would have to do. Quiet as a bank inside, the store had only one row of cane-backed chairs lined up against a mirrored wall. Two powdered elderly women stared openly as he walked to the display of shoes at the back. One admired her shapeless foot in a plain black shoe, the other murmured: "They're very slimming, Bert." Boxes brimming with lavender tissue paper lay in piles around the women. He would make a bigger pile.

Anxious to get on with it, he strolled among the shoes, picking up several and stroking the leather. He decided to start with wingtips. "I'd like to try a pair of these," he said to the thin man bent over the woman's bulging foot.

"Sir?" The man inclined from his position without making a move toward him.

"These—in a 9 narrow," he said, commanding all his courage to look the man in the eye.

Yoder waited until the salesman had turned toward the back of the store before grabbing a pair of patent leather tuxedo shoes and holding one aloft. "And these—I want to try a pair of these, too." The man nodded and turned silently away, giving him a long look before disappearing. In this kind of store the customer was always right.

Yoder sat on the edge of the chair, not wanting to spoil the velvet with his wet jeans, and shed his shoes. The rotting leather had lost its shape. The blackened laces were knotted all along their length, like notches on a sword that told of a warrior's battles. He hid them beneath his chair and stretched his legs, wiggling his toes, waiting for the salesman in his grey wool suit and maroon tie to kneel before him. The man unlaced the black and white wingtips as if handling a piece of fine china. His manicured hands struggled to slip the shoe onto Yoder's ragged foot. Yoder kept his own hands locked behind his head. After a few awkward moments, the man stopped, holding one of Yoder's feet in his hand. "Perhaps a $9\frac{1}{2}$ then," he suggested.

"I always take a 9."

"Perhaps in this shoe you need a slightly larger size, sir."

"Let me try the other one."

Yoder stared at the swirl of blond hair covering a creeping bald spot, while the salesman made a pointless effort to ram the shoe onto his foot. The moment stretched and Yoder considered leaving before things went any further.

"I'm afraid you need a $9\frac{1}{2}$ in this one as well, sir."

"Do you have any oxfords? I'm looking for a pair of brown oxfords."

"I can show you a few styles in brown."

"Good. Bring them all."

For the next half hour Yoder watched the man's jaw tighten as he slid shoe after shoe onto his feet, lacing them with brisk strokes, tying a perfect bow on the top of each one. He felt the flashes of pity needed to sweeten any act of humiliation. He felt democracy at work. And he did nothing. Sat still as the man laced and unlaced. Asked questions about the fit, the leather, the price. As the pile of boxes began to grow around his chair, the man stopped answering, stopped selling and kept his head bowed low over Yoder's feet. He tried on a dozen pairs of shoes before sighing, "I was really looking for something in a size 9."

The salesman let a pair of suede loafers drop. "Look, I'm on salary." His voice strained with control. "You can do this all day long if that's how you get your jollies." There was a marked and heavy pause. "Sir," he added. Yoder stumbled from the store as if he had binged on cheap wine, and awoken to find something restored to him, something destroyed.

The streets were empty. Everyone on the phone again. With any luck, his brother's line would be open. Yoder mumbled Sam's name and cringed as violins and horns blared onto the line in the middle of his sentence. The song ended and another which sounded just like it had started when Sam's voice interrupted: "May I help you?"

"Sam? Hey, Sam, it's Yoder."

A pause at the other end. "Yoder?" Sam repeated, as if it were a word so long out of use he'd forgotten its meaning. "That really you?"

Same Sam. "Why would I lie about a thing like that. Listen, I'm standing here in a phone booth and—"

"You all right? Where are you?" Another pause. "Say, listen, Yoder, is this one of those phony credit card calls? Look, tell me where you are and I'll call you right back because honestly, the last time you did this the FBI called me. No kidding. I don't want them calling me here. So give me your number and I'll call you right back."

Yoder held the phone slightly away while Sam sputtered to a stop. "Sam, I'm calling from fucking Newark, fucking ten blocks from your office. I used a dime."

"You're back? I wrote when I heard about the amnesty. I sent it to that Toronto address—did you get it?"

"I've been back a while. Sam, I need a place to stay. Can you help me out?"

"Have you seen Mom and Pop, yet? Yoder, you should let them know you're back. How long have you been back?"

"Sam, I can hardly hear you with this traffic. Could you come and pick me up? I'm downtown."

"How'd you get there, Yoder?"

"I hitched."

"That's what I thought. Feel free to hitch right on over to my place. It's the same apartment I was in last time you needed a place to stay—only now I own it. I'd pick you up but I've got a meeting in about two minutes."

"Skip your meeting, Sam. How many times have I asked you to skip a meeting?"

"No comment. Check with the caretaker; she'll let you in. You can figure it out, Yoder. See you tonight."

Yoder circled the condominium complex, hoping to recognize Sam's place from among the dozens of identical windows and balconies. The buildings loomed up from patches of crumbly snow, as oppressive as barracks. Sam paid a lot to live here. He considered himself some sort of urban pioneer and every summer his letters had made mention of the fact that he was getting a tax deduction and not mowing a lawn.

Yoder paced the perimeter, peering into living rooms for signs of Sam's possessions. A few times he startled an old woman, a maid sweeping the kitchen. In several apartments the T.V. flickered though no one watched. Turning a corner, he recognized a hilly mound planted with willows that dipped down to a small pond. Sam's apartment faced this view—in fact, it centered on it. Through the window he saw a room papered in a metallic zig-zag pattern. How could he forget that wallpaper? He remembered a sliding glass door on the second floor that might be open. Sizing up a balcony hanging low from Sam's second floor study, Yoder ran, jumping and catching hold of the iron railing.

After six shaky chin-ups he was stopped by a voice that could call the races at the Meadowlands. "Hey, stop! Hey, whatcha doin' there?" Nothing like a Jersey girl. "You up there. Stop!" the woman shouted.

Slinging his body onto the balcony, he watched the tiny woman in a pink sweatsuit and curlers run toward him, waving her arms. "I'm callin' the cops," she shouted. He hoped she would leap onto the balcony in pursuit but she stopped a few yards short, her feet planted apart and her little rabbit face screwed into a frown. "What do you think you're doing?"

"Breaking and entering." He smiled down at her but she wasn't kidding.

The woman held onto her curlers as she strained to peer up at him. "Who are you?"

"Zorro," he hissed, leaning over the balcony and raising his eyebrows.

"I don't think so. I'm callin' the cops."

"Do you know who lives here?"

"I know you do *not* live here." She crossed her arms over her chest and he heard her gum pop.

Yoder held his hand up to silence her. "Wait. Don't tell me. Let me guess." He put his fingertips to his forehead like a bar lounge swami. "His name is Samuel. Yes, that's it. Tall, stuffy, trustworthy type. Drinks scotch."

"You know Sam?" Her voice lost a little of its lady-cop snap.

"Sort of. He's my brother."

She didn't miss a beat. "So does your brother know that you're breaking into his apartment?"

Yoder jumped from the balcony, landing so close to the woman that a small squeal escaped her lips. "He knows."

"Look, I'll have to check this out with Sam. You'll have to come back with me while I get my key."

She walked several paces ahead, pushing her short legs to their limit. He followed, imitating her indignant stride. Jersey girls were a breed unto themselves. They'd terrified him in high school, overwhelming him with their perfume, their bodies, the tight whispering circles they formed in the hallways. He got good grades, but they were smart about life— tougher than he, with souls as practical as Tupperware. This woman seemed as familiar as a sister.

She unlocked a door at the other end of the complex to the unholy sound of a child's piercing cry. "Comin', baby," she called, shooting Yoder a look that put the blame squarely on his shoulders. "Mama's comin'." Inside she scooped a pudgy boy from his playpen. Red-faced and furious, he beat his fists against her head as she tried to calm him with reasons. "Mama's workin', hon. That's right. I'll be right back. You be a good boy. Want a cracker? Yeah? All right, Mama'll get you a cracker." Without taking a breath her voice lowered an octave. "Hang on while I give Sam a call," she said, disappearing into the kitchen.

The boy looked frantically back and forth between the

kitchen and the door; his little face folded in on itself. His chest began to heave, like a race car revving up at the starting line. "Hey, kid," Yoder said, "don't go doing that now." What he didn't like about children was that they made him feel like an adult—awkward, tongue-tied, as insufferably solicitous as his parents' friends in the neighborhood. He moved uncertainly to the playpen and hefted the boy into his arms. Alarmed, the boy's eyes widened and he twisted away, his body surprisingly muscular. "Your mom's coming right back with a cracker." Yoder heard the sing-song in his voice and wondered where it came from. What told him to bounce the boy like this—to keep him moving? "How about a ride?" He remembered how much he'd loved riding on his Uncle Dan's shoulders, how happy it made him to be taller than everyone in the room. Lifting the boy's legs over his head, Yoder sat him back on his shoulders and bounced over to the window. No sound from the boy. Bouncing back, he raised his eyes from the floor to see the boy's mother standing in the doorway, a reluctant smile on her face.

"Nice work," she said. "Come on, cowboy, back to the ranch with you." She plopped the boy into his playpen and motioned Yoder out the door. Outside she paused, counted to five—and like an orchestra conductor, gave the downbeat precisely when the boy began to howl.

Hurrying back across the yellowed lawn, Yoder kept pace with the woman, watching the heavy brass ring she clenched in her left hand. Without curlers, her dark hair remained pinched into cigar-shaped bundles and bounced with each step. She'd smeared a bit of green eyeshadow on her lids. "I never heard Sam mention a brother," she said, raising her left eyebrow into a V, keeping the other impossibly flat and still. A fancy move, obviously one she'd practiced.

"I never heard him mention a caretaker."

"I'm Rita Delvecio. Your brother and I are friends. Why didn't you just come and get a key? You scared people, peeking into their windows like that. I got calls."

"Ah, don't sweat it," he said, giving a grin away. "It'll give them something to talk about at dinner. If they're so afraid of other people, why do they live on top of each another like this?" He could see she didn't follow this line of thinking. No place for the Merry Pranksters here.

She ushered him down the hall to Sam's door as if to the principal's office, unlocking it with a precise, proprietary movement. "If you get locked out again," she jabbed the key toward his face, "come to me first."

"Yes, ma'am," he said, ducking under her arm to enter the apartment.

Sam had bucks—and no imagination. The apartment looked a little like the lobby of a Holiday Inn. Since he'd last been here, Sam's comfortable furniture had been replaced with chrome and leather. On the walls were framed posters of the New York City Ballet and the Sante Fe Chamber Orchestra, Georgia O'Keefe's skull of a cow looming large over a pink and blue desert. Instead of books, his shelves held a Bang & Olufsen stereo system that must have set him back a few grand. None of the purple geodes and conch shells gathering dust on the top shelf had the broken edges or imbedded grit of found objects. Yoder turned one in his hand, remembering Sam dragging home his butterfly net full of shells day after day during summer vacations in Atlantic City. He'd lined the garden with them, edged the driveway, filled tabletops inside the tiny rented cottage. Each year Sam wrapped some of the best specimens in newspaper for the trip home. But these shells still had a gold label, "Gifts from the Sea," attached to the underside.

A clock was ticking. Yoder headed down the hallway toward the kitchen. He opened the refrigerator and the food nearly tumbled into his arms. Good old Sam. Yoder stood before the open refrigerator, momentarily paralyzed by greed and hunger. Impossible to eat it all, all at once. He sprung the lid on a tin of imported mints and popped several into his mouth, letting them dissolve into the peculiar pleasure which is chocolate. He ran his finger along the glossy surface of a wedge of cheese, scooping the yellow softness into his mouth. Chocolate and brie was an inspired combination. Somebody should make a candy bar for adults—sell it wrapped in gold foil with a fleur de lis stamped on its surface. He grabbed a fat leg of fried chicken, doused it with salt, and opened a beer, continuing down the hallway.

The bathroom was Sam's crowning achievement; as big as a small bedroom, it was the cosiest room in the apartment. A deep brown carpet covered the floor and wicker chairs lounged in the corners. Fat towels were stacked on top of an antique bureau and an erotic Oriental print hung over the toilet. He had to hand it to the Chinese: They knew how to make sexual acrobatics clinical and sensual at the same time. He guessed that women probably loved to stay with Sam for a chance to get at his bathroom.

Yoder tore the meat off the chicken leg and searched for a place to throw the greasy bone away. Confronting himself in the full-length mirror, he straightened to stare at his ragged body. Denim hat smashed on his head, some kind of oily stain on its brim, corduroy jacket hanging limply off one shoulder, blue jeans stiff with dirt and road salt. Throwing his shoulders back, Yoder turned to glance at his profile. It was better—in profile he looked more like a man of the road than a bum. He needed some clothes. A car. Bucks. Josh had stuffed his pockets from time to time but he was as close to dead broke as he'd been six years before. Back then, he had company. Now all the old hippies were wearing Calvin Klein.

Pouring the beer down his throat, he pitched the can into the basket and peeled off his clothes. Naked, moving his toes through the deep nap of the carpet, he faced himself again in the mirror, staring with disappointment at his small body, which seemed to twist inward in search of warmth. Moving closer, he pulled at his skin. It looked stretched and old, as if it had been used before he got it. The unbelievable was beginning to happen: Tiny wrinkles knitted the skin beneath his eyes and around his mouth. Proof that he was getting on with it. The wheels were turning; he was changing, moving steadily up until finally he would be out.

Experimenting with the dials on the shower massage, Yoder settled on the thickest, most pulsating stream of water. A plastic dispenser installed inside the shower held compartments for shampoo, conditioner and soap. Turning each of the little spigots, he sent blue, yellow and green ooze down the side of the tub where they mixed into a pile of goo. Was Sam having trouble spending all the money he earned or did he really need a machine to help him take a shower? When the water had churned into steam, he backed in, resting his head against the tile. How long had he been cold? Opening his mouth wide, he let the water fill and spill over, let it run across his eyelids, pound his chest. Soap foamed into lather in his hands and he scrubbed himself red and tingling, cleansing away the staleness that lurked about his body.

Wrapping up in a big towel he sat down to attend his feet. They looked amphibious and strong, as if they might swim off without him. He took scrupulous care of them, keeping the nails clipped and clean, cultivating callouses. Someday, he hoped to grow a permanent layer of hard skin over his feet so he needn't ever be concerned about shoes. He brought Sam's terrycloth robe up to his face and inhaled, smelling the sheets he'd once helped his mother bring in from the line on wash day. The smell of sunlight. He slipped the robe on, hiking it up over the belt to keep it from trailing on the ground.

Padding back toward the kitchen, a rush of sighs escaped his lips, rapid and involuntary as a convulsion. Yoder steadied himself against the wall and thought about survivors— of plane crashes, kidnappings, natural disasters—of the way they looked in the newspaper in clean clothes, faces freshly shaven. A bath was best when it had real work to do. Water and food and soft cotton were good things. Wall-to-wall carpeting was a good thing. Was this a truth he'd overlooked all these years? Deep down inside, did everyone want wall-to-wall carpeting?

He decided to get drunk. There would be plenty of time tomorrow to fight with Sam. Sam's generosity brought out the heckler in him, and though he once vowed to resist, he saw no point to it now. He was on the lookout for anything weaker than himself. Behind the sticky half-bottles of Drambuie and Grand Marnier, he found a gallon of Seagrams in a jug with a pour spout. Yoder downed a tall one, poured another and headed straight for the couch. "I see someone finally taught you to position speakers," he said aloud before closing his eyes.

Bare black limbs enclosed a winter sky. A woman emerged from the trees. She pulled back the thin, ragged blanket to show him the baby. Its face was long and pointed, like a lizard. It opened its mouth wide, like a fish.

Sam's face hovered over him as if he were a patient in intensive care. "When they asked him what he missed most about Canada, he said: Canadian whiskey. Right?" Sam held the scotch bottle aloft. "Yoder, for God's sake open your eyes, I know you're awake." Sam's hand, accustomed to greeting clients, shot out as soon as Yoder sat up. His arm tightened around Yoder's shoulder. "Great to have you back," he said. They were buddies. Good buddies. "You look great—really. What were they feeding you up there? Really—you don't look a day older. Hey, we could give Mom and Pop a call. It's only 8—they're still up. What do you say?"

Sam exhausted him totally. He believed in keeping a conversation going even if he had to do it all by himself. "No way, Sam. And I'd appreciate it if you didn't mention that I'm here."

"Don't be like that!" Sam sounded like an elementary school teacher explaining the virtues of sharing. "They want to see you, believe me. You're going to see them, aren't you? Yoder, you've got to go see them."

"Sam?" A woman's voice came from out of the darkness. "Have you got oregano?"

"In the refrigerator, Rit," Sam yelled back. "That's Rita. You've met, I heard. I couldn't remember if you ate meat anymore so I asked her to fix us something veg."

The woman who hated him for catching her in curlers. She'd tried to make him take her baby. "I'm not hungry," Yoder said.

"Once you smell Rita's spinach lasagna you're going to want some."

His heart sank at the thought of another spinach lasagna with another couple he didn't trust.

"We go out." Sam raised his eyebrows in a particularly unappealing leer. "Actually, she mostly comes in. She likes to cook for me. What can I say?"

"She's probably just after your money, Sam."

"What money?"

"Looks like you're doing pretty damn well. I hardly recognized the place. What did those Altec speakers set you back?"

"You'd appreciate the sound, Yoder. They're so sharp, I had to replace all my records." Yoder thought of his own collection, wilting in his parents' musty basement all these years. "Actually, it's going real well for me. Tax bracket's killing me but I'm not complaining."

Money looked good on Sam; he'd become a Martini and Rossi ad, his black suit tailored somehow to give him shoulders. He'd lost the beleaguered look from eight years back when he'd helped run a storefront legal clinic, before he'd decided that the only person he wanted to help was himself. Sam was probably having his shirts hand-laundered. No doubt he'd taken up jogging.

"I'm broke myself."

"Big surprise." Sam punched him lightly in the arm. "Hey, sorry, that was low. Having a little cash flow problem, are we?"

"We aren't."

"What'd you say?"

"Forget it, Sam. I don't want to talk about it."

"Hey, look, if the Democrats don't screw up the economy, you'll be able to find work. Hey, Carter's a Bob Dylan fan, did you hear that? I thought of you when I heard that."

He hadn't heard. Surely, this was the end. "It's not that simple, Sam."

"You're not in any trouble are you?"

"Somebody stole my wallet."

Sam held up both his hands. "I'm not gonna do it Yoder, so don't ask."

"Don't ask what?"

"When you called, I knew this was going to come up. In the long run it's not the right move for you. Let me tell you why. I know I sound like Pop, but you're not getting any younger. You coast by much longer and nobody's going to touch you."

"I didn't choose to have my wallet ripped off."

"Look, stay with me while you get settled. I can talk to some people. Have you got a suit?"

"Don't make me laugh, Sam."

"We'll find you something. Anyway I think that's the best route to go here."

"Except that I'm not staying. I think I'm going to head out West."

"Haven't we had this conversation before? Last time you were going to head out West, you ended up in Canada."

Not such a bad idea—Canada. "Aren't I always good for the money?" It sickened him to whine like this, to argue about a couple hundred bucks with someone who spent that on bathroom toys in a week.

"That's not the point. I wouldn't be helping you out by just handing over some money. I really wouldn't."

"You really would."

"Enough, Yoder. All right? Now, just relax, this is a night to celebrate. Stay right there. I'm going to give Rita a hand with dinner."

Maybe the President listened to Bob Dylan but some things hadn't changed. America's "A" speech still sounded the same. And Sam could still deliver it without blinking. Something made him slip off the couch and follow his brother down the hallway. Sam turned toward the bedroom and pulled open a dresser drawer. Yoder slid into the kitchen.

"Easy on the oregano," he said, conjuring up a smile.

Rita dropped a fat noodle on the floor. "You scared me. I didn't know you were awake."

"I'm not. This is just an illusion."

"I was gonna teach your brother how to make a Harvey Wallbanger. Want one?"

"Nope, I'll just grab a beer."

"Say, thanks for playing with Jo-Jo this afternoon. He's such a little baby—can't stand to be away from me."

"No problem." Yoder opened his beer and moved away, unwilling to meet her eyes. It was like this sometimes with dreams; sometimes he'd be angry at Sal for days because of something she'd done in a dream.

"He liked you. You could see it. The problem is he really needs a dad."

"Sorry, not available," Yoder said as lightly as he could.

"Hey, he's on his feet." Sam barreled into the kitchen holding a roll of bills.

Yoder held out his hand, trying not to smile too broadly. He knew Sam would weaken if he had a moment to think it over.

"Oh, no. This is the maintenance fee. Caretaker gets on my ass if I don't pay on time." Sam shook the bills in Yoder's face. "A hundred bucks a month I pay for upkeep on this place. See what I mean, Yoder? Nothing comes cheap."

"Your brother's an excellent tenant." Rita winked at Sam. "He always pays in cash." She took the money and feigned stuffing it down her blouse. One of those women who learned to flirt by watching Gidget reruns.

"Would you look at those socks!" Sam pointed at Yoder's feet. "One green, one black. Same old Yoder. Great to have you back."

"Got a family reunion comin' up?" Rita asked, sliding the soupy pasta into the oven.

"Not if I can help it," Yoder mumbled.

"If I have to drive you over there myself, you're going."

"Sam." Rita had the verbal kick under the table down pat.

"No, I mean it. Mom keeps asking me if I've heard from you. And Pop—oh, my Lord, you don't know about Pop."

Rita looked stricken. "Sam, not now," she said.

"Well, he's got to know some time."

"I'll go in the other room, then," she said.

"Know what?" Yoder barked, causing them to shut their mouths and stare at him.

Sam poured a beer into a tall, funnel-shaped glass. It took him a very long time.

"What about Dad?" Yoder repeated.

"He had a stroke, Yoder. A bad one—about a year ago. We didn't want to tell you because of all that FBI crap when you first left. Mom thought you might try to come home."

"Fuck that. How is he?"

"Well, he's better. It left him paralyzed on the left side for a few months. He lost his speech for a while—he was like a goddamn baby, Yoder, pointing and squirming when he wanted something. He looks older. His speech is still a little slurred. The paper kept him on part-time, but he's on his way out."

Yoder stared at the bubbles in his beer, absorbing this information which had, in a matter of seconds, changed his feelings for his father.

"Why didn't *you* tell me, Sam? Jesus—didn't anybody stop to think I might have wanted to know?

"Hey, like I was saying to Rita: In our family, no secret is too small to keep. Pop didn't want anybody to know. Mom insists on calling it a 'cerebral-vascular incident.' Besides, with you gone, we had to redefine the family dynamic. I'm not saying you're not still part of the family—you are—but it made more sense to act like it was just the three of us."

"That works out just great for you, doesn't it, Sam?"

"We only did what was best for Mom and Pop."

"Fuck you all, is what I have to say to that, Sam. What if he'd died? That happened—I knew guys who had someone die while they were in Canada and nobody told them cause they were protecting them or some bullshit like that."

"Yoder, we never thought we'd see you again. We had to accept that you were gone."

"Well, I'm not. I'm back. How do you like that? I'm back in the family, OK? So just get used to it."

## 10

CRAMMED BETWEEN NEWARK and The Oranges, the town where he'd grown up had remained placid while all around it real cities heaved with smoke and sirens and light. Streets were named for the faceless Presidents—Harding, Coolidge, Hoover, Taft—and American flags hung limply from six flagpoles in front of an aggressively colonial court-house. Fiscal conservatism and civic pride turned the old fire station into a youth center with nothing but a ping-pong table, a soda machine that was always empty, and concrete block walls plastered with Army-Navy recruiting posters. The best thing about the town was how easy it was to leave. The Atlantic Ocean hit the shore just a few toll booths down the Parkway. And from his uncle's apartment in nearby Jersey City, Yoder could see the Statue of Liberty wearing away. She *was* smiling, he'd decided, and like the Mona Lisa, the only real issue was why.

Yoder got off the bus several blocks before his street, uncertain whether the route still ran by the house or turned up the Parkway toward the City. The grocery store where he'd learned to steal was gone, but the modest houses overloaded with grillwork, awnings, weather vanes and eagles still squatted on the hill, distinguished from one another only by lawn ornaments and signs warning "Beware of Dog." Beneath his feet stretched the old cracked sidewalks, somewhere his initials set in concrete, entwined with Susie Merton's.

Each August the tiny yards had been draped with Chinese lanterns and Christmas tree bulbs for the Block Party—a night of intoxicating energy, of too much orange pop, snooping in strange bedrooms and crossing the street without looking both ways. His mother and father, transformed into exotic unreachable adults, huddled with the other parents around the barbecue, sipping martinis. At some point, very late, out of the darkness came their voices: "Susan, Yoder, Debbie, Douglas, Sam," and sorting themselves out they returned to the right houses and their own beds, unable to sleep with the heat and excitement.

Only his parents had not moved on. His father was "content"—his mother's phrase implied some deep character flaw—to remain at his job as linotype operator for the Bergen County paper. Content to remain in their first house. Content. Yoder learned to despise the work that left his father worn as his antiquated machinery at the end of a week. His father regarded the newspaper as a factory and put words together day after day with little regard for their meaning. He took pride in the fact that typographical errors rarely appeared in the editions for which he was responsible, and in the mornings he read the paper like a proofreader. Yoder remembered the day his father had pieced together the headline "President Kennedy Assassinated." He told of looking at the words spelled backwards on his typestand, unable to move, thinking of the number of combinations he'd made from those same letters and how surely this combination should never have been made. The whole event seemed to confirm something for his father, something he'd been born knowing that made the rest of the world seem like children. In this, Yoder knew he and his father were alike.

Yoder hurried up the sidewalk, averting his gaze from passers-by. A familiar, comfortable paranoia accompanied him on these streets. Here, where everyone knew his mother

he'd always felt out of place. In Newark or the City people
expected a stranger. Sometimes he thought the only explanation was some cosmic mix-up by which he'd been sent to
New Jersey, instead of to a white star on the other side of the
universe.

Home was a chalky green split-level house with a rangy
sumac in the front yard—a terribly dull place to live out
one's life. Yoder could count the end of his childhood from
the day exhilaration at the sight of this house had turned to
dread. But in Canada he had a recurring dream of running
toward its yellow light, bounding up the steps, reaching to
open the door and catching sight of a different family
through the window. The woman, bending to pick up something by the couch, was not his mother, and he was lost on
his own street. Now he smiled at the sight of her cut-glass
bottle collection cluttering the front window. Filled with colored water, they grew cloudy and dark with particles of
fungus when she neglected them. Yoder remembered staring
at the sumac through each successive color, deciding finally
that he preferred the world washed blue in summer, eerie
yellow in the winter.

The hinges groaned when he pulled the bundle of mail
from the box: bills, a letter from his mother's sister, and a
flimsy tabloid titled "Aries Speaks" with an elaborate drawing of a ram on the cover. "Lose Weight the Zodiac Way."
However strange he might be, his mother would always be
more strange.

Pressing the cracked doorbell, he counted 2–4–6–8. He'd
sent scores of letters to this mailbox, postmarked from towns
all across Canada, and always he envisioned these steps,
these squeaky hinges, his mother's hands reaching out the
door in cold and in heat. Her infrequent letters were newsy
and polite. His father never wrote. His father. A mysterious,
acute sense of responsibility had kept Yoder awake all night
on Sam's couch. For exactly how much of his father's sadness—and now, his sickness—was he responsible? Yoder
turned to go, his feet skipping the first two steps, his heart
pounding as desperately as it had all the nights he'd run
from them while they slept in their narrow beds. But the
mailman, ambling up the street actually whistling, shamed

him and he turned back, reminding himself that she would
come slowly, setting down the iron, wetting her fingertips to
smooth back her wispy hair as she surfaced from the solitude
that engulfed her days.

The lock turned. Yoder faced the door. Her first unre-
hearsed reaction was important. She stood before him a moment, her eyes betraying no surprise. He stared down at the
crooked part in her braided hair, at the grey twisted into the
black. "Yoder," she said finally, as if it were the saddest word
she knew. Her soft arms pressed his face against her fleshy
neck. He smelled onions and talcum.

"Sam was right," she said. "You haven't changed."

His eyes shot skyward and he tossed the mail onto a stool
in the hallway. "I asked him not to tell you."

"He means well. Besides I knew you were coming long
ago." She had melted a little, he saw now, become a pale
shade of her own mother, a resemblance he'd not noticed before. And she had dressed up, a red skirt, a polka-dotted scarf
at her neck.

"How did you know?"

"Never mind that now. Let me look at you."

Fluttering about him, she chattered in her nervous way,
touching and poking as if fitting him for a suit of clothes. He
paid attention, wondering if she'd say the word: "As far as
I'm concerned, I don't have a second son," she'd said that last
night.

Dark in the living room, the curtains drawn against the
afternoon. Little china statues of boys in flat-brimmed hats
and blond girls with sausage curls cluttered the mantle. A
coffee table that looked new was ruined by everything
around it—the electric blue couch worn dull, the Naugahyde
lounger mottled by wear and grease from his father's hair.

"We're glad to see you, Yoder. I've made stew."

A good sign. He loved her stew and she knew it. "You've
painted in here."

"You like it? I was so bored with that blue. I've always
liked a deep lavender. Your father calls it puce. I imagine
you're hungry. I'll fix us something."

She hurried out of the room. Yoder let his head drop back
and released a long breath. She stood as close as possible

without touching him, as if wanting to define the space between them. He'd half-expected a party, balloons, Sam and
Rita jumping out from behind the piano and his father lighting a cigar. Ill at ease, he floundered, then wandered, opening
doors and staring in at the lifeless room. Since he'd been
gone, these scratched wooden floors and pebbly walls had
lost their physical reality, become something he'd dreamed
with unusual clarity. In truth, they were more quiet and
plain than any dream. Even at the door to his own bedroom,
the anticipated emotion did not come. Stripped of his belongings, it had the spartan appearance of a hospital room,
the white chenille bedspread stretched tight across the un-
used bed. No trace of the intense hours he'd passed here—on
his worst days tucked into a ball in a corner of the deep
closet, a blanket pulled over his head. He felt oddly envious
of those days when, reaching for depths he had no reason to
fear, he'd been fierce in his misery, proud of his loneliness.

Before the last door off the hallway, he hesitated. If any
room still had power, it would be this one. Yoder pushed
lightly on the door and stood on the threshold of the tiny
pink bathroom, seeing thin rivers of blood run between the
square tiles, collecting in a pool by the bathtub. Ten years
ago he had watched it all from this floor, his head resting on
a towel, his body curled around the toilet.

Suicide takes only a minute. Open the mirrored cabinet,
second shelf, grab the blue box, break the plastic cover. Slip
out a shiny new blade, test it once, twice, against the tip of
your finger. Then silently, without thought or hesitation,
draw a broad X across the ridges of your veins.

The papery edges had welled instantly with his thin blood,
ruining his arm. Immediately there was regret. A terrible
distance, like a boat pulling away from a dock, a widening
gap, a scream that can't reach the other side. Like drowning,
a wave of air between him and rescue. He'd fought against
fluttering eyelids, as the sound of his whimpers muted and
the blood ran through his hands like water. He'd held on to
his body, touching head, feet, groin; his chest heaving in air.
It was nothing more than letting your mind wander. Just
that fast, just a second to catch it, and then nothing you
could do to make the next breath come. He remembered

thinking: It takes a quick mind to stay alive.

Pulling back the sleeve of his shirt the way one checks a wound under a bandage, he traced the humped white scars. The sensations swarmed, still immediate, still a dream: the heady blood smell, the animal sound of his gasping, the single shriek. His parents had known instantly, broken down the door, saved him.

"Yoder," she was calling. "Where are you?"

The cold water hit his face. "Coming, Ma," he shouted back in his old way, grabbing a towel from the hook on the door and wiping his face against its musty surface.

A plate of saltines and American cheese slices had appeared on the coffee table. He bent to pick it up. "Let's go in the kitchen."

"Now, Yoder," she said, "I don't take company in the kitchen."

That was nice. If not her son, then an honored guest. "Come on. It's too gloomy in here," he insisted.

Yoder took his place at the kitchen table while she fussed with the coffee on the stove. Few things had changed. The tin canisters with their dark lemons and blood red apples chipped in the same places, the toaster that had to be held down to brown on both sides. "You got a microwave."

"Your brother has been good to us." His mother took a seat across from him.

"That's what he's good at." He picked at a slice of cheese, tearing off little pieces and letting them melt in his mouth. "So, what's new around here? How's the old neighborhood?"

"Here? I don't know much anymore. People stopped talking to us." He narrowed his eyes, daring her to blame this, too, on him. "It's a whole new group on the block now, younger," she added quickly, meeting his gaze. "But let me think. There *was* news about Dougie Roderman a while back. From around the corner—remember him?"

"Sure." Freckle-faced creep. Bully.

"He's in jail. Bad checks, I think." Victory rang in her voice. "And the Linfield girl—I guess she's doing very well in the City. Publishing or P.R. or something. Has a fancy place uptown. Mrs. Osterman says you couldn't fit a bridge game in it—but nice. If you like that sort of thing."

"And we don't."

Her eyes drifted toward the window. "I like a yard."

"What about the Mertons? They still live around here?" He tried to keep his voice even. Susan's face had re-entered his daydreams: Her billboard lips—her hair falling across her left eye.

"Heaven knows. Mrs. Merton and I haven't spoken since you know when," she said, dismissing him with an odd official smile, like a clerk at the unemployment office. "*She's* around though. I see her at the Shop-Rite. She has a son, I believe, but she's not married as far as I know."

He felt momentarily disoriented, as if the world had braked and everything had shifted to make room for a new possibility.

"She's ill, you know," his mother continued. "Some muscle disease. Virginia Osterman told me she heard they had to put ramps in the house."

He tried not to picture her. She came streaking down the alley and disappeared behind the Strommen's house. He saw her laughing at him, her hair in her eyes. Saw her body rolling with his across the red pile carpet in her parent's living room—made for their love-making, Susan always said.

"We don't speak." His mother dropped an ice cube in her coffee and they both watched her stir.

Sliding his wrists off the table, he cast about for a way to change the subject. "So what do you say when people ask about me?"

"Mostly, they don't ask." She leaned in and whispered, suddenly a schoolgirl. "It's like you died, Yoder. I just say that you're searching."

His laugh echoed in the quiet house.

"Is that funny?"

Suddenly he was very tired. This house on a cloudy day had always exhausted him. "It might be easier just to lie," he said.

"Well, sometimes I do. To people who have no sense."

"What do you say then?"

She gave him her smile, a sly one that stretched the muscles and revealed a child. "I tell them you're a priest." This was why he loved her; she rarely left the house, inventing a life whenever she needed one. "They think it's amazing. 'Yoder?' they say, 'You must be very proud.' I hope you don't mind. Sometimes I just get tired of defending you." She leaned forward across the table, her chin resting just inches above the shiny white formica. "Besides, you are the one who inherited my spiritual side."

Now was not the time for an argument about the difference between spirituality and fear. His mother believed in belief; lived in fear of finding heaven closed because she had not embraced the pearly gates, or transubstantiation, meditation, astrology—whatever was offered as the true path. She'd become a Catholic just in case.

Yoder stood, sucked in a breath. Not enough air in this house. "Tell me about Dad. How is he?"

"I don't really know, Yoder."

"Well, is he better? Sam said he only works a couple days a week."

"Oh, he's around all the time but I don't see him. He gets up first and has his toast, then sits out there and reads the paper. I take my coffee in here and do my work. He comes in exactly at noon for his lunch and I go back into the bedroom and read. He takes a nap in the afternoons. When he works, sometimes he's too tired to eat dinner. He's five years from his pension but I don't think he'll make it. The bills, Yoder." She shook her head and punched a cracker with her fingers, splintering it on the plate. "All he wants to do anymore is play solitaire."

"Sam says that sometimes happens with a stroke—loss of motivation, I mean. Sam says Dad's a lot better than he was at first."

She shrugged. He felt like slapping her.

"So how did it happen?"

Her eyes swept past him as if she'd forgotten who he was —her gone look. She seemed to communicate with great difficulty from a great distance. "It happened right here," she said, "on a Sunday morning. He was reading the sports page and I heard this rattling. I turned from the sink and here's the paper slipping from his hands. Then he said my name. It was all drawn out like a record slowed down. By the time we got to the hospital he couldn't speak."

"You know, I just heard about this yesterday."

"Don't use that tone of voice with me."

"Why didn't you tell me?"

"When you left this house, you said you didn't care about this family."

"What if I'd gone to 'Nam, damn it, and all you had left was my graduation picture? Would that mean I cared?"

"Your father couldn't take any more trouble."

"Why do you insist on believing I left *you?*"

"I'll only say this once, Yoder, because you are a guest in this house and you are always welcome." She held a breath, and then spoke quietly. "I lost my cousin Frank to the Second World War; I wrote letters to boys who never read them; I listened to the planes going overhead and prayed to any God I could find not to let a bomb drop on my house. Your Uncle Dan was never the same after that war. But never, never, would it have occurred to me to refuse my country. Your family is like your country, Yoder. When you turn your back on it, it owes you nothing." Steel in her. A strength he'd inherited but not earned.

"Ma, do you remember how you walked me to school the summer before I started kindergarten? Do you remember how you told me over and over again to stand on the curb—not in the street; to look both ways; to wait—even if everyone else crossed the street—until I felt safe? I was taking care of myself, Ma. Like you taught me."

"We lost you just the same."

"Jesus, I thought you understood. Shall I go over it again? Would it make any difference? I had to do something, Ma. That summer it all sickened in me. I couldn't sit still with it. I had to move. I tried to imagine myself killing or killed in that crazy place. Myself, my friends. I had to do *something*. Why am I talking about this? It doesn't matter anymore. I thought at least you understood."

"War is a sin," she said, reaching out to pat his hand. "It's not how God intended us to live. You understood that long before I did. But you can't expect your country—or your father—to thank you."

"What about you? Do you think I was right?"

"That's a question I've decided I don't have to answer."

"It's important."

"You've buttered your bread." She walked out into the living room as if alone in the house. Her long braid lay across her chest and she stroked it as if she embraced a complacent, faithful animal. In his memory, he saw her like this, prowling the house dreamy and withdrawn. Her outburst sounded practiced. He wondered whether she'd been preparing it all these years. The imitation wood clock chimed the hour and he thought of her days here with only its ticking for company. The kitchen was so small and clean, her war over cracking linoleum and grease such a daily victory. Yet he liked it best when it was messy and full of smells: Onion skins on the bread board, tomatoes bubbling over onto the hard white shine of the stove. Was it possible to spend an entire life winning the wrong battles?

When she slid back into the kitchen, she held an envelope in her hand. "This came for you," she announced, putting on her glasses to study the postmark. "Over a month ago."

On the back of the envelope, a yellow cow jumped over a purple moon. Sal. Yoder reached for the letter but she drew it back, holding it across her chest like a shield. "Why didn't you call, Yoder? Why didn't you let me know you'd come home?"

"I'm here now, aren't I?"

"We never told the FBI *anything*," she said, her voice quaking. "They came on Thanksgiving, on Christmas, even to your grandfather's funeral. Like buzzards." She spit these last words out. "And I never missed a birthday, Yoder. There are six years of presents in that closet." Her arm lashed out toward his room. "Open them. Go get those presents and open them."

"Ma, later."

"I want you to open those presents!" Her voice had strength but her body collapsed into the kitchen chair.

"Ma," he said, putting his hand over hers.

"You don't know what it's been like, Yoder. You don't know."

"Let me have the envelope." She let him slip it from her soft fingers. He could see her rounded back trembling beneath her red sweater. "Here," he said, ripping a paper towel from the roll above the sink and setting it down in front of her. Nothing was harder for him to watch than the way her fingers quivered below her eyes as she tried to stem the tears. She never allowed herself to cry in front of him. "I'm going to take a little walk. All right?"

"Stew's almost ready," she said, nodding her head to indicate he should go. "We'll eat just as soon as your father gets home."

He grabbed a beer from the refrigerator and headed for the door with Sal's letter.

"Yoder?"

"Yes, Ma?"

"Just tell me. Are you all right?"

"Don't worry about me," he said, popping the tab and easing out the back door.

A rusted gate made of wire so thin he could bend it between two fingers kept evil out of the yard. On the other side of the gate lay the alley. Yoder closed his eyes and held his arms out straight from his sides, walking the thin line of a ditch which ran down its center. Only a few inches wide, it collected the refuse of the seasons, blooming green in summer, orange with leaves in the fall.

Eyes closed, he walked, remembering to veer right around the Rinaldi's garage and braced for the barking of their dog. It came on cue. He gave himself a point. He walked wide to the left near the Strommen's house, the childless couple whom everyone had feared. Their garden was legendary, their yard always littered with wheelbarrows and an assortment of ceramic bunnies. The neighborhood kids had assumed the worst of these old people without children, daring one another to ring the Strommen's doorbell on Halloween, spreading rumors of a torture chamber in their basement. He opened his eyes and peeked. A pile of lawn chairs capped in sooty snow spilled out into the alley. Behind them, a red and white striped swing set. The Strommens were gone. Dead, he wondered?

Pleased with his mastery of the alley, he broke into a run across the old vacant lot where they'd played Statues in the dark, where he'd tested his homemade bombs while Benish stood mesmerized with fear and admiration. It was potholes and blacktop—a dry cleaner's parking lot. Down Harrison Road at the bottom of the hill lay the elementary school. Gravel crunched beneath his feet as he entered the playground, a park of stones connected to a small baseball diamond. Yoder wrapped his hands around the cold metal of the jungle gym and chinned himself easily, then again. Watching his hands on the bars, knuckles cracked and dirty, he felt the same eerie jump in time he'd experienced earlier that afternoon staring at the bathroom tile. With a blink he could change his rough hands into tiny forerunners, into the hands of an eight-year-old, struggling against this same bar in what was a wholly different life. It was as if he'd grown monstrous, rushed into grimy adulthood while his childhood waited here, still small. He snapped his finger against the bars, setting off a hollow ring.

Oh, how he'd loved her. His first memory was of the silkiness of her hair against his cheek as she held him, for comfort over some tragedy long forgotten now. He'd catch her staring at him while he ate his lunch or bent over his baseball cards. Knew she was trying to picture him old enough to leave her. He resented that look, the way it silenced the part of him that understood why she took to the attic for long hours on weekends, never explaining what she did up there among the boxes and the dust. He wanted to know why she had never visited him in Canada.

He pumped his legs and set his body swinging out over the gravel until he picked up enough speed to fly, landing in a squat and sending up a flurry of stones. Once, he'd been the uncontested champion of this maneuver, landing within inches of the swing set. Today, he brushed himself off and walked. With his arms looped around the chain links, he watched needle-sharp rays of the sun splash out from behind the school's smokestack. He let his legs drag in the sand, wishing childhood had been good enough to want it back.

In the room at the end of the building he'd suffered for love of his English teacher, enduring *The Wind in the Willows* just to please her. It was always the English teacher, he realized. No one ever broke a heart over the history teacher, the art lady. Down the hall, he'd learned enough chemistry to make small bombs out of charcoal, potassium nitrate and sulfur. Sam had taught him to ride his bicycle no-hands on this playground, the two of them circling in the gravel, at first quiet with fear, then screaming. He'd had an intimation that day of what it felt like to be cool. Riding no-hands was cool. It felt great, and once you had it, you never wanted to feel any other way. After that he understood why those born to cool sometimes acted like jerks.

His father's health had begun to fail shortly after Yoder left the country. At first, no one seemed to connect the two events. But each time his mother sent money, she sent news of his father's arrhythmic heart and high blood pressure. Dread kept Yoder from holding an image of his father in mind for more than a moment. Instead, he saw himself, leaning into the blue-and-white Chevy, cavalierly relegating his father to a hospital bed. He toyed with missing supper; never going back. A crippled man, Scrooge-like, pointed a bony finger at him and coughed.

Yoder reached into his jacket and pulled out the envelope. No letter ever measured up to the heft of a sealed envelope in his hand. He could live for days off the anticipation. But this letter had been waiting long enough.

*Dear Yoder: I'm dashing off just a note to you at your folks in hopes they still live at this address and that you'll get this—of course, if you're reading this, then you've gotten it—so why mention it—a metaphysical puzzle for you, in case you're in need of one. I'm sorry it turned out so badly. I was just confused that night and my life is not the same. I AM NOT THE SAME. But I never dreamed I'd ever treat you that way. Please let me know where and how you are. Please write. I can't stand thinking of you just disappearing again. Please can we be friends. Love, Sal.*

*P.S. Crock has been looking for you. He pesters me every week about where you are. Can I give him this address?*

He read it three times before returning to the lines: *I am not the same, please can we be friends. Please can we be friends, I am not the same.* His heart lifted in his chest, like he'd gotten a Valentine from the smartest girl in the fourth grade.

Gritting his teeth, he told himself he was not cold. And with no books to carry, no baseball mitt or coronet case to juggle, the run home for supper would be easy. *Crock pesters me every week*. Yoder took a last sour gulp of beer and heaved the can into the sunset.

HIS FATHER'S CAR was in the driveway. Not the same car he'd seen six years back but they were all alike. A Ford—always—usually a ratty station wagon loaded with rags and ladders and paints. Yoder took the front steps in a leap. The house smelled beefy. The television droned from the back bedroom.

"I'm home," he said to no one.

His father was sure to be in front of the T.V., arguing with Cronkite, driving even Yoder's mother from the room. The summer before Canada, Yoder had taken to watching the news with his father, and had grown fond of Cronkite. He suspected that his affection was actually a misplaced longing for Walt Disney, whom Cronkite resembled, and who had brought him reassurance each Sunday night of his child-hood.

They'd sit in the back bedroom, together for the only time all day, and devour the news. During commercial breaks, his father would tell war stories that made WWII sound like one drunken furlough. Nothing but hijinks. Best years of his life. Yoder called up a ghost of himself—in cut-offs and a Jethro

Tull T-shirt—brandishing a beer toward the jumpy hand-held footage of bandaged soldiers sloshing through swamps. A disappointing washed-out green. Utter gut-wrenching confusion. *Can't you see what's happening?*

Afraid of what he might see, Yoder hesitated in the doorway. His father sat on top of the bed, fully dressed. Though he belonged in the easy chair, with the paper on his lap and a Bud in his hand, at least he was not in his pajamas. But he was thin, terribly thin, his nose pointing awkwardly out of a face that had lost its cheeks. A black stubble shadowed his jaw line; he hadn't shaved—that wasn't so serious. His hair had thinned, and lightened—become not grey but neutral, transparent. He'd let it grow long, a plume of it reaching back from his forehead. The most striking change was his posture, his back comfortably slumped instead of ramrod straight. The word elderly came to mind. In his left hand he clutched a remote-control device. The television blinked crazily between channels.

"Dad?" Yoder asked, wishing too late that he could erase the doubt from that word.

"Well look who's here." His father spoke without taking his eyes off the television. Relieved at this indifference, Yoder stepped into the room. He'd been expecting a stranger but he knew this son-of-a-bitch very well.

"Sit down, sit down." His father patted the bedclothes, which had the rumpled, grey look of being left unmade for days. Yoder moved closer, compelled toward some sort of embrace, but was able only to pump his father's arm mechanically. Soft, the skin loose, his father's hand felt like a woman's. "How long are you staying?"

"Just for the night. You know me, always on the move."

"Sure, sure." His father began to nod but produced only a slow jerking, like a spasm in his neck. Yoder winced, afraid he might not be able to raise his head again. Somehow it snapped back into position but on his father's face was a smirk of self-disgust. "So what do you think of your old man now?"

Yoder glanced at the television, drawn to a chorus line of dancing cereal boxes, ten pairs of legs in fishnet stockings shuffling under life-size Wheaties cartons.

"You know what's happened, don't you?"

The legs kicked higher. He was unable to say the word.

His father kept talking though both fixed their eyes on the television. "That's right. I couldn't feel a thing on my left side for six weeks. I remember saying to your mother: 'Where's my arm? I lost my arm.' Then the speech was gone, too. No warning. No warning."

"It's been, what, almost a year now, Dad?"

His father pushed his spongy fingers against one another, trying to make them snap. "It's nothing—a year's nothing to me now. Goes by without thinking about it."

"You look good to me," Yoder said, managing a weak smile.

"Hah! Now I know it's bad."

Yoder traced a worn spot on the rug with the toe of his boot. He had wanted to say something nice. "You need anything, Dad? Can I bring you your dinner?"

"I don't eat in bed, Yoder." His father changed the channel. "Your mother will call me."

Dinner was a parody of the old days when Yoder would slouch sullen in his chair tearing his napkin to bits, while his father delivered himself of whatever troubled him: The traffic, the Mets, the union, the morons who run things. But tonight, it was his father who ate in silence, his forearms resting flat on the table. Yoder's mother asked polite questions about Canada.

"I hear Toronto's very clean. Didn't I read somewhere that the Canadians are a very clean people? No litter and such. Did you find that, Yoder?"

"It's not Newark if that's what you mean."

"More peas?" She held a spoonful aloft.

"No thanks," he said, "I'm full." The peas landed on his plate, smack in the middle of the gravy he was trying to sop up with a piece of bread. His mother cooked the way he listened to music—obsessively, fixating on an ingredient—pimentos, canned salmon, green olives—and cooking with it almost exclusively for weeks at a time. Rebellions were handled with gestapo tactics—food forced onto every plate.

Suddenly his father remembered his lines. "So what are your plans?"

"Don't have any, " Yoder answered, hoping the spin he put on the words would lead his father into combat.

"Don't. Have. Any?" A white shadow outlined his lips. Yoder wondered when he'd taken to drinking milk.

"Martin, give him some time." His mother's arm circled the back of Yoder's chair.

His father was picking his teeth. "I could use some help unloading a batch of downspouts from the car when we're through here."

A quivering mass of strawberry jello threatened his plate. Yoder grabbed his mother's wrist, intercepting the spoon. "I said I was full."

"Father?" She dropped the jello into the mess already on his father's plate. The trouble with everybody wanting to make things just like they used to be was that things were just like they used to be.

"Why do you *do* that?" Yoder asked.

"I like to see my boys eat well." A warning in her voice— and her company smile. "Eat up that meat, Yoder."

They had all stopped eating, the overhead light harsh on their faces. He spun his beer can in circles on the table. Suddenly it felt like the lunch counter at the bus station. "So how have you two been?"

His mother opened her mouth and made a little sound, then shut it again.

"Something must have happened in six years that you'd like to talk about. Your job, Dad, how's your job?"

His father composed himself like a talk show guest who's answered the same question too many times. "Paper's converting to computers. It's the end of my trade. Simple as that. But like I was telling your brother, as long as they put out that afternoon edition, they'll need me."

"How long's that going to be?"

"Ask your mother here. She's the fortune teller."

Yoder glanced at his mother; she wasn't smiling.

"Hasn't she told you? She's got everyone in the neighborhood trompin' through here to get their fortunes told. Doesn't need a priest anymore. Gets her answers direct."

"Sam understands," she said. "He's found the tarot very helpful to his career."

"You're kidding, right, Ma? What have we got here, Madame Leona?"

"You sound just like your father." Yoder sank back in his chair, momentarily derailed. The further he ran, the more his father rose in him, like a ghost who wanders unbidden into the lives of rational people. Heredity was a fact. He turned on his father. "How would you feel if she never read your newspaper?"

"Don't make me mad, Yoder. A newspaper's got facts in it. All's in those cards are foolish dreams and mumbo-jumbo."

"How would you know, Martin?"

He could see this was old territory, something they could fight about when they wanted company. "Look, Ma," he said. "Would you read my cards after dinner? Open mind, I swear."

She had turned away from them both to stare out the window. "Your father won't see it, but it's like a conversation with yourself."

"Yeah, well, whatever. Read my cards tonight, OK?"

He helped his mother wash up and they gossiped about his father—just like always. "What did you think?" she wanted to know, as if they were buying a car and had finally gotten out of earshot of the salesman. He couldn't tell her that his father reminded him of the dried shell of an insect, shed because it was no longer of use. He gave her his version of a pep talk, wishing for the first time to be more like Sam—good at pep talks, unable to distinguish what he believed from what he said. Alone with her in the kitchen among smells of soap and cotton, he wanted her to tell him what to do, wanted to tell her about Ruth and the baby who'd been visiting him in dreams. But she was his mother. "It's so nice of you to help with the dishes," she kept saying, and he realized he probably never even carried his plate to the sink when he lived here. The other women in his life had not been so easy on him.

Yoder wandered out to the garage, pausing before the open door. In the glare of the light from a single bare bulb, he watched his father move among his things, touching table saw, aluminum fishing boat, hammers in their pegboard cradles, drills, like a blind man reminiscing.

"Haven't seen this old place in a long time," Yoder said lamely to announce his presence.

"So you've come back." A man with no interest in conversation, his father threw out little topic sentences, inviting him to tackle a subject, but Yoder knew never to expect a dialogue. He let the opening pass, inclining toward the station wagon and peering in the windows. "Your mother's real happy about that," his father said. Did he mean the new car or the fact that Yoder had returned? "Let's get this done," he continued. "You get on the back, Yoder. And we'll just set them down over there against the wall. Watch now, they're dusty."

"Are you sure they'll fit?" Yoder asked, slipping immediately into his role as younger son, apprentice, helper.

"Of course they'll fit."

"They must be eight foot, Dad."

"I don't need you to tell me how to do it, Yoder. I just need you to help me get it done. Now, be careful sliding them out of there. Don't scratch up the car."

The downspouts didn't fit. His father's back remained rigid as he bent at the knees to lower them to the concrete and tried to kick them into place against the wall. Each breath sounded considered. Yoder thought fast, hoping to come up with a solution before his father had to acknowledge his mistake. They would fit across the open beams in the ceiling where the fishing boat was stored. But he didn't want his father trying to lift them up that high.

"Maybe you should get the tape measure so we can find out just how long these things are," Yoder suggested.

"I will if your mother hasn't stolen it away again." His father gave the downspouts one last kick. "I keep telling her that a tape measure is a tool; it belongs in the garage."

After his father shuffled off, Yoder struggled with the awkward load, using the step ladder to reach the ceiling, sliding each pipe up onto the crossbeams. When he finished he felt hot and satisfied.

"Now what?" his father barked from the doorway, catching him with one foot on the ladder.

"I think this will work out better, Dad. See how they fit up there on the ceiling." His father looked at the pipe and bowed his head, sliding the metal tape in and out of its container. Yoder realized his mistake. His father would never be able to get them down again. "When are you going to do this project?" Yoder asked, stepping off the ladder.

"Should have been done last fall. Your brother might give me a hand. I can't remember if he said this weekend was good."

"Why don't you let me take care of it for you tomorrow?"

"Thought you were leaving."

"I'll leave Friday."

"You know how to do downspouts?"

"I should. You and I did them together about fifty times."

"I did them, if I remember." His father collapsed the ladder and set it back against the wall.

He turned to go, slightly relieved. The last thing he wanted to do was work on another house. "Let's just go inside, Dad. We can figure it out later."

"Freezing my damn ass off," he heard his father mumble.

"What?"

"I said no sense freezing our asses off out here."

Yoder couldn't remember ever before hearing his father curse.

"Looks like she's ready for you," his father said, nodding toward the kitchen and shaking his head. A candle had been lit at the kitchen table, now covered with a black cloth. The flame burned in the window, its reflected light bouncing off the curved tubing of the dinette set. The kitchen no longer smelled of stew, but of incense. Jesus, he thought, was this full circle or what?

Suddenly he had a vision of his mother in a turban and the sequined robes of a charlatan. Yoder hoped he could keep a straight face, if not the open mind he had promised. What a mysterious woman. He felt a certain pride—how many middle-aged women learn to read the tarot? How many can hold their heads up to the whispers in church; snub the FBI at picnics; insist that their son the traitor is serving God somewhere in the Yukon? A moment later she entered, gliding a bit more than necessary. She still wore her red skirt and sweater though it was possible she'd put on lipstick. He couldn't quite tell in the dim light. Straight-armed before her, she carried a small oak box with a mirrored top. Its sides were made of wooden bars criss-crossed like a log cabin. She set the box ceremoniously in the center of the table.

"Wash your hands, Yoder," she said, taking a seat at the table. He did as she asked, wondering if he'd always feel like a child in this house. "Before we begin," she said, "let me assure you that the tarot is an ancient and honorable practice. It has nothing to do with witchcraft or the occult." Her voice was strictly professional; her speech was obviously designed to allay the fears of her matronly customers. Why did people need a deck of cards to talk to themselves? "One way to think of it is that tarot uses the language of symbols."

"Hmm, dangerous stuff."

"Please."

"How much do you charge for this, Ma?"

"Not now, Yoder." Her arm swept past the box with practiced grace. "If you'll just open the box and remove the cards."

The box seemed to be one solid piece. He couldn't push the top off with his thumb. A second look confirmed his suspicions.

"Look at it carefully. Don't assume anything."

He was playing Sixties games with his mother. Was this progress? Turning the box in his hands, he admired the workmanship and the sleek oiled wood. The mirror flashed in the candlelight, bringing him fragments of himself. He checked for cracks, latches, a false bottom, and began to feel irritated by her steady gaze. "Here, you do it," he said finally, thrusting the box across the table. "You're supposed to be the mystic."

"Significator," she corrected him.

"Very clever. Then what's the significance of this stupid box?"

Placing her thumb and index finger on either side of the base, she slid the top two wooden rungs easily off a groove. Nested in velvet was a pack of oversized cards, their backs a deep blue field of stars like a summer sky. It was a neat trick, a nice opening. From someone his own age he might have appreciated it. "You have to realize, I've played these games before," he said.

"For a veteran, you didn't do so well. I've seen 60-year-old women figure out that box in no time." Cradling the cards in her left hand, she took up her speech again. "Now if you'll cut the cards into five piles and shuffle each pile three times, we'll begin. As you shuffle, I'll ask you to consider a question you'd like the reading to address."

"When am I gonna be rich and famous?"

"That's rather frivolous, but all right."

"How about what's going to happen? In fact, that's exactly what I want to know. What the hell's going to happen next?"

"Concentrate on that."

Shuffling the cards, he began to feel curious about what they might reveal, a little worried about discussing something so personal with this woman, his mother. Since reading *On the Beach* in junior high school, he'd played a recurring mind game. What if the bomb should drop right now, while I'm sitting here or filling my car with gas? Suddenly he could concentrate on nothing else. Could see only the blast, hitting right that moment, the candle setting fire to the curtain, flames climbing the walls, sealing him there for all time to be discovered like some citizen of Pompeii with his mother and his future laid out before him.

"That ought to be enough," she said, drawing him back to the kitchen and her dark eyes glazed with impatience. Taking the first pile from his hand, she turned over ten cards. "The question is: What will happen to you next?" Leaning in close, they stared at the pictures spread out on the black cloth. His eyes focused immediately on a skeleton dressed for battle, carrying a banner with the insignia of a rose. "DEATH" said the black letters at the bottom of the card. "I don't know," she said, after staring at the cards a long moment. "I'm sorry. You don't know."

"I can see the cards. My days are numbered, right?"

"No, no. This card simply means transforming change. That's why I can't be more specific. I can tell you that you're waiting for a message from someone." She pointed to the Ace of Pentacles, a five-pointed star in a circular frame surrounded by two fully flowered poppies. "Also, I see broken promises." Apparently she saw them in a crescent moon, beautifully rendered against an open sky. "There was some sort of fight before you left Canada. And there's a strong warning here about trouble with the police."

So that was it. She was throwing her voice—like Soupy Sales. "Look, Ma, you can just ask me what you want to know. I'm not in trouble. Everything's fine. Not even a parking ticket." Best not to mention the argument with Steven. She'd earned a point but he didn't want her to know it.

"Then why are you here?"

"I wanted to see you."

She gave him a look: Don't lie to me. "I'm just responding to what I see in the cards. Now, I need another question."

"Let's go back to fame and fortune. Specifically, fortune."

"Yoder, we don't have it. You didn't ask your father, did you?"

"Ask him what?"

"Sam said you needed money."

"Goddamn Sam. You always listen to him, but he doesn't always know what he's talking about. He really doesn't."

"Let's look at the cards," she said, turning over eight more pictures. "Oh, see, look here. Good news. The World card— fulfillment, the end of a cycle, usually involving the material world."

"You think that's why I'm here, don't you?"

"Yoder, this is a very good card. It's number 21. A magic number. Sum of the first six numbers, product of 3 times 7. Twenty-one is the perfect number."

"That's not why I'm here, Ma."

"I'd say you're going to come into some money."

"All right, fine. I suppose it says I'm going to take a long trip, too."

"That's not in the cards so far. Next question."

Suddenly reluctant to meet her eyes in the candlelight, he put his hands to his face, feigning weariness. "All right. So is there a woman in my future?"

"Remember to concentrate as you shuffle."

"And does she like to dance?" No predicting what his Catholic mother-turned-gypsy might want the cards to say.

She began talking even before she finished laying out the

cards. She seemed not to study them at all but to read them as one does an eye chart in the doctor's office. "There she is—the Queen of Wands." The card pictured a dark-haired woman holding a sunflower and a tall green staff budding into flower at its tip. Lila. "She's in a warm place—the South, in the country, maybe. But a loss is implied here." Her pudgy finger tapped the 10 of Cups, which was upside down. "Of a friend. Some difficult choice is involved."

Interested, he peered at the card. "She's kind of cute."

"She's a symbol, Yoder. Shall we go on?"

Something about her serious and direct manner and the flickering light made him consider the question he hadn't settled by walking away. "I can't think of another question," he said finally.

"Take your time."

"Oh, hell, I don't know—will I ever get married or, you know, have a family?"

Again she stared at the cards a long time, then raised her eyes to bear down on him. "There's no point in trying to fool the cards. I think you're being less than honest with me, Yoder. I feel you already have a child in the world."

"Forget it!"

"There will be others, two others in the future with a different woman. Perhaps one you marry." She paused, for effect, he guessed. All her mother-tricks still in operation. "The King of Wands, here, represents an honest, faithful, generous man. It could be your card, Yoder." The young king wore a helmet, with an eagle mounted on its brim. The King looked like Josh, he realized, not himself.

"Let's get one thing straight. I don't have a kid."

"You don't have to raise your voice."

Susan, he thought. "She has a boy," his mother said that afternoon. After Susan he'd been careful. Obsessed, Sal always said. "At least not as far as I know."

"We can interpret the cards many ways. Perhaps this means you've been creative in some other area. You have one more question coming."

"I don't want to hear any more, Ma."

"We'll just see what the cards have to say, then."

The last pile held four cards. She pointed to the Seven of

Pentacles. "This card indicates risk. But as you can see, it's next to Temperance. Gamble, but gamble wisely, in other words. Ah, and here we have The Fool. I expected it to show up in your reading." Dressed in jester's breeches, the Fool carried a hobo's bundle over his shoulder. Gazing into the sky, he was about to step off a precipice. "The Fool is Fate," his mother said softly.

"Tell me something I don't already know."

"Look at the card, see how he's stepping off the cliff but watching the sky? This card represents choice. I'd say the future is entirely up to you."

"And that's it?"

"That's everything, dear."

Flushed, like a performer after her bows, she sank back into her chair, and he had a vision of her youth that disappeared before he could make much of it. "One other thing, Yoder. Get your eyes checked. It came up several times. I'm sure Dr. Baker would see you. Do it, won't you? Just to be sure."

Did he already have a child in the world? That would explain why Susan's parents had refused to speak to him all those years ago. He'd been so certain about love then, and when Susan disappeared there was no one in the world whom he could trust. He'd headed for the bathroom, and when that wasn't the answer, had set aside a part of himself to keep watch, determined never to be fooled again. Had he already sent himself into the future? Was he the fool, letting Josh down for the sake of some false principle?

"The tarot is very powerful," his mother said, watching the confusion on his face. "I've learned a lot since I started studying. I've learned how much I already know. For example, I should have known you would run away, even though you assured me you wouldn't go."

"Ma, I didn't run. I left. Some people go live in England. You don't say they ran."

"You're a Scorpio on the cusp like me. You keep your secrets. Even when I was pregnant, I knew you'd be something special when you came."

She had never spoken of his birth to him in any way before. "Meaning what?"

"You were conceived under a full moon, did you know that? I remember there were three planets visible in the sky. At the time I was very interested in astronomy. We left Sammy with the Ostermans and your father took me to an observatory. That was a night! We don't get clear skies like that anymore. Imagine how it must have been for the ancients!"

The tender place where he kept his feelings for this man and woman ached. They'd had a date. Looked at the stars, his father's arm gentle on her shoulder, their bodies liquid with awe. He remembered shivering beside his father on clear nights while he pointed out Ursus Major, Orion, the Pleiades. He recalled no passion in his father's voice. But it could very well have been there. He, himself, had probably turned it into a tedious lesson.

"Your father and I were on the same wavelength that night," she continued. "The next morning I knew I had conceived. I told your father and he made some remark, but I was right."

"Why didn't you tell me this before?"

"You never wanted to hear it, Yoder. Don't you remember forbidding me to bring out your baby pictures?" The pictures had only reminded him of his helplessness, of being small and weak and utterly dependent. He thought of Lucy, nudging her calf to life with her loose pink tongue.

His mother's voice was still in the room but she had disappeared. "For months I hardly knew you were there. You seemed to arrive all at once. I grew overnight somewhere during the sixth month." He wanted her to stop. Something hurt and he wanted her to stop. "And you were so quiet. At times I was beside myself, fearing I'd lost you. Sam—he was fighting to be born, but you rarely moved or kicked." She stared at the flame in the window, as if talking about someone who was far away. "And, oh, how you wanted to stay! Two weeks overdue and even then we had a terrible time getting you to come out."

"Oh, god," he said, a mounting grief making him whisper. "God, oh god," he whispered, laying his head on the table.

Y ODER COULD NOT wake up the next morning. His little
bed assumed the precarious safety of a raft adrift in a cold
steel ocean of sharks. Whenever his eyes opened and he saw
the heavy blue light that was neither morning nor afternoon
press in through the window, he forced himself back into a
feverish half-sleep. His challenge was to remain in suspen-
sion, letting men and women who did not know one another
romp about in his dreams, sometimes swimming, sometimes
stacking boxes in a skylit warehouse, or gathering in an
operating room built of bamboo to await the delivery of the
last child of an old crone they all seemed to know. He was on
the edge of these dreams, assisting or passing by. Though in
the case of the jungle baby who was handed from lap to lap,
fed grapes and milk and chocolate by those who held him
briefly, Yoder was the doctor. He pulled the wet head of the
creature from the old woman's body and he was not
ashamed.

Yoder let his eyelids flutter, sensing a presence in the room.
His mother slipped in through the doorway in her good wool
coat, her purse dangling from the crook of her arm. He pre-

tended to sleep. Her spicy perfume peppered the air over his bed. Her hand brushed across his forehand, cold as charity, and then he felt the moisture of her lips. She hovered over him a moment before tiptoeing from the room and he wondered what she saw in his tired face. For a second he thought to call after her, to say: "Mother." But if the kiss remained a secret, he could keep it with him always. Like the memory of his body in the ocean, its imprint would be a comfort that time could not take away.

His mother had visited him in dreams that night. Yoder struggled to bring the dream into focus but recovered only a sense of the dream of her: She frightened him because she herself was frightened. He was growing tired of these visions of babies and mothers. Ruth hounded him even into his dreams. Awake now in that hopeless way the body has of giving in, Yoder threw off the covers, wanting suddenly to be up and gone. But something kept him poised on the edge, unable to start the day. His mother leaning over his bed had caused in him a flutter of terror. A memory from infancy? A memory. Without thinking, he grabbed a hank of hair in his hand and felt his heart hurtle against his chest. A memory relegated to darkness. His mother standing over him. Mutilation. He squeezed his eyes shut, as if calling back a dream, tugging on the memory that lay just out of reach. His hair. Yoder opened his eyes and let out a long sigh, laying still a moment longer, quiescent with disbelief.

He'd been one of the first in his school to grow his hair long—as a tribute to his musical idols, the Kinks, and a way of marking the distance between himself and the Frats and Greasers. His parents allowed him to grow it to the juncture of his neck and shoulders before ordering a haircut. He marveled that it took them so long to object and only later realized they had begun to be afraid of him.

When his thick hair had curled past his shoulders, he wore it pulled back in a rubber band and this seemed to incense his father even more than his defiance. Yoder suspected that his father gave the order though his mother carried out the crime. She had waited for him to fall into a drunken sleep one Saturday night, then crept into his room and cut his ponytail off at the rubber band, leaving a jagged cap of hair ending in the middle of his skull. He had to wear hats the rest of the school year.

Later he strained to imagine her as she stood over him that night, watching his chest heave, the sewing shears trembling in her hand. Sam tried to convince him it was no different from the days their mother had sat them in highchairs and clipped their hair around inverted mixing bowls, but Sam didn't know anything. Surely, he'd been orphaned. When he'd learned about xenogenesis in biology, he'd drawn comfort from the possibility that he was an original being sprung from parents to whom he had no actual connection.

Memory had dulled his anger like the pain of a toothache by Novocain. He knew the boy for whom this betrayal had been final, who actually hoped orphanhood was more than metaphor, but he'd left him behind on the bathroom floor of this tiny house. Yes, she had done a terrible thing, but indignation and disbelief are for the very young. He'd topped her long ago and yet—he held his face in his hands for comfort at the thought—all this trouble had come because he'd tried so very hard not to do a terrible thing.

As he pulled on his clothes, laundered mysteriously in the night and folded neatly at the foot of his bed, Yoder remembered the presents. He should not open them without his mother. She was very big on holiday rituals, hoping, he imagined, that the whole greeting-card spirit would be contagious and they would all finally get it. The rules specified that the packages be stacked on the low table in the living room, that his mother sing "Happy Birthday" as she carried each gift to the birthday boy, who always sat in the lounger with his feet up. But curiosity sent him to the closet where the dusty packages languished in a blue plastic laundry basket. Clues. What had she wanted to give him all these years?

Most of the packages were wrapped in tissue paper, dressed up with curly silver ribbon. One had the words: "All You Need Is Love," printed over and over in block letters on shiny red paper. Poor John Lennon. Yoder wished him well, hoped he didn't often ride in elevators, didn't have to hear second-rate strings crucifying his melodies. Each gift was labeled with a little sticker noting the year.

Yoder sat on the floor and spread the packages out around him, chronologically. Nineteen seventy-one was so ridiculous it made him smile. How hard she was trying in those days! The year she'd disowned him, and the year she wrote him nearly every week. On the back of a blue chambray workshirt, she'd embroidered the cover of Dylan's "Self-Portrait" album. Duplicating the colors exactly, Dylan's face melted into red and yellow, his eyes burned out of the cloth. In places where her handiwork was sloppy, he could see the image drawn freehand in blue ink. The stitches had been laid on so thick that, when he put it on, he felt the weight on his back.

In 1972, a Bible—white leather cover, gilt edges, the words of Christ in red. The year his mother turned Catholic. On the flyleaf she'd copied out the part of the Beatitudes she obviously thought was meant for him. *Blessed are the meek for they shall inherit the Earth*, it read in her unbalanced, childish hand. The meek don't want it, he thought, setting the Bible aside.

In '73 and '74 she lost her nerve: A heavy sweater and an electric popcorn popper. He'd moved around so much in those years that she stopped writing. In '73 the suicide dreams had started, dreams of slipping over the line and not coming back. In '74 he'd gotten his scar, an S-shaped gash just below his knee that had never healed properly. He'd ripped his leg open on a barbed wire fence while trying to sneak back across the Washington State border in the dark. A trail of blood led back to his tent in the woods and he'd had to move every day, certain he was being hunted. He'd indulged a fantasy of living out his years in the woods like Crusoe. Envisioned a treehouse, elaborate and impossible. When the leaves fell, he traveled east, landing at the Farmhouse, grateful for the company of the others. He discovered that most dodgers had been wounded while logging, or farming or working in the Canadian oil fields. He felt more at home among them once he'd acquired his own.

Even before he unwrapped 1975, its size and shape brought him the elation, rare after age five, that comes from getting exactly what you want. The flimsy paperboard case was covered with stickers and faded magazine photos made into a collage by someone with appalling musical taste: Jefferson Airplane, Deep Purple, The Moody Blues. But the guitar inside was a beauty.

How he'd missed the physical comfort of a guitar in his arms, the distraction of keeping it in tune. Writing songs had once informed his future, allowed him to take his own counsel, speculate a move. He'd stumble on a chord progression and mess with it. Later he'd overhear something on a bus or come across some words he liked, and the spinning would begin. At one time, the walking bass had been the soundtrack to his life—a pulsing, demanding eight-to-the-bar. His tempo had slowed; he heard acoustic melodies, but without a guitar, he couldn't write a song. He wanted new strings, a tortoise-shell pick. A real case. He'd need money. But at the moment it felt good simply to want something besides a meal, a bath, a ride, and someone who had not forgotten the few things he could remember.

Yoder heard the front door push against the rug and his mother's keys drop into her purse. "Ma," he called, "thanks for the guitar."

She appeared in the doorway, her coat hanging off one arm. She was dressed, he noted with surprise, in a red sweatsuit. "Oh," she said, her face young with disappointment, "I was hoping I'd be here to watch you open your presents. The shirt still fits, I see. That man is just so awful looking, I don't understand why he's such a big star. Yoder," she said breathlessly, "why didn't you wait for me?"

"Hey, I've still got one left," he said. "1976. I'll get it."

"I was just at my aerobics class."

"What's that? Another diet, Ma?"

"I thought you'd sleep in," she said, turning away from the door.

Yoder grabbed the small package from the bottom of the basket and set it out on the table in the living room.

"I know what this one is," his mother said. She was hanging up her coat.

He pushed back into his father's lounger and folded his hands in his lap. "I'm ready," he said, forcing cheer into his voice. "Aren't you going to sing?"

His mother smoothed back her hair and fussed with an

arrangement of dried flowers on the table. "I don't think so, Yoder. Just go ahead and open it."

Unaccountably disappointed, he ripped the paper in long strips like orange peelings. A homely brown photo album. "Family Fotos" stamped in gold on the cover. The photographs had been pasted neatly onto the black pages, beginning with the thin, sleepy infant and ending with the last event of which the family could be proud: The awkward 11-year-old graduating from elementary school third in his class. In every photograph, a dark-haired boy with three moles in a triangular pattern on his cheek stared directly into the camera as if insulted. Insulted at the Shore with a shovel and bucket; insulted before the Christmas tree; insulted to be interrupted while he rode his rocking horse to Mars.

"Don't you want these anymore?" he asked when he'd seen enough.

"No, you should have them," she said. "Sometimes I think you forget that you were a happy little boy."

"Was I?"

"Yes, you were my joy." She wandered off into the kitchen and he knew he had to get out of there. She was making things up again, fantasizing a child that did not exist. The photographs were proof, and she wanted to get rid of the evidence. He thought of her in the dime store, waffling between the black cover and the brown, then sorting through the shoeboxes in the attic, confronting the photos that betrayed her, slipping each under the plastic, sealing it up. She never spoke to him of his childhood, never reminisced, because it always came out the same—a little boy lost on his own street. A little boy on his way to a birthday party, so lost in the silver ribbon on the present he carried that he'd floated right past the barrier set up on the sidewalk and plunged ankle-deep into freshly poured concrete. Though the street stood empty, he knew that behind one of the gauzy window curtains a woman, like his mother, watched, nodding her head, saying to a child in the corner: "What a strange little boy."

He looked again at the photographs. His eyes were alive at the beach in Atlantic City. He had loved the little cabins stocked with just enough plates and forks, the red striped cabanas, the burly gulls, and fish washing up silver at his feet. His mother and father, dreamy and detached, read paperbacks on the endless bed of white sand, unconcerned about his hours, their chatter drowned in the sound of the waves. He and Sam had built the world's best-defended treehouse fort out behind the cabin. There had been moments, he saw now, perhaps whole years of happiness. When had he fallen out of love with the world? The photos stared back like an accusation, a promise he'd neglected to *fulfill*. He had to get out of there. But first he had to see Susan, to find out if the jungle baby in his dream was his own son.

His mother stood with her hands on her hips in front of the stove, waiting for the tea kettle to boil. "Ma," he said. "Where does Susan Merton live?"

"I couldn't tell you," she said, turning her face away and letting the kettle scream.

"Ma," he said, "the kettle."

She didn't move but stood facing the wall while the kettle's wail accelerated, nodding her head, eyes closed, getting ready to give him what he wanted.

Except for the wooden ramp curving up from the sidewalk to the front door, Susan's house was exactly the kind of house she'd made him promise they'd never live in. A stark, pinched green box on a block of shabby houses with porch lights cracked. That she lived in the old neighborhood at all shocked him. It seemed nearly illegal for someone of his generation to live so close to parents and parish. His boots thumped against the boards of the wheelchair ramp. In his jacket pocket, Yoder's hand settled around the iron star he'd pulled from Josh's door and he ran his finger over its rough edges.

After a second knock, a boy opened the door. Yoder could not speak. He'd come during the day, thinking that the boy would be in school. He didn't know what to make of the blond hair falling in the boy's eyes, or the way he wore Susan's full pouty mouth. "Is this Susan's house?" he stammered. "Is your mother's name Susan? Is she home?"

"Yeah, and no, she's not." The door had opened only a crack.

"Do you know when she will be home?"

"Are you the insurance guy?"

The first and last time he'd be mistaken for an insurance salesman. "I'm an old friend. I just wanted to say hello."

"She's supposed to be here but I don't know where she's at." The boy kept looking over his shoulder as if listening to instructions from another room.

"You mind if I come in and wait?"

The boy led him into a small living room filled with anemic plants drooping over tables and windowsills. Strips of yellowed vinyl traversed the carpet, leading to the rooms beyond. An instrusive piney odor—air freshener or Pine-Sol —hung in the air.

"I'm supposed to lock up when I go back to school. See," the boy said, holding up a ring of keys.

"I'll leave if your mom's not home by then. My name's Yoder," he said, studying the boy's face to see if the name registered, but the boy concentrated on the keys, watching them rattle against one another. "What's your name?"

"Ricky."

"Ricky," he repeated dumbly. What did you say to a kid? What did you say to a kid who might be your kid? "So what grade are you in Ricky?"

"Sixth."

"Sixth." Yoder calculated quickly—it was possible. "So, you like school?"

The boy shrugged. "I gotta go make my sandwich. If you want to wait that's OK with me but you gotta take your shoes off if you're going to walk on the carpet." The boy ran off, leaving Yoder alone. They had not recognized one another. Ricky had blond hair, but then, so did Susan. The way he averted his eyes seemed familiar. Yoder slipped off his boots and followed the murmur of the television into the kitchen. Ricky stood two feet from the set, slathering peanut butter onto a bagel.

"What's on?" Yoder asked.

"My mom's soap opera. I watch it for her when she's not

here. She hates to miss. Hey, I just remembered. She's at the doctor's. I don't know when she's gonna be back." Ricky poured a stream of Coke down his throat, holding the huge plastic bottle with both hands. "I gotta watch this," he said. "Marion's about to confess. I knew it was her that did it."

"Did what?"

"She killed the old guy—Harrison or something like that."

Without looking away from the set, Ricky layered a ring of Fritos onto the peanut butter and crushed them with the other half of the bagel. Yoder realized that his one lasting memory of his son might be of this hulking child guzzling Coke in front of the T.V. set.

Yoder pulled out a chair, threw his jacket over the back and stared at the television. People demanded respect for their television habits. Just as he'd been expected to let his roast beef cool on his plate while his grandmother mumbled grace and crossed herself, her fingers fumbling at her sunken chest. Without commercials, there might never be conversation in America at all.

"I bet she's gonna kill herself," Ricky said when a commercial finally burst on. The television appeared to release him after holding his body in rigid attention, while Bill told Marion he had no choice but to take the evidence to the D.A. "She's probably going to Hollywood for a sitcom. That's why so many of 'em get killed on these shows. I don't know why they can't just move. I mean, people move all the time. Why can't they just say: 'Oh by the way Ronnie got transferred to Philadelphia.'" The words came out slightly mangled by the mess of peanut butter in Ricky's mouth. "So, how do you know my mom? You a vet?"

"You mean, like a veterinarian?"

"No, you know, a veteran."

"No, I'm not. Why?"

"I don't know. You got long hair, I figured you were probably a vet. Besides, most of the guys my mom knows are vets. Doesn't it bug you having all that hair in your face?"

"I've been thinking about getting a haircut."

"Yeah, you should," Ricky said. "I bet lots of people think you're a vet. So how do you know my mom?"

"High school."

Ricky found this very funny. His face eased into a kid smile. "Really! You went to school with my mom? What was she like?"

What could he say? That she was awkwardly beautiful. Laughed too loud. Smoked dope before school every morning. Had perfect white feet. Thought Frank Lloyd Wright invented the airplane. "She was fun. Your mom was a lot of fun." Yoder stood and turned to look out the window at the April sun on the ivy. Buds coming back. He began to think he shouldn't have come. Still, he found himself wanting to touch Ricky's shoulder.

"Cool shirt," Ricky said. "Who's the guy?"

Yoder looked down at his chest and realized he'd forgotten to take off 1971. "You want it? Here, take it."

"You're gonna give me your shirt? Cool."

"The guy's name is Dylan. Bob Dylan."

"Oh, yeah, my mom's got some of his records. Don't you like him anymore or what?"

"I like him."

"Then how come you're givin' me the shirt?"

"I don't know. It looks like it might fit."

"Thanks," Ricky said, taking the shirt and holding it out in front of him. "I mostly wear T-shirts but maybe I'll put it on my wall."

Suddenly he realized how his mother might have felt that morning, seeing her carefully wrapped presents tossed about the bedroom floor. He'd give her something before he left again—a pretty scarf, maybe. A candle.

Ricky's green corduroy pants stopped just short of his ankles. Every few minutes he tugged on his thin sweater. He was a nice kid who didn't know how to dress. Peanut butter ringed his mouth. "So, Ricky, you doing OK? I mean, in your life. Are you happy? You and your mom getting along OK? I know your mom's been sick and I just wondered if things were all right."

Ricky kept chewing. Kids wouldn't make small talk but real questions were also out of bounds. "You sure you're not from the insurance place?" Ricky asked. " 'Cause I know my mom would kill me for talking to you like this if you are."

"Do I look like I work for an insurance company?"

"How do I know you're not an undercover guy or something? Like you knew my mom was going to the doctor today and you came here to try to get it out of me how sick she is and how much dough we got."

"This isn't a T.V. show, Ricky."

"Stuff like that happens in real life," Ricky insisted. "It's in the papers. Besides, what do you care whether I'm happy?"

"I guess because I care about your mom."

"Then how come I've never met you before? I haven't, have I? Sometimes I can't keep track. Darn, I missed it," Ricky said, leaning into the T.V. again. "Did you see what happened? My friend will have caught it. He never misses either. His mom and my mom actually talk about this stuff on the phone. If I were a girl, I wouldn't waste my time in school. I'd drop out now if I were them."

"Not all girls grow up to watch the soaps," Yoder said.

"I know, some of them are doctors, right? Just like some blacks can be doctors. But most—most of them have babies and watch the soaps. That much I know."

Yoder shook his head. It started so young—arrogance masking ignorance. It got so old. Definitely one of his own favorite tricks at that age. He stared at Ricky, looking for clues the photograph album could not give him. Happiness is the ability to be sufficiently deceived. Could such a belief be passed along, one man to the next, like a strong chin or flat feet? "That's how you got here, isn't it?" Yoder said. "Somebody's got to do it."

"Too bad it wasn't somebody with money who did it to me is all I got to say."

Yoder wanted to ask Ricky what he knew about his father but it was too eerie. Better not to be an undercover agent just in case the truth did come out. Ricky wiped down the counters and hosed out the sink with practiced ease. Why did he care about this boy only if he was his son? He wouldn't give the kid a second thought otherwise. Wouldn't be sitting in this ugly little kitchen with its lime green cupboards and the poster on the refrigerator that said: DIET IS A FOUR LETTER WORD. Wouldn't have this intense desire to know about Ricky's friends or whether he'd read *Twenty Thousand Leagues Under the Sea*. Maybe you had kids so you could care about somebody, even someone you would be bored to death with otherwise. Was that why the mothers of murderers looked so pissed on T.V.? Why the mothers of boys killed in 'Nam looked like they'd been swindled?

"So your mom knows a lot of vets, huh?"

"Yeah. I don't know. I like some of them. They've got neat stuff, grenades and stuff. I don't know. Some of them are weird. I wish my mom wouldn't hang around with them sometimes."

"Why?"

"My friend says they go crazy all the time."

"Haven't you ever done something crazy? Maybe when you were really mad at someone?"

Ricky shrugged—his number one gesture. "I broke a window once. Once I ran away."

"OK," Yoder said, "Think about how you felt afterwards. The more you think about what you did, the more you can't believe you did it, right?" He marveled at the tone of his voice—like an assistant principal. Like Sam. From the quickening in Ricky's movements, Yoder knew he was on the right track.

"Yeah," Ricky said. "I took my mom's wallet and then I was afraid to go into the store so I just got hungrier and hungrier. I don't know why I didn't just go into the store."

"I think it must be like that when you've been in a war," Yoder said. "I bet you think about it a lot and you can't believe you did it and there's no way to check it out. See how that might make you a little crazy?"

"I guess. I thought you said you weren't a vet."

"I'm not. But I've thought about it a lot. That can make you crazy, too."

Ricky looked at him with impatience and fascination. Yoder remembered the feeling, those days just before you gave up on adults. "Old people are always telling you stories, right?" he said.

"My mom's always saying: 'It's for your own good, Ricky.'"

"I know," Yoder said. "I think it's better to be like the trees."

"Trees?"

"Trees are real old and real beautiful and they keep their

stories to themselves. They know, but they just shut-up and
let the wind blow."

"Hey, that sounds like a song," Ricky said. "Let the wind-
ind-ind-ind blow." Ricky was doubled over, playing air guitar
when the front door banged open. They both froze. "Hey,
Mom's home," he said. " I gotta go help her."

Yoder heard a man's voice and a lot of racket and then he
heard Ricky: "Thanks, I got it." He felt like bolting, as if he'd
snuck into her house through an open window and was about
to be caught. "Hey, Mom," Ricky said from the living room,
"There's some guy here to see you. He went to high school
with you or something." Yoder could hear Susan's voice but
he couldn't distinguish any words. "I know, Mom, I will,"
Ricky whined. The door slammed and Yoder heard the hum
of an electric wheelchair. He turned to face Susan as she
rolled into the kitchen.

Her hair still fell past her shoulders, but it was not the
yellow cream he loved to see splashed against his own black
hair on the pillow. Everything about her had darkened.
Something adolescent still lurked about her face, but deep
circles like bruises aged the skin beneath her eyes. Like all
confined people, she was pale, except for the tip of her nose,
which looked raw and reddened. Yoder battled a brief clutch
of guilt—their petty crimes and arrogance had somehow
caused her illness. Susan's expectant smile gave way to an
unbecoming pop-eyed gape. "Not you!" she said, letting her
head drop over the wheelchair.

"Hey, Girl," he said, the words out of his mouth before he
could stop them. He'd always called her Girl. She'd always
hated it, wanting to run with the strongest and toughest.

"Ever hug a crip before?" she asked. "Just come over here
and squat and let me get my hands on you." He did as she
asked, feeling like a child embracing a huge doll. Her body
had gone soft as if her muscles had jellied.

"How did you find me?" she asked.

"My ma knew where you lived."

"Your mom! That's a joke. I see her in town and she acts
like I'm Tarantula Woman. God, look at your hair! You
always did have gorgeous hair. Sit down, Yoder." But he
could not. He leaned against the stove, crossed to the win-

dow, crossed back. Susan wheeled over to the refrigerator
and pulled out two beers. The kitchen shrank, her chair
spanning the distance between the refrigerator and the table.
"I'm not supposed to drink, but what the hell."

"Don't drink on account of me," he said quickly. "Actually, I
don't want anything. I just stopped by to say hello."

"I must look terrible." Susan pulled the rubber band out of
her hair and shook her head until the limp strands fell
around her face. "There. That might be more like the old
Susie Cream Cheese."

Her nickname, lifted from a Frank Zappa song. Now her
body had gone soft as cream cheese.

"The last time I saw you was May 1966," she said. "I know
because I wrote about it in my diary. What a little girl I was."

"You disappeared. I couldn't believe you just left."

"I was A Runaway," she laughed. "Sometimes I wish my
kid would run away. He's a nice kid, though, don't you
think?" A drool of beer meandered down her chin. Yoder
thought of his grandmother, how hard it had been to eat with
her after she'd lost all feeling in her face. The flecks of
chicken, the exclamations of gravy glued to her chin had
made him laugh though he did not want to laugh.

"It hurt me when you left, Susan."

"I heard what you did." She grabbed for his wrists and he
drew away. "Hey, sorry," she said.

"That's not really why I did it."

"I didn't think so. I figured it had to do more with you,
than with me and you. I'm glad you did such a lousy job of
it."

Yoder paced in front of her, crossing the tiny kitchen in
three strides, watching his feet. "Why did you leave?"

"Who knows. I can hardly remember that girl. Though if I
squint, I either see two of you—my eyesight's gone bad with
this thing—or I can just about see you in your leather jacket
leaning against a tree, burning holes in a leaf with your cigarette. I loved that jacket."

"I want to know why you left."

"Yoder, it was nothing. Who knows why kids do things? I
couldn't handle my folks getting on my case anymore. You
were going to college. I don't know. It seemed obvious at the

time." Her eyes drifted toward the television and he felt foolish. All his fantasies put to rest by the realization that she kept one eye on the television, very skillfully making conversation without missing a single vital second of the drama that really mattered.

"So that's it? That's all? You just felt like walking?"

"You look disappointed. Did you think I'd fallen in with a cult or something?"

"No, I thought maybe you were pregnant. Then I heard you had a kid."

She made no attempt to hold back an ugly, derisive laugh. "Why is it that guys think the only reason we do stuff is 'cause we're pregnant? Oh, you are really something, Yoder. Does Ricky look like you? No, he doesn't. He looks like his father, Yoder. His dead father."

Relief and sadness, just like in the hospital the night he'd tried to kill himself. The same unresolvable mixture. "I'm sorry," he said.

"Are you? How sorry?"

"Well, Susan, I'm sorry for you—for the loss—I didn't know him."

"No, you didn't. And do you know why? He hated the likes of you. Ever hear of Khe Sahn?"

"Oh shit," he said, spinning around in the tiny kitchen. When you hit a land mine, Walter had told him, the explosion was so loud it made you a deaf man if not a dead one.

"Is that all you have to say, Yoder? Shit on you, is what I have to say."

"Susan."

"What?"

"Don't do this," he said. Once he realized that his fear was written in his eyes he had to force himself to look at her.

"I'm real proud of Tommy, Yoder. I wish he was here to know it."

"Susan, I didn't kill him."

"Yes you did!" The accusation burst from her like a bird shooting from long grass. Her upper body thrust forward, as if determined to leave the wheelchair. Yoder lunged and caught her in his arms. She had terrific strength, pushing against his chest with her forearms. "Why weren't all you bastards over there helping?" she screamed.

"Shut up, Susan."

"Why Tommy?" she screeched. "Why not you? You bastard."

He squeezed her shoulders, sent her a brutal message with his eyes. She wasn't supposed to love anyone better than him. Least of all a baby-killer. Skin-head. Crazy fucking soldier. Shake it out of her. Shake her. Shake her. Her voice. Her eyes. Frightened.

Yoder dropped his hands, as if her body suddenly surged with electricity. "I'm sorry. I can't stand to hear this from you," he said to the linoleum. "We should be on the same side."

Susan let her head fall onto his shoulder. "I know," she whispered. "I know it was all a terrible mess." Yoder ran his hand down her hair, tangled and warm as the wheatfields, looking for the thrill this privilege had once given him. She was his wild one, his hurricane, his sweet, his girl. "When I'm feeling really pissed at Tommy," she said, "I sometimes think: What's so brave about getting blown up in somebody else's jungle so some chick who can't walk a straight line has to raise your kid all by herself? Sometimes I think Tommy just wanted to leave behind a piece of himself before he went off to die." Shaking off his hand, she straightened. "And, hey, it worked. Ricky looks just like him."

"He's a good kid," Yoder said quietly.

"I worry about him, Yoder. I want him to be proud of his dad. I want him to have money and a pretty little wife and a house in Fort Lee. I want him to take me out to a fancy restaurant when I'm old and wearing too much rouge." She gave him a moment to look at her. She lowered her voice. "I've tried to teach him that his father was a hero."

"Why?" Perhaps she would have an answer that made sense.

"Why?" she repeated, angry again. "Why do you always ask me questions I can't answer? Why? Because a boy needs to look up to his father and know he was a good, strong man. That's why."

From the girl who'd stolen a pair of downhill skis and poles right off the floor of a department store, who knew how to let tears glisten in her eyelashes when the cops were around, this was a disappointing answer. He liked her better at 16, raw and easy, a white scarf at her neck, breaking all the rules. Time to go. He could hardly breathe in her grimy little kitchen. A film of grease coated the inside of his mouth. "Don't worry about Ricky, Susan. He's got you to teach him about courage."

She patted her wheelchair. "If learning to cook eggs when you can't see the top of the stove from your wheelchair is courage then maybe I've got some. Actually I think courage is having a mother like me and still eating eggs." She laughed, a version of her old wild hoot, when they'd go flying down the street at midnight, drunk, powerful, waking up the dead. "I suppose there's a kind of courage in loving," she said, her head turned toward the window.

"What's wrong with you, Susan?"

"It's a nerve disease. Sometimes I can walk. Then I'll have like an attack. I've got scars on my nerves so everything comes out wrong. Here, I'll show you. Try to pick up that glass," she said, pointing to a blue plastic tumbler. Yoder grabbed it and Susan shook her head. "No, I said, *try* to pick it up. You can't do it. When everything's working you either do it or you don't. Now watch me."

Susan sat forward in her chair and stared at the glass as if memorizing it. Abruptly she raised her hand, moving it forward through air suddenly thick as jello. Her trembling arm missed the glass by about five inches. She made three more attempts before connecting. Behind her, on the television, a woman in a red dress put lipstick on over her lipstick. "Everything's like that when I'm sick," Susan said. "After a while, very few things seem worth the trouble. That's why I like the soaps. They do it all for you."

"Marion confessed."

"So I heard. You know, I've told Ricky straight out: 'I'm living through you so make it good.' The trouble is, he likes it here with me. Never even wanted to go away to camp. Tell me where you've been, Yoder. Did you ever get to Europe? Remember how we always talked about throwing ourselves off the Eiffel Tower?" She said E*eefil*.

"It wasn't so great," he lied.

"Have you seen Montreal?"

"I've seen it."

"Do they really speak French there? Did you see the World's Fair?"

"I hated Canada, Susan."

"You're famous here, you know that?" she said. "I got involved with Vet stuff for awhile—trying to get Tommy's benefits. I was the only one who actually knew you but everyone knew your name. I kept telling people that you weren't afraid of anything in high school."

A woman mourned a pair of overalls. Without Clorox, the toughest spots did not come out. "Look, I don't want to keep you from your programs any longer. I just wanted to say hello."

She looked at him like she'd been slapped. "Here I don't see you for ten, eleven years and now you're leaving. Well, I don't blame you. I'm just a mom on AFDC who likes to watch the soaps. Not your kind of girl anymore, am I?"

"The only one I ever thought I'd marry."

"Yeah? That's sweet. Now that you're back you should take a scissors to that gorgeous hair of yours. Won't help you with the ladies anymore."

He wanted to take something from her house, the glass swan in the window sill, the magnetic ladybug on the refrigerator, the scented stationery he imagined perfumed a drawer someplace in her bedroom. His hand itched in his pocket. "This is strange but, do you have anything I can have? I'm not sure what I mean. A picture maybe or...."

"Well, I've got lots of pictures of little Ricky. That's why I named him Ricky—'cause "I Love Lucy" was Tommy's favorite T.V. show."

"Never mind," he said. "Let's do this in reverse. You take this." Yoder pulled Josh's star from his pocket. "It's a lucky star, but it only seems to work for people I give it to. So you take it and tell Ricky goodbye for me and you take care of yourself Susan."

He'd wanted to marry her, to work at the pickle factory, wrestle on the living room floor, drop kernels of popped corn onto her little pink tongue. His well-developed sense of the tragic began with her disappearance. But there was no tragedy here, just the stupid luck that sometimes blessed the young and kept them from their shallow dreams, forcing them underwater where there were electric blue fish, and orange ones.

Susan held the rough-edged star up to her chest. "It looks like a medal," she said. "About time I got a medal, right?"

Outside, the whole world had changed—trees closer to the earth, snow just hard dirty water. He agreed with the Zen monks that Enlightenment meant not coming back for another go-round. Still, a part of him had wished for this boy to be his own. He understood a little better what it felt like for Ruth to want a child. There was real pain in the loss of something you'd never had. *You've thrown the worst fear/ That can ever be hurled*, Dylan sang, *Fear to bring children/ Into the world.*

------

*I don't know where he came from, literally. When he was a baby, people made jokes about the mailman and I couldn't blame them. He just doesn't look like us. It had never occurred to me that I would have to work at liking my own child. Of course other women know, but they won't tell you. The Church teaches that we are all brothers and sisters and that's the way I like to look at it.*

*I should feel worse about everything than I do, but I've spent so many hours and days thinking about him that I can't work up much enthusiasm for it. I'm looking down a long corridor of my own. Luckily, early on I learned not to get in the habit of comparing my children to others. Eventually they'd come up short and I'd feel responsible and all the fun would go out of it. From the start I figured my boys had their own fish to fry.*

*He doesn't know. I never told him—not even after he came home. I didn't want him to be drafted—not even for a desk job. It was selfishness. I kept quiet, letting Martin go on about "our problem" as he called it, until it started to take its toll. I was putting a photo album together for Yoder—pictures from when he was small—and I felt exhausted by the thought of all our* days together, all the times I'd bundled him double so he wouldn't catch cold, the songs Martin sang him in hopes he'd turn out musical, the hours listening to him sort out the big world, trying not to worry over his black eyes and bruises. Too much work and all our hearts in those boys, I told Martin, to see them gone to waste on such a war. I told him I'd been sending Yoder money. He turned on me like a dog then. Let out twenty years of hate. I nearly left him. And then his heart went bad.

After Sam was in school and Yoder and I were alone together, he would follow me around, saying, "What if it wasn't?" to nearly everything I said. I'd say the sun was out—he'd say what if it wasn't—I'd say it was raining—he'd say what if it wasn't—I'd say then we wouldn't need our umbrella—what if we did—I'd say maybe because we only had one leg. And when Martin would come home and ask him what he did that day, Yoder would tell him we'd gone out in the rain and met a man with one leg.

The problem with being a mother is not enough time to yourself.

**13**

"WELL?" HIS MOTHER asked, her face a mask, unreadable, regal. She sat bent over the kitchen table, polishing her nails. Her hair lay loose across her back.

Yoder pulled open the refrigerator door and let it shut again without registering any of its contents.

"Did you get the answer you wanted?"

"Her kid is named after Ricky Ricardo—not me," he said, meeting her presumptuous eyes. Had she seen it in the cards, or simply wondered all these years if something between him and Susan explained his behavior in the bathroom?

Her hands held out stiffly before her, she scrutinized the polished nails as if for faultlines. "I'm sorry."

"Why? I told you I didn't have a kid. You're just ticked off because the cards were wrong."

"The cards aren't wrong." He startled as she took his face in her hands, pressing his cheeks lightly with the palms of her hands. "You're more like your Uncle Dan every day. He'd still be alive if he'd had a family of his own." She let a hand linger on his cheek, as if he were made of a rare alabaster she could admire but not possess. "Your father and I have discussed it. You are welcome to your old room so long as you're out looking for work." She puffed a bit on her nails. "And no drugs."

"I'm leaving tomorrow, Ma. I've got some possibilities out West."

"West? What's west?"

"Where's Dad?"

"In bed—playing solitaire. Go to him, Yoder. We'll talk after dinner." He watched her dip the tiny paintbrush into the sticky red polish, watched her address her long, vaguely frightening nails with a meditative breath, like a Japanese calligrapher about to stroke rice paper.

Before the picture window, and the cut-glass bottles rimmed in scum, he paused to collect himself. The sun had sunk behind the skeletal trees; the sky shone in afterglow— opalescent winter colors: dove grey, cream, rose. The houses looked exhausted, their lawns matted, dead brown. Someone's garbage can, blown over in the wind, rolled aimlessly down the street.

He often thought that his Uncle Dan should have married his mother. Not only would he have made a superior father, but his mother loved him more. She lit up whenever he arrived—unannounced—for one of his infrequent visits. She called him "Handsome Dan," and he did look like an ad for yachting clothes or French vermouth in his white linen jackets, Panama hats and polka-dot bow ties. He was a sailor and a salesman, a bartender and a dozen other things. Always just back from some adventure—in Iowa or India— bringing yards of shiny material for his mother, hats that looked ridiculous on his father and soft grey elephants with bells in their ears or flutes of painted wood for him and Sam. "Just came by to put my feet under your table, sister Leona," he'd say, breezing in to turn their house into a party. He told long funny stories of near disaster, which Yoder identified at an early age as elegant lies. "Uncle Dan has always had an imagination," his mother would say with a dismissive wave of her hand.

The only time Yoder ever saw his uncle's apartment in Jersey City was the day after he died. His parents made him wait outside in the hall of the apartment building while they carried the television set and boxes of books out of the furnished rooms where Uncle Dan had gone to sleep and not woken up. Yoder caught a glimpse of the yellowed front room—cracked shades pulled down over bare windows, a tarnished floor lamp and a threadbare armchair. The shape of a stain on the wall above the chair still came to him in dreams: a buffalo, its head down, its belly and legs bleeding into the carpet. He left that afternoon more saddened by the apartment than by death.

With one blow he could shatter her bottles, watch the colors coat the window, glass splinter his hand. The earth was struggling toward spring—awkward and ugly as an adolescent. He felt as if someone had died and now that the funeral was over, it was time to go on home.

"Yoder?" She lumbered into the living room, carrying a dusty beer case. "I've been saving these for you," she said, thrusting the box into his hands. "I almost sent them to Toronto but I was afraid they'd break."

Heavy. Dusty. He'd never seen the box before. "My records?" he asked, incredulous and hopeful.

"No, no. Sam took those away years ago."

"Took them?"

"We had no use for them here, Yoder."

"They were mine. I asked you to store them for me."

"We didn't ever expect to see you again. Go ahead, open the box. I imagine you've forgotten all about them."

Whatever the box held, it couldn't begin to compensate for the records Sam had stolen from him. Classics, every one: The marbled paisley disc of Dave Mason's "Alone Together," like bad SpinArt at the fair; Blind Faith's one album debut and demise; Firesign Theatre; Bo Diddley; Little Richard; early Elvis; Sonny Terry; T. Rex; "The Velvet Underground and Nico" with the banana cover by Warhol; "Trout Mask Replica." All procured at no cost from record club subscriptions Yoder once held under phony names. The estates of James Joyce, Jack Kerouac, and Dmitri Shostakovich (there seemed no limit to what a computer would believe) all owed the record clubs a bunch.

Instead of records, the box held lumpy objects wrapped in newspaper. "Kennedy In Berlin," "Tonto Talks"—this box had survived intact from childhood. Yoder unrolled a pale pitted conch shell and held it up for inspection. He set the shell aside and unwrapped a second package, revealing a clam shell thick as his thumb, edged in purple, its underside chalky and heavily striated.

"Remember?" his mother prompted.

"Yeah," he said, tossing the clam shell back into the box. "I remember. These are Sam's, Ma. Not mine. I was the one who got picked up for setting off firecrackers under the boardwalk. Remember?"

"Oh," she said, licking her lips and looking toward the kitchen. "For some reason I thought they were yours."

"Jesus, Ma." He let the box hit the floor and watched her disappear, puzzling out the years. Which one had cried so hard when left alone as an infant? Which couldn't learn to tell left from right? Which son disgraced her? Which bought her a microwave?

"You know it's all changed now," she said finally.

"What is?"

"Atlantic City."

"Everything's changed, Ma."

"No, I mean really changed. They built a casino right on the boardwalk. They say there will be more. Your father's all for it, of course. I won't go there. I wouldn't know where to look."

"Dad taking up roulette now, is he?"

"Cards," she said. "He keeps telling me that by the time the other fellows at the paper are ready to draw a pension we'll be living in Miami Beach. I didn't know you could make money on solitaire. I'm not worried. You know your father."

His father had always been big on get-rich-quick schemes. If he'd had money, he'd have speculated on the market. As it was, he entered sweepstakes and raffles, invested in an Air Force buddy's failing chain of do-it-yourself car repair shops, and played the horses. When Yoder and Sam were young, he'd taken them to the races every week. It was clear even then that his father went mainly to watch the horses straining at the gate, highstepping around the practice ring. He liked to say he had more respect for animals, with the exception of cats and blue jays, than for any human being. From him, Yoder learned the fine points of betting and how to read the racing form to balance out his hunches. Later, it was a source of embarrassment to him that their most intimate moments as father and son had come over a tip sheet.

"Don't you want to live in Miami, Ma?"

"I want to stay right here. It's a good house." She drifted off, leaving as she came. "You can have your old room," she said.

While Yoder floundered just outside the bedroom door, rehearsing how to ask for trainfare to Tucson, he realized that his father wasn't playing solitaire. Propped up in bed with the white bedtable that reminded Yoder of his grandmother, across his lap, he turned cards over in short rapid sequences. "Win. Win. Win. Lose. Win," he muttered. The tremor in his hands was new.

"What's that you're doing?" Yoder jammed his fingers in the back pockets of his blue jeans, the gesture an echo of adolescence that he couldn't restrain.

"Blackjack," his father said, without interrupting the relentless turning of the cards. "Your mother's not the only one who sees a fortune in the cards." He laughed a stupid little laugh and Yoder felt embarrassed for him. "Working a system. It's Whitey's system really. They've got a casino at the Shore now. If I play it steady, Whitey says I should bring in two, three hundred a week. Conservative."

"You giving up on the horses?"

"This is real money we're talking." His voice was full of the adult impatience Yoder remembered from childhood. "A system, Yoder. Not funny money. A scientific system."

His father had apparently forgotten that their hours at the track had been spent in pursuit of "science." He seemed determined not to acknowledge Yoder's presence. Yoder watched him play a few moments and then gave voice to an idea he'd given absolutely no forethought. "Look, I'm leaving tomorrow. So I'm going to do those downspouts now."

"Don't bother. Sam will take care of it."

"I told you I'd fix them. I just need to know if there's any special way you want it done."

"Sam knows how I like them done. Leave them be, Yoder. It'll be dark soon." The cards slapped against the bed tray.

"You're never going to forgive me, are you?"

"Win," his father said, triumph sparking in his eyes. "How about that? Five in a row."

"The President did. It's acceptable these days. Everybody's doing it. It's the coming thing."

His father cut him off. "Help your mother with dinner, Yoder. Don't look for trouble where there isn't any."

"Dad, I'd like to start over."

"Little late for that."

Slap, slap, the cards. Whapata, whap.

"All I'm asking is for you to let me help with the fucking downspouts." No reaction—they were long past the time when his language could get a rise out of his father.

"Then stick around if it's so important to you," his father said with equanimity. "You can help your brother next weekend. That's not what you had in mind though, is it?" Whap. Whap. Shush.

"Helping Sam?"

"Sticking around."

"You want me to move in next door, Dad? That make you happy?"

"That would make me a dreamer. Am I right?"

"Look, I'm leaving in the morning. And I'm doing those spouts before I go."

"You gonna do them in the dark, smart aleck?"

The downspouts his father had scrounged from some junkyard were squared off at the ends—the gutters rounded. It took Yoder a long time to fit the two together, working high up on the ladder whose every shifting in the spring-softened ground caused his heart to drop. Perhaps he would die out here doing this job, but if he did, at least his father would be the one who felt guilty. Using a flashlight propped up in the gutter, Yoder drilled holes for the fasteners to secure the spouts to the side of the house. Dogs barked, and the headlights of cars heading home for supper swooped past him. Working without gloves in the twilight, his hands stiffened in the spring chill and the sweat cooled on his body. From his bower atop the ladder he watched the stars and streetlights coming on. He was tempted to scramble onto the roof, light up a Camel straight and contemplate the mystery of Susan's body, just as he'd done that last summer. But he was too tired to scramble, too winded to smoke, unwilling to confront what had happened to that young, strong body.

After Susan had disappeared he'd spent a lot of time on the roof—smoking, searching the sky for patterns, trying to understand what he'd done. He didn't have a feeling for mortality then. In actuality, he had not believed he would die—the razor and the blood more proof than revelation. Armies took advantage of that beautiful delusion—and countries used to war had to recruit their soldiers younger and younger.

As he bent the metal into shape with his father's tin snips, he fought off memory. His job was to imagine a future. Fate hadn't played her card—he'd been watching for signs—but not even the tarot gave him any real clue. Back in Canada he'd imagined crossing the country by train, dropping off here and there in Nebraska, Montana, Oregon—just in case some spot might strike him as a good spot. But he had forty-eight bucks—enough for a bus ticket to the Bronx. He imagined the ladder arching backward toward the spongy earth—landing with a solid sound, pinning his body beneath the bars.

He'd put in a lot of roof time in the days just before he'd made a sharp right on his way to New Mexico, and ended up in Canada. Up here he'd caught the only breeze in town—the only breath. The idea had been born in him, but was impossible to claim in his father's house. Sal was moving out, guys kept dying on the news. At the time it had seemed the bravest thing he'd ever done—leaving without their goodbyes, or their blessing—a romantic gesture to spare them the separation.

"That's fit's gotta be tight." A voice below him, straining to shout. Yoder leaned over and saw his father standing by the euonymus bushes in shirt sleeves and slippers.

"It's the wrong shape."

"I know it's the wrong shape. That's the art of it. Come down, Yoder. The neighbors will be thinking we've lost our minds over here. Come down from there. Your mother's waiting dinner." Yoder felt his father's hand on the ladder—feared for a moment he would come after him.

"Why won't you let me do this for you?"

"Don't shout."

"If I don't shout you can't hear me."

"Shut your mouth and learn something. Off to the left there, Yoder—over the Strommen's house." His father pointed past him at the sky. Castor and Pollux. Focused lights in a boundless dark—there as they had always been on chilly spring evenings—just to the left of the Strommen's house.

"Too bad we don't have a telescope," Yoder said, remembering his lines, remembering how he'd strained to see the constellations so familiar to his father's eyes, how he'd wanted their mystery to be as compelling to him—worth shivering for in the dark.

"Comet's coming back in another ten years," his father said. "Won't need a telescope then." As an infant, his father had been no more than awake in the presence of Halley's Comet. But he had been told its stories—how it cast a shadow at midnight, how its tail took up half the sky. "Not many can say they've seen the comet twice in a lifetime. Course maybe I won't make it either."

"You'll make it, Dad."

"How could I have guessed what would happen to this world?"

Yoder leaned over the side of the ladder, looking for his father's eyes. There was so much distance between them in the dark.

"You know how they say 'forgive and forget?'" his father asked from the ground. "Well, I *can't* forget."

———————

*He's named after a buddy of mine in the service. Last I heard, Phil was living in, I don't know, Ohio. Someplace. Iowa. Someplace I'm not likely to be passing through, you can bet on that. He sent a Christmas card five, ten years ago. Said I should stop by and see him if I'm ever passing through. Meet his wife, Babette. Babette! Can you imagine? I don't want to know his wife, see those waterjug ears of his popping out of his two kids.*

*I imagine the name's been hard on Yoder. We were under*

*pressure with Sam—backed down and named him for Leona's father. But when the second one came along I decided he was mine to name and I kept my promise. Phil and I had this agreement to name our kids after one another. At the time I thought it would be a great joke on Phil that I give his last name to my kid. Drinking too much bourbon in those days. We sent the bastard a birth announcement and I never heard a damn thing until 20 years later I get a Christmas card from Ohio. Iowa. Him with two kids named Milton and Edward.*

*When Yoder was small I explained to him about how he had a special name. Finally when he was around ten, I told him about Phil. How he and I won the war singlehandedly. How we saw the world and it didn't cost us a damn penny. How we'd play poker on watch with machine gun shells. Yoder sort of slouched off the way he does, looking at me like I'd sold him out. "He's just some guy?" he said. Like it was dirt. "You named me after some guy in the Air Force? That's it?" Kids will do more damage to your heart without trying than any woman, any war. That's why I like dogs—they're smarter than most humans, they do what they're told, and the only way they ever let you down is by dying.*

---

SALVATION ALWAYS COMES from an unexpected quarter. The next morning as Yoder swirled brown sugar into his Farina, plotting a story that would convince his mother to give him bus fare to Santa Fe, she looked up from her newspaper, lowered her bifocals and saved him.

"I almost forgot. Someone called for you. He sounded like a vacuum cleaner salesman—syrupy. He said his name was...." She drummed her fingers on her lips as if to coax out the name. "Just a minute. I wrote it down. I'll get the paper." She returned with a matchbook cover, squinting to read the writing on its back. "C-R-O-C-K," she spelled. "Crock?" She checked the matchbook, certain she could not have gotten it right.

"He called here? When?"

"Something wrong with that?"

"No, I just don't know why he'd call me. When did he call?"

"He didn't seem to know you were here. He was trying to find out. I didn't let on. I told him I'd give you the message if I heard from you."

"Thanks, Ma, but it's no big deal." Sal, he figured, Sal had caved in and given Crock the number.

"I don't tell anyone anything since that FBI came to your grandfather's funeral."

Didn't they have anything better to do? He was still incredulous when he thought of slim men in dark glasses waking every morning with hopes of nabbing him. She weighed the matchbook in her hands like evidence. "Who is this Crock?"

"Old friend. Mind if I call him?" He didn't say long distance, didn't say drug dealer.

She gestured toward the living room. "I'll pack you a lunch. I imagine you'll want to get an early start."

Crock hadn't left a number but it was easy to find; anyone who stays in the same place for six years is a sitting duck. He answered the phone like a bookie with three deals on hold. "So it's you," he said with a snort. "I'd just about given you up for dumb. Jersey? You're still in Jersey? Hell, I had some business to talk," he said, "but I guess you wouldn't be interested."

"Talk," Yoder said.

"Let's just say I've taken up pottery." There was a pause. "If you know what I mean," he drawled finally, chuckling into the receiver. Dealers had in common with 10-year-old boys a love of secrets and codes. "I'm talking to investors—thought you might want to know."

"Taking up pottery" was a scheme for smuggling cocaine, one Yoder had heard about for years but had never actually seen work. Cocaine was concealed in a clay out of which pottery was made. Transported across the border as Mexican imports, the pots were later crushed to reveal packets of pure cocaine. It surprised him that Crock was still so small-time; he needed only two grand, promised a return of ten. The deal went down in three days.

"Count me in," Yoder blurted, recklessness rising in him like a bad habit. He liked the daring of Crock's scheme, and its elegance. He thought briefly of volunteering to drive the shipment across the border.

"Noon on Monday, my house," Crock said. "Don't fuck up, Yoder. Be here with the cash. And be on time. I don't want you around when it's going down. Understand?"

Drugs were God's way of saying I'm sorry. Yoder agreed with Ruth that nature had all the bases covered: Birds for music, trees for grace, the moon and sudden rain to keep you honest. Grass, coca leaves and peyote were for the pain. Yoder turned from the phone to find his mother hesitating in the doorway. He let the smile drop from his face, tried for an early morning calm he didn't feel. "What is it, Ma?"

"You tell me."

"Great news, actually. A guy I knew in Michigan might have some work for me. I gotta think it through. I might be staying here a couple more days if that's OK. I think I, ah, I think I need to go for a drive."

"The keys are in my purse." She moved to touch him but seemed to think better of it. "Remember what the cards said about trouble. You've got that look."

What had the cards said about money? Two grand was an impossible amount of money. He'd led Crock to believe he had bucks, and like a good businessman, Crock had remembered. Tossing the keys off his hand into the air, Yoder slipped out the door and into his mother's old blue Fairlane. When he'd left for Canada, the car had been brand new. Now it was beat-up and rusting along the bottom of its heavy doors. Kleenex box on the front seat. Flashlight, emergency flares and paperback novel in the glove compartment. His mother never wanted to be stranded without something to read. The ashtray was mysteriously full of cigarette butts. Evidence of a secret life? A lover? Yoder resisted the urge to peel away from the curb, to take advantage of the power only a 350 with a two-barrel can put out. He wanted money. Enough for one clean deal, a car, and a new case for his guitar.

Yoder roared through the intersection of the town's main crossroad, a bit giddy behind the wheel. When he'd lived here he hadn't known that the world was full of places this dull, that most lives in America were lived between the bank, pharmacy, church and cafe on the four corners of Main Street. He wheeled by the Shop-Rite and slammed on the brakes, executing a U-turn into the parking lot. He needed something to chew on—pretzels or peanuts, and his mother had mentioned that Susan shopped here. It was a fantasy of his to run into an old girlfriend at the grocery store, to see a lover's name on the roster in an office building or get pulled over by Sammy Benish, who'd wanted to be a cop even in grade school. He wondered if these kinds of reunions happened routinely to those who'd stayed.

In pursuit of junk food, he slunk down the aisles, checking back over his shoulder, automatically preparing to lift whatever he could. A woman seemed to be following him. There were mirrors in all the corners. Forget it, he thought and headed for the counter with his peanuts and cheese. In the checkout line, he flipped through a copy of *Rolling Stone*— studying the photographs of bands called Fog Hat, Journey, Rush. Where were the Rolling Stones? He heard a woman's voice raise above the acceptable grocery store level and craned his neck around the people in front of him to get a look. The woman seemed to be creating a disturbance at the front of the line. He could see the cashier—a girl with blue eyelids—nodding impatiently as she bagged the woman's groceries—about ten cans of cat food and a double bag of chips.

"You live around here?" the customer asked in a painful singsong.

"Yeah, yeah I do," said the clerk.

"You do? I do too." The woman's voice rose in excitement, like a child meeting someone who shares the same name. "Boy, we're in the same neighborhood. I thought so, 'cause I've seen you here so much and walking sometimes too." Short and plump, her glasses slightly askew, the woman had the unguarded face of a retarded person. Bag in hand she inched away from the counter, still talking, obviously reluctant to leave. "Maybe we could get together sometime, huh?"

The cashier suppressed a giggle, looking up from under her bent head to smile knowingly at the next customer. The tension in the line rose as everyone did a mental check: Would I get together with her if she asked me? Mercifully the woman left, struggling to roll down the top of her grocery bag, nearly running into the glass door on her way out. Yoder heard the clerk mumble to the next customer. "Maybe I could go over and visit her in The Home sometime." The clerk rolled her eyes. "I don't know why she always talks to me."

Yoder pushed past a well-dressed couple and a teenager in line in front of him. "Beggars can't be choosers, lady," he murmured, bolting out the door with groceries spilling out of his arms.

"Hey, he didn't pay!"

Yoder heard confusion bubbling into action and double-timed to his car. Squealing out of the parking lot, he wished only that he had grabbed another package of Monterey Jack.

A cruel and stupid world—that's what Ruth hadn't thought through. She hadn't been a skinny kid who loved animal books and the coronet, who didn't have the courage to defend that kind of love, who crouched behind bushes to avoid the big kids with eyes on his lunch money, who once had to share a crawlspace under the fieldhouse with a dead squirrel, counting to 10,000 without skipping any numbers to block out the irresistible smell of decay.

With ten grand he could drive until he found some place that felt familiar, get a dog, and listen to the music everyone else had forgotten. With ten grand he could find a spot in the desert too barren for anyone to care about. Sink in. Forget that the world wanted a disco beat, an MBA, a condo over-looking the blight. Start some kind of life. What had the cards said about money? Something about cycles, fulfill-ment. Gamble but gamble wisely, she said.

As he pulled up to the light by the elementary school it hit him. *Twenty-one is the perfect number.* Like tumblers drop-ping into place, like the way Sal's body fit against his, like his favorite boots hugging his feet, like so few things in his life, this felt right. Twenty-one. All he needed was a stake. Cruising past the elementary school he watched two kids on bikes circling the playground—hatless—blond—careless with laughter. Brothers, he guessed. Old lady fate, he whis-pered, strike me blind. When he opened his eyes, the brothers were still there.

"I need to get into Sam's apartment," Yoder shouted over the noise of the electric drill Rita held with both hands like a jackhammer. He found her working on the front door lock of an upstairs apartment. The hallway smelled of bacon. If I had some bacon I could have bacon and eggs, he thought, if I had some eggs.

"Didn't Sam give you a key?"

"He was going to, but he forgot." He flashed his hobo grin but she didn't seem in the mood for charm.

Rita wiped the back of her hand across her forehead. She couldn't possibly be sweating. I'm busy, she was saying, can't you see that? "Gotta check with Sam first."

"He's here?" It never occurred to him that Sam might sleep in late on a workday, linger with a lover over coffee.

"Here? No, he's at work." She set the drill down and started to close the door. "I'll give him a call."

"No, wait," Yoder said, pushing against the door it keep it open. "You'll never get ahold of him. He told me he'd be out of the office all day."

"I can't let anybody in without tenant's permission. Even Sam's brother." She gave him a small smile and he decided to run with it.

"The truth is, Rita, I wanted to surprise him. You see, I've got this box of shells—that he collected as a kid. I wanted to leave them in his apartment as a surprise."

"Shells? That's sweet." Rita dug into the pocket of her jeans, stretched tight across her narrow hips, and pulled out the ring of keys. "I guess it'll be all right. But wait until I'm through here. I gotta come with you to lock up."

Gingerly, he plucked the keys from her fingers. "Don't bother. You're busy. I'll bring them right back. Really. It's too cold out. I'll be right back."

Men, he'd noticed, didn't know quite to do with a bedroom. Sam's smelled of permanent masculine disarray—the bed unmade, closet doors thrown open, tennis shoes and a burgundy sweatsuit in a heap on the floor. Again he was grateful that living on the edge had made him a watcher. He could never tell when he might need to know what made someone tick, where the scotch was kept, which drawer held the money. Tired as he'd been that first night, he'd watched Sam disappear toward the bedroom, dig down into the top drawer of his dresser. Even as a kid, Sam liked to keep his money where he could smell it. He always had a jar full of pennies on his desk—and never complained when Yoder helped himself to a handful.

Yoder inched the top drawer open and pawed through Sam's flashy jockey shorts and neatly rolled balls of socks, looking for something hard. He tossed the socks over his shoulder, scooped the underwear out onto the floor. Imagined Rita tiptoeing in to check on him; Sam bursting through the door with an early headache. Where was the goddamn money? Sam never let him down. Finally, his hand closed around a slim plastic billfold of traveler's checks. Unsigned. Sam, the perfect businessman, always prepared for a little impromptu trip to the home office. Sam, the perfect fool, keeping blank checks in his dresser drawer. Yoder counted quickly—nearly a thousand bucks. He took it all, put back half, took it out again, stared at the clean blue bills, counted out five hundreds and buried the billfold in a heap of handkerchiefs.

The editorial writers said that his generation grew up with a willful disregard for the law. The law was a joke. It kept criminals in office and everyone else out of work. The CIA lied; Nixon lied; even the war was against the law. Eventually you just went with it: bought marijuana, joined a record club with a fake name, evaded the draft. Stole from those who cared about you. He looked at his tired skin in the mirror. You dirty little wasted piece of shit, he thought.

It saddened him that the place he'd been happiest as a child would be ruined in memory by what he was about to do. His understanding of innocence rested on images from summer vacations in Atlantic City—home of Miss America —that other woman who wore a crown and stood tall for her country. How fitting that a casino be erected right alongside the boardwalk and the swimsuit competition. America loved beautiful, silent women standing tall, loved hot dogs, and money.

Yoder had loved the boardwalk at dawn, the fearful white sun rising out of the ocean to light the empty beach, the shopkeepers sweeping, the sensation of being backstage and watching the day prepare for its great performance. Allies at the Shore, partners in skee ball and beach soccer, competitors at the penny arcade, he and Sam had passed the long days together, days punctuated by the custard, fudge, peanuts, salt-water taffy and hot dogs they ate without regard for meal times.

Eventually Sam discovered girls, and Yoder learned from him, noting how they loved to watch Sam comb his greased hair into stiff ribs ending in a perfect duck-tail. Then one summer, Sam deserted him for the scent of girlish bodies. At night, from his bedroom window, Yoder watched the amusement park on the steel pier decorate the sky. The ferris wheel, circling in the dark, promised deliverance, and he began sneaking out to roam the carnival grounds. Sam put his arm around a girl and walked off into the future without looking back. Yoder realized that, even in those days, he had preferred to sneak out.

Bravery in the name of the law made you a hero. Courage in defiance of human law was criminal. He'd cast his lot with the criminals six years before. In the eyes of America, his pardon was no more honorable than Nixon's. His father could not forget, and the others could live with themselves only if they made him into a hero. There were no heroes this time, but he understood why the mothers and fathers, the vets and dodgers needed to believe in heroic choices. No one wanted to feel like a criminal. Yoder lifted a perfect conch shell off Sam's top shelf and wrote out a note, stuffing the feeble excuse for an excuse inside the shell. He pulled the door shut behind him.

Though convinced that fate responded neither to prayer nor to good intentions, Yoder practiced the game of "21" on the bus the next day all the way to Atlantic City. Dealing hand after hand onto the seat, playing against an imaginary dealer as he'd watched his father do, he won twice as often as he lost. Occasionally he paused to look out the window, watching banks of smokestacks staggered like pipe organs against the horizon give way to the water of Raritan Bay and the greening hills of South Jersey. The other passengers were members of a senior citizens group from Philly and they reminded him of Josh's chickens, gabbing and gobbling on about limits and systems. Slots were the game of choice. A

woman in a white linen suit claimed she'd use her winnings
to send her granddaughter to Bible camp. "So I always lose,"
the man behind Yoder said to no one in particular. "So what?
Columbus took chances. Roosevelt, he took chances."

He didn't know many old people. Most put him off with a
smugness he imagined came from having survived so long.
He felt they eyed him greedily, their hands little claws, wanting something. Across the aisle, a clear-eyed woman with
hair spun like cotton candy, watched him openly, making little ticking noises of approval. "You should have split on that
last hand," she said finally.

Her voice, soaked in alcohol or age, attracted him. "What
do you mean, split?"

"What system are you playing?"

"The Fool's system," he said, thinking of the tarot card, a
man stepping off a cliff with his eyes on the heavens. "I don't
have a system."

"Oh, my dear," she said, reaching out to touch his knee,
"you've got to have a system. I've used Scarne's for 20 years.
I've kept books, you see, so I knew exactly how well it
works." Eyes narrowed, she clicked her tongue, as if sizing up
a racehorse. "You're good, but you should never sit down at
the tables without a system. Look, just remember this:
Always hit under 12, never over 17, split with everything but
a pair of 10's, leave the table as soon the dealer wins more
often than you do. Here," she took his hands in hers. "I'm
lucky. Now, my luck rubs off on you."

I'll take it, he thought, but I don't need it.

When the heavy door closed behind him, he took a deep
breath and jumped beneath the noise and the lights. The casino stretched before him, irresistible as the carnival at
night. A ringing blinking clanging glaring penny arcade for
adults. Greed all dressed up to look like fun. Yoder stood
alert and still, as if he'd parachuted into dangerous country,
and tried to get his bearings. The muscle of the place, he saw,
was tucked away above the mirrored ceilings; there were no
clocks or windows to mark the passing of the day. Though it
was not yet noon, barmaids in fishnet stockings scurried between the tables and slot machines. Fleets of women in peach

pantsuits buzzed among the machines, armed with paper cups full of silver. Those with the determined look of addiction did not stop even to scoop their winnings from the tray. They yanked the golden arm until nearly out of breath, some playing five machines at once, as if the big money could be won the American way—with persistence and sweat. No one smiled, or presumed to have a good time.

Yoder approached the cashier with the antagonism he usually reserved for the law. As he countersigned the traveler's checks, he considered for the first time the possibility that Sam might be on to him by now, that he'd been followed, that phone calls had been made. He didn't care what happened; he just wanted to win a little first. But the cashier slid bills across the counter without ever looking at him. He walked away from the window feeling bitter and reckless and lucky. This was America at its best: Highrollers lost money right alongside the ladies from Jersey City. Some bought drugs with their winnings, and some went home with a heavy purse and a story to tell at the church supper.

A barmaid who didn't look old enough to drink pointed him toward the blackjack tables—like half-moons, edged in polished wood. Behind each stood a dealer in a red brocade vest, trading little wooden chips for cash, keeping up the pretense that it was just a game. "And over there, behind the baccarat," she said, a slight Southern drawl giving her voice an unexpected elegance, "are the suicide tables." She ran her eyes down his body from his faded jacket to his blackened boots. "Thousand dollar minimum." With nothing to guide him, he had to follow every sign. He felt certain he'd be at the $1000 table before the night was over.

This early in the afternoon the casino lacked the flamboyance he'd expected—the mannered mobsters fingering hundred dollar bills, the whores in black lamé. It seemed a tame and desperate place: Old women battling the slots; a cluster of codgers shooting craps, razzing one another like kids playing twilight games. The blackjack tables looked neglected, sedate, diminished by the gang of decorative women crowding around the roulette wheel. How many were addicts? How many belonged to men whose "business trips" bought them furs, and left them alone to play roulette while the ocean roared in the sunlight just outside?

Yoder walked the rows of blackjack tables, looking for a fresh game, an empty $25 table—the red-backed cards spread out in a double fan across the green felt. He sized-up the dealers, settling on an Oriental woman whose sleek hair brushed her cheek when she moved. In her face he spotted vulnerability: She was a mother, perhaps. A jilted lover. Sliding onto a plush stool, he offered her a new $100 bill, rough and proper as linen. She let the money hang in the air between them, her eyes on the table. "Drop it," she hissed. His first mistake. He let the bill fall. Money was so sacred here, you weren't allowed even to touch it.

Without meeting his eye, the dealer said, "One hundred," picked the bill up by one corner as if contaminated, flipped it, smoothed it flat and dropped it into a hidden compartment. She dealt the first hand, her slender fingers barely touching the cards sliding from the lucite shoe like water. He won, lost, lost, lost, won again, playing by instinct, making every move with the assurance of a seasoned gambler. Stick, hit, split, never over 17, never under 12, he thought, but mostly he tried not to think. The speed of the game made it easy, cards and money on and off the table every thirty seconds.

Though several people stopped to watch and one man played a few hands, Yoder and the dealer played alone for most of an hour. They never spoke. Their hands performed the sign language, and Yoder understood the practicality of ritual, how it freed you and swept you up. A smile trembled on the dealer's face whenever she hit blackjack, but it was fleeting and not triumphant. Yoder felt certain she was on his side. At one point, he had cleared $700, ten minutes later he was down to 8 chips. When he felt his concentration slipping, he thought of Sal. He hated himself a little less when cast as a knight avenging her honor. He wanted to use Crock to work his way back to her; he wanted to use Crock. Mesmerized by the cards sliding onto the table, by the inner voice that seemed to give him instructions, by the sensation of being in the right place at the right time, he kept playing. After a while, even the money lost importance. Like a bad joke endured for the sake of the punchline, he cared only for the next hand, and the next. He wondered if dealers had trouble sleeping at night.

In two hours he doubled his money. Even the dealer smiled when he left the table. He staggered just a bit, dizzied by the black flashing red and the furious math. The casino had filled out while he'd been at the table, noisy now and crowded, like a party with an open bar. Across the room by the wheel he spotted the woman from the bus, nearly ran to bring her his success, but inside the casino she suddenly seemed a competitor. The $1000 tables beckoned from a panelled room with its own bar. So far he'd refused all drinks though the offers increased the longer he played. Now he wanted a double.

Yoder stopped just outside the cordoned-off playing area and assessed the serious circle. Each player kissed a thousand bucks goodbye with every hand lost. It was possible to blow a fortune in ten minutes. None looked capable of sustaining such a loss. A young black woman, her hair twisted into a shiny knot and fastened with a diamond clip, came closest to his idea of a high roller. Next to her, a clean-cut man in a sportcoat looked as if he were about to do something very stupid on his honeymoon. The dealer had silver hair and a face of stone.

It took guts to sit at this table. Time to find out if he had any. No hands shook. He couldn't detect any sweat beading up on the woman's fine dark skin. He walked as casually as possible past the pit boss, knowing it wasn't paranoid to sense keen eyes on his every move. And when he reached the table, sliding onto a stool without meeting any eyes, he felt the heat. From a distance the players looked cool, but he knew that the only reason to throw away money like this was for the heat. You could only find it on the edge, when the stakes were all or nothing. Like Russian Roulette. Like Walter enlisting just to find out if his number was up. Deserting because the war had become a gigantic video game: The little guys who got blown off the screen were sometimes his friends, sometimes the bravest men in the village.

Yoder had enough money to play exactly one hand. The dealer gave him a single chip, his face betraying no scorn. Yoder held it between two fingers as if delivering a blessing and made himself a deal: Win, and there's more waiting in

Michigan. Lose, and the border's just a day away. If America couldn't come up with the bucks, it was all over.

Yoder placed his chip carefully on the green felt, keeping his eyes on the dealer's delicate fingers. The dealer seemed too involved, too personally interested in winning. Yoder could not look at the other players. He could scarcely breathe. The Queen of Hearts fell at his feet, followed by an eight of spades. The old lady's rules told him to stick. He scrapped the table for another card, drew a two, won. Each little round chip represented a thousand dollars and now he had two of them. The honeymooner stood to leave, managing to order one last scotch and soda. Yoder watched the man's hand dart out to place a bet before he could stop it. It was criminal to walk away. One more win and he could pay Sam back, buy a plane ticket and a dozen white roses. The woman fingered a tall stack of chips, tossing them on the felt like play money. The next hand would be his. And the next.

He placed the bet—one chip, one thousand dollars. The cards flew into place, one hand looking so much like the next. Yoder hit twice, resting at a perfect 20, praying to a god he did not know for it all to be over. But when the dealer turned up an Ace and the Jack of Diamonds, he saw the road back to Canada stretching before him.

"It's fucking rigged," he mumbled.

"Sir?"

"That's your second blackjack in four hands."

"If you'd like, I'll call the manager, sir. Otherwise I'll ask you to leave the table."

He saw the dealer nod toward the men in tuxedos. The woman put her hand on his shoulder, an almost imperceptible pressure leaning him off the stool. "Better go now, honey," she said. The guys in penguin suits approached. Yoder jumped to his feet, two steps ahead of them all the way out the door. He ducked into the shadows; the night wind made him shudder. He wanted a cigarette, a Lucky Strike like Goldie used to smoke. He wanted a cup of coffee with cream. Out on the boardwalk the steel pier sat in darkness, nearly invisible. It took him a moment to realize that the lights of the amusement park were gone.

*The wolf just slunk through my living room with my goddamn
per diem under his sheep's clothing. He was laughing at me the
whole time. He was always this urchin, creeping around the
edges of the family. When we were growing up, I kept expecting
to come home one day and find the place cleaned out and him
sneaking down the alley with it all tied up in a bedsheet. Now
it's happened.*

*At least I got my shells back. Rita feels responsible. Isn't that
always the way? Responsible people feel responsible, even for
the likes of him. I collected every damn one of those shells. I
suppose Mom figured they belonged to Yoder because he was
the sensitive one: the one who wrote songs and slit his wrists.*

*I tried to be supportive when he took off for, what, Ontario?
I'd done my time about two hours from here, just before Vietnam got rolling. I knew the Army was no place for him. He
wouldn't last a minute. Not that he isn't strong. Christ, that guy
has been through it. But the rules and regs would have killed
him—if not the pathetic way that war was fought. He never
liked me. Even as a kid I knew I just didn't make it with him.
Sometimes it hurt and sometimes it made me think. But I
always felt I should look out for him. He was too raw; he read
too many books. He used to embarrass me—he didn't pretend.
No social graces, Mom used to say.*

*But you know, he's played his last card. I won't be singing his
tune again. He walks around with his head bent so low to the
ground that he can't see there are people who care about him.
There are no noble savages. You make your compromises somewhere. Maybe not in the usual places where us conventional,
boring types cave in. But you make your compromises. And the
biggest compromise of all is the one where you end up with
nothing because you've sacrificed nothing.*

15

SHE SAW HIM first. He felt the surge, the air electric between them. Standing on the platform, waiting for the Lake
Shore Limited to roll in, he caught her staring, studying him
as if trying to remember where she'd seen him before. He
never knew how to react when his eyes met another's purely
by accident. Even with someone neutral, an old woman or a
mailman, the uninvited relationship left him confused, more
lonely than ever.

The woman tried to hold his eyes. Yoder craned his neck off
to the left, examining the tracks with feigned intensity and,
moments later, realized his mistake. Obviously, the train
would arrive from the other direction. He spun in place, a
full circle, trying to make it look a spontaneous, playful act.
When he checked on the woman again, she seemed absorbed
in watching her toes tap out a little rhythm on the concrete.

She did look oddly familiar, like he'd seen her in a movie
or lusted after her in freshman Poli. Sci. She wasn't pretty;
she had sharp elfin features, skin as pale as his own. No
make-up. Attractively odd. Her metallic red hair reminded
him of a cat he'd once fed. Cut short as a boy's, it fell in little

points around her neck. The Cat Woman wore a long sheep-
skin coat open to the wind, and looking at her he realized it
was kite weather—a friendly breeze on his face, the morning
sun slanting across the tracks. Mostly she looked clean, one
of those people who woke without the sand of sleep in her
eyes.

Every two minutes he wanted to call Crock. Wanted to hear
again about the money, how simple it would be. He'd decided
not to tell Crock he had only a grand, betting on the pressure
of the moment to help Crock figure out that a grand was
better than nothing. When he caught the bus to Penn Station
that morning, leaving his mother with a kiss on the cheek
and a flimsy story about a line of imported china, he was
seized with rollercoaster dread: The sickening resignation
that hits just after you've been strapped in, and are out of
control. Pushing past the crowds, Yoder returned to the station in search of a phone, placing his hand flat against the
newly washed glass doors. Candy wrappers littered the floor,
rising and falling in the current of rushing feet.

Some woman was tying up the phone. Yoder flipped his
dime off the flat of his thumb, catching it six, seven, eight
times. More out of habit than interest, he stared at her body
lounging against the phone booth, half-turned toward him,
one worn leather boot crossed over the other. In her face, a
pink-powdered vacantness. In her voice, pure New Jersey
bite. "Can you believe it?" she kept saying, shaking her head.
Try me, he thought. She turned her back to him, eased the
door closed behind her. As the weather grew warmer, his
staring threatened to grow out of control. Everywhere he saw
hungry eyes—others who hid their loneliness through the
winter until in spring its ugliness burst forth like a boil. Was
Cat Woman lonely too?

A bored New Jersey whine announced the arrival of several
trains: "BostonPhillyWilmingtonNewportNews"—an incan-
tation so monotonous that Yoder nearly missed his call. Out
on the platform, he checked briefly for the white coat, then
sidestepped an enormous black woman juggling suitcases
and two tired little boys, and swung up into a bright orange
car.

Commuters jammed the entryway. Yoder rose up on his

toes, looking for an empty seat. He didn't want to be near smokers or card players, wanted to be near the bar. Mostly, he wanted to sleep away the hours until his transfer in Ohio. But as he moved from car to car, holding his guitar case high above his head, it became clear that he'd be lucky to get a seat at all. There was something frightening about humans fighting for space. At any moment it could turn into Dr. Zhivago: thousands of fur caps and dark coats vying for those fifty seats on the train out of Moscow. Zhivago had made it, but Yoder always remained with those left behind in the dying city, some, he imagined, crushed under the train's lumbering wheels.

Just as he was about to sink down into the crowd, he spotted a pair of impossibly empty seats toward the front of the car. Snaking around the overburdened people in the aisles, Yoder pulled himself forward by grabbing onto seat backs. With a final lunge he swung down into the aisle seat, bashing his guitar case into the knee of the man across the aisle.

"Hey! You squished my hat!" A little girl who looked destined to appear in Kool-Aid commercials sat in the window seat. She'd been deftly hidden from view by the tall seatbacks. General principle: Just because you can't see it, doesn't mean it isn't there.

"Sorry," he said, arching his back to retrieve a black felt cowboy hat with a braided yellow band. Don't scream, he thought. Don't start to cry on me. The train lurched forward. Without another word the girl set to work punching and bending her hat into shape. Her feet, in red tennis shoes to match the bows in her pigtails and the flowers on her sweater, barely hung over the edge of the seat. She worked with the pure concentration Yoder envied in children. Her face, moon-shaped and freckled, was as American as ambition.

"You alone?" he asked.

The girl nodded, staring straight ahead as if remembering instructions about strangers on trains.

"Great," he whispered, slouching down into his seat, relieved that her mother wouldn't be returning to oust him into the aisle.

"My name's Sunshine," she said quietly.

He coughed back a laugh and a vision of her parents hovering just behind her shoulders in beads and batiks, wrinkles like sunbursts streaming from their eyes. Sunshine, Moonglow, Prophecy and Omega-we'll-call-her-Meg. A whole generation would be changing their names as soon as they could get a court order.

The smoke stacks and apartments and faded billboards of Newark flickered by. Yoder relaxed in his seat, relieved as always to be moving. He never tired of beginning a journey, but he was running out of places to go.

"I'm going to Ohio."

"Hmm," he said closing his eyes.

"My mom's meeting me there. She's gonna take me to Cedar Point."

Yoder leaned out into the aisle to see if maybe someone had jumped off the train. He wanted a different seat. Knots of people in big coats huddled by the exits, squatted on suitcases in the aisles. The car hummed with discontent.

"You ever been to Cedar Point?" she asked.

"What's that—a lake?"

"No!" Where did a little girl learn such contempt? "It's a Family Fun Center," she explained. "They have rides and horses and a Shoot-the-Robber game. I won my hat at it last year."

"Yeah? How many did you have to shoot?"

"Three."

"Did they fall backward off the ledge with their feet sticking straight out?"

"You've played it!"

"Sure, but I never won a hat."

Sunshine looked pleased. "That's OK. If I win another one —another black one—you can have it."

"Great. It'll come in handy next time I rob a bank." Yoder clutched his knapsack full of cash to his chest, feeling like a Saturday matinee hoodlum. "Listen, I'm going to try to sleep. It would help if you'd be quiet."

Sunshine beamed. He was the Mad Hatter; she wanted to tell him everything. "In here? You're going to sleep in this racket?" On her knees, breathing down his neck.

Lifting the hat gingerly off her head, Yoder covered his face like a cowhand. "Do not talk to me," he muttered from beneath the hat.

"OK, but what if you snore? Can I tell you to be quiet?"

"I mean it."

"OK, but when my dad snores . . . ."

"This is not going to work." On his feet, Yoder scanned the car for someone with whom he might trade places. The car was a mess: Hot dogs shuttling up the aisles, people sucking on Cokes like fans at a Mets game. Yoder sat back down and turned on her his most adult glare.

"If you won't leave, I'll be quiet," she said, suddenly ready to bargain as if for her life.

"I'm staying right here," he said, sobered by her small and absolutely serious request. She couldn't be any older than seven. At her age he'd been afraid of night monsters in the closet. "Look, how about if I sing you a song?"

Hauling the guitar onto his lap, he strummed the strings lightly, picking out the chords for "Mr. Tambourine Man." As far as he was concerned, it was Dylan's only children's song and, for that reason, one that might endure. Sunshine sang along on the chorus, absently, as if reciting a familiar nursery rhyme. For the first time Yoder felt curious about the children his generation was raising. They would grow up knowing the words to all the songs on the "White Album," the poems of cummings and Ferlinghetti and Blake.

Yoder watched Sunshine press toward the window, humming the chorus. Her head looked like a small cantaloupe that would fit easily into his hand. She would probably be a lot of fun at an amusement park. What kind of mother meets her kid in Ohio? And where was her father? Who would send such a sweet-eyed kid on a train all by herself? He curled away from the girl though he didn't feel like sleeping. *You better go, honey,* the woman at the blackjack table had said. He would write Sam a letter, let him know he'd get his money back, double it even. Get him to look at it as an investment.

How had he come to this? How did all these people with mustard on their faces manage what he could not? He'd missed something. In the same way, he'd never learned to make a capital K in cursive because he'd missed school that

one day. How does one get food, shelter? He hadn't been paying attention when they explained the rules. "You just don't
want to listen," his mother would say. He was still waiting
for someone to pop out of the bushes and surprise him with a
set-up that made sense.

Sunshine was doing a terrific imitation of a mother in a
spirited conversation with her rag doll. Why didn't he want
to talk to her? General principle: You start talking to kids
and you'll be sorry an hour later after they've started in on
what they want for Christmas. There was more to it—something about her name, her incontrovertible dependence—
just bugged him.

Yoder felt a hard poke in his shoulder and jumped slightly
in his seat. A well-scrubbed teenager with the deferential
smile of a maitre d' leaned over him from the aisle. "I'm
making a food run for this section," the boy said. "Just wondered if you two wanted anything."

Yoder grabbed the boy's shirt sleeve. "See my eyes. They're
closed. Doesn't that mean anything to you?"

"Sorry." The boy moved off quickly, inclining into the seat
ahead. Sam was the same way at that age—always on the
lookout for something to organize. General principle: Never
encourage those who see group discomfort as a chance for a
sing-along.

"You didn't ask me." Sunshine's hands were folded in her
lap.

"What?"

"If I wanted something. You didn't ask me if I wanted
something."

"Hey, you gotta speak up. I'm not in charge here. Maybe
you can catch him on his way back."

"But I'm thirsty nooow." The beginning of a whine. He
could hear it in the way she made "now" into two syllables.

"Look, I'll get you something in a while, after the babies
have had their bottles."

"What babies?"

"Never mind."

"You're a funny kind of man."

"You're right about that," he said.

• • •

When he hit the bar car, Cat Woman was there. Even without
the white coat, he recognized her spikey hair, her feet planted
firmly though the train rolled and shook. She was dressed
like a normal person—nice tight blue jeans hugging her ass,
creamy turtleneck and a good old soft flannel shirt. Yoder
hurried into line behind her. She jingled coins in her pocket,
thring, thring—thring, thring. He clung casually to the
counter for balance. While he searched for something unexpected to say, she turned around and looked straight at him.
"Someone was staring at me," she said flatly. "I wanted to see
who it was."

Up close, her green eyes were cast with darkness, like the
sky warning of a tornado. "Not me," he objected, raising his
hands in protest. "I mean, I'm standing behind you so I can't
help looking at you, but I was more looking *through* you, if
you know what I mean."

"No need to explain," she said, turning her back to him.

Before him lay a discouraging display of manufactured
food—hard little doughnuts with colored sprinkles on their
topsides, gummy Danishes, chips and chips and chips, and a
bowl of standard-issue shiny apples. Everything wrapped in
plastic. After the bomb, houses would be made from burger
pods, with Saran Wrap windows and drinking straw beds.

"I'll have a Bloody Mary and an apple, please." Cat Woman
drew a bill from a soft cloth purse, black with pink roses on it
and a drawstring like the band around the kid's hat.

"That's some combination," Yoder ventured. His short
laugh turned into a snort.

She looked at him as if her were from space. The next moment he leaned forward to say: "Give me a beer, a grape pop
and two Twinkies," and couldn't do it. "A Pabst if you've got
it," was all he managed. He decided to come back for the
kid's order in a few minutes.

Cat Woman took her mix and the little bottle of vodka to a
booth in the corner. As she eased herself down, she looked up
at him and very deliberately stuck out her tongue. He made
up his mind, the roll of bills in his knapsack giving him courage. Walking toward her, he wished he were taller.

She didn't look up as he stood before her, watching the
vodka slip down the side of her glass in waves. She stirred

the mixture langorously, tapped the spoon twice against the rim. She had delicate wrists, long fingers, the reckless grace of a debutante slumming it in blue jeans. Yoder drew hard on his beer.

"To Seattle!" she said, raising her glass.

"You're going all the way?"

"Who wouldn't? The rest of the country drives me crazy. Ever noticed how they're not the same—oceans? The Atlantic's like a big old lake. But the Pacific is wild. It bites!" Her fingers snapped just an inch from his face. She laughed and he thought of a cat tripping across piano keys. "And you," she said. "How far do you go?"

The simplest question struck him as provocative. "As far as I can."

"No fair. Groucho Marx said that first."

She looked too young to know Marx Brothers' routines. "Actually, I'm just going to Michigan," His voice cracked— out of practice.

"Live there?"

"I've got business there."

"You don't look the type."

"I'm helping out a friend . . . in the import business." This is the first lie I'll tell you, he thought.

"The import business? What is this, an old movie? You do look sort of like that guy, what's his name—Peter Lorre. Come on, roll those eyes, let's see."

He had never been good at allowing women to tease him. He was having a hard time keeping up—watching her eyes dart about and her fingers tap the table top, flutter to her hair or finger the button on her shirt. Each breath caused her breasts to swell beneath the flannel shirt. No bra.

"So, where are you from?" she asked.

"Nairobi," he muttered. "Isn't everyone?" Her eyes widened but she did not back away as most people did when Firesign Theatre lines leaped out of his mouth. The cues were buried in the shallows of his subconscious. He could no more keep from reciting the next line than the actor who's done too much "Pygmalion" in summer stock. "Nowhere at the moment," he said, meeting her suddenly avid gaze.

"Nairobi?" she laughed. "So you're staying in Michigan, then?"

"I don't think so—I've already lived there once."

"Man Lives in All 50 States," she announced, sketching a newspaper headline in the air. "Wow, I didn't mean it to be such a tough question."

He reached to pick out a hair floating in his beer glass and she wrinkled her nose. "Yours, I hope," she said.

"I've got nothing against other people's hair."

She leaned forward, stage-whispered: "Checked out the bathrooms yet?"

"Should I?"

"They're great. Real roomy, with a little couch, double sinks. You can wash your hair no problem. Three days on this thing, I'm gonna be crazy to wash my hair."

Who was she with her too-skinny legs drawn up to her chest and her eyelids shining in the fading light? A small scar by the side of her mouth, shaped like a crescent moon, did just enough damage to her looks to give him confidence. "So, you think the bathroom might be a good place to toot up?" he asked.

Silently, she repeated his last words. "You mean, coke?" He thought she looked a little impressed but not too much, which was good. "What's that like?" she asked. "I've never heard a single thing that would make me want to try it."

"It's great," he stalled a moment for a description. He'd been broke for so long that getting high was a dim memory. "It's where the term 'rush' comes from," he said. "That's it. An incredible rush of blood, all internal like an implosion. And when it's over," he spread his arms, "I always feel like I've been pulled from a burning building."

Hoods dropped over her eyes. She spoke from miles away. "If that's what it feels like, no thanks," she said so solemnly he could barely make out her words.

"Hey, what did I say?"

"Ever come home from a funeral and flip on the T.V. and see some jerk on Carson cracking jokes about the morgue and it sets you off again—just the words?"

Not knowing what she was talking about, he didn't know what to say. "I don't watch T.V."

"Good," she said, as if it were all settled. She sank back in her chair and showed him her white teeth.

Perhaps she was crazy. Though impressed by her intensity, he could make no sense of it. Random explosions issued from her, followed by stunning silence. It had become very uncomfortable at their little table. She was examining her nails, running her thumb over the uneven ridges, perhaps determining where the next bites should come. Yoder could feel the contours of her nail, the pressure on her thumb as it rubbed across the rounded tip. The very center of him was drawn into the tiny plane on the edge of her fingernail. Twisting away, he drained his beer and looked out the window, somewhat surprised to see houses and hills flipping by. The flat land had begun to rise into the mountains of Pennsylvania. Whenever he was moving, even through country as impressive as this, the marigolds and dogs on chains, the yellow crumbling trim and cyclone fences seemed made to be left behind.

"Look at that!" he said. Going by was a perfect sycamore tree, alone in a tilled field. Bare of leaves, its tangled skeleton held a pulsating orange sun which seemed to have paused there on its way out of the world.

"Now that's why I ride trains," she said. When she bit into her apple, it left a bit of white foam on her lower lip. Extending the exposed section toward him she asked, "Want a bite?" and there was no mistaking her intentions.

"Not right now," he hedged.

"I'm sorry about shutting down like that. I'm sure you don't even know what you said a minute ago. My father was recently in a fire. He killed himself, actually. Words like 'burning building' set me off. New York was a bad place for me to be. So many sirens. I stayed with friends and at night they left a fire burning in the fireplace. I couldn't sleep. I had to sneak downstairs and put it out with the teapot."

"Killed himself?"

"It's not a story that I tell to strangers. In fact, I don't tell it much anymore at all."

"Jesus, I'm sorry. I can understand why it's hard for you to talk about." He was scrambling, going for a correct response. For some reason, it hurt that she thought of him as a stranger.

"Oh, no," she said, "it's too easy. I've got it down—the five minute version, the full-length album version. Whenever I needed strokes, I'd haul out my story."

He took pride in his skill at this very thing, though he bought sympathy with stories he invented completely. He'd been an orphan, his father had died of cancer, his best friend run down by a car, his childhood marred by drownings and lost dogs. Imaginative suffering was an art form he was prepared to defend. He hoped she wasn't going to insist on berating herself much longer. She was so pale and pretty. He did like looking at her, did like the comfort of her deeply breathing presence. So many questions. If he were as open as he pretended he'd ask them: Are you married? Have you given up on men? Do you believe that to be too conscious is an illness? Does it rain every day in Seattle? How far are you prepared to go?

"So, does it really rain every day where you live?"

She rolled her eyes. "I'm very tired of that question. Isn't there something else you'd rather know?"

"Yeah, are you married?"

"No. But thanks for asking." She shifted her focus to something just over his shoulder. Yoder braced himself for the lover approaching in mountain parka and cowboy hat. But when he turned around, he saw Sunshine eating up the ground beneath her, tiny clenched fists swinging in time with her pigtails.

"There you are!" she shouted, pointing him out to the whole car. "Where's my pop?"

"Sorry. I got to talking here."

"You left hours ago. You left when it was still light out." When it comes to letting the world know you're angry, it helps to be young.

"Are you two together?" Cat Woman lowered her voice, purring at the girl.

"Till Ohio."

"What's in Ohio?"

"My mom. She's taking me to Cedar Point."

"Is that right?" Yoder saw Cat Woman's eyes glaze over. "Your wife?" she asked in the voice all adults use to exclude children.

"No. It's not like that at all. We don't even know each other," he said a little too quickly.

"We do too!"

"You're right, Sunshine. You're right." Yoder rummaged around in his knapsack for change. "Look, I'll be right back with your food."

"A beer, a grape pop and two Twinkies," he said to the woman behind the counter, feeling only slightly less foolish this time. Rocking impatiently on his heels as the attendant searched through the Cokes and 7-Up, he kept checking on Sunshine. Say something nice, kid. You owe me, he thought. But he knew that wasn't the case. He owed her in some undefined, irritating way. He added a chocolate-covered doughnut for good measure.

Balancing the pastries and drinks on a tray, he turned to walk back to the table when he was stopped still by the vision confronting him: the two of them sitting next to one another at the end of the darkened car, the woman's head bent slightly to listen to the girl. A yellow light over the booth lit the top of their heads and the girl's legs were swinging lazily. He felt separated from them in time and space, as if hovering slightly above the scene. Yet he could see them with extraordinary clarity. They were lovely, both pale and fierce. Both had improbably light eyebrows that made their eyes look fully open. Yoder had the frightening sensation that he had done this slow turn once before, moved in this exact way toward the child and the woman, his family. The impossible association stuck with complete authority. His family. He set the food carefully back down on the counter and walked quickly and silently out of the car.

He stood in what looked like a phone booth, his hands curled inside the pockets of an overcoat that was not his own. Made of a dark fur, it had little animal heads with beaded red eyes hanging from around the collar like the stole his grandmother wore at Christmas and to funerals. Snow slanted across the road in front of him, piling up on the windows of

the booth. Periodically, he wiped traces of his breath from
the glass with the sleeve of the coat. A white car appeared
and he watched a woman emerge, holding a blanket-
shrouded bundle. He pushed against the glass door and
struggled out, sinking to his knees in a snowdrift. His bare
feet gathered frost on their edges like slabs of frozen meat.
The woman called to him. His feet burned with the cold. Before he could answer, she tossed the bundle toward him and
sped away, leaving the child in the air.

"Hey, buddy. You OK?"

A tall black man stood over him. "There's some chick outside lookin' for you," he said, tugging on the brim of his
leather cap. "Man, she was 'bout to come in here." The man
wheezed a short laugh, raising his eyes in sympathetic
amazement. "Chicks," the man said as he opened the door to
leave. "A man can't get any peace."

The train. Still on the train. Yoder spit into the sink and
ran his tongue across his teeth. Spinning, he scanned the little bathroom and spotted his knapsack slouched against the
wall. Digging to the bottom, his hand settled around the roll
of bills. Idiot, he thought, pulling out the fat hunk of money.

Suddenly, Cat Woman rose up behind him in the mirror,
wearing the white coat, her bottom lip flushed with blood.
"I've never been in a men's john before," she said, letting the
door slam shut behind her. "Isn't that ridiculous? There's
still this one taboo place. I mean, I really had to get my nerve
up to come in here. It's not nearly as nice as ours." She ran
her hands along the countertop as if it were made of Italian
marble. Yoder shoved the money back into the knapsack,
wondering how long she'd been watching. "Why is it that
men have to stand together to piss and we get privacy? Is it
only the sitting down part that's supposed to be embarrassing? You look tired."

She'd come for an explanation. He needed time to think of
one. "Let's get out of here," he said.

"No, let's stay. I like it in here. It's private."

"And orange."

"We could lock the door." A seductive smile eased onto her
face.

"What if somebody needs to take a piss?"

"He can go to the next car. There's a john in every single one. Believe me, I know. I've been up and down this whole sucker looking for you."

"What time is it?"

"After midnight. It's dead out there. Listen, I'm not following you around. I just didn't want you to miss your stop."

The realization that he'd overslept always brought him fully alert. He'd make a good fireman for that reason, he thought, or a good soldier. "Where? Did we pass it? Where are we?"

"Calm down. It's not for another hour. But I didn't want you to miss it. Plus you left your guitar under your seat. It's just outside."

He put his hand on her shoulder. "Thanks." It was an extremely nice thing to do for someone who'd walked out on you a few hours before. Too nice, maybe. "Where's the kid?"

"Gone. I got her off the train a little while after you left. Met her mom."

"Was she mad?"

"Who?"

"Sunshine."

"Confused, I think."

"It feels like one of those things I'll dream about later," Yoder said, rubbing his hands across his face. "Seeing her waving at me across a big auditorium. Running after her with a Twinkie."

"If you live right, you don't need to dream," she said. He winced; she was younger than he'd thought. She poked at her hair in the mirror. "I'm Lee. Who are you?"

"My name's Yoder."

"Really? Sounds Scandinavian."

"It's not." He saw that her ass tucked neatly into her blue jeans like a heart.

Lee pushed the lever on the door to LOCK. "I don't want to sleep all alone out there with strangers. After the lights went off I closed my eyes for a while and when I opened them the conductor was standing over me, staring. I told him to take a picture."

It came back to him, her fingertip running across her thumbnail. The pressure. "If you want to stay in here, it's all right with me. It won't be the first time." He put his arm around her shoulder and she leaned into him, filling the space beneath his arm.

"It won't?" Her voice rose in disappointment.

"Nope. I've slept on bathroom floors quite a bit."

She had freckles on her shoulders and her skin was very pale. It surprised him that her pubic hair was a soft red—the color of her eyebrows. There was not time to notice much more. Within minutes she'd spread her coat across the floor and they had rolled onto it, the fleece keeping them warm. Unbuttoning her shirt, he was struck again by how thin the lines are which divide a life. One minute you're alive, but let your eyes wander off the road to gaze at horses in a field and you're a goner. This afternoon he could only stare at the buttons he now fingered playfully. He took one in his teeth, pulling her flannel shirt off.

Lee's hand rested cool on his back. Frantic, she curled around him as if moving into some position long-established between them. She licked his earlobe and he grabbed her buttocks. Firm buttocks gave him confidence. Her breasts felt like clouds. "Wait a minute," he whispered, taking her by the shoulders, "I don't have anything."

"It's all right," she said.

He knew he'd have to take her word for it. No stopping now. "Watch your head," he managed to mumble as she climbed atop of him, eyes open, her body floating upward as if levitating. They were rushing. He forced his breath to be long and slow, thought of the desert. She rubbed against him like a dog in the grass.

The train shook. Ear to the ground, he could appreciate the purely mechanical nature of the motion, swaying left, right, left, right, as gravity resisted the mass moving through it. What seemed lulling from a cushioned seat was loud and fast and frightening up close. Yoder began to mimic the double-time movement, rocking her, rocking her. It should always be like this, he thought, like a piano duet by two people who don't know how to play, each inventing their own part, bent over the keys, frantic to keep pace, out of tune and laughing, satisfied and breathless at the end.

"This is like something I would have done when I was a kid," she said, rolling onto her back, knees bent, her feet in the air.

"Wish I'd met you ten years ago."

"You know, something you'd do just to say you'd done it. Oh, god, that was good." Sighing, stretching her limbs out long, she looked like all the girls he'd loved when he was twelve. "Say your name again. I can't believe we just did that and I don't remember your name."

He spelled it for her, wanting a blanket, a nap with her head on his chest.

"Yoder," she repeated, as if learning a foreign language.

"So how old are you now?" he asked.

"21."

That number again. Younger even than he'd thought. She pulled her jeans on more matter-of-factly than he liked but left her shirt unbuttoned and flopped down beside him on her stomach. He smoothed her hair around her ears. She had led him like a sleepwalker. She had come for him.

"You were hot," she said.

"Hot?"

"Like lightning." Deliberately, she kissed him with more passion than had just passed between them. What a corny thing to say. He pulled her across his chest. "No, no, forget it. You'll miss your transfer."

"So what," he said, seeing Ann Arbor's slushy streets, the wind blowing leaflets and junk food wrappers against his legs. "Why don't you come with me for a few days? I'll show you Ann Arbor."

"You have a place to stay?"

"Sure. The guy I'm meeting will put us up." Maybe, he thought. Why was he complicating his life like this?

She frowned down at him for a few moments. He tried to compose his face but realized that he had no idea what would convince her. He felt a little like a pastry in a bakery shop window. "Let me guess," he said. "You'd rather remember me as someone you screwed just so you could say that you did."

Abruptly she stood and faced the mirror. Leaning in close, she ran a finger under one eye, then stepped back to pose for herself. "I've got things to do in Seattle."

"What things?"

"There's just people, things. Someone's staying at my place and they're sort of expecting me."

"A lover?"

"A friend."

"Hey, whatever. I'm just some guy on a train. Forget I mentioned it. Let's shake hands and promise to write."

"It's not like that. I'd like to come with you. You know how with some people, after five minutes you've got them figured out? I haven't got you figured out."

"Then get off this train and marry me."

"But I don't have a thing to wear."

"How about if we just do the honeymoon? Then later, in the privacy of your own seat, you can make up your mind about the ceremony."

A rapid pounding on the door brought Lee's hand to her mouth and Yoder to his feet. "Open up!" a man's voice shouted. "Open up in there before I call a conductor." The words were slurred—a drunk—a sleepwalker.

"This unit's temporarily out of order, sir," Yoder said, inflating his voice. "You'll find one working in the next car." The man swore and moved off. Pleased with himself, Yoder looked to see if Lee was impressed, but she was still studying herself in the mirror.

**T**HEY HELD HANDS that morning, slouched across leatherette chairs in the Ann Arbor train station. Yoder called Crock from Toledo to see if they might sleep at his place, but Crock wasn't home at 2 o'clock in the morning. He called again when they reached Ann Arbor, let the phone ring 25 times, tried not to think anything of it. Tried to concentrate on Lee's thumb rubbing back and forth across his knuckles as she dozed in her chair. Yoder found himself apologizing for the uncomfortable chairs and the Muzak and the pale coffee. Lee insisted that she didn't mind, that she'd dreamed the whole thing already, even the way they used his knapsack as a pillow and her coat as a blanket. She told him that she liked hearing him breathe.

They ate runny eggs and home-fries at Dino's, a place near the hospital that was always open. Around them, nurses nibbled donuts and whitened their coffee; interns slouched over stacks of pancakes and limp bacon. Yoder told Lee how he used to steal food from hospital trays when he didn't have any money. She said that was nothing compared to what women could do when they had to. She told him that she lived on a houseboat left to her by her father, that she worked in a secondhand store by the docks, that she wanted to be a singer. He told her he was a songwriter and she believed him.

"Maybe we can team up, make Big Money," she said, snapping her fingers to turn her last two words into a concept. "I'm very interested in Big Money."

"Music is not the way to make money."

"I know. If I don't have a recording contract in my pocket in five years, I'm going into real estate. I think I have a talent for real estate. It's in my blood, I think."

"As in: Your father owned half of Seattle?"

"Daddy was a fisherman," she said sternly. "My mother *should* have been in real estate. Everybody always said that. I stayed with her winters and we used to go to open houses and bargain. She was practicing, she said, for when she went into real estate."

"So did she?"

"No, she died five years ago."

"I'm sorry."

Silence at the breakfast table. How to proceed? He wanted to know everything. Didn't want to be careful or polite. "What will you do with all your money?"

"Buy a marina," she said, ticking items off on her fingers. "Travel. Get my own island. Buy lots of shoes."

Yoder thought of the roll of bills at the bottom of his knapsack. That was how you came by money in this world. You sold off some part of yourself that you thought you wouldn't miss, and you bought shoes.

They hit the streets under a clear sky splintered with light. The hour just after dawn was his favorite for walking. Civilization slept late, and the world could be re-formed according to his whim. Walk barefoot down the middle of State Street, spit on the statues of statesmen; hear the stoplights clicking over pointlessly, blinking like red-eyed Cyclops. Walking in the morning made him believe he had a tiny bit of a secret that wouldn't do anyone else any good. His arm around Lee, Yoder took the empty streets with confidence, pointing out old haunts and landmarks: The bookstore where Sal had worked, the Orange Julius whose fluorescent lights were a comfort he couldn't explain, the stone lions guarding the

Natural History Building. He repeated the story told to freshmen: How the lions would rise up and roar if ever a virgin walked by. Lee said that made her feel better about never having gone to college.

The traffic began to heat up and students tumbled into the streets. Yoder steered Lee toward the Arboretum, a rolling expanse of land planted with specimens of trees gathered from around the world. When he'd studied here, the Arb had seemed a sort of tree museum meant for browsing, and by the time he'd left, his only church. He wanted Lee to know this place, wanted it to be something they had between them, no matter what happened.

Inside the iron gates, the air seemed saturated with the stench of spring. A soft breath on the land swept dark pink crab apple against tight-fisted lilacs, sprays of forsythia. Buds beaded up along the branches of elms like clusters of grapes. Yoder paused at the top of the grassy bowl. Eight winters before he'd learned to speed down this icy slope on a cafeteria tray. It looked smaller, less treacherous by half. In patches the grass had greened and as he descended clods of loam stuck to his boots. It was almost barefoot weather. The rigors of spring training lay just ahead. Each May he put his feet through their paces until they toughened and could take him anywhere—across July asphalt, mossy river bottoms and the spit and bottle caps of back alleys. Fueled by the steep hillside and a sudden desire to see the woods alone, Yoder broke into a run, leaving Lee to follow him along the path into the trees.

White oak, Douglas fir, tamarack, loblolly pine. Hemlock, aspen, hawthorn, juniper. Ginkgo, basswood, catalpa, birch. Weeping, weeping willow. The names he'd memorized in forestry school wove themselves into a chant he recited whenever he walked in the woods. Even tangled and gawky as they were in early spring, these were things worth living for, these old trees that harmed no one and the small yellow flowers that spread out beneath them. Yoder pointed out those few he could recognize by the skin of their trunks and Lee was delighted with the idea of knowing their names.

"Do you know flowers?" she asked.

"No, just trees."

"Well, I'm going to learn those then. You wouldn't believe the flowers we get in summer."

You wouldn't believe how young you look right now, he thought. He wanted to be with her, for it to be that simple. But if she came with him to Crock's place, he would have to explain, and if she didn't understand, everything would be spoiled. Lee ran ahead on the narrow path and Yoder vowed to return to the Arboretum with her before she left for Seattle. Vowed to use his profits to find her again. A lot could go wrong in that time: Lee could get married or choke on a fishbone and die. Her boat could sink; her plans could change; she could meet someone else on a train. Things were moving fast, usually a good sign, but he'd lost the thread. What had seemed so simple—this one deal, quick cash, an appointment—had become an annoyance. The last twelve hours stood as the best twelve since he'd come back.

"Will you be all right here for a couple hours? I have to meet that guy I was telling you about."

"Sure," she said, "It's great here. Reminds me of home; it's so green."

"We'll have a place to stay tonight, I promise." They could both use a good sleep. Lee's eyes looked bloodshot and small. "Meet me by the arches at 2 o'clock."

She ambled off down the path, her hands fingering the tips of branches as she passed. By some perverse logic he began convincing himself that she would not wait. What motivated Lee was still a mystery, but if she was enough like him to like him, she was enough like him to split. She nearly always had a smart-ass smile on her face, a smirk, like she didn't believe a word he said, like everything had a double meaning, like they'd met before and she was waiting to spring it on him: I'm the girl you ran circles with in the rain; I'm the one whose bicycle you stole; the dark one whose face you touched in the alley; the one whose letter you kept in your pocket until it bled in the wash and only the word "soon" remained.

Yoder cut through the forsythia bushes separating the Arboretum from the cemetery and hurried up the curving asphalt drive past the woods where the oldest graves were found. If he believed in being buried, he would want to be buried here. The traffic didn't penetrate. Even the wind kept still in this part of town. The markers, mostly white and crumbling in this section, broke up the landscape like the saguaro cactus of New Mexico, stone silent but strangely aware.

Mathilde's grave was surrounded by a grove of twisted oaks, the kind that made him believe in fairy tales. Whoever she was, she had died on the day of his birth. Ten years ago, he'd found that profoundly significant. On her gravestone had been sculpted a small relief of what he presumed to be her face. There were no other graves beside her, no husband or children. He often wondered whom she had left behind to erect such a sweet stone.

Nearby, workmen in overalls and bright orange caps bent to their task, disturbing the absolute privacy he required of this place. He'd always walked here when he had thinking to do. He tried to shut out the sound of metal against earth, the scrape and thud that signals our final obligation. He hated the empty graves and the stones already marked with a birthdate and an open question. He'd walked here six years ago in high summer, cicadas humming in the damp darkness, the trees alive and quivering, pausing before the graves of children—and soldiers, the stiff little flags and the arithmetic angering him. He'd walked here and spoken to Mathilde, trying to make sense of a voice that said: *run*. He came back here now in communion with a new voice he did not trust, a voice that wanted him to stay.

As always, he touched her face, the pitted granite of her nose, the blackened hollow eyes. The artist had fashioned earrings in the curve of her ears, knobs of pearly stone that made him certain a pair just like them lay rattling about the bottom of her coffin. Perhaps Lee would think to wander here later this afternoon. Perhaps be drawn to this grave as he'd been one morning a lifetime ago while taking Blue for a walk. He wanted to tell Mathilde that he'd found her. Found the woman. Found the woman. *She lives in a warm place, the South maybe.* His mother had been wrong about a child, right about the money. Was she right about the Queen of Wands? He listened for the trees to rub their branches together, whisper a blessing or a warning. He heard a dog bark, felt the sun rising into afternoon. Down on one knee in this singular ritual of prayer, he asked for her blessing and then hurried away, afraid to be late, afraid to be on time.

On the street again he made a slight detour across dormitory lawns to cross the highway by way of the Ho Chi Minh bridge. The reason for its nickname was lost to him now, though he remembered watching crowds of fellow freshmen chanting HO, HO, HO CHI MINH, VIET CONG ARE GONNA WIN as they stormed the bridge on the way to an anti-ROTC rally. At the time, the cheering had seemed no different from the pep rallies of the generation who had gone before, and he had walked resolutely against the mob, returning to his room to drink beer and listen to Dave Mason albums. Two years later, those same people had saved him.

As he passed by the stone lions, Yoder heard an insistent hiss, loud like a stage-whisper, silly like a kid's game. He turned toward the marble steps of the Natural History Building, interested. Standing with his legs spread wide, his hand shading his eyes as if the world were flooded with light, was a man in a suit. A man in a suit with a red beard the color of weak tea. Goldie. Alive and well. Goldie. Yoder wanted to hug him. Instead he waved casually. "Spare change?"

"Christ, it is you." Goldie had him by the shoulders, slapping his back and staring at him as if he expected him to disappear. "Whenever I'm in this part of town, even though I know better, I look for you. Even though I know you've disappeared forever."

Looking at Goldie's hair trimmed above the collar, at his cheap corduroy suit and snappy tie, it seemed it was he who had disappeared. Yoder had never known Goldie to wear anything but jeans and something appropriate from his T-shirt collection. He could think of nothing to say. "So, Goldie, what's with the get-up?"

"First things first. What are you doing here?" Goldie lowered his voice, looking over his shoulder only half in jest. "Are you a Fu-gi-tive? If so, we gotta get you some clothes."

"It's old news, Goldie. We got amnesty. I've been back a few months."

"I assume you want to be back."

"Don't..."

"...Assume. Anything." Goldie insinuated his eyebrows

with skill. "Lots of guys who weren't even drafted went over the line after you, just to get outta here."

"I know. Toronto was like a refugee camp for WASPs. How'd you get out? You had a low number."

"I almost bought it. I didn't have squat, no letter, no rap, no scam up my sleeve. Tell you the truth I went in there half hoping they'd draft me. Thought I'd shut the old man up— you know, do the one thing *nobody* expected. Anyway, a guy in line, like two seconds before the blood pressure test, says: Squeeze your butt. So I did. Went sky high, and I drank coffee and inhaled Luckys for three days to keep it there." He paused, studying his shoes. "I usually tell the story like it was the hardest fucking three days of my life. A picnic compared to what—four years?"

"Six."

"Jesus."

Nothing could redeem the silence. It was small talk or nothing. "That your job-hunting suit, Goldie?"

"Nope. I'm a lifer, now. I evaluate bastards like you to see if we can put you on the dole. The Department of Economic Security. It kills me. All these people with resumes up the wazoo out there don't have jobs, and I do. I keep expecting one of them to say, hey Jack, move over, I can do that better than you. I like to think of myself as the Robin Hood of the System." He took a short bow and Yoder noticed he had bread crumbs in his moustache.

"Sounds awful, Goldie."

"What better to do with an anthropology degree? Besides, I've got Responsibilities."

He remembered that Goldie couldn't get a fried egg out of the pan without breaking it, ran his cars into the ground because he never bothered to learn how they worked, liked to spend afternoons at the movie theater watching the same show over and over.

"You'll have to come out to the house sometime. Jan will go nuts. You remember Jan—well, of course you do. We got ourselves married." Goldie was good at making fun of himself; he was swinging his arms and sticking out his front teeth like a yokel. "Really, come over for dinner, only don't come tomorrow."

"Congratulations."

"Got time for a beer?"

"Always got time for a beer."

"I still drink at the old Stand-Up Ernie's—"

"Jesus, that dump?"

"You'd never recognize it. They call it the Beanery Bar now, but *I* remember."

It was already pushing noon. He couldn't believe that Goldie was standing right there before him and he was about to give him the brush off. He'd missed Goldie perhaps most of all—for his junior-high silliness, his impossible good cheer.

"Hey, we don't have to go to Ernie's." Goldie was reading his silence. "You name it."

Yoder reached to touch the thinning nap of Goldie's lapel, then drew back, repelled by its implications—dry cleaners, darning, tie racks. He didn't want to have a beer and reminisce. He wanted to live it. "Can't," he said. 'I'm already late."

"I'm in the book, then." A muscle in Goldie's face twitched under the skin. "Under Arnold J. Ward." He'd never before heard Goldie's real name. "Call me some time." An invisible cigar materialized in Goldie's hand, Groucho crept into his voice. "Call me Arnie."

"How about if I call you Goldie?"

Goldie flapped his overcoat like a sideshow hawker and backed away down the sidewalk. "So, I'm gone. Off to do good deeds and white collar crime—steal some paperclips for the missus. Call!"

Without the snow to soften them, the houses on Crock's block looked blighted. As he ran toward the house, he again felt uncertain about the changes. Had time tampered with the easy grace of the frame houses, or had he simply been young when he lived here? Where was the wisdom in doing business with someone who didn't notice that the world had changed? He wondered what Goldie would think of his partnership with Crock. It was a crap-shoot; he could get ripped off, or he could get rich. Just let it go down smooth, he whispered as he hopped the fence separating the alley from Crock's backyard.

Grass grew between the chipped bricks on the back patio.

Two lawn chairs were pulled up to a rust-spotted table. Two open beers. Had the meeting begun? He was curious about the other investors. Yoder approached the house, startling slightly at a burst of music from a stereo abruptly turned up way too loud. He moved closer. Heard a crash and a shattering of glass. He slid up to the patio, knocking over a bulging bag of garbage, and pressed his nose against the sliding glass door.

A chair upended. A bare bulb swinging from the ceiling, the stained-glass shade in pieces on the table. On the floor, in a heap, the crumpled body of a woman. Crock stood in the archway between the living room and the kitchen. Yoder couldn't see his face. A rock 'n' roll bass line shook the house. The Stones. The woman began inching her way up the door jamb, hand over hand as if on tiptoe. Crock's arm sliced the air. His hand cracked across the side of her face, knocking her head against the wall. Her head bounced. Twice. She sank to her knees. Crock touched her shoulder once and ran from the room, tugging at his hair.

Yoder leapt at the door, his fists pleading with the glass. "Let me in," he shouted. "Open the door!" He flew against the glass. "Open up!" The door trembled and he couldn't see anything and he couldn't get in.

Suddenly Crock stood before him, his leather jacket slung over one shoulder. "Beat it, Yoder," he said, pulling hard on a cigarette. "What are you, blind? Get out of here."

"Let me in or I'm calling the cops."

"This is none of your business. Get lost, I'm telling you."

"Let me in."

"Wrong."

"Crock, I saw what you did."

"Your timing is for shit, Yoder. You're late. Deal was supposed to go down at noon." Crock slid the door closed behind him and stepped out onto the patio. The cigarette shook in his hand. Yoder smelled liquor, sticky sweet, on his breath.

"Fuck the deal. What's going on here?"

"I said it's none of your goddamn business. Listen, you got the money? Maybe I can still arrange something."

"I wouldn't let you arrange my next crap."

He grabbed Crock then, by the shirt, and heaved him into

the rough stucco wall. Crock raised his fist, and Yoder hit him in the stomach, bringing him down on his knees. He watched as Crock folded in on himself, and caught his eye before Crock sank beneath the pain. He felt satisfied. Righteous. If he wanted, he could hit him again. Yoder stared down at Crock's insect arms wrapped around his middle. He felt tall. He felt the privilege of compassion. Without a word, he slipped into the house and locked the door behind him.

Yoder hit the volume control on the stereo and in the silence he heard the woman sobbing. Alone with her, he was aware of being a man, the enemy, a stranger. He remembered his own hands on Susan's shoulders, shaking her. "You all right?" he asked from the other side of the room, reluctant to move toward her.

She nodded her head, but with it buried in her knees he couldn't tell if she meant yes or no.

"Look, can I take you somewhere?"

"Is he gone?" Her voice a whisper from a dream.

Crock was disappearing—leaping over the back fence toward the garage. "Seems to be," Yoder said.

Black tears streaked her face. "I need a tissue," she said.

And some ice, he thought, going into the kitchen to get them. Dishes were piled in the sink and half-cooked eggs cooled on the stove. Every cupboard door stood open and a piece of toast lay on the floor, Crock's cat, Starman, quietly licking the butter off the top. No ice in the freezer. He turned to grab paper towels and a damp rag and he saw his wallet lying on top of a pile of papers next to the phone. Just seconds before he saw it, he knew it would be there. Slime was slime. Two twenties inside—the fifties and hundreds missing. He couldn't be certain whether the wallet had slipped— or been taken—out of his jacket pocket that night. It didn't matter. All he could think about was Sam.

Yoder kneeled down beside the woman who still sat crumpled in the doorway. She blew her nose then lay the cloth across her blue jeans and rested her cheek on the cloth.

"I'm all right," she said, lying badly. "You can go now. He won't be back for hours. If there's some message...." She looked at him for the first time. A bruise was yellowing on her cheek. Ugly, this hidden blood.

"Message?" he said, letting his voice rise into a shout. "You're gonna give him a message? Here's a message: Tell him the deal's off and I'm gonna kill him the next time I see him."

"That's not a thing to joke about with Crock."

"No, I suppose not. I suppose he's got a gun now. What are you doing here? Do you know what you looked like when he was hitting you?" Suddenly he was afraid for Lee. What had he been thinking, leaving her alone? "Look, you need some money or something? Here, take this." Yoder dug a handful of bills from the knapsack and slipped them between her feet.

"Please leave me alone," she said.

He stood, spun, unable to get hold of the situation. The room was such an incredible mess. She was a mess. "You tell him he can't get away with this. Not with any of this. On second thought, don't tell him anything. Just get out of here." She watched him with the same expectant terror he'd seen on her face through the window. "I'm going, OK? But you go too." At the door he turned back, remembering why he'd come inside in the first place. "I'm sorry he hurt you," he said, disappointed by the impotence of words.

Outside he heard birds. The sky was a watery blue, striped with high sketchy clouds like paint peeling off a fencepost. A Tom Sawyer sky. He staggered down the driveway to the sidewalk. Sometimes his mind simply seized up like the engine of Eliot's dirtbike, locking into the position of its last function. The woman's head crashed against the wall again and again. The spin, the hair, the black tears, again and again.

The first time he'd been beaten up, two kids had rolled him in an alley behind a grocery store while he was still in grade school. They'd taken his tennis shoes. Brand new high-tops. Took them right off his feet on a cool October evening. He had to buy a new pair the next day and that record remained unbroken: two new pairs of shoes in a single week. He remembered how the soft night had turned ugly, the puddles smelling of gasoline, asphalt burning into his hands when he fell. One guy pressed a heavy rubber rod against his throat while the other one went through his pockets and took off his shoes. It was the shoe part that had bothered him the most.

He'd had to walk home through the rainy streets and the spit on the sidewalk, and just minutes before he'd been happy about the peach sunset and the black trees and the cars throwing out fans of raindrops gleaming in their headlights. He'd kept quiet about it, telling his mother he'd forgotten to get the milk and kept seeing it run in the street, mixing with the dirt, the rain and the broken glass. Later, he told Benish that there had been a gang, a struggle.

An elderly man walked past him, his beagle straining toward the trees on the boulevard. Things happened and everywhere people sighed over lunch. On the freeway, someone sneezed. How could people walk around as if nothing had happened? Things happened. Sal lived just a few blocks away. Be home, Sal, he thought. Be home now.

ONE PROBLEM WITH dropping in on people all the time
was that he frequently saw them at their worst. Yoder hoped
Sal would be home but more than that he hoped she would
be home to him. The back door hung slightly open. Through
the dried stems of last summer's morning glories clinging to
the blackened screen, he could see Sal moving about the
kitchen in her aimless way. He couldn't decide if she was
humming, or if he simply expected her to be humming. She
drifted toward the sink, ran the water for no apparent purpose and shut it off again. He was astonished to see her belly
rounding hard beneath her lilac-flowered dress. Sal clipped
something from a hanging basket in the window, chewed ab-
sentmindedly on a piece and began chopping the rest into a
large wooden bowl. She *was* humming.

Yoder knocked twice on the shaky door frame. Sal dropped
the knife, and he saw her perfect round eyes accept that he
was on her doorstep and not hesitate to move toward him.
Her stomach came between them when they hugged. Up
close, she looked tired.

"Glad to see me, Sal?"

"You know it." She kissed him on the forehead, suddenly ten years younger, suddenly the girl on the stoop. He peeked into the iron pot rumbling on the stove. Inside boiled a muddy stew. "What's cooking?"

"Well," Sal looked at the ceiling and laughed. "I don't exactly know."

"I'll have some then."

"I figure I should cook it, whatever it is, at least a couple hours. Will you stay?"

"That's up to you," he said, wondering if she'd forgotten that he always wanted to stay.

"Then stay," she said. "Stay for dinner," she added quickly, and he saw the line she'd drawn between them. "You look different, Yoder."

"Do I? How?"

"I'm not sure. Can't you feel it? Are you all right?"

"I had a horseshit morning." He searched for words to tell her about the woman, her face composed and ready like an actress who'd done the scene before. But with the sun coating Sal's kitchen like marmalade, and the smell of garlic on her fingers, he couldn't bring himself to intrude that much. "I'll tell you about it later."

Sal laughed and he didn't try to figure out why. Sal laughed all the time. Though he knew it was her way of not looking at things, it had never bothered him. "You know, I was thinking about you the other day," she said. "We had a spring rain and I was remembering that time in the cemetery—that time in the rainstorm. Remember? All that mud. And we threw mudballs at the gravestones. Yoder, don't you remember that?" Sal was shrieking and he was glad to see her but he didn't remember.

"I remember the time we got caught in the rain on our bikes," he offered. "Your T-shirt got soaked and we were almost in a couple collisions with horny drivers. I remember that."

With her hands on her hips drawing the lilac fabric across her stomach, she looked ridiculous, like one of those heavy-bottomed dolls that can't be toppled. "I'll never forget it," she said. "It was the first time I realized that as far as I wanted to go, you'd go farther. I thought: Now this is gonna be fun."

"So much for first impressions."

"It was fun, now come on."

Why did women always decide he was fun after their relationship had ended?

"You haven't said anything, Yoder."

"About what?"

"I'm going to have a baby."

Sal patted her stomach and Yoder felt lost. He looked out the window as if he could look past the houses and the greening lawns, the alleys, open garages, telephone poles, elm trees, into the solemn blue sky and the moon pale as a choirboy. He pushed the elastic air and it came right back at him. "I can see that. Big changes in your life."

"He's a wonderful man," she said, revving up again. "He's truly wonderful. Maybe you can meet him. He's not here right now but how long are you staying?"

General principle: Regard things as if they were about to disappear. "Just passing through, Sal."

"No. Stay a while. I'm sorry about last time." She dropped her eyes and Yoder felt his body tense in the anticipation of justice. "Did you get my letter? Stay. I want to know what's happened."

So do I, he thought. Send me the man who can tell me just exactly what's happened. "Actually, I could use a place for the night." He remembered waking up to those eyes. "I'm traveling with a woman though, so I wouldn't want to put you out."

Like a best friend, she didn't flinch. "Something serious?"

"I don't know what it is. I met her on the train coming out here."

"Then you're both welcome. Everybody's welcome." Sal had been flying around the kitchen, opening cupboards, measuring flour. Now she shaped a shiny roll of dough with her fists, hitting it deliberately and hard.

"What are you doing?"

"This? It's bread, Yoder. I figured since you were staying, I'd make bread."

"Just like that? Just throw stuff together and it turns out to be bread." Feminine and mysterious, bread baking seemed an ordained skill, unlike making pizza dough or pie crust.

"So what's this lady's name?"

"Lee. She's a lot younger than we are. Believe it or not, I think she's after me."

"Oh, Yoder, let me give you a hug. You say that like it's never happened before."

"Been a long time, Sal." He did not move toward her.

"Well, where is she?"

"In the Arb somewhere, I hope. She wanted to stay and wander around. You know how it is when you first see that place."

"A spring morning at the Arb. How romantic." She said it in a way that drew them together but didn't exclude Lee.

"You know, Sal, I miss this kitchen. It's the sunniest damn kitchen I've ever been in. You got a funnel pumping it in or something?"

"Since you're not going to ask, I'm going to tell you. His name's Jerry. I met him at the co-op. He's, like, the manager of the co-op." She flipped the dough and began kneading it from the other side, her hair swinging dangerously close to the sticky surface. "Oh, and plus he plays drums in a band."

"Watch your hair."

"You might like him, Yoder. You might."

"So you're going to marry another man, eh, Sal?"

She stopped, her eyes confused, as they'd been that night in the blue light of her porch. "After all this time, you're jealous?"

"A little."

"Is it the marriage part or the baby part?"

"I don't know."

" 'Cause if it's the marriage, relax. We're not getting married."

She flopped the dough, exhausted and pale, into a darkly stained bread pan, pushing her hair from her eyes every few seconds. "Now, let's see." Abandoning the bread, she disappeared into the next room. Yoder heard her talking but couldn't understand any words. Sal's kitchen had exploded, flour everywhere and half-full cups of tea. A necklace of red peppers hung over the stove and a dog-eared copy of the *Vegetarian Epicure* lay open on the table. In Sal's kitchen, things like Comet and salt were hard to come by. She never bought ketchup but she had lemon pepper, no milk but maybe papaya juice. What's-his-name must have stocked the kitchen.

Sal drifted back into the kitchen carrying a stack of photographs, thumbing through them and making little noises to herself as she walked. "We went camping last fall and took some pictures. There he is." A burly man stood up to his waist in fast-moving water. He carried a log in his hands, held high over his head like a rifle.

"What are you going to do with a baby, Sal? Teach it yoga?"

"You expect me to know? When it comes, I'll know. I think I'll miss being pregnant, though. It makes me think about us, you know, all of us. How we were babies once and our mothers were young and scared and felt us kick in the night. I've been seeing my mother a lot. You know how she is. But it's different now. We've got things to talk about."

"My mother's reading tarot cards for the neighbor ladies."

"I love it."

"I don't."

"When are you going to cheer up, Yoder?"

"Right now. You're cheering me up, Sal."

"Good. Wanna feel her?"

"Her?"

"Definitely."

A sudden shyness made him hesitate. When she took his hand and laid it flat against her stomach, he was unprepared for its firmness and his desire to know her body in this new way.

"I'm never alone anymore," she said.

Soon there would be a little girl, kneeling on a stool at the sink, making messes just like her mother. She'd be spacey and charming and have a laugh like a song. "I'm glad for you," he said. They had all grown up. Everybody had grown up with guns and babies to prove it.

His thoughts drifted out the hole in the screen door, landing disembodied in the kitchen in Rydertown. Josh and Ruthie were fighting. Josh tugged on his hair. Ruth looked old and hateful in the coastal light. He watched Sal pick dead leaves off an ancient Swedish ivy. The window sill was lined with slippery egg-shaped avocado seeds, their roots ex-

ploding in jars of water. "We never talked about children, did
we?"

"We were children, Yoder."

"Was that the problem?"

Sighing dramatically, she lowered herself into a rocking
chair, her legs spread wide like every pregnant woman he'd
ever seen. "We talk about this every time I see you. Let's not
talk about it now."

"No, it's important. Whatever I did, I don't want to do it
again."

"Yoder, you can stay here. I don't care what you do. I'm
distracted with my baby. Nothing much bothers me."

"That's not what I mean. It's this woman, Lee."

"I should have known. When you're in love you don't look
suicidal—which you don't, but you worry all the time. Go
get her so I can meet her."

"Was it that I wanted too much?"

"Yes." He hated the strained patience in her voice.

"How much is too much?"

"Too much is you and I walking in the Arb at dawn, making love in the pine needles, whistling bird songs and the
next morning you disappear for three weeks. And then suddenly you're back sleeping on my doorstep with roses and
poems. Too much is letters from Canada that make me crazy
because I have no reason to expect I'll ever see you again.
That's too much."

"Which part?"

"Yoder, I love you. But it's not something I can live with
every day. It's not." Her voice was stern. "I need someone
who stays."

He knew all this. They had talked about it one hundred
times before. But he had to remember that Sal couldn't
speak for the whole human race. Lee's long legs had wrapped
around him, her eyes pulled him in. She took as much as he
could give. In the intensity game, so far they were even. Perhaps age would be his friend in this. Perhaps he would be
like a cat that's easier to love once it calms down and prefers
sleeping in your lap to chasing motes in the light. Sal had her
hand on his knee and he placed his own over hers. Right then
it seemed there could be nothing more beautiful than their

hands sheltering one another on faded blue jeans in spring light.

"Listen, I'll be back in an hour or so."

"I won't be surprised if you aren't, but I think I'll call Jerry. We'll have a party waiting."

Yoder was fairly sure that he wouldn't like Jerry, but it would be easier with Lee at his side. Lee. It was a wind name. Maybe he'd write a song about her. Then again— maybe not.

The rough granite arches bordering the Arboretum picked up the failing sunlight in particles that sparkled like stars in a miniature universe. Bits of green poked through the flabby snow, insistently returning. Yoder was tempted to take off his boots and run his toes through the mud. Cars whizzed by at his back. He spotted Lee at the base of the hill beneath a jack pine of remarkable breadth, talking to a woman with hair the color of milkweed. The woman jostled a child in her arms.

Yoder wanted Lee to see him first, to run toward him with a look that proved Sal wrong. But her back was turned and she did not hear him coughing. Watching her hands fly between hips and hair, he saw that she listened to everyone with her whole body, her eyes narrowing, fingers snapping with excitement. To everyone—not just to him. Knowing her body had little to do with knowing Lee. Keeping up with the meaning of a first fuck was like trying to comprehend Dylan's best lyrics; it changed on you every time you thought you understood.

A loud bob-white whistle, another gift from forestry school, did the trick. Lee waved vigorously. He plopped his hat on her head, slightly askew. She looked like Peter Pan then, and he took his hat back.

"Meet Laurie and Shawn," she said. The woman regarded him with disinterest. Vegetarian, he guessed, single mother, forgets to water her ferns, hates men. "She was just telling me about this place. I bet we walked three miles."

Of all the disappointments of the day, the fact that Lee had explored this place without him stung the most acutely. "That's nothing," he said. "This place is at least 80 acres."

Turning his back on the woman and child, he pulled Lee away. She frowned and bent to ruffle the boy's hair. Soon she would learn to read his signals, to know that his abruptness indicated not anger but desire. Desire or possessiveness? What if she could read him already and just didn't like what she saw?

Walking up the hill, she talked about Laurie, her troubles with her husband—he winced at his error—her ambition to become a chef. Lee knew more about the damn woman than she did about him. The sun slanted across her face, igniting her hair and he tried to calm down, to enjoy the rhythm of her words tumbling out all twisted up with excitement.

"I guess you make friends easily," he said finally.

"I meet people easily—obviously. But I'm not close to many."

"How come?"

"Must be by choice. Most things are."

You going to get close to me? he wanted to ask. Everything had changed; he felt unsure about what he wanted to do next. He had a knapsack full of cash but he couldn't think of anything to buy.

"How'd it go with your mysterious business?"

"Tell you about that later," he said, trying for a lightness he did not feel. "Right now we're talking food. An old friend invited us to dinner. We're going to stay at her place tonight."

"Her place?"

He shrugged, offered a smile and took her hand. "We were lovers—a long time ago." He held his breath, unable to pre- dict her reaction to plain truth.

"I like a man on speaking terms with former lovers." She gave him a friendly poke in the chest.

"All right," he said, his spirits lifting as if they had both passed some first test, "then you're gonna love me."

Sal answered the door with a cabbage in her hand, her hair now bundled up on top of her head, golden wisps lit with rainbows curling around her ears. "I don't believe it," she squealed. "You actually came back." When she saw Lee she stumbled momentarily but recovered, introducing herself and shooting a glance at Yoder that seemed a reprimand.

She led them into the living room and Yoder felt momentarily lost. It looked like the rec room where he'd copped his first kiss in junior high school: a freestanding formica bar, an aqua vinyl couch, blond trapezoidal end tables and an incredible collection of ugly lamps made from angular steel tubing. Since he'd been here in February, Sal had chucked all their old furniture. "It started when I found the lamps in a junk shop," Sal explained. "Before I knew it, I'd created a nightmare out of my childhood."

"I love it," Lee gushed. "Very retro."

"Very what?" Yoder asked.

"Never mind, Yoder," Sal said. "It's beyond you. What's important is that it was all incredibly cheap."

Jerry looked like his photograph, only taller. Rosy-cheeked with thinning hair and a full beard, his booming voice seemed designed to let Yoder know who was in charge. Jerry began referring to Lee as "Little Lee," a nickname aggravated by the hint of a Southern accent in his voice. The third time he did it, while handing Lee a beer, Yoder glanced at Sal and was met with a wince and a shrug that made all love suspect. She knew. Knew this man, this family she'd run toward, was a compromise. That one look was enough to reassure him that the level of their own relationship would remain intact, off the scale, enshrined somewhere.

Jerry leaned back expansively in a frayed butterfly chair, pulling Sal down into his lap and patting her stomach proprietarily. "I hear you did some time in Canada," he said.

"Canada's a beautiful country," Yoder conceded, hoping to bore the impending conversation to death.

"Then why did you come back?"

"Darling, he didn't *want* to go in the first place." Sal stroked Jerry's back as if calming a dog. "It was horrible for him. He couldn't work there and ..."

"Don't tell me how tough he had it," Jerry snapped.

"...missing everyone back here," she finished weakly.

Out of the corner of his eye, Yoder saw Lee rise out of her chair. "So what kind of music do you play, Jerry?" he asked quickly. "I used to work the bars around here a bit."

"Sally mentioned that."

"I didn't know you lived in Canada." Lee stood beside him, arms crossed over her chest.

"Hell, this man's a Sixties hero," Jerry boomed. "He wasn't about to let them scalp him." Jerry rubbed his shiny head. "Mine never grew back. Sally thinks I should sue the Army."

So old Jer was a vet. Sal's living room was the last place he expected to run into one. Time to start telling people that he'd spent the years between 1968 and 1973 in a hospital bed, paralyzed with amnesia and indifference.

"What else don't I know about you?" Lee gave him a wink, a social one to hide the seriousness of the question. One he decided to ignore.

"Lots, believe me. Isn't that what this is all about?" he said, grateful to see Sal waving them over to the table.

She brought out a steaming platter of whole wheat spaghetti crowned with chunks of slimy tofu. "The soup turned out just awful," she said with a shrug. Sal sat next to Lee and tried to direct the conversation toward her, but even she could not keep Jerry from saying his piece. Yoder was accustomed to extreme reticence from vets. It was a silence he understood. But Jerry seemed to be one of those people who talked on buses and in elevators, who talked to keep the feelings away. The only thing working in Yoder's favor was that Jerry was a sucker, of the school that ate spaghetti by slurping the strands from plate to mouth. This made it difficult for him to talk, but not impossible.

"Where I came from we didn't have draft lawyers," Jerry was saying. "Just chicken farms and a hell of a desire to get out of town. I was one of those guys who got the shivers when J.F.K. talked about what you could do for your country." He'd heard this before, back in New Jersey, between commercials. "When he got wasted, I thought, man, we can't let those barbarians get to us like this."

Lee stared at Jerry, her fork frozen in midair. She'd been eleven years old in '66, sixteen when Yoder left the country. She had just missed it.

"So where were you when you heard about Kennedy, Jer?" Sal was playing Hostess, trying to be diverting. "I remember feeling happy because my civics test was cancelled. Isn't that typical?"

"Were you drafted?" Lee asked, her attention like a beam of light on Jerry.

"Enlisted. No question in my mind where I belonged."

"Jerry was mostly in Saigon," Sal said, her eyes on her plate.

"I was gonna show them what America was made of. Eighteen and I didn't know squat."

"You don't meet many people who were actually there," Lee said quietly.

"Most guys don't talk about it. What I can't stand is not talking about it."

"I understand that." Lee looked around the table for support. "I get that way, myself. Just talking sometimes helps."

"Pass the bread," Yoder interrupted. Don't encourage him, he thought. He shifted in his chair, unaccustomed to the bulge of his wallet in his back pocket.

"I knew some incredible guys over there." Jerry's beard dripped spaghetti sauce. Teach the man to eat, Yoder thought. "Unfortunately, I got real good at writing letters to other people's mothers."

Any minute now Jerry was going to start in about how it would have been all right if America had just been allowed to win. About how everybody who wasn't for them was against them. The phone rang and Yoder jumped, mumbling "I'll get it." Sal pushed him gently back into his chair. "Yoder, it's my phone. I'll answer it." While Jerry talked on, Yoder played with the pile of tofu he'd corralled into one corner of his plate, watching the soft larva worm their way up between the tines of his fork.

"Someday, after the big shots are dead," Jerry was saying, "the truth will come out."

"Who cares," Yoder said, almost without intending to speak. The truth is exactly what won't come out. It doesn't apply. It doesn't matter.

Sal slipped back into the room, her lips pursed as if she had something to say. But she turned her attention to Jerry, like a wife who feels her husband needs the approval of her complete attention.

"Who *cares?* A hell of a lot of guys made of better stuff than you or I—that's who cares." Jerry seemed to be measuring his anger. "You know pal, I don't know how you people did it. I couldn't have split knowing I might never see the folks I cared about again." Jerry devoured a piece of bread, littering his beard with crumbs. Bastard. Sal hanging on every word. "Follow me? Never run these rivers. Never eat a dog at Tiger Stadium." Jerry put his arm around Sal. "Never look into these blue eyes. That's what would have stopped me."

How much did Jerry know? "I tried not to think about that too much," he said, not pointing out that the same risk lay behind Jerry's decision. He looked at Sal, her arms crossed over her chest, her mouth set against him. She still took it personally, still believed he'd run from her. He wanted no part of an argument but before he walked out of Sal's life, he wanted her to know the truth.

"I don't think men should be made to kill other men," Yoder said, remembering the calm anesthetic sense of well-being that had propelled him down the sidewalk after bringing Crock to his knees. The sun was on the edge of sinking, burning itself out through the living room window. Sal looked sweet and bloated. "But, I was in love at the time..." They'd fought that last summer, watched too much television from their sweaty bed on the floor. Neither wanted to do the dishes. Sal had been reading about astral projection and spent hours in the dark trying to leave her body. "...so I'm not sure that I did the right thing."

Sal gave him a small private smile. "That was Crock on the phone," she said. "He's coming over."

"He's what?"

"He's coming over."

Her whisper made him raise his voice. "Did you tell him I was here?"

"Yes, that's why he's coming over. Isn't that all right?"

"No. It's not, dammit. Come on, Lee." Yoder pushed out of his chair.

"What's the matter?" Lee was looking from Sally to Jerry and back for an explanation.

"You got a problem?" Jerry barked.

"Never mind. We just have to go. Right now."

Lee seemed in no hurry to move. Wasn't he making it plain enough? When she started thanking Sal for dinner, apologizing and rolling her eyes, he could stand it no longer and pulled her toward the door. "Later, Sal," he yelled over his shoulder, feeling as if he did indeed have a child on his hands. Maybe you needed to look down the throat of a gun, or face two hundred cops in riot gear to know what "move" really meant.

Outside in the dusky light, the streetlights popping on all down the avenue, Lee shook free. "Why are you running?" she demanded. He kept going down the driveway, calling back to her, wishing he'd explained everything. "Trust me, OK? I'm in trouble."

He saw that she had stopped still in the driveway. He stomped his feet and waved his arms. "Come on." Though the spaghetti lay heavy in his stomach and he knew he was not getting through to her, he could not stop. Money was involved and he was the one who had it. Crock was the one with the gun. He trusted that Lee would get her legs back and kept running. Crossing the street and shooting down the block, his boots pounded against the slushy pavement until he heard the sound of car tires squealing as they do only in desperation.

He turned in time to see Lee's body bouncing off the hood of a black car with no lights. She flew through the air like a rag doll, her arms wings, her back arched as if someone had tied piano wire around her middle and was tugging on her from above.

His thoughts were selfish for an instant—don't take her—then he felt the threat to her private and only life which set his body trembling. Everything in him willed her to land on the grass, to miss the hard edge of the curb, the bone-crushing pavement. Telekinesis it was called—time to find out if he had it. The world flipped the way it did on acid—became alien—everything shimmered like a heat mirage—colors stretched to their limit—no sound. The illusion was momentarily gone, like photographs that show how you really look when you're drunk, or mummies who refuse to speak no matter how long you stand over them, asking.

Lee landed in a clump beneath an elm tree on the boule-

vard. Across the street in seconds, he tried to make sense of
her body. Saying her name over and over, uncertain whether
he was saying it out loud. She was conscious and she was not
bleeding, at least not on the surface. "I'm all right," he heard
her insist and knew she was the real authority but for the
first time in his life he wanted someone wearing a uniform to
say it also.

From the corner of his eye he registered Sal coming to the
door and disappearing and knew an ambulance would be on
the way. Lee lay on her side, one knee drawn up to her chest,
the other so crooked he didn't want to ask about it. Struggling out of his jacket, he felt unsure where it should go—
over her chest, over her leg, under the leg? Where was the
goddamn ambulance? He heard, then saw, a woman whose
hair was hidden under a paisley scarf kneel down beside him.
"She came out of nowhere," the woman said. "Thank god I
wasn't speeding. I'm a careful driver. I hope to god she's all
right. Is she all right?"

In what he considered a superhuman act of restraint,
Yoder told the woman to go inside and check on the ambulance. He did not scream: "You should have had your lights
on, you idiot," the way he wanted to, remembering the truck
driver with Tundra's body in his arms, looking like his truck
had been borrowed to do some awful deed that he couldn't
comprehend.

Lee was quiet, staring straight ahead the way people do
when they see the line drawn firmly in front of them for the
first time. Vacant, as if listening to a voice explain the rules:
Line's invisible. Can be thrown in your path at any moment.
Hiding won't help. We've got cancer and fires and planes
dropping out of the sky to take care of that. Praying might
help; we aren't going to say for sure. He'd made that line
dance for him, change colors, multiply like streamers.
Though he'd wanted to die, he'd succeeded only in destroy-
ing his will to die. It left him a prisoner, unable to use the
escape clause, waiting like everyone else for the snake to
spring from nowhere, wrap itself around his throat and drag
him away.

"It was so stupid," Lee said quietly. "I didn't look."

"Don't talk."

"That's the first thing I ever learned, to look both ways."

Look at her now, he thought. She'll never be the same.

The red beat of the ambulance made everything worse, setting off his instinctive desire to run. The flashing light brought crowds, winter coats thrown over nightgowns, dark shapes drawn to the sight of the sacrifice that would keep them safe for the night. God as Dracula, letting blood so the world might sleep. Yoder scanned the crowd for Crock, wanting someone else to blame.

When the ambulance came, he rode with her. When they examined her in the emergency room, he sat beside her not letting go of her hand. When they announced that Lee had broken her leg and wheeled her away, he helped her to hold her own hand and whispered his favorite Dylan love line in her ear. He told Sal and Jerry to go home and he was grateful when they allowed him to wait alone.

A voice announced that visiting hours were over and tired people in loud clothes began streaming toward the elevators. Yoder walked in the opposite direction. At the end of the hall he took the steps down to the next level, walked it, kept winding down. When it looked as if he would overtake a teenager struggling with an I.V., he stopped to gulp water from a drinking fountain. Cowardice tasted sour and thick. On the third floor, he spotted a crowd of people waiting by the elevators and turned a corner to avoid them. Veering to the left he found himself facing a wall of glass. Before him lay ten or twenty infants, each in a little cart lined up against the window. Most slept, hands curled next to their mouths, knuckles the size of pearls. Behind them, shadowy nurses moved in blue light.

They were as alien as rabbits. Each one a different shade of red. Even the two black babies seemed to glow as if each cell were charged and ready. For what? He didn't want them to know about days like this when love hurts and there's blood and fear. He wanted to talk to the babies more than to anyone. How is it? he wanted to ask. What do you dream of? Dark nights on the water, the sound of the heart beating time with the blood? Does one heart whisper to the other all those long months: Listen child, here is what this heart knows. Was that why the infants looked old, sighed deeply?

Years ago, he'd walked into the darkness of Notre Dame expecting beauty, and encountered a presence that seemed to use up all the air and sent him running for the light. That same ecstasy filled his chest now. He heard it in the woods at dusk when fireflies winked their silent song. Ahhhh, he heard them sing, ahhhh. It was the sound on the mountain when Josh walked his land alone, and was not lonely.

Kneeling, he peered at the wrinkled face of one infant who seemed to struggle inside his tight blanket. The baby broke into a scream, setting off a chain of choking cries. There was no point in protecting them. They knew from the start about loneliness and fear. Two days old and wailing like a widow, or a peasant who's lost his village. Some slept, blind. His child would not be one of those. Later that night on the couch on Sal's porch, he dreamt of eyeless salamanders groping among the rocks of a shallow pool, some floating on their backs, their faces genderless as infants.

Frightened by the babies' cries he ran back up four flights of stairs to look in on Lee. The flood of parking lot lights made her sleeping face ghostly pale. Her hair was dark with sweat, plastered in spikes against her neck. He watched for her chest to rise and fall, then left, walking through the loud streets, leaping at headlights glaring around a corner, trying not to despise the music pouring from the bars. The students who laughed along the streets in couples and groups seemed aberrations.

He tried to remember the man who had boarded a train the day before with money on his mind. Now there was a woman asleep in a strange bed, her body broken from the mere knowledge of him. He stopped by a streetlight and turned his wrists to the air, exposing the greyish worms that snaked across them. Do something right, he hissed. Anything at all.

**18**

O N THE PLANE Yoder kept stealing looks at Lee's face
turned toward the window and the clouds erupting below.
Her silence made them strangers. Her hand lay in his like
soap in a dish, unmoved by his apologies, the strokes he
made to follow the curve of her fingers. Though it pained him
to be shut out, he was impressed by her ability to ignore him.
Now and then she spoke without turning from the window,
bursts of unconnected thought like a radio program blasting
through onto another station. "How will I climb onto my
boat? There's only a skinny little ladder."

"I'll carry you. I'll build something," he whispered.

"It seems like a dream—flying through the air. Did you see
me? You seem like a dream."

He spent the morning after the accident handing out
money—to the hospital, the airline, the taxi, stripping down
his fat roll of bills, thinking once in a while of Sam. He wondered if there would be any point in staying past the first
day, past buying Lee groceries, building a ramp for her boat,
repairing the surface damage. Yoder expected punishment
but there was no way to predict its arrival. Instinct told him

to cut his losses. But Lee was not easy to leave. In the hospital, her eyes looked as wide and young as an animal caught in headlights. He hoped she would not be needy for long, but one glimpse of her bloodless face that morning told him that she needed him now.

Sal had convinced him to go. He'd returned to her house after walking late into the night, the streets tugging at memories he resisted like sacrilege. Alone in the apartment, they'd held one another in the old way, forehead to forehead, arms slung around one another's neck. Before sleep had come talk, tears from Sal, and his envy of how easily she found release. He remembered little of the conversation, only Sal's maternal gaze sorting things out for him, urging him not to turn away. Her words had flowed over him, soothing in their cadence, their meaning lost almost immediately. He knew what he wanted to do, and for once he had the money to do it. He would fly Lee home and head out across the water for Vancouver. When the money was gone, he'd drift down toward Mexico—life was cheap there, he'd heard.

Below, the twisted scar of the Rockies slid by. Yoder gulped back a Coors and tried to explain about Crock and the cocaine. Lee listened without turning from the window, wincing when he got to the part about the woman's head hitting the wall. When he was through she said only, "I see," and then, "I forgot who I was. I just ran." He didn't try to explain the suspicious elation, the gratification it brought him to sink his fist into Crock's stomach. Aggression was its own reward. It had a visceral payoff that pacifism could not touch. Stepping in where he did not belong and doing bodily harm had felt good. The implications of that knowledge made him wish he could drift forever in the landscape of the second sky.

At the Seattle airport, he helped Lee to her car—a yellow Volkswagen she called Fever—and was pleased to see her shake her body in a little dance at the sight of it, twisting her leg on the plastic stump that now defined the bottom of her foot. Her whole being had revived when she spotted Seattle looming in the distance, lumpy and green. The sun on the mist turned Puget Sound into a bowl of light. Perhaps she would be all right.

As they sped out of the city, Yoder caught a glimpse of Seattle's huge harbor—white ships, and the cranes and machinery of a major port. Lee did not actually live in Seattle, it turned out. She could not live there, she said, because the islands hovering nearby always made her want to leave. She lived an hour closer to the ocean in a high, windy town at the end of a long forested highway. For most of the drive, they used the radio as a distraction, Lee feigning complete attention to the news and the blur of trees out the window. Yoder kept his foot light on the gas, fighting an urge to rip down the empty road.

Port Townsend lay on a bay off the Strait of Juan de Fuca, named for a Greek sailor fabled to have discovered the waterway to the Pacific. Lee was possessive of such facts about her town, relating them with a civic pride as puzzling as whatever caused people to boast about a football team. Wide enough to give the illusion of an empty horizon, the Strait was crowded with islands, the nearest one just forty minutes away by boat. But as far as Lee was concerned, she lived at the edge of the world.

She insisted that he drive through the broad sunny streets terracing the hill which overlooked the harbor, while she pointed out the houses of people she knew as if Mr. Bruback or Millie Barnes were names that meant something to him. Most were clapboard monstrosities cluttered with Victorian gingerbread, turrets, patterned shingles and wraparound porches, their yards sprawling with rhododendrons. Like the fussy old houses at Cape May on the Jersey shore, they showed evidence of an overzealous restoration—paint wet with color, pots of flowers hanging from every eave. At first glance the town did not seem to suit the woman he'd fallen for on the train. It seemed a Western version of his own home town, polite and insular, though the wind off the water quickened the air, encouraging deep breaths and a feeling of spaciousness. An uncomfortable coincidence—the streets were named for the Presidents here as well—reinforced his feeling of having landed in a mirror image of home. Here, the greats straddled the hill, bisected by those whose names would otherwise never be spoken.

But when they finally made their way down to the water,

Yoder caught a bit of Lee's excitement. A stone breakwater protected the harbor, forming a small inner lake for the motorboats and sailing cruisers clinking and rocking in the sunlight. As Yoder watched them bob in the water, the sun bursting out of a cabin windshield, he felt a sense of recognition, much like when he'd learned to read, when crooked lines had come into focus and he said "A," and knew its meaning. Not deja vu, but a sharp sensation of nostalgia for a past, spent here, where he might have felt at home. A pair of yellow cats lolled in the dock. He heard a flute weave its way around the sound of a power sander, an irregular hammering, and motors coughing back gas. He saw himself sitting on Lee's boat in the evening, his skin tanned and warm, casting notes from his guitar out over the water to make someone tip their head and listen as he listened now, pausing with Lee's suitcase in one hand to help her struggle down the steps.

Scattered among the pleasure boats were what looked like old dead motorboats strung with laundry, their chimneys drifting woodsmoke, and simple cabins rising out of wooden rafts floating on banks of logs. Crowded with morning glories starting up makeshift trellises, firewood, windchimes and rainbow decals plastered on every possible surface, they looked like retirement homes for old hippies. He thought of how happy Sal would be in a spot like this where life took place out-of-doors, on the water, slowly. But it was wrong to be thinking of Sal with Lee on his arm, swinging her white plaster leg forward with a thud, a pause, a thud.

"There it is!" Lee pointed to a wreck of a boat at the end of the dock closest to the breakwater—a true houseboat with a boxy cabin and a real hull curving into the water. "These others are called floating homes," she said. "They don't go anywhere. Of course, neither does mine, but it could."

The boat's swollen hull was a soft pink that Yoder realized was actually a sun and salt-faded red. "The Lee-High" was painted in gold letters across the stern. The name was a tribute to her, she said, and a pun on the name of the college where her father had been expelled for drinking, after which he'd come west, gotten hooked on the sea and started what Lee called a "two-bit" commercial fishing operation.

Lifting Lee onto the boat was not easy, the cast adding

clumsiness as well as weight. Yoder wanted it to be effortless, even romantic, but he couldn't keep from grunting and nearly fell, depositing Lee abruptly on the deck. He expected her boat to resemble the houseboat he'd seen in a Sophia Loren movie—nautical, stripped-down, shipshape. Instead, Lee's place looked more like a set for "Arsenic and Old Lace." A real velvet couch—dotted with doilies like his grand-mother used to make—crowded one side of the narrow cabin. Next to it stood a porcelain lamp with cracked yellow roses twining up the base. Milk glass and painted china vases, rusty chewing tobacco tins and old cracked teapots cluttered the kitchen shelves. A photograph of Lee and a man he presumed to be her father covered the door of the small portable refrigerator. The man had Lee's delicate nose and pale skin, and looked unwilling to relinquish the spotlight to the freckle-faced girl in cowboy boots who sat on his lap.

Lee threw herself onto the couch, placing the back of her hand to her forehead like a heroine in distress. "You like?" she asked.

She obviously did. His neck tightened. "Sure. It's cozy." And hot and close, he thought. "Is there a bathroom?"

"It's back there." She gestured toward shore, missing his innuendo. "Have to use the harbor facilities. There's a shower with plenty of hot water. Except on weekends," she added, more disappointed about this than he. "Let me show you the bed," she said, hobbling across the cabin at terrific speed. But the room tucked into the bow of the boat was empty of everything except decoration. From the ceiling hung a dozen wooden puppets, their strings taut, bringing a knee into a bend or opening a painted jaw. There was a soldier in gold-braided coat and cap, a ballerina, a one-eyed pirate and a sea-hag whose tiny wicker basket spilled dull silver fish. Stuffed animals tumbled out of the corners. The strawberry pink room caused his stomach to twist: A twelve-year-old lived here.

Oblivious, Lee pulled a bed down out of the wall, setting up its metal support with a quick kick from her good leg, throwing herself off balance. A peach and green patchwork quilt lay across the unmade bed. All the women he cared about loved patchwork quilts. He thought of lying on the hay under Ruth's quilt of blue stars. The house would be framed in by now, the birds coming back.

They slept like children that night, bundled in the lumpy bed, the boat rocking just enough for comfort, unlike the train whose speed kept sleep at bay. Lee wanted his arms around her and nothing more, so he took the blanket in his teeth and bit down hard. He woke once, and in the light of the full moon, he caught the yellow-eyed bear staring.

Yoder left the next morning before Lee had even tossed in her sleep. He returned with wood and nails, groceries and the mail, and set to work building a ramp from the dock to the stern of the Lee-High. Lee lay inside on the couch in an over-sized chenille robe with fat roses trailing down the front, scattering the mail around her, reading aloud now and then from circulars. A long mid-morning silence turned out to be a nap, for which he was grateful. That meant she couldn't watch him floundering as he tried to build the little bridge he'd envisioned to get her on and off the boat without his help.

The sun on his back came and went, a coastal wind speeding clouds across the sky. He loved wind over water; it woke him, the ocean scent carried in the air like bait. The boats docked next to the Lee-High seemed to be pleasure craft and so he passed the day in solitude, removed from contact with the other residents. He hoped the occasional knot of tourists, talking loudly and wandering the docks as if attending an exhibit, would think the boat his own.

As he bent to sand the siderails smooth, Lee called out to him. Twenty Questions: What did he like for breakfast? What did he know about fishing? Did he cook, do plumbing or own jogging shoes? Had he been to Woodstock? Had he been too wasted? He answered her questions honestly since he could not guess what she wanted to hear. As he ran the sandpaper, cupped in his hand like a catcher's mitt, back and forth across the cheap pine rail, he told Lee that he preferred showers to baths, meat to vegetables, Willie Nelson to The Eagles, making love outdoors to anything.

"Do you like parties?"

"Only if I can dance."

"Kids?"

He hesitated. "Kids are great."

"I'm too selfish for kids," she said. "What three places would you like to visit in the next ten years?"

Yoder put down his hammer and tried to call up images of alluring destinations. Morocco? Haiti? New Orleans? At the moment the idea of having to go anywhere at all frightened him. "I pass."

The finished project looked humble, endearingly crude, he decided. Sloping up from the dock, the ramp was hinged to accommodate the boat's gentle rocking. Skeptical at first, Lee thumped across it again and again, like a kid with a new trick. Silently he thanked Josh for teaching him to see possibilities in wood and nails.

When they ducked inside and sat together on the high-backed couch for the first time all day, the sun had just slipped away. "One more question," Lee said.

"Then it's my turn."

"Will you stay until my cast comes off? Will you stay with me that long?"

"I'm used to living alone," he hedged.

"But I'm not sure I can manage alone. Remember, you offered to marry me."

Her smile. "Does this mean I passed the interview?"

"Part One," she said, moving closer to him on the couch. "Part Two is more, well, more hands-on, shall we say."

The next morning Yoder walked Water Street from the harbor all the way to Point Hudson—a spit of sand on the other end of town just beyond the transient docks. The town seemed to lean out toward the water. The big sky offered no shelter. No restraint. He had a spring in his step, as if something lifted the air, moving him ever so slightly forward. Men smiled, let their hair fall about their shoulders. He glimpsed a woman, tan and barefoot, her blonde hair tied in a bandanna, leaning out of the cool interior of a Volkswagen van, and felt perhaps he'd only been asleep all these years.

Along the row of red brick warehouses and shops, he heard Dylan's voice slipping out a doorway and felt safe, as if among his own tribe. Briefly and fully happy. He strained to catch the harmonica riff, strained for the lyric, but only the voice remained. His was one of the few voices Yoder liked to hear outdoors. It did not offend the trees or overpower the crickets. Only Dylan could sing the word *you* into an accusation and a caress, just short of crooning, a harmonica sound.

As a kid, drawn to the fancy houses on the hill, he'd looked in the windows on night walks and seen men and women shouting and the blue indictment of television in every room. Life was life, he'd decided, no matter where you lived it. But here, surrounded by people who had chosen the quiet of the water, life had a chance to shine. He saw a town at work, but not too hard. A bumper sticker: "I break for hallucinations." A bald eagle's nest, and a Tree of Heaven—right downtown, growing out of a retaining wall, overlooking a parking lot where the sound of a saxophone could be heard in the morning. When he returned he told Lee he would stay, his decision tinged with obligation, the comfort of the water rocking beneath them, and hope.

Entering another's life as a lover meant learning to appreciate the loved one's smallest obsessions. Watching Lee perform simple tasks kept Yoder busy for days. She never untied a shoe; talked in whispers outside on the boat deck; put salt on her cantaloupe, catsup on her eggs; sang little ditties— snatches of camp songs and radio jingles—without warning; kept her clothes in a cardboard box; saved glass jars, twist ties and paper bags; thought indoor green plants were wimpy; remembered nothing about her grandmother but a pair of silver hairclips shaped like feathers, and wanted to be famous so she could meet Bette Davis. What Yoder liked most was the way she shrugged off life. It was ridiculous to her in some deep way. She made faces at it and went on adding teapots to her collection.

Was she or was she not beautiful? Women who loved him were beautiful. Anyone's palm on his cheek in that intimate way. Anyone's eyes up close. There was, in the beginning of love, a tendency for the loved one to fill up his vision, to overpower any room. Watching T.V. in early love was ludicrous. Even music shrunk before the skin, the eyes that knew him, the stunning presence of another human being who had opened to him. With Lee on the couch drinking coffee, her words lapping over him, it was as if he sat before a white flower the size of a circus tent. She took up all the space.

She was beautiful in the morning, waking clean and soft-ened. "Hold me," she would say, and he could not understand how she rose and managed her life without him, so childish and needy were her mornings. He imagined her coming to life suddenly while behind the counter at the store, scaring customers with a laugh, her movements quickening, the talk pouring from her, charming them completely.

Yoder took to stroking the scar that hugged the corner of her mouth, telling her it looked like the bridge he'd built, stretching from one lip to the other. It was good to be touched in the places that hurt, she said. Only those who loved you could do that. She told him that she loved him nearly every day—sometimes a whisper, once a shout. It seemed like breathing—her loving, and it seemed she loved him no better than anything else. When she did something domestic—like fold towels with snapping precision—he was fascinated, relieved, on his way to being bored with her.

A few days a week, Yoder hung around the store to help Lee write prices on the piles of junk. He got a kick out of charging a dollar for a Monopoly game missing Boardwalk, Marvin Gardens and both dice. Normally he avoided stores because they brought out his greed, but in Lee's store he felt immune. The tobacco-stained shirts, toothpick holders shaped like cows, electric Saran-Wrap dispensers with crooked metal teeth, plastic roses, and the shoes—bins of them without partners, chewed-up and smelling of stale peanuts—only saddened him. After a few hours in her store, the world seemed full of greedy children, opening presents on Christmas morning and smashing them before dinner, always wanting more.

When Yoder visited Lee at work, he understood why her boat looked like an explosion in a Salvation Army store. As proprietor of the town's thrift shop, she was allowed first pick of the discards. She seemed most attracted to the relics of the Ozzie and Harriet era, a sort of insistent cheeriness created by pastels and animal likenesses worked into every-thing. "Look at this teapot—only one chip!" she'd say when she brought her box of junk home at the end of each week. She started bringing home clothes for him—vests, wide silk neckties, a pinstriped shirt and a pair of red suspenders—an outfit she called a "Forks tuxedo." He'd need it for the Fourth of July, she told him. He started wearing it right away.

She seemed to take pleasure in building a heritage out of a stranger's discarded past. The puppets, she claimed, were a gift from her grandmother, though he suspected instead an impressive find at the store. "Daddy didn't leave me anything but the boat," she said one morning as they sorted through a box of Lazy Susans and fondue pots. "He didn't think about that when he set that fire. My whole childhood got fried. My Beatrix Potter books, my grandmother's shawl from England, my first drawing—you should have seen it—a salmon. I drew a salmon. So what are you? Romanian or something?"

"Thorian," he mumbled.

She squinted at him. She squinted a lot—probably one of those women who would go blind needing glasses.

"Never mind. A little of everything. Nothing."

Silent Russians, stoic Finns, a rumor of French aristocracy —everything watered down to nothing. In Yoder's childhood vision of heaven, a grey line of people ranged across the sky. As he moved down the line, great-uncles and tattered ancestors, standing silently in order of arrival, raised a hand, nodded, but Yoder could never tell if they actually signaled to him. Lee's love of chipped teacups and faded photographs of some other family's reunion seemed an optimistic version of his own rootless sprawl.

As he unpacked a load of galoshes, Lee called him to the front of the store. A handsome kid, lost in a suit jacket several sizes too big, leaned against the counter. "This is Wesley Dexter," Lee said, elbowing the kid and clowning. "We just call him Dex."

Yoder nodded and looked at the floor.

"He's a mill rat, but he plays piano. And he's a songwriter like you, Yoder."

The kid never took his eyes off Lee. *Friend* was such a lying little word, meaningless without a context. Yoder guessed that Dex had it bad for Lee.

"You two should get together sometime," Lee went on. "Dex knows everybody in the music scene around here. Don't you, Dex?" Yoder couldn't read the meaning behind Lee's big sister act. They'd spent the past three weeks virtually alone. This was a new equation.

"Lee tells me you opened for the Turtles, or somebody, once," Dex said, his eyes eager, willing to be impressed.

Why had he lied? So she'd know he was serious about music, believe he'd been around? "Some guys I knew did a gig with them," he said. Lee opened her mouth to protest.

"You ever meet, like, Dr. John?" Dex pressed, not about to be dissuaded by the truth.

"I don't know anybody famous." Yoder reached for Lee's hand, relieved when she offered it without hesitation.

"He's magic at the keys." Dex hunched over an invisible piano, pounding out notes, a Dr. John smirk—like the Cheshire Cat on acid—on his face. "But mostly I'm into Keith Jarrett. You heard of him? The guy's galactic. You had any of your songs recorded? I'm working on one called 'Fear of Disco.' The idea is that pretty soon you'll go to a concert and see like, robots, playing the mechano-music they're trying to put over on us. You know what I mean?"

It wasn't exactly overthrowing the military-industrial complex but at least the kid was angry. "I do," he said. "I do know what you mean."

At work again in the back of the store, Yoder re-folded sweaters he'd folded that morning so he could eavesdrop on their conversation. Lee had dropped her voice but Dex spoke recklessly, as if they were alone. "So, how come we don't see you at Lobo's anymore?" he asked. Lee mumbled something. "Bruce is back in town," Dex said. "We've been jamming. You should come and sing with us sometime."

"Maybe I will," Lee said.

"Heard anything from Andy?"

"No," Lee said, "Nothing."

"Friend of my brother's thought he saw him. He was hiking in Olympic and he saw this guy trapping. Said he looked just like Andy, only with a beard, I guess."

Yoder watched Lee lean over the counter, whispering to Dex, her forehead wrinkled with urgency. Was Andy the guy who'd preceded him on the boat? The guy who'd left a pair of boots in the back of the closet, and the books on gun collecting and aviation? They had traded love stories, but Yoder hadn't mentioned Julie or his enduring attachment to Sal. No doubt Lee had held back on the recent past as well.

"Tell your brother to give me a call at the store," Lee said as Dex swung out the door, his shoulders huge in the coat. Yoder slipped on a wool sweater emblazoned with green ducks. Too ugly, he thought. Just too ugly. Time to hit a real store, spend some money on clothes.

Soon he was doing all the cooking. Lee survived on chow mein noodles, cold rice, peanut butter and grapefruit juice. But she loved his meals and he loved to watch her eat. Ungraceful as a laborer, her jaw moved decisively; her eyes rarely left her plate. She acknowledged his conversation with polite nods, but it became a challenge to distract her from a meal. When he introduced her to feta cheese, her delight was so great that he knew in this way, if no other, he would be in her life always.

The first time she watched him cook she applauded a clumsy omelet flip and he realized how easy she would be to impress. "That's nothing," he said. "I learned to do that when I was just a kid."

"About my age?"

"Hey, I was barely in high school. I got the work ethic early but I lost it just as fast." He told her about being a malter at a diner on the Jersey shore. "The head cook was a drunk. Nice old guy—guzzled gin out of an army canteen. He taught me everything: How to water down malts, fix a grilled cheese that's seen too much grill." He explained that cooking was the only job he could get in Canada—bars, joints, Chinese places, truck stops. "Vegetarian places don't pay much, but they'd always hire me because I look like one of them. Eventually they'd drive me crazy with their tofu and their Indian music."

Lee's omelet had disappeared. "When Sally brought out that awful spaghetti with the tofu I thought I'd be sick. And I was so hungry."

"You can never be sure what's going to come out of Sal's

kitchen." He thought of the baby in Sal's belly—something in the oven, his mother always said. Lately, everywhere he looked he saw pregnant women. On his walks, it seemed half the women he met strode along the street leading with their bellies, tank tops stretched over basketballs.

As the days melted into June, Yoder rarely needed shoes, rarely wore anything but a pair of cut-off jeans Lee brought him from the store. The fog that snaked up the Strait dissipated a bit earlier each morning and the sun shone hot as he'd dreamed it in winter. He began to fish off the end of the dock, most mornings accompanied by a retired woman named Betti-with-an-i. Boredom was the main thing you needed to understand about fishing, Betti told him. And for that reason, fishing was good practice for growing old. She taught him how to fillet a flounder in under five minutes and they developed a grudging friendship of necessity.

The first Sunday in June, Yoder sat on the dock making circles in the water with his feet and watching a cormorant on the breakwater dry its wings. Lee had told him that the Chinese once fished with the birds, placing a ring around their throats to keep them from swallowing. The thought of those tasty fish being plucked again and again from the bird's throat had put Yoder in sympathy with the cormorant. He'd been up at dawn, admiring a cracked sunrise sky, engorged with veins of pink and gold. The marina had smelled pleasantly of gasoline; he'd listened to the metronome of pulleys clinking against masts, and thought perhaps Ruth was right, perhaps life was beautiful.

He felt Lee's arm encircle his shoulder and he smiled up at her without opening his eyes. She squeezed his chest and her nipples hardened beneath her thin shirt. The cool plaster of her cast pressed into his thigh. "I love the smell of your body," she said, her face burrowing into his neck.

"Sorry, but I can't do anything about it."

"No, no, I really do. It's sort of nutty. If I was blind I could find you anywhere."

Her smells were of shampoo and sex. After they had laid in the sun, her skin smelled like sheets dried in the wind. Yoder grabbed her good leg. "Remember I told you that you looked like a girl I knew in high school—the girl who had a horse and somehow it made me think she was experienced. Have you met anyone who looked like me?"

Lee bent her head around to study him. "Certainly not," she said.

"I read a story once and the idea of it was that everyone has a twin somewhere in the universe. I always liked that idea."

"Sounds boring."

"I even made up a planet called Thor and told people that's where I came from." A planet covered with trees—catalpa in flower, sycamore, oak—the trees of his childhood. Just like the doomed planet in *The Little Prince*, but instead of being suffocated by baobab, Thor was sweet with trees.

"I thought you liked being alone." Lee dropped her voice, and eyes. This coyness when she needed reassurance was the youngest thing about her. "I thought you'd be getting itchy by now, cramped in this little cabin with me. When I get this damn thing off, we'll go camping."

"I don't believe in camping with a tent," he said, rubbing his hand across her back. "Sleep under the stars or stay home."

"So, you believe in an afterlife and you want to take a buddy with you."

"No."

"I think you do." She stretched and threw her arms back over her head. "Let's get a burger tonight, maybe go to Lobo's. I don't feel like cooking do you?"

"No, I don't. Do you?"

"No. Do you?" She said, slapping his shoulder.

"Do you?" he laughed.

"No, do you?"

"Do you?"

"Do you?"

"Do you?"

The accident, and his part in it, were never mentioned, though Lee's cast was always a weight between them. She refused to use a crutch. "You are my crutch," she said, and he did not like it. One night she awoke screaming, and in her thrashing kicked Yoder hard in the jaw. She claimed no memory of the dream but Yoder noticed her watching whenever he rubbed the sore place.

"**D**ROP THAT DOUGH," she said. "I've got news."

Lee stood watching him spin a pizza crust off his fingers. Her belief in his ability to cook had propelled him to the brink of culinary disaster. He hushed her, needing to concentrate. The crust was too thin; it wobbled out of shape with each spin. She thumped up and down the cabin, impatient with his show. Her black sundress revealed her early tan and the pale freckles she'd collected across her shouders. Tight in the bodice and flouncy on the bottom, the dress covered her cast so her halting walk seemed awkward and spastic. He made her wait just a moment longer than necessary, relishing the attention, then set the limp oblong failure on the counter and turned to listen, holding his hands in the air before him, like a surgeon awaiting gloves.

"I've got an engagement, as they say." She curtsied, pulling her dress out to the side. "I'm going to sing at P.T.'s harvest festival—first weekend in August. For pay!" Lee punched him in the arm.

"What? Singing country?"

"Singing blues. It's just a big party—a big excuse to party.

I'm nervous already. I think I'll get a band together. Bruce and Dex, maybe. And," she had him by the shoulders, "I'm going to sing one of your songs."

Lee didn't wait for him to respond but went off in a little fit of excitement, rattling on with words that weren't as important as the feelings behind them. She was like the sun on the water; she could dazzle anybody. His heart felt big, stretched by learning to make her happiness his own. Lee deserved to be on stage, not for her voice, which was strong though unremarkable, but for the earnest way she wanted to be there.

He reached for her, moving his floury hands over her black dress, the powder flying off in the air behind her like ocean spray. She hummed the theme song from "Hogan's Heroes," and ran her tongue along his gums. Soon they were dancing. The dress would come off, the pizza would wait, they would toss together in their careful passion, a style of love-making they were perfecting, defined by the stiff grey deadness of Lee's left leg. He could make love to a woman who could only move one side of her body but he could not write her a song to sing, not in a month. He hadn't written a word since he'd crossed the border. But this was no time for honesty.

He began to spend a part of each afternoon sitting out on the boat deck, legs propped up on the railing, his notebook limp in his hand. Staring out across the breakwater, focusing on something until it disappeared, he approached catatonia but looked deep in thought. Words floated before his eyes, at times loud and insistent. A chant: *Elbow, elbow, elbow. Magenta, magenta.* He wrote them in his notebook and they drifted across the pages, in places as interesting as bad poetry, but mostly they did not add up. Canada lay just across the Strait. He imagined he could see it across the breakwater: A big empty country where Humphrey wasn't dying of cancer while Nixon spilled his guts on T.V. A quiet country where men weren't shooting women in cars. A country where nothing was expected of him.

On days when Lee closed the store early and came thumping down the dock in early afternoon, Yoder found himself cursing her silently. He never felt so glad to see anyone but there was always a shift. It was never as peaceful as his mornings alone with the windchimes and the unmade bed and the rocking on the water. Sometimes he feared he'd fallen more in love with the boat than with Lee, though he knew that the longing of mid-afternoon could not be satisfied by wood and paint and nails.

He called her The Stump and chronicled her exploits up and down the Pacific Coast in little stories he wrote while he was supposed to be writing songs. Sometimes he delivered the stories to the store or hid them on the boat, making her take the lid off all the teapots and peer into all the jars to find them. Lee began calling him The Hump in retaliation, for the stooped way he moved down the dock. "Like an orangoutang in the zoo," she said. Soon after, he stopped writing the stories, called her Lee and put an end to the cartoon couple they'd created out of themselves.

When Lee's band started to rehearse, she pressed him for the lyrics, the music, anything she could take back to them.

"Can you hum it for me?" She'd been watching him "work" for half an hour; he wanted to push her overboard.

"I don't hum."

"What's it about?"

"That would be giving it away." He clutched his notebook to his chest. In case Lee should try to check his progress, he hid the notebook in a different place in the boat each night. She would find doodles, drafts of Stump stories, letters, little rhymes and chord progressions, but there were no songs.

"Is it about me? Let me see," she teased, grabbing for the notebook.

He let his voice rise into a shout.

"All right. You don't have to yell," she said. "Jesus, Yoder, everyone in the marina can hear you."

"Then let them hear this: You're the hotshot around here. Write your own damn song. And the rest of you—stop throwing your goddamn garbage in the water. It makes me sick."

When he wrote about love these days, his images were of loss, of love as loss. He wrote: *Bodies joined. Hearts bound with string. My mind reconsiders everything.* And: *I sprout*

*wings, eat seeds of light, try my backspins, cut the night. Glide
along and be my breeze. Heavy flight's the end of me.* He finally
resorted to showing Lee some obscure Dylan lyrics which she
thought had promise.

Walking into town each morning, Yoder watched the Whidbey Island ferry pull into the city dock at the foot of Water
Street—a white spot becoming a ship with apparent magic.
He watched the cars roll down the ramp and away, watched
foot passengers carrying blankets and portable radios
saunter on and off. Twice daily a ferry left for Vancouver.
He'd stared into the water too long from a boat that never
moved. He wanted to be out in it, wanted a glimpse of ocean.
He pocketed a ferry schedule, but to Lee he proposed only
that they make the short trip to Whidbey Island. Lee looked
at him without speaking, as if waiting for him to come to his
senses.
     "Daddy's there," she said flatly. "I mean, his cabin was
there. It's where he died, Yoder." She seemed irritated that he
didn't know the details of something she refused to talk
about.
     "Then, I'd like to see it," he said, feeling a little like an
older brother who knows what's best.
     "You really ought to see the island," she allowed, softening.
"We could have a picnic at Deception Pass."
     There was a bit of the tour guide in her; he'd sensed a
similar tendency in others who lived here. Shopkeepers volunteered lengthy histories of their storefronts. While she
waited for a fish to bite, Betti confided century-old gossip as
if it still scandalized "certain elements" of the town. Yoder
feigned an interest in the view from the Pass and Lee reluctantly agreed to go.
     The battleship hull of the old ferryboat flattened the waves
so the crossing felt like a bus ride. Lee worked at being
cheerful, primarily by remaining in constant motion—pacing the wide deck, leaning out over the water, clowning. Her
hair flamed in the sun. Yoder hung back whenever he could,
to get a look at her from a distance. Out in the breeze, moving across the water, he could make her into the mysterious
woman on the train, so strange and distant he'd forgotten to

be shy. On the houseboat, with everything so close, he couldn't see it.

It still pained him to look at her cast, dirty now, wearing away at the toe, so he led her away from the railing, inside to an ugly little booth by a window. Hot and still, the cabin had an abandoned feeling: Everyone with any class was outside catching some sun. Yoder bought Lee a Coke and plied her with questions about her father. She loved him so well, she couldn't resist telling his stories. Irish, a drinker, a loner, he'd actually run away to join the circus. By the time they docked, he'd convinced her to drive him by the ruins which lay around the west side of the island.

The cabin, or what remained of it, overlooked the island's main road, shielded from the highway by a stand of Douglas firs. On either side the land fell away into farmland, leaving the foundation alone on a small rise. Charred ends of wood, broken glass, fragments of twisted metal—it looked like Detroit after the riots. Lee told him that she'd combed through the remains on the day of the memorial service she held for her father's fishing friends. "I thought I might find his glasses, or his shotgun, but there was nothing," she said as they stood a safe distance away on the sunny roadside. Yoder put his arm around her, feeling as inadequate as a teenager. He couldn't pretend to feel her grief, though a vision of his own father kept intruding on the scene.

Traveling across Canada, he'd prowled through deserted and vandalized cabins, drawn to the scrap of newspaper or the bent spoon that testified to a moment of comfort. He always imagined the owners in a better place. Surely they'd moved on and found a city apartment made of brick or a farmhouse with a fence painted white every spring. Here, the sunlight falling on the blackened wood seemed as callous and final as the sea.

"You OK?" he asked.

"Should I be? Yoder, he was my family. I don't understand suicide. I don't get it."

"We should talk about it sometime."

"Why?"

"Because I do understand it. I do get it."

"No!" she shouted, jumping suddenly in the air and landing hard, her fists clenched and her eyes closed tight.

"Wait a minute, Lee. Calm down. I'm here, aren't I? It was a long time ago."

"But you might feel like that again sometime." Her voice just the other side of panic. "That's how it works. They're called repeaters. Daddy was one."

He took her hands and held them tight. "Not me, Lee. I hung a big fat price tag on my life six years ago and it ain't coming off."

And when he said it, he knew it was true.

"I'm going to take a little walk," he said quietly.

"When you lose your father you'll miss him, you really will." She rubbed the top of her head, making her hair stand on end.

He walked away, leaving her alone for what seemed like the right reasons. Though Lee had not spoken of it since, he imagined that as soon as he was out of sight, she had bent and rubbed the cinders between her fingers and felt something. He saw her this way now, slightly bent toward the ground.

Yoder regarded the day Lee's cast would come off with a thorny ambivalence that made it hard for him to prepare a celebration. Though happy for her, and happily rid of that reminder of his culpability, the day marked the end of his commitment to stay. She'd confused him, quietly claiming the space in him left empty by loss. Lee filled that space and carved out more—he had room for Betti-with-an-i; for Tuna, a congenial retriever who lived back behind the post office; room for long mornings alone on a boat that never moved.

Lee suggested that they spend the day at the zoo in Portland, but zoos made him nervous. The primates pacing left him wondering what it meant to be human. He wanted to see the ocean, see whether it made the Atlantic look like dirty dishwater as Lee claimed. And he wanted to drive through Olympic National Park to see the rain forest—the only one in the northern hemisphere. He'd read of the giant firs and spruces, mutated by water into spectral beings, triumphant, dazzling and green. Lee agreed to show him her favorite beach, just around the bend of the country near a town called Neah.

Yoder gathered weeds from the field behind the dump, filling all the vases and teapots with Queen Anne's Lace, grasses and Black-Eyed Susan. The boat looked like a prairie. Feeling calmly domesticated, he loaded Fever with blankets and beer. Day At The Beach: A scene that lived in memory; Ma, Dad, Sam and their dog Salty; peanut butter sandwiches, beach balls and something pitiful about his father's white chest and his mother's bruised thighs; the sun always a little too bright. But like so many things in this time with Lee, the sense of archetype comforted him; the routine excited him. Whenever he did something normal, he felt happy.

Lee was waiting when he pulled up to the clinic with a wilted bouquet. She limped down the sidewalk, her leg pale and rubbery like canned asparagus. "They asked me if I wanted to keep the cast," she said. "Can you imagine?"

Fever crawled behind logging trucks up Highway 101, past a crescent-shaped mountain lake, literally to the end of the country. At the general store in Neah they walked down a bumpy trail of stones and tree roots the size of fists to a lookout high above Cape Flattery. "You can't go any further west in America," Lee announced. Her sense of drama was nearly as well-developed as his own. But moments and places that demanded obligatory emotion made him itchy. His interest lay in the drama that might unfold between them on the beach. "They gave this place the right name," she said. "It looks beautiful, but the boats that believe it, sink right to the bottom."

"I'll keep that in mind," Yoder said.

A bit further down the coast they pulled Fever into the bushes by the roadside and followed a makeshift trail through the woods towards the sound of the Pacific. Impatient with her slow tender steps, Yoder pushed ahead, suddenly unable to wait another moment, even for Lee. He felt the strain of being close to the end of a journey, a sudden exhaustion coupled with a burst of energy that pushed him toward arrival. Once he hit the coast, he'd have come as far as it was possible to go in America. He could give up and lay spread-eagled in the sand.

A first glimpse of ocean, below a rise of dune or a parting of the forest, carries such joy and calamity in it that Yoder thought surely it was memory—a distant unconscious remembrance of birth, of emergence into light and roar and earthly beauty. The Pacific had eluded him for years. He'd never glimpsed it from American shores, though he'd walked the beaches near Vancouver. There he'd found the ocean cold and flat—a steady presence without power to inspire.

Here, he felt joy. After taking in a breath, he ran to it. His legs pushed across the grey sand toward the water. The sunlight skidded over the waves, a careless scattering of brilliance that testified to god in the world. He let the water slam against his legs, foaming up cold and stinging. When he turned and opened his arms to Lee, he saw his pleasure mirrored in her face. He felt aware of how beautiful they were on this beach—how anyone would think so—his skin dark, her hair holding light.

Lee was right; this ocean was wild. Huge rock promontories shot out of the water just offshore, one large enough to support a row of pines. Whole tree trunks, bleached white and resembling bones, lay piled at one end of the beach. Madroños lined the cliff like dancers and lovers, their smooth limbs bending into gestures so human he could never feel lonely in their presence. They walked the beach, back and forth, again and again, neither wanting to be still, charged with an energy almost sexual in its drive and resistance to completion. Yoder skipped sand dollars across the waves. Lee bobbed for rocks, examining each chosen one closely before discarding it. Another small relief; she was not a hoarder of marine memorabilia—a habit that could become annoying so close to the ocean. They poked at the strange stringy bits of flotsam littering the shore and carved out hieroglyphs in the wet sand. It was entirely possible, he realized, that before the end of day they would build a sand castle.

He loved her for bringing him here, for being skinny and red-haired, with a face like a fairy from a children's book. He loved her, or the ocean, or her boat, or the slanting western light on the red bricks on Water Street—or something. He

loved something in this world this day and it felt clean. No
need to balance this love against the cruel heart of things. He
caught himself thinking: Someday we'll walk this beach and
say: We were young here. The thought had the authority of
prophecy. He embraced the commitment it implied. And saw
his mother holding him—his small body straining against
snowsuit, boots and scarves—holding him just one moment
too long whenever he wanted to leave.

He was afraid to let Lee out of his sight. He imagined the
waves claiming her in a decisive sweep, tossing her onto the
rocks, her eyes forced toward the sky, her neck at a crazy
angle. Worse, he feared that the water might take her while
his back was turned, without a ripple, leaving a clear horizon
and an empty beach. But Lee was an excellent swimmer.
Yoder reminded himself that he was the one without stamina
in deep water.

Watching Lee in the ocean was to fall in love with all
women and their capacity for abandon. He'd never known a
woman so at home in her body. Moving without fear into the
surf, she dove in a high arch, emerging slick and powerful as
a dolphin. She swam laps against the waves, finally stretching out on her back to float so quietly it seemed like prayer.
She needed no partner and that made him want a part of
whatever lit her face in the ocean.

They shed their clothes and lay at the water's edge, letting
the surf slam into them. Lee's new leg began to redden. Yoder
tried to find a pattern in the waves, counting the intervals
and keeping track of the direction of approach, but could de-
cipher none. He licked the salt from her earlobes, and told
her he wanted to live beside the ocean so they could always
make love tasting salt.

"Where'd you get this scar?" She traced the gash on his leg.

"In the war." He thought of the cartoon from the war years
—Johnson's stomach marred by a scar in the shape of the
country of Vietnam.

"Molotaw cocktail?"

"Molotov," he corrected her, batting her hand away. The
scar still tingled when touched, or mentioned. "After V. Molotov—World War II Russian guy. What makes you think that?"

"I know you radical Sixties types," she teased.

"No. You don't," he said with as much authority as he could. "There never was any type."

"Oh, right, I forgot," she said. "You were all individuals, digging each other's uniqueness." Lee rolled over and lay on her back, closing her eyes to the sun.

"Spare me the Sixties," she'd said once, and it had wounded him more than he cared to admit. He knew what she meant; he felt the same way about The Depression. His parents had used it against him, implying that if he was a truly worthwhile human being, he'd have been alive then. As soon as Lee had learned that he'd not been to Woodstock, had not marched on Washington, did not know any big-name rock stars, she'd stopped listening. The reality of slogging one's way through those times in ignorance and naivete was worse than boring.

"So how come you didn't just go to jail?" Eyes closed, she reached out to pull his hand into hers.

Surprised by her question, he sat up to consider an answer. As far as he could tell, Lee thought him neither a hero nor a coward. It was all just dusty history and it didn't matter. "It wasn't like checking into a motel, Lee."

"That's what my brother was going to do."

"Your brother? I didn't know you had a brother."

"You don't know a lot of things."

"I wish I could tell you about those days," he said, turning to face the ocean. There was a pattern to the waves, he was certain, he just could not read it. "There's practically no way to do it without lying." Lee's eyes were closed but she had a smart-ass smirk on her face. She nodded vigorously in agreement. Fuck you, he thought. "We used to play this game when we were stoned. We'd mix cornstarch and water into this mush, and at a certain point the surface tension became variable—a solid one moment, and a liquid the next. The whole time is like that for me. I think I've got something solid in my hands and then it runs right through my fingers."

He threw pebbles at the waves, breaking their crest. In her indifference, he saw the horrible way the generations deny one another. "I know I sound like a folksinger, but I hate it when people say we were irresponsible. We were responsible toward a *new* world. Some of us. Not me, but people I knew. Everyone was trying to imagine—sometimes, hallucinate—a new world. Because this one wasn't right—and it still is not right. Someday it's going to rot out from under us—just like your boat."

"The boat's fine."

"It never goes anywhere, Lee. It would crumble out there."

"Just leave the boat out of this."

"It isn't even a boat, really."

Lee put her hand on his knee. "Are you happy here with me?"

"I told you never to ask me that."

"I'm asking." All the laughter was gone from her voice.

"I am," he said.

"Then stay," she said. "Stay another six weeks. Stay." She took his hand and held on to it.

They were getting up together in the morning and eating off one another's plates in restaurants and reading aloud from *Mrs. Brewster's Last Love* and the other strange old books she kept on the boat. Life was more complicated than this. She would want part of his life and in return she would give him part of hers. Perhaps they should just keep their own lives and make the best of it.

"I'll think it over," he said, brushing his hand across his forehead.

"Thanks tremendously."

"No, I will. I'm taking this very seriously. Just one question: Who's Andy?" The way her eyes flickered out over the ocean told him he'd evoked a ghost. "Those are his boots in the closet, right? Look, Lee, I've got people in my past who I can't quite let go. I think we should talk about it."

"So talk."

"All right," he said. "It's no big deal, but Sal, well, she's more than an old friend."

"I knew that."

"No, I mean, we were serious. I still love her in that way you'll always love some people." He wondered if she was old enough to appreciate this, and if someday this would be how she would think of him. "I'd understand if you have someone like that in your life." To a point, he thought, only to a point.

"Anything else I should know as long as we're playing Truth or Dare?"

"There was a woman in Canada. Mostly she was my good friend. She had a son who really liked me, for some reason." On the verge of telling her about Ruth, he hesitated. How close they'd come, body and soul, in the barn. The intensity of that night still plagued him. What had felt right, was actually so wrong. He wasn't sure anymore why it was so wrong. He decided to hold back this one ghost. "Your turn," he said, his arm tightening around her shoulder.

"Andy's my brother." A victorious little laugh, one he decided not to hold against her.

"What happened to him?"

"Beats me. He's not dead, but it's like he's dead. And even if I knew where he was, I don't think I'd want to see him."

"What did he do to you?"

"It's what he didn't do. He'd been staying on the boat with me after Daddy died and then this spring he just disappeared. I had a terrible year, Yoder, until I met you. I just want to forget about it." She lay back and thrust her feet toward him—one pink, one pasty white. "Sometimes it makes me get so clingy around you I'm afraid I'll drive you away. It's not like me."

"Keep in mind, I've never left anyone first."

"Neither have I," she said.

"Then it's a showdown."

She was quiet a moment. "You left Sally."

"No, I did not," he said firmly. "I left the country. She could have come with me."

"Sorry. None of my business."

"Jesus, revisionists everywhere. I hate it when she says I left her."

"I said the same thing to Andy." She hesitated. "He's about your age, you know. When he went in the service, they cut off all his hair."

"Drafted?"

"I guess. I wasn't paying much attention in those days. I knew there was a war and I knew Andy didn't want to go. When he told me he was going to Vietnam, I had to look it up

on the map. After he came home and started working for
Daddy again things got really bad. He was drinking. Doping.
Forgetting things. Daddy said it wasn't safe to have Andy on
the boat, so he let him go. Daddy just went crazy after Andy
came back. He just...oh, forget it. We're at the beach—give
me another sandwich."

Yoder handed her a second peanut butter and marmalade
on rye. She opened the sandwich and layered it with potato
chips. It was so nice to be with a woman for whom food
wasn't a religious issue. Yoder thought of Ricky and his careful routine with bagels.

"So where do you think your brother went?"

"I don't have a clue. Somebody's always thinking they've
seen him but I never get any word. I don't care that much.
I'm pretty mad at him. I think he's why my dad set the fire. I
really do." Yoder flinched; he could not dispel the notion that
he was somehow responsible for his own father's decline.
"But I wish I knew if Andy was all right. He could be dead,
too. Then I'd be all alone, wouldn't I?"

Yoder lay down in the sand, taking her in his arms. The
rush of the waves was a comfort, pierced by the gulls spinning overhead and calling. Eyes closed, he saw Lee, like a
series of snapshots: Holding out a rock for his inspection;
naked in the water; diving and tossing spray from her hair;
eating a peanut butter sandwich as if her life depended on it.

It was the kind of day designed to work and it left the part
of him that stood back and watched feeling wary. Nothing he
could put his finger on. Just a vague distrust of happiness, an
awareness that there is always a price. Already he'd lined up
lies for Lee's big night. He wanted to be able to tell her the
truth about her singing but knew he'd use the lie of omission
if he needed it, knew he'd soften it all with the lie of love.
Could one be both sad and in love? Could love, not the loss of
it, but love itself make one sad? Could happiness make one
sad? In any event, happiness depended upon ignoring everything except what was making you happy. He was used to
looking for the deception behind the happiness but this time
he decided to try to let it fly. He pushed the sand with his
heels until he made two deep trenches. Then, he buried his
feet.

---

*Someday you might want to know why. I can't give you an honest answer. Love's involved, but not in the way you might normally think (although I have no idea how you normally do anything). Love, and death too. I didn't die once when I wanted to die, and a second time when everybody else thought I should. I lived—but not forever. Life was two up on me; I owed.*

*Love and death then, and something else that I hope you learn sooner than I. Being responsible—a grown-up—means more than making money. It means being able to respond. To your own true feelings. To the world you were born in. To life. Some people will say I was a coward, but a very wise woman once told me that there's a kind of courage in loving. And that, my dear unknowable one, is the truth.*

---

**20**

WHEN HE WOKE, he knew it was Monday because Lee
was gone. Yoder lay still, an undercurrent of panic pinning
him to the lumpy bed as if he lay deep in the weeds smelling
bear. Something terrible would happen unless Lee came
home to sit beside him. The soldier and the sea-hag spun in
slow circles over his head. The Queen Anne's Lace had
dropped flowerheads on the floor like snow, and the yellow
petals of the Black-Eyed Susan had shriveled to a brittle
paper. He let the boat rock him down. It needed a thorough
cleaning, but he didn't feel up to the job; it wasn't his boat
after all.

His project for the morning was to dismantle the ramp. He
set about hacking it apart with a mounting reluctance. He
hadn't taken shop in high school, had no footstools or nesting
endtables of which to be proud. This ramp was it, unless he
counted the rabbit hutch he'd pounded together for Jamie or
the entire goddamn floor of Josh's house. The sky had been
clear for three days. It was the kind of day just asking to be
killed hanging out on a boardwalk: Sand between your toes
and the smell of Coppertone; hustlers, and women whose

bodies took unbelievable curves right before your eyes. Sabretts. The Midway. Here, if he climbed the hill or walked into town, at best he could look into the quiet deep of the Strait. From Lee's boat, he couldn't see a thing.

Not until the little bridge had been reduced to a pile of lumber and bent nails on the dock did Yoder realize that, without it, he felt stranded. The houseboat seemed miles away. He hadn't learned to make the little jump from dock to boat. Not that he couldn't—but he didn't want to *have* to jump. All weekend Lee had stared at him, mouth slightly open, waiting for his answer. Patient—as one is patient with a stutterer. She said nothing, but he felt the weight. Looking at the splintered boards and bent nails, he realized that he should have left the ramp in place. Now he had no claim to the boat, and there were no visiting rights for inanimate objects.

A family of ducks, whose spring brood looked nearly ready to fly away, bobbed by in search of scraps. Yoder fed them whole wheat nut bread, glancing up between tosses at the sailboat that had been anchored off the end of the breakwater for the past few days. Painted the blue of the sky and water, he imagined the boat would disappear altogether on the horizon. Its owner, a bald, deeply tanned man who looked about 60 years old, did even less than Yoder did in a day. Yoder had watched him sleep in a yellow hammock; eat watermelon, spitting the seeds over the side in what looked like a private contest; fish; read dozens of books at one time, piling stacks in a circle around him on the deck; and play harmonica, badly, in the evening.

After a nap that lasted longer than he intended, Yoder assumed his position on the front deck, guitar in hand, notebook by his side. He wanted to try to write about the beach—about the coarse grey sand and the graveyard of bones; the beautiful way the waves abandoned themselves on the rocks. About how he couldn't stop looking at Lee's pale leg. He wanted to write about loving her. The ferry blew the four o'clock whistle—a fog-horn bellow nearly as evocative to him now as the sound of a train in the dark. Yoder put his feet up on the railing, closed his eyes and saw Lee alone by the roadside as he walked away from her that day on the island. She managed a remarkable happiness that seemed authentic. Why couldn't he put that into words? Whenever he tried to write about happiness he grew restless, pushing the notebook aside, overcome by a desire for sleep.

He picked out a tune, feeling heroic and ancient as always, looking down at the strings as if cradling a child. A melodic line developed. He moved it along, trying to use speed to lift the tune out of sadness. He heard something between and beyond the chords. He had it. Had it. Just out of reach. His fingers moved along the strings, liquid and sure. The guitar became an instrument—like a divining rod or a metal detector. He was using it to find what lurked at the edge of the notes. Feeling became physical became music. The cry of a harmonica reached him and he smiled, thinking of how Dylan had learned to sing the sound of the harp, and then he realized he'd been joined by the man across the water. Yoder tipped his chair upright, put his feet firmly on the deck and played fast and steady, pausing to let the old man carry a solo, then charging ahead as he caught a whiff of a new direction, his fingers racing against the strings, which had not been so good to him since the sessions with Josh on the mountain.

They finished in a running crescendo and Yoder let out a whoop, waving his hat at his new partner. "Play me one," he shouted. The man began a whining blues cry. The blues was a guilty pleasure, like comforting another man's lady. The cause of the heartache nearly worth the pleasure of the cure. The old guy cupped the harp in his hands and bent over double, letting the music batter his body about, pulling the notes out long. Yoder stood and gave him a two-finger rock concert whistle.

The man bowed slightly from the waist and motioned to him, tracing a path in the air that indicated he should walk down the dock to a rowboat lashed to the piling. Yoder grabbed his hat, pulled the door closed, and ran. The houseboat diminished as he rowed away from the dock and he felt the relief of open water. He saw that the man on the sailboat was not bald, but had white hair cut so short his scalp had tanned beneath it. Standing at the stern with his hands on his hips, he wore navy blue boxer shorts and a smile. His face was a mask of wrinkles, pouches, and intersecting white lines where the skin did not tan. Jimmy Buffet thirty years from now.

"Good go," the man said, catching the rope one-handed and tying it to the stern with practiced ease. The sailboat looked to be in perfect shape, the wood trim highly polished and the ropes on deck coiled like sleeping snakes. "The name's Joe." He extended his hand to help Yoder up the ladder. "Beer?"

They had been out of beer since the beach. He was drinking it too quickly or they both were. Buy a case tonight, he thought. "Sure," he said, swinging himself on board. "I'm Yoder."

"What kind of name is that, now?"

He shrugged. "Never got a real explanation." Never asked for one, he realized. By the time he was old enough to care, he'd stopped asking his parents anything personal. Deep in his orphan phase, he'd missed his chance to be filled in on all kinds of things: What his grandfather did for a living; when his ancestors came to this country—from exactly where, exactly when. Did his mother nurse him; did she walk the floor? She'd said once that he was a sleepy baby but he didn't know how to take that.

"Good enough. So is it a woman then?"

Confused, Yoder didn't answer, offering instead a tight, cautious smile.

"You were playing the blues," Joe went on. "That usually means some kind of woman trouble."

"I was? I thought I was playing a love song."

"Wouldn't be the first time that love gave someone the blues." Joe's glassy round-the-block-and-back eyes testified to the life of unencumbered self-indulgence to which Yoder had once aspired. That life included a fondness for the Loved-Her-And-I'm-Leavin' blues. The tune born in Yoder that afternoon was profoundly lacking in that kind of drama. It was not, as he'd discovered, the kind of love that inspires a good song lyric. It was better.

"Think what you want, but I'm not needing the blues right now."

"Suit yourself. So, where'd you learn to play guitar like that?"

Yoder could not meet his eye. Joe reminded him of someone; his questions implied a judgment; his eyes searched out what was hidden. "I'm barely any good," he said, examining the chrome on a set of winches.

"Depends on why you're playing, I suppose. I thought you were first-rate."

Something broke inside him, a wall crumbling, a few bricks slipping and sending up dust. "Thanks," he said, shifting his weight, his hands finding their way into the back pockets of his jeans. Joe ducked below deck and Yoder let himself smile out at the late afternoon sun turning the water to silver. First-rate. A stretch—but if the old guy liked his music they might play more together. It felt good to play off a fearless—if unreliable—harmonica line.

"I see you out there quite a bit," Joe shouted up from below deck. "You permanent?"

"I've been here a few months. The boat belongs to a friend of mine." He hadn't been able to say girlfriend since he was twelve. Lover sounded good only in the movies. "She's permanent."

Who did Joe look like? The tender, paranoid part of his heart feared the worst. Whenever he felt this sense of dim recognition, he imagined the suspect would turn out to be someone he'd pissed off in a parking lot, a guy whose fancy mailbox he'd blown up, the dog catcher who'd kidnapped Blue, and found that his mail had been mysteriously forwarded to Tucson.

Joe returned with two bottles of Mexican Tecate. "It's a nice little harbor," he said, dismissing it neatly. "Came up from Monterey last week, myself. Heading on toward Alaska. I like the idea of Alaska. Know what I mean?"

"No. I don't."

"Good. Then you can stay a while. Have a seat, Yoder."

Joe's idea of Alaska, it turned out, was nothing more than The Last Frontier. Yoder had heard that said about so many places, from North Dakota to outer space, that he wondered why the idea that men had done it all had ever gotten started. "Eighty percent of the prison population is Eskimo. Think about that if you don't believe it's the Wild West." Joe talked on about an oil pipeline that would create boomtowns all along the Alaskan coastline. "Now, a person can stand to live in a boomtown because you know it'll blow itself up before you get sick of it. In the meantime there are plenty of bars, women and cards. You go in for bars, women and cards?"

"Some. But I like this boat of yours a lot better." From his seat at the stern, he could see the entire marina, and the Lee-High looking half-sunk, way down at the end. He felt a faint thrill at the prospect of watching Lee make her way down the dock to discover him gone. He tried always to be home for Lee; she said it made her day to know he'd be there to listen to her stories and sift through her box of junk.

"Yeah, she's a good old boat, but you're young," Joe continued. "Go to Alaska, I'm telling you. Sign on for a year or two and you'll make more money than you can spend in twenty."

It took him a moment to pull his thoughts back from shore. "If I want to be cold, I'll go to Canada," he said, tipping his head back to let the beer pour through him. "Besides, I've had it with those kind of schemes."

"Drugs, you mean."

Yoder studied the man closely. There was someone else in his life this emphatic, this invasive.

"Greed got in on a good thing pretty quick," Joe continued, as if Yoder had concurred. "Don't look at me like I'm some kid. Drugs have always been provided. You're a musician, you should know that. What do you think they were growing in the Garden of Eden? Any paradise worth the price of admission is gonna have something for the pain. Myself, I've got a little something set aside for that last trip out. If it turns out I have to hallucinate my own heaven—which I suspect will be the case—I'll be equipped."

"You mean acid?" he asked, not certain he wanted to hear the answer.

He nodded. "Do it once a year on New Year's Eve. Get my priorities straight. You?"

"Not in a long time." He'd assumed acid was something you eventually gave up. That there came a point when you didn't want to know any more. First his mother, than this guy. Everyone over 60 had suddenly gotten so hip. "You ever do MDA?"

"Heard about it," Joe said as if they were discussing late-model cars. "Heard it makes you love Richard Nixon, freeways, mosquitoes, everything. I don't need that much love in my life but from the looks of those wrists of yours, I'd guess that you do. Ever sail on a boat like this?"

"Nope. Not on any boat."

"Afraid of the water?"

"Not at all."

"Care to go for a ride? The wind's up. We'll cook ourselves some dinner. You can tell me more about this woman friend of yours. I'll sail."

He said nothing. Joe turned on the engine and Yoder moved over behind the wheel to keep the boat pointed toward shore while Joe raised the sail. As Joe tugged on the rope near the mast, the huge sail billowed out and rose in fits and starts until the wind pushed it to one side and kept it full, a white bowl of air. Yoder felt a moment of hesitation as he often did before he was about to get exactly what he wanted. Joe yanked the sail tight and maneuvered out into the Strait where the spinnakers Yoder had admired from a distance suddenly loomed in on them. He loved it immediately—the wind rippling the canvas, the shiny efficient hardware, the whorl of the coiled rope. Yoder watched Joe's movements with the sails but could not discern the reasons behind them. He seemed to sail absent-mindedly, steering with a foot or a finger on the wheel, his eye on the horizon— a gaze that suddenly seemed the essence of nobility.

The Western sky was the sun's true territory. They sailed away from the setting sun at a fast clip. The water turned seriously blue; the sky opened up like a clamshell. As the marina, the harbor, the town and finally land itself sped away from him and blurred into just a green horizon, Yoder felt the wind fill his body until he was light. He thought of the way Lee's body fell away from him in sleep, how her muscles gave way and she grew heavy in his arms until she was lost to him. The clouds fled in one direction, the water in another. Everything in motion. Only the illusion of the hori-

zon remained firm. Yoder felt his body flirt with the water. It
would be so simple to roll off the deck, to hit the water passive and limp and be carried under the roiling waves without
a fight.

It took forever for the sun to set. The moon rose across the
way in readiness, while the sun grew bigger and rosier, wob-
bling out of shape only at the very end when it dropped like a
hot coal into a well. They ate dinner—a kidney bean and
vegetable concoction Joe had made up by the gallon. Yoder
heated the stew on a little alcohol stove which swung on
hinges with the rocking of the waves. The windows above the
stove looked directly out onto the surface of the water and it
dizzied him to see how violently the boat rose and fell.

He fed Joe the whole story, embellishing out of habit, making the accident bloodier, Crock more threatening, Lee a better singer. He stopped short of telling him about Ruth, afraid
Joe wouldn't understand his refusal. Joe listened without response, as if hearing a familiar tale. Like everyone else, he
seemed most interested in Canada. Yoder didn't know how to
explain that it had been like every other time in his life:
Bleak and cold with a couple of sunny days, great dogs and
kind women in-between.

"I was in the Philippines after Pearl Harbor," Joe mused,
picking his teeth with a fingernail apparently left long for
this purpose. "Grim," he said. "But your war—at least the
version I watched on T.V.—didn't even look that good. When
they're just about issuing dope with your dog tags, I guess
you gotta think twice."

"Thinking twice doesn't sit too well with most people."

"You don't look like a fellow who wastes much time worry-
ing about that. Sounds like it's not sitting too well with you."

"Look, I lost six years. Lost a woman and any chance I had
of getting a job that wouldn't make me feel like a robot." Lost
my dad, he thought. "I was going to do what Kerouac did in
that book. You ever read that book? Sit up on a mountain
somewhere and spot fires."

"Smoky Bear. Sure."

"But I never finished school."

"So go back."

"What I'm finding out is that it's hard to go back." Joe had fixed his eyes on him and they never wavered. "I thought I did the right thing. But now I'm not sure. And when you're not sure what the right thing is, then it's easier just not to think about it. And then you do stupid things, maybe wrong things, and you start losing track of why you're here at all. But if you don't mind, I don't want to hear what you think."

Joe waved this away. "What about this Lee? You say she's in love with you. Do you love her?"

There was an echo in Joe's voice. The word *love her* rang over and over. He had thought he'd loved Susan, had loved Sal. This was different. It didn't have need attached to it. He remembered the way Lee had tipped her head toward the little girl on the train and how it had frightened him.

"How far out are we?"

"You in a hurry?"

"She was expecting me a long time ago."

"To tell you the truth, I was hoping we could head on into Seattle. Take us until around midnight, I'd guess. A buddy of mine lives there. We could play some music. You game?"

He loved this boat in the dark. The huge white sail almost glowing; the sneaky soundless way the bow cut the water; the air thick on his face like terrycloth. "No, I gotta get back."

"You'd like the music. My friend plays sax, congas. We could be back day after tomorrow."

"Maybe another time."

"Won't be another time. Be here now, pal."

Be where? Where did he want to be? Right now he wanted to be exactly here. Exactly on this boat in the dark. But tomorrow, next week? "Can't."

Joe looked annoyed. "I forgot that people have other people to answer to."

"I don't exactly answer to her," Yoder said, irritated by the implication. What was the nature of the connection? Not long ago his body could have washed ashore at Lee's feet and she would have been nothing more than horrified. How did it alter body chemistry so that a name heard years later made your mouth dry? What made it weaken at the center, break into loathing or daily indifference?

"Look, I promised to take a lady friend to dinner on Friday myself. My friend's a first-rate jazzman. First-rate. Let's just do it. We'll radio your friend so she won't worry. What do you say?"

"I say turn the boat around!" A slip in his voice, the panic showing through. He could see the drums set up in the basement apartment. It looked like hell and smelled like reefer. Joe and his friend knew about abandon. The music was hot and sloppy, the music filled in all the empty spaces. "Just take me back to the harbor," he said with resignation, feeling like a dry alcoholic at a party.

Joe shoved the tiller hard away from his body, spinning the boat on its heel until it stopped dead in the water. Wordlessly he started the motor and scrambled toward the bow to lower the sail. Nimble and sure-footed, he stood astride the deck while the boat tossed in the waves. Yoder tried to keep from imagining him pitching off into the black water.

As they motored back toward what now seemed like home, Yoder realized that the conversation was over. He watched Joe steering with both hands on the wheel, his eyes darting between his instruments and the darkness. He felt light-headed from the beer and the strange sensation that he was looking at himself. He made his way toward the front of the boat and lay down on the deck to watch the stars. When he did, he was nearly sick.

The stars appeared close and impossibly present. The boat seemed to be floating in space. In the future he knew he would sense the stars shining in daylight. The blue dust of the afternoon was just a kindness to disguise the fact that he was hurtling toward the stars and they had been there forever. He pounded his chest to get his breath, fearing out of nowhere some doom knitting itself toward him: The ringing of the first traitorous cell gone bad; Lee's sandal slipping on a stair; his father, pausing, short of breath as he lowered into a chair. If God was in the moon, then judgement took place in the stars. The sky was filled with accusations. The constellations re-formed—the dots connecting him to the well of darkness in which he seemed to be moving. The brightest stars had pinned him to the deck, passing through his body and circling the world until he was strung like a bead and could not move, only circle on the beam of starlight, a burning heat on the wound where it entered just below his heart.

"Close your eyes." Joe's voice came from across the water. "Close your eyes." They felt locked open. Like plunging into water, he dove into blackness, holding onto an iron cleat as if it might keep him anchored to the earth. The darkness behind his eyes was full of color but he was not dreaming. He could hear water sloshing against the side of the boat and felt a breeze in his hair.

An image of Joe at the helm, attention focused on something in the distance that Yoder could not understand, grew behind his eyes like a shadow at dusk. They were afloat in a rowboat painted yellow on the inside. The weather was fine and clear. Yoder set down his oars, leaned over the side and looked into his reflection mirrored perfectly in the still water. Someone he recognized but could not place. "Dad?" he called, like he'd called out from the bathroom the night he'd soaked in his own blood.

Someone answered: "Hang on, son."

Yoder was sitting beside his father in the concert hall. The orchestra thundered—horns and percussion—a battle, he thought, or a storm. But his father heard something more. Yoder squirmed in the hard seat and stared. His father's delicate glasses flashed in the light. Yoder searched for clues in his father's thin face, something that might calm his pounding heart when he confronted his own face in the mirror. He saw that the man in the next seat was not his father, but someone separate—mysterious and unreachable. He moved to touch him and the scene dissolved into color.

He saw a small boy sitting cross-legged on the ground surrounded by ferns. Everything a soft and hazy grey, like an old, poorly filmed home movie. The boy leaned into a bowl of fronds. Put his hand out to touch. The boy sat on the ground before a mound of snow. White in the sun. White and clean as the shaved ice in the grocery store. The boy thrust his hands into the ice, and he *was* the boy, the cold burning into his fingers. Out of the ice, with something like delight, he pulled a shining bunch of round red radishes.

The rowboat toddled along behind them like a loyal subject all the way into the harbor. Joe helped Yoder climb down into it, and put the oars in his hands. Still drowsy and confused, Yoder rowed away from the sailboat, slowly and carefully toward shore. The darkness separated into shades of grey; the waves sloshed conversationally. He aimed for the screaming green lights on the breakwater. The wind on his face roused him. "What the hell was in the beans?" he shouted back to the sailboat but Joe had disappeared. Magic mushrooms, he figured. And too late to mutiny.

He crept down the dock, aware of each creaking board, his accordian headache, and the general rumble that marked his progress toward the Lee-High. A few lights shone out from widely scattered boats but he was glad to see that the light was not on in the bedroom of the Lee-High. He was hoping Lee would be asleep, hoping for a few minutes to himself to look through the photo album that lay at the bottom of his knapsack. He wanted to see if there was a picture there—an old black and white of himself as a toddler—out in the backyard by the fence, by the ferns.

In the hallucination he'd been looking over the boy's shoulder from a height, as if from his father's viewpoint as he'd snapped the picture. Yoder felt less certain of the radishes. That vision had been in color, had seemed less remembered than lived, as in a dream. He did not know what to make of the image. If it was not memory, if the boy was not himself, why did he feel so intensely his long moment with the ferns, his happiness over radishes?

He ducked into the cabin and found Lee washing out clothes at the kitchen sink, her hands spattered with purple dye released by a shirt she twisted in her hands. She turned to face him, and he searched for a sign of rebuke. He was reminded of the way Ruthie looked at him that first night, like he was a ghost with dirty feet.

"Been for a ride?"

"How'd you know?"

"Spies." She neither smiled nor glared at him. She looked distracted, as if making conversation while she attended to matters of importance.

"We got so far out there, it was like being nowhere." He watched the purple water swirl down the drain like Easter egg dye. "Sorry."

"For what?"

"For making you worry."

"Who said I worried?"

He put his arm around her shoulder. She fit under his chin like always. Neither had grown in his absence. She smelled of bleach.

"Yoder, I have to talk to you about something."

So this was how it was going to be. No tears, no shouting, just ice. They were going to learn how to fight but she was going to choose the weapons. "What's to talk about? I came back, didn't I? If you're angry that I was gone then we've got problems. Besides, it was out of my control. First I'm on his boat shooting the shit and then we're going for a little ride and then before I know it we're out so far we might as well go to Seattle. We didn't, you know. I made him turn back."

"Interesting technique." He felt the first grain of hate solidify, like the sand particle that invades the oyster. "Apologize first so I don't get to say anything. That doesn't happen to be what I wanted to talk about. Actually, I wanted to apologize to you."

He felt momentarily thrown, stuck way out on a defensive limb where it was hard to back down. "Well, great," he said, smiling broadly. "I accept your apology."

"You haven't heard it yet. I did a terrible thing. You left your notebook lying open on the deck and I read it. I don't have to tell you what I found."

"Stump stories?"

"Why did you lie to me? You know, I really don't care whether you're a songwriter or a postman. What's the point, Yoder?" The soggy purple shirt hit the floor. "What isn't a lie about you?"

He fought an urge to run, find the notebook, see how much she knew. It was fuzzy, what he'd told her. He felt naked and he didn't want to be forgiven.

"I'll tell you something," she said, her voice shaking slightly. "If I ever have children I will not be telling them about Santa Claus. They can believe in animals that talk if they want, or even in imaginary planets, but there will be no wonderful man who comes in the night to bring them their heart's desire."

"Wait a minute. I only made you one promise. And look,"

he spread his arms wide, "I'm still here."

"You said you'd never left anyone first." She jabbed her finger toward him, her hands wet and reddened.

"That's right."

"You said you were writing me a song. No song, Yoder. Just a letter to some chicky saying you've been thinking about her and how maybe you shouldn't have left so suddenly. I imagine you're terrific at leaving suddenly. That's fine. If you're gonna go, I don't want to know about it. Just do me that favor."

"Slow down, Lee. What letter?"

"Ruth—somebody named Ruth."

"I never sent that letter. I was just . . . ."

"Don't explain! I can't stand it if you explain."

"Lee, sit down." She was pacing the tiny cabin with such determination he was forced to get out of her way every few moments. "I'm sorry about the song. Today I . . . ."

"There's a letter in there for me too, isn't there? Where you explain that it's all about love and death. And how people will think you're a coward. I know what that's about. Don't explain that one away. Don't!"

"Lee."

"You can't kill yourself, Yoder. You can't."

"What?"

"I love you. Doesn't that mean anything to anybody?"

Suddenly he understood, and his heart reached for her. She'd read a letter meant for no one, meant for a circling soul who'd been haunting his dreams. A little boy perhaps, who loved radishes. "Lee," he said, "listen to me. I didn't write you a letter. I wrote you a song; it just doesn't have any words."

AT THE FARMHOUSE, Fourth of July had evolved into a kind of bitter victory party. The idea was to have a terrific time at the expense of America, celebrate what they'd left behind and how much it didn't matter. They'd toasted marshmallows and burned Nixon in effigy. One year Georgia had read a short history of war resistance in her earnest, quavering voice while "Masters of War" soared in the background. Walter and Bobby played horseshoes and Yoder pitched a rusty fastball into Jamie's mitt. Another hot July evening, they'd endured a tedious revisionist play about the American Revolution starring Steven as Thomas Jefferson wrapped in an American flag and wearing beads. The message was rejection, but someone always lit a sparkler, snuck a hotdog in town, remembered a parade.

Now it appeared he would spend his first Fourth of July back in America with Lee, and Lee wanted to spend it with her friends. A woman named Cinda had organized an all-American barbeque with a Port Townsend twist. There would be volleyball, beer, chicken and contraband fireworks over the water, but the celebrants would be in costume. The theme was American Heroes, and Lee had decided to go as a cleaning woman.

She prepared him for the party with little capsule histories of the people he would meet: A woman who ran marathons and groomed dogs; a band called Heavy Angels whose members dressed in lamé and claimed Carol Channing as their spiritual leader; a boat builder; an herbal healer; a weaver who believed polyester to be carcinogenic. The convoluted tales of affairs and betrayals reaffirmed his belief that meeting a lover's friends too early in a relationship only served to reveal something you didn't like about the person. Lee's crowd sounded young and aggressively disaffected. He was afraid he'd find himself repeating his mother's all-purpose admonishment: "Keep it up and it just might stick."

At dinner a few days before the Fourth, he tested the water. "How would you feel if I didn't go to this party?" he asked, rolling a salty corncob in the juice of an incredibly tasty local tomato.

"Well, I'd be disappointed," she said. "I'd have a good time anyway, because I like these people. When it comes time to dance, I'd probably dance."

Irresistible, she was, in this mid-summer light. He focused on a bit of corn stuck to her chin. "Good answer," he said. "Then you go and I'll stay. Independence Day."

Something had shifted since the night they'd fought, and talked until daybreak—a radical resettling, like boulders tumbling into a new configuration because a single edge has eroded away. Since he'd revealed his growing intimacy with the child who lived in his dreams, Lee had stared at him more, talked to him less. She had mentioned Ruth's proposal only once in the weeks that followed. Out of nowhere one morning she'd rolled over in bed and placed her head on his chest. "Don't you think it's nice that she wanted you to be the father? I think that's a compliment." He'd asked what brought that to mind and she told him she'd been looking at his collarbone, how he wore it on his body like a necklace. Something had been released in her. She left him more easily, watched him less intently, stopped waiting, he felt, for the answer he couldn't give. When he asked if it would be too cold to spend the winter on the houseboat she told him she was making no plans.

Yoder made Hot Dog Surprise—a bizarre recipe that he found in one of her cast-off cookbooks—for Lee to take to the picnic and felt a tug of jealousy as he watched her walk away with her arm around Cinda. He had no idea how to pass the day, but he knew he wanted to be alone. The boat and the harbor were clearly out. The code of silence had been cancelled; kids and coolers spilled out of the cabins, and old folks set up lawn chairs on the dock.

Yoder closed up the boat and took the keys to Yellow Fever intending to indulge a vague desire to see the ocean again. But before he'd revved into third gear past the high school, he knew where he wanted to be. Sometimes he thought that if he simply followed the trees they would take him everywhere he needed to go: India to see the banyan, Greece for the olives. He'd collect the yellow explosions of mimosa on the Côte d'Azur, hunt the swollen baobab in Africa, taste the fruit of the durian—indescribable, he'd been told, like onions and apricots. Olympic National Forest held the only jungle in North America, and he wanted to be in it.

Crawling up Highway 101 behind pop-top campers, and convertibles full of teenagers, Yoder set his sights on a mountain peak capped in clouds. "Crybaby Mountain," Lee called it. The road appeared to run right into it. A strange oblong cloud of fog hung low over Lake Crescent, visible for miles as the road twisted higher and turned back on itself. The trees opened to reveal meadows and water, then closed in next to the road, cradling him. Fever was a foolish little car, the engine threatening ruin on the steeper climbs, but it felt good to be behind the wheel. He spun a Kerouac fantasy: Drive all night; coffee at a roadside joint—red neon in the rain; sleep under the stars; catch a sunrise and drift his feet through the dew. Mexico. Vancouver. Alaska. Alone in a car for the first time in months, he sang, humming the melody he'd hit on the day he met Joe, when for the first time he seriously considered life without Lee.

After he rounded the curve of the country, the landscape took on a rugged, end-of-the-world look. Aside from abandoned billboards, and trailer homes sunk into the trees, there was no sign of civilization until he hit Forks. To his amazement, men—and a few women—dressed in pinstripes and red suspenders, milled about the main street. Lee had warned him about Fourth of July in this part of the world. Had he worn his tuxedo, the guy at the gas station might have thought he belonged there.

According to Lee, the Hoh River was the best entry into the rain forest. A small sign marked the turnoff a few miles south of Forks. Yoder held his breath in anticipation. But the trees on either side of the gravel road had the shaggy look of a logged forest. Entire slopes had been clear-cut, the sun blasting onto the brown grass. Tree trunks spilled down the hillside like matchsticks. Yoder looked for signs of the red alder. It would be the first tree to return in a clear-cut forest here— a fact pulled from deep memory. He felt a peculiar anger. This was rain forest. And not only was it not raining, there were no big trees. Above him, a clear view of marshmallow clouds. Off to the right, the Hoh River, shallow and moving swiftly, flitted in and out of view. He drove faster.

Twenty miles in, the sky lowered. Douglas firs and hemlock soared two, maybe three hundred feet in the air, straight as masts, their upper branches forming a canopy across the sky. Club moss hung a thick fringe from the shoulders of these trees, further clamping off the light. Rain forest. No mistaking it. It looked as if an ocean had been sucked away, leaving a vast undersea kingdom exposed to the air, everything dripping with seaweed and algae. Traffic piled up behind him.

The road ended abruptly at a parking lot that seemed an affront to the silent authority of the forest. He slammed the car door and walked. Men and women with chubby-legged toddlers milled about, music blared, tents sprouted American flags. Dinner campfires blazed like flares; Yoder could smell wine-soaked chicken broiling, and burgers. Lee and her friends had gathered around picnic tables by now, a little drunk, giddy with friendship. He'd brought an apple and the last beer.

Sixteen miles in from the campground lay the glacial fields of Mt. Olympus—icy blue, he imagined, cold enough to freeze a man's blood. If he walked all night, he'd see a sunrise over ice and snow in July. If it got cold enough, maybe he'd see the gods. He decided to head for something called Happy 4 Shelter, five miles upriver. Mostly he wanted to be away from other hikers and the sounds of celebration.

As soon as he entered the trail, the campground noise receded; the forest became almost perfectly quiet. Around him loomed huge swaybacked firs, the twisted limbs of vine maple, and lacy hemlock overhead on branches way too high. The air felt cool though it seemed as heavy and moist as his intuition of the jungle. He took slow deliberate steps, as if scouting prey, holding his breath in hushed anticipation, his heart sounding loud in his chest. The leaves of the black cottonwood applauded. The names were coming back to him —each paired with a spidery textbook drawing and the facts of shape, texture, seed, leaf. When he first learned the names, the forest had changed for him; he'd felt accompanied. Many trees here were strangers.

He stopped still and listened to the rare silence. An eerie luminescence, like he'd seen only in Walt Disney movies, made the woods seem like one glowing organism. This was some kind of factory of green. Every growing thing growing things. The trunks and branches growing fur; moss and lichen giving the trees an animal shape. When the wind passed through, the forest breathed as a single being. Suddenly he wanted to be in it, striking his own path through the jungle. He wanted to let it close behind him. His mother always said that she needed to be alone in church, so she could hear what was meant just for her.

Up ahead, off the trail to his left, the heaved roots of a Douglas fir made a cave big enough for a man to sleep in. Yoder stepped off the trail into the undergrowth, the forest floor giving way beneath him. Immediately he felt surrounded. A huge tree lay in his path, swathed in mosses, like a dead whale washed ashore. Yoder straddled it and ran his hand across waxy shelf mushrooms the size of endtables. There was columbine and yellow monkey flowers. He heard a peculiar whistle, too perfect and regular to be human. Spinning in place, he tried to detect movement, eyes, but found himself alone. The forest drew him on, as if some destination lay just a few yards further. Now and then he glanced back over his shoulder, spotting landmarks in the green. Each step took him further from the trail. He felt uncertain of the need for caution—this was, after all, a national park. And yet it was the wildness here that propelled him forward.

Surely trees were the oldest living things. He spoke to some of them as he passed, for he felt he had been spoken to. It was like praying, talking to these trees. With no thought for hunger or future or night, he moved through what seemed an endless exhaltation of green. This was an exquisite stage for light. Filtered through the tallest firs and spruce, it bounced off the leaves of the understory forest, was misted by the moss, cut into lace by ferns. The jumble and wreck of the forest floor opened to him, a hidden path revealed one step at a time. The rushing of the Hoh River receded as he pushed further into the thickening forest. "Ho, Ho, Ho Chi Minh," he chanted incongruously. "Viet Cong are Gonna Win." He was lost and he knew it. He was flirting. He didn't give a damn. He kept walking. Some part of him had always wanted to be swallowed up.

As the sun drew back to let night come, the forest began to change. Exhausted light trapped under the arching branches took on an opacity, making him strain to see his way. In the failing light, the forest seemed funereal, the trees suddenly draped in crepe. Yoder paused to listen to the heavy silence, certain he heard the crunch of the forest moving behind him. The dryads are here, he thought—men with the power to inhabit trees. He felt a trill of fear; stopped looking at the details and tried to get a sense of the whole picture. The light falling like a curtain. The forest moving behind him. Some of the oldest trees in the world, just waiting. He'd hoped to reach the campground before dark by curving toward the west and joining up with the trail close to where he'd entered. But he had no reference point in the monotonous trees and found it difficult to define a curve. He was snow-blind in so much green, dizzied, without depth perception.

Estimating that he'd left the trail an hour before, Yoder began counting seconds into minutes, learning an interval he could use to measure time. He couldn't think about what might happen if he didn't find the trail in 60 intervals. No weapon, no matches, no compass. No brains, he thought. He picked up a hefty stick, waving it before him like a machete. Heard the electric insect sound he associated with jungles. He was far from alone. How much he'd romanticized the forest. If put to the test in these woods, he would lose. He longed for the hard lines of town, bars casting a warm light into the street, bodies closing around his in a crowd.

Behind his reasons for going to Canada lurked a terrible loneliness that wanted company. A loneliness so profound it could be soothed only by extremes of itself, the way an addiction demands to be fed. And behind the good reasons and the loneliness was fear. Fear of such a jungle as this, of night loosing danger, of a heat so wet his skin was always cold and of the need to kill, and to rejoice in silence, kill again and rejoice until death and life became inextricably bound. To at last be united with his father and all fathers before him, so saddened by learning to be men that they could not look children in the eye.

He imagined a swamp-creature, stinking of rotted vegetation, sliding slick arms around his body, squeezing. He imagined bear. He imagined that a night spent out here would never end. Propelled by terror, Yoder crashed through forest, needing to run. Out. Flailing his arms, he darted past the enormous dripping trees. Moss brushed against his cheek. Flying squirrels swooped low over his head. *Ho, Ho, Ho Chi Minh,* said the river. The trees slipped into darkness. A branch slashed his cheek. He kept running until he ran straight into a green man with his hands around the throat of a small dead animal.

The man wore Army fatigues and a knit cap covered with leaves. Mud had been applied to his face, very carefully, like clown-white on a mime. His feet were wrapped in cloth, tied with rope at the ankles. Yoder turned to run in the other direction.

"Ain't nothing back that way," the man said, his voice even and friendly.

Yoder backed up a few steps. "I'm already lost." He raised his arms in a gesture of surrender.

"I can see that." The man had loosened his grip on the animal's neck. It was just larger than a cat and definitely dead.

He pulled a piece of chamois from his knapsack and wrapped the little body. "Marmot," he said. "Met his match." Was it his imagination or did the man's lips curve into a smile of pride? "All right now, you want to get back to the campground, right? You're just about a mile northeast, I'd guess. These woods are deceptive. Even when you've been around them like I have."

"You a ranger?" Yoder asked. A foolish hope, but worth a try.

"I'm not wearing a Boy Scout uniform, am I? You got a compass? A flashlight?" The man gave him a look of parental impatience. "It's going to be dark as a deadwagon soon. Follow me. I'll walk you to the trail." With his compass, he set them a course about 30 degrees off to the left. Yoder hung a few steps back, remembering *Deliverance*.

"My name's Gunner," the man said. What kind of a name was that? Swedish? If so, this Swede had black hair pulled back in a ponytail, exactly like his own. "What takes you so far off the trail?"

"The trees," Yoder said weakly. "I couldn't help myself. Once I got in here, they just pulled me right off."

"You can die out here acting like that," Gunner said.

Gunner's pants were held up by a canvas belt from which hung knives, leather pouches, rope and a small ax. On his back he carried a large frame backpack, also green. A box of Triscuits poked out of the top flap.

"You say you like trees?" Gunner said, as if silence hadn't fallen between them. Both watched their feet. Toppled logs seems to rise out of nowhere in the deepening darkness. "Biggest Douglas fir on the planet is over in Queets." Gunner paused to pat a tree whose drooping branches seemed to be weeping. Rain, Yoder realized. It was raining. "Here's a tree with all the time in the world. You know the Sitka?" Gunner asked.

"Sure," Yoder lied. He'd seen it only in books—*P. sitchensis* —and hadn't recognized it here. "I've studied forestry," he said.

Gunner stopped abruptly and turned, his eyes squinted up with interest. "*You* wouldn't be a ranger, now would you?"

Again Yoder held his hands up like a prisoner. For some

reason, in the darkening jungle the gesture came naturally. If he had become a ranger, he wouldn't be here now, shivering in the mist. Wouldn't be lost, his future dependent on the good will of this slow-talking man whose body seemed to disappear into the fabric of the forest. "Nope," he said. "I never finished school."

"Don't play around with me now," Gunner said.

"Really, I'm just a dummy lost in the woods. And I'd appreciate your help," he added quickly.

"Yeah, trees, you can't beat 'em," Gunner said, setting off into the woods again, his compass held straight in front of him. "When the wind blows hard they seem to dig it, like a backrub. When I sleep outside I look for the big old Douglas. Nothing better than the bed they make for you with their old brown needles."

"So, you stay out here sometimes?" The stunning silence of the woods was no longer comfortable. Yoder felt compelled to make conversation, to keep this strangler of small animals talking.

"All the time," Gunner said.

All the time. "What about bears? I heard there's bears out here."

"I've got protection. Besides, I mostly sleep in the day, when they do. Sometimes I hang out at the campgrounds. As long as I'm gone by morning the rangers can't catch me."

Yoder wanted to ask him why. Why would he live out here alone with these spooky mutated trees, but he knew the answer. He felt the same way about highways. What about love, he wanted to ask. Don't you ever fall in love with some camper in a flannel shirt and want to put your arm around her and walk out of here?

Under the canopy of trees, it was fully dark. They walked slowly, picking their way through the underbrush. Coyotes howled, followed by owls, the hissing of wind. Gunner fell silent, hunching slightly forward to read his compass. Yoder heard the river. He found himself squinting to separate darkness from darkness, Gunner's shape from the limbs of the trees. Suddenly they were caught mid-stride in a glare that cut the dark like a flash popping off in an empty room. "Down," Gunner commanded. "Get down." Gunfire rumbled in the distance. Gunner dropped flat to the ground, in one motion like a gymnast. Yoder crouched low beside him, his mouth open to the spectacle in the very distant sky. "Incoming," Gunner said in a hoarse whisper. "Can't see," he said. "Can't see a damn thing. They always come at night."

Looking up through layers of leaves, branches and needles, Yoder picked out bursts of exploding white far above. These could not be bombs or guns, though Yoder realized he might not recognize the sound of a gunblast. Cops, soldiers, hunters and criminals shared that special knowledge. Gunner seemed paralyzed with stillness, all muscles on alert, as primed as a jaguar before the pounce. Gunner motioned with one arm, "Keep low," and Yoder noticed the beautiful gleam of gunmetal in his hand. His eyes, no longer empty, had a hard shine like marbles or petrified wood.

A terrible, terrible mistake had been made. Gunner thrown back to some other time in some other jungle; Yoder unable to offer a more logical explanation. Gunner held his gun cocked in the air before him, his hand jerking with each blast from above. Yoder kept his eye on the gun, too afraid to move out of its range. This was a nightmare he'd brought on himself. How many times had he imagined a jungle, guns, the sky torn with unholy light, and he on his belly, shriveled up with fear? Now it was real, a forest and a crazy man with a gun, the sky torn with unholy light.

Then he remembered: Fourth of July at the campground. Fireworks under the stars, kids and their dads oohing and ahhing, awaiting the finale in the bedazzled sky. It was how we celebrated war, with harmless bombs so beautiful no one thought to fear.

"Gunner," he said, "It's fireworks. It's the Fourth of July, man. It's the fireworks at the campground. We must be close."

"Damn right, we're close, too close, and that ain't no fireworks."

Yoder listened, heard guns—and fireworks. "No, it's fireworks, really. We've just got to go a little further and you'll see."

"I'm not moving. Go if you want to. It's your ass."

The explosions intensified, rapid fire blasts vibrating

through the ground and the air. Gunner held the gun with both hands, aiming into the darkness.

"It's 1977. America," Yoder shouted. "It's safe here."

"It ain't *safe* anywhere," Gunner said.

When he heard Gunner's breath coming in short bursts like a runner at the finish line, he knew it was over. If he lay still, perhaps reality would return like wakefulness after deep sleep. Gunner would orient himself and they would find the normal world waiting for them at the campground. But as the minutes grew long, the silence took on an edge. He wondered if it was foolish to lie beside this crazy vet in the dark. Perhaps Gunner wouldn't remember. Yoder listened to him gasping like a dog in pain and realized with a rush of sympathy that the man beside him was terrified.

Yoder began to talk, softly, as if to himself, letting the words build a bridge in the dark. "I like willows and oak. A stand of old oak makes you believe in fairy tales. I like sycamore—they're grand. They've got those incredible leaves— bigger than my hand, some of them. My sentimental favorite, I suppose, is the catalpa. We had one in our front yard on Seymour Avenue back in New Jersey and it was like snow in June when it dropped its flowers. One year I collected a whole cigar box of them. I figured they must be valuable but they just got brown and shriveled up to nothing. A girl in the neighborhood used to scoop up those white flowers and toss them in the air to float down on us, over and over. Her name was Ronda. Ronda Ratner."

"They always come in the dark," Gunner interrupted, rolling onto his back. "They always come when you aren't ready. Once, I thought I was dead. And then I wasn't."

"Exactly."

"So now I'm always ready." Gunner turned his head to look at Yoder for the first time. "I take it you weren't in 'Nam."

"No, I wasn't," Yoder whispered, hoping Gunner wouldn't hear him or wouldn't care.

"Get lucky with the numbers?"

"No."

"Neither did I," Gunner said. "I drew 64. The Beatles had that song out about 64 back then, remember? I thought that was pretty funny because I never expected to make it to 64."

Suddenly all business, Gunner hopped to his feet. "Still might not if we don't get out of these woods before the cougar catch wind of us." He picked up the rope that had fallen from his belt and wound it back in place. Yoder noticed for the first time that Gunner had a mole on his cheek, right near his mouth. He reached up and touched his own.

"How long were you there?"

"Apparently part of me is still there—I thought you were a friend of mine. You're supposed to be old, in some rocking chair, before you have more dead friends than living ones. I haven't found anybody back here who seems worth the trouble. Friends are trouble, no doubt about that."

Yoder looked up into the trees. This was not like Josh's land where you could live among the trees. This was a place to hide. "I went to Canada," Yoder said. Gunner seemed not to hear him, intent on adjusting his pack. "I ran," he said, putting a little more force behind the words.

Gunner looked at him briefly. "Yeah, well, we were all running pretty fast back then."

"I didn't want to die in a jungle like this."

"It's not like this there," Gunner said quickly.

"I'm sorry." Land mines, land mines. He could hardly talk to a man 25 or older without stepping on one.

"For what?"

"For thinking I know what it was like over there."

"You're right, you don't. You see trees. I see someone behind the trees." Gunner held a low branch aside for him to pass by. "But then I don't know what it was like to sit up there in Canada and be called a criminal. I don't know what it was like to rot in jail. I don't know what it's like to be stinking rich now and guilty. I don't know what it feels like to be twenty years old today and just not get it at all. I don't know how anybody gets along with anybody in this country anymore." There was a light rain falling like a clock ticking. Yoder kept his eyes on the ground, walking in Gunner's footsteps. "If you want to know the truth," Gunner said, a threat of laughter in his voice, "if I'd had any guts I would have deserted. But I couldn't leave my friends. I've never had friends like that in my whole blessed life. I did the only thing that made sense, given who I was back then. Now I just gotta

find a way to live with it." Yoder strained toward the sharply
fallen silence. Just the crush of the forest beneath their heavy
bodies walking. "See, 'cause, I know what I did over there. I
know what I did. No matter what anyone else says or thinks,
I know what I did. It's what you do that counts, not why, or
why not, or what somebody else thinks about it. Your life is
what you do." Yoder remembered the first months away from
home when he'd been uncertain where to draw the line.
What *could* he kill? An ant, a chicken, a celery stick? He'd
had trouble eating, trouble sleeping in grass. "I learned my
job pretty well in 'Nam," Gunner said. "So now I bury small
animals, I spot fires, sometimes I lead lost dummies back to
the path."

The path appeared before them—a grey haze hovering
over an opening in the forest. Gunner stopped at the edge of
the clearing surrounding the trail. "You know the Indian leg-
end about the cedar tree?" he asked without any interest in
the answer. "There was a man who did good deeds all his life,
and when he died, he got turned into the cedar. The Indians
around here, they couldn't have survived without the cedar.
For them it was like the spirit of good men come back to
help." He stood aside to let Yoder pass. "When I die, I'd like
to sink my roots right here in this soil."

"Is there anything I can do?" Yoder said. "You need anything? Money, or . . . ."

Gunner stared at him, as if trying to read his features in
the dark. "You could give me your boots," he said finally. "I
lost mine a few days ago in the river."

Yoder bent down and unlaced his boots, looking at them a
long moment before handing them over. "They're all yours,"
he said. Gunner pulled off his cloth slippers and Yoder
wrapped his feet, tying the rope just tight enough so it hurt.

As he walked away, he thought about what a terrible thing
it was to be lost. Like The Lady and The Tiger—all choices
were wrong because you didn't know what lay behind the
door until it was too late. What mattered was what you did
next. For a long time, future had been a word without meaning. But here in the forest it had a shadowy form, like a boat
that didn't go anywhere, but could. Like a lady in the harbor
that lets you know you're home.

My brother's out there somewhere walking around in Yoder's shoes. I can't get used to that name—Yoder—no matter how long I live with it. I know that Yoder saw Andy in Olympic. Yoder doesn't agree. We went over it and over it. I showed him Andy's high school graduation picture but he didn't see any resemblance.

Andy piloted a helicopter in the war. That explains the name. His letters were full of strange names: Fox and Runner and Blackfoot and Western. Yoder says that he has friends with strange names too: Crock, Goldie, Speed. It seems so Sixties, those nicknames. I just call my friends by their right names, except Dex of course, but who could call him Wesley?

Andy and Yoder are alot alike. I thought of that right away when I met Yoder. They both want to know everything, and when their eyes focus on you, you feel as if you know everything. I've even told Yoder that I love him like a brother. He thinks that means I don't feel enough passion for him. I said: 'You think this is all an act?' What I mean is that I feel related to him—like we have the same blood.

Then there's the part about burying animals. You should have seen Andy with animals. He loved animals almost more than people. I used to tell him he should be a vet. I mentioned that to Yoder and he said: "He is a vet." It was almost a good laugh for us. We didn't laugh much after the Fourth of July. Yoder can turn so quiet and moody. It took him two whole days to tell me about seeing Andy. I said: "Why didn't you wake me up and tell me right away?" He said he wasn't sure he was going to tell me at all. So I go, "It's my brother we're talking about here." And he goes: "We don't know that for sure."

I could feel Yoder pulling away those days right after the Fourth, tucking back into himself, like a diver right before he straightens out and plunges into the water. I knew he was getting ready to leave me—but in that healthy way that people have to separate a little when they love each other as much as

*Yoder and I do. You can't be all bound up together. Both of us were feeling a little suffocated.*

*I didn't know how far the leaving would go. I didn't know how serious it was for him, or that it would be the best thing that could happen for us. I didn't know any of that then. Yoder claims that he did—that he could feel everything shifting, like an earthquake, and that he was glad because he knew when it settled again, we'd be on firm ground.*

LEE CUT HIS hair out on the dock. His fishing buddy came by to watch. "You'll be gettin' a job next, I suppose," Betti grumbled, letting a hank of hair drift off her hands into the water. No point in telling her this was just a trim, that just enough was coming off so that he could not pull it back into a ponytail at the base of his neck. "I'll have the fish to myself, I suppose." She had shuffled off then, the ratty man's sweater tied around her waist dragging on the dock. Maybe some kind of work with trees, he had thought, and the idea took hold with the persistence of a hunger for fried potatoes or the siren call of red wine. When Lee took his hair in her hand, he fought a buzz of panic, just as he had when Ruth had washed his hair a lifetime ago by kerosene light. This time he knew its origin, and with his breath he could beat it back as if extinguishing a slow-spreading grassfire. His hair curled up around his ears now. When he saw himself in a mirror, he looked younger than he'd ever been.

Yoder stared back up the hill at the town blazing with summer. Autumn would be too much—too many sweeps of color—maples and aspen burning themselves out until just the pale tamarack broke the green hills. He knew he might change his mind before nightfall, but at the moment it pleased him to make a plan. He wanted to spend Christmas with his parents. He'd known it since he stood by Lee's side staring into the remains of her father's house. He pictured himself a skinny, bemused Santa, a latter-day saint with a knapsack full of toys for Ricky, and Rita's kid, for Jamie, and for Sal's baby girl.

Lee would go on stage in an hour. When she'd left that morning, wearing a slippery green dress that looked a little cheap in the daylight, she'd been so caught up in the details of her stage-fright that she hadn't noticed his quiet shoving off. He gulped his coffee, dressed quickly in his pinstriped shirt and red suspenders and hurried up the hill.

He got a ride immediately from a sprinkler salesman named Abel. Abel was on his way to Port Angeles; he had a sales call, and a favorite restaurant he wanted to hit for lunch. Abel talked non-stop, like after-hours radio, and Yoder let the words roll over him as the old trees flickered by out the window. Abel talked about his family (four boys), his weight (fluctuating) and his own lawn. "It's green as an Irish heart," he boasted. "Sometimes I take customers to see it. My lawn always makes the sale." Abel smiled benignly the entire ride—except for one frightening moment when he turned to face Yoder, his voice shaking with anger. "You can't just water a lawn when it's turned brown, you know. People don't understand that. You have to water when it's green and healthy. You have to water ALL THE TIME."

The festival was being held at old Fort Worden—a state park where once there had been barracks and tree-house lookout stations, and where a radar dish at the lighthouse still searched the sky for planes over the Pacific. As Yoder climbed over a rise framing a shallow grassy bowl, he felt momentarily dizzied by the spectacle below. Some sort of psychedelic Brigadoon had emerged from the mist, spun out of color, drums and the ubiquitous leaflet. Long-skirted women with braids thick as a fist danced among children painted up in blue stars. Mimes in tuxedos. Movement. A perfectly ordinary man in a clown nose and scuba flippers. Fabric flamed out behind leaping bodies, tambourines flashed from the folds of skirts. An anemic dulcimer tried to hold its own against an unseen saxophone. Congas. Bells. Movement. Bodies flat out in the grass, attendant to the sun.

Like a huge square dance, the scene transformed itself every few moments into a new configuration. Yoder let his feet slip down the hillside, smiling in spite of himself at nearly everyone he passed. As he moved through the crowd, the faces swirled one into the next and he saw Eliot dancing, and Goldie with hair down to his shoulders, Sunshine, Trucker, Jamie and Lila. Saw the Jack of Hearts, The Sad-Eyed Lady, Napoleon in Rags and Louie the King. He began to feel he might disappear altogether into the crowd, become invisible, unable to separate from the men and women for whom he had a sudden sentimental rush of affection. He'd seen them all somewhere before. But not for a long, long time.

Tables had been set up all along the perimeter of the festival and no cause was left uncovered. The Greenpeace seal mooned out from a stack of T-shirts. Rivers, redwoods, and referendums needed saving. Whales were nuked or not. Yoder felt the tug of a saving strand of cynicism and held on tight, remembering what he hated about do-gooders, dues, newsletters, marches and bumper stickers. The strained friendliness of the proselytizer repelled him like a politician's handshake. It looked as if altruism was once again loose on the land, but he knew that the pushers and addicts, wife beaters and lost ones, the liars, cheaters and thieves were simply waiting at home for their better selves to return. Lingering over the literature—slicker now than it used to be—scowling at the attendants, he got his sensibility back.

He bought a falafel and a cup of iced Red Zinger to hold him until he could find the beer tent. With an eye out for Lee, he walked by palmists holding hands, reflexologists rubbing feet. A tendril-haired boy blew soap bubbles past a quilt on the grass where an old man who looked like Mr. Natural threw the I Ching. Hardly anyone wore shoes. When we have a celebration, he thought, this is what we do. Crepe paper streamers shimmied from trees. Women and men danced alone, hands in the air, clapping out the beat, as Dylan's greatest anthem blasting from a set of speakers in a tree,

built to its romantic, irresistible chorus. The dancers shouted
the lyrics into the air, as if the gods could be made to hear.
How does it feel? To ask the question, you had to know the
answer. He turned away, afraid the dancers might link arms,
snake through the crowd carried away with bliss, and that he
might join them.

Further down the circular path, Yoder drew in a breath,
stopped on the slope of the hill and stared. Beneath a banner
emblazoned with the insignia of the Vietnam Veterans of
America, a half-dozen vets stood like a dark wall against the
make-believe pageant whirling along behind them. His first
impulse was to drop his eyes, walk quickly away, as if they
might jump him. A rowdy-looking crew. Not a bare head in
the group: black berets, bandanas, camouflage hats and caps.
Most wore jackets or vests loaded down with medals, badges,
buttons, pins and tiny American flags. No passers-by drifted
over to their table; they seemed separate, a tiny scream in a
quiet room, silence in a crowd. They seemed not to notice.
One who was missing a front tooth shook a pack of Camels in
each man's face and much was made of the tapping, tongue-
ing and lighting of smokes. A fat guy whose hat read "The
few, the proud, the Marines," drew hard on a diet soda and
gestured wildly like a man who could tell a good story. A guy
in full camouflage eased down into a folding chair. Yoder
could see the pink lip of an artificial limb beneath the hem of
his blue jeans.

A man with a face soft and jowly as an infant's rose to tell a
story. The others were ready, slapping his back and calling
out to him. Yoder caught only scattered phrases, their sense
lost in the space that separated him from the men. Quinn the
Eskimo walked by eating a taco; two shrieking sisters linked
arms, intoxicated with their own beauty; a spaced-out kid
muttered along, his eyes glassy with confusion. Yoder
strained toward the veterans, standing closer to the path but
unwilling to risk crossing over. The story seemed to make
them all jumpy. The circle tightened, the card tables piled
with literature momentarily abandoned. He heard many
voices and hard laughter. A man in a wheelchair circled the
group, as if looking for an opening, as if pacing. The button
on his jacket read: *If you haven't been there, shut yer mouth.*

Yoder wished Gunner were here to walk with him up to the circle of men. He wanted only to circle the circle—like the man in the wheelchair. The story took a turn for the worse. The men broke from center in a flinch of memory. Yoder took a step backward and the tears came. The fat one hugged the guy in the wheelchair. Yoder pulled the tears across his face with the back of his hand. His eyes searched the crowd for Lee. Little stages had been set up throughout the festival. He couldn't spot her. He could scarcely see. What was this feeling? Pressure in his chest flooding his eyes. Any moment he would be sobbing. The Marine's eyes were shut tight as if in sudden pain. Something about these men in combat boots and worn-out skin. Toothless saluted the crippled one; a little silver gun pinned to his beret flashed in the sun. Something about friendship, how time moves on. *Unpredictable flashes of himself—showing up somewhere else.* Yoder took a step forward.

He had done what he had done. Had lost more than he could say. He wanted these men to think he had guts and principles both. Not enough principles for jail, he thought. Not enough guts for 'Nam, they would say. It took guts *not* to go, he wanted to tell them. Like them, he'd become a reminder of what everyone just wanted to forget. Gunner seemed to understand. But these back-slapping men whose literature denounced what their fellowship celebrated, couldn't even see him standing so close outside their circle he could hear them breathe, as he stuffed pamphlets into his back pocket, slowly.

With a long look backward, Yoder disappeared into the crowd, hurrying now, hoping Lee's music would lead him to her. The sun seemed stuck in the sky but a slight breeze off the point carried the heat away. So much color. A man with a David Crosby moustache lit into a slice of watermelon, spitting the seeds out as he walked. He heard a banjo, a flute, a rattling of bells as if someone were dancing in ankle bracelets. He passed a woman juggling Campbell soup cans. The apex of Western civilization, Josh had argued long ago, was the week John and Yoko spent in bed feeling up peace. He wanted to see Lee's face, wanted her to recognize him in a crowd, wanted to reflect the light in her eyes right back to her.

On a little joke of a stage beneath the only trees in sight, Lee blew sharp breaths into a microphone, pausing to listen for something no one else could hear. He'd watched so many singers prepare. It tended to make them either bitchy or withdrawn. Lee was acting like a pro. Watching her huddle with the musicians, stride across the stage in her cowboy boots, adjust microphones and levels, he realized how much he didn't know about her. There was probably a lifetime of knowing in some people.

Dex, dressed in another overgrown suit coat, was killing time at the piano. The others looked young and harmless. Yoder wished he had the nerve to be up there with her, wished he were the kind of lover who could come right out and play her song. He moved up as close to the stage as he could bear, hiding just a bit behind a woman's straw hat, uncertain whether he wanted Lee to see him before she began to sing.

Dancers started to materialize about halfway through the first set, swaying like wilting flowers to Lee's throaty blues standards. She dropped her nervous gestures and found her pace. He clapped harder. It didn't matter that he'd heard better singers—C.V., for one, probably the most versatile singer he'd ever known. Lee had conviction and plenty of stage-magic. The make-up and the lights and the aura she assumed simply from being on stage made him marvel that he even knew her.

Passion began with longing—and grew in the imagination. Love grew into compromise; it lacked imagination. He had nothing but admiration for those who could do it. Ruth loved Josh, the best friend there ever was, in that long way. But for the one thing Josh couldn't do. Children, he realized, were the imagination of long love. The light flickered through the trees onto Lee's face. Her voice coaxed "Mocking Bird" to life, and Yoder stood still before the stage while couples swayed around him. Despite the dripping heat and the dancers grabbing the real spotlight and a thousand fantasies circling like gulls behind a tuna boat, there was a thread that stretched from the stage to his heart, a thread that might stretch across time and separation, across a whole continent if need be, and keep them connected like the smile Lee gave him in the middle of the song that found its mark in the crowd.

He made up his mind.

Who was he to say whether or not it's doom alone that counts? That was Dylan's line. Not his.

---

*The first thing I heard was the birds. They do the job of dogs out here—this was before we got Cotton, our shepherd. The jays screech and put up a fuss when someone approaches through the woods. I was picking tomatoes in the garden, thinking we had more than Josh and I could possibly eat. I heard the birds, and then I heard shouts. He came running up the road, waving his arms over his head and calling my name. He startled me. I get so used to the quiet, especially when Josh is on the road with the band; it's just me and the birds and the cottonwoods.*

*For some reason, I was frightened. I ran into the house and put the lock on the door. I don't know what I was thinking. He's so unpredictable, I guess. I've gotten so I don't trust extremes in anyone. Some of that is just Josh talking through me, but I spent enough years in the city to know we are never truly safe with one another.*

*I talked to him through the screen door. He looked like he did the first night I saw him—wild and dirty and frantic, with exhaustion behind it all. I thought: Does this man never change? He asked for Josh. I told him that I was expecting him any time. Then he said the strangest thing. "Ruthie, get your quilt," he said. "Bring it out here in the sun."*

*I walked around the house trying to think, figuring that he was probably broke and needed a place to stay. I decided we could do it again for a while. I was a little bit in love with him, you see, though I couldn't admit it. He listened to me. He wanted to understand every shade of my feelings. He made me dig to come up with how I really felt about fate and front-wheel drive. Back in March when he left the first time, I'd made tea and eggs, waiting for him to stumble downstairs like he always did, sleepy-eyed and looking like a boy. After the food got too cold to eat, it dawned on me that he was either gone or dead. I realized I'd driven him away.*

*I unlocked the door. He was out there in the long grass, stark naked. Here, I hadn't seen him in months and he's out there, naked. I laughed and he heard me—just turned his head, real casual—"Don't laugh," he said. "I'm very sensitive about my body. Bring the quilt." It hit me that he had come back to give me my baby. I ripped the quilt off the bed and ran out into the grass. It was a remarkable day, humming and alive, everything clear. The grass looked like a field of neon. We lay beside one another facing the clouds. A perfect sky. Neither of us said a word.*

*I knew he was waiting for me to make the first move. Suddenly it was a huge thing, as frightening as any time two people confront one another that way. I said: "Are you sure you want to go through with this?" He said. "I'm here, aren't I?" I pulled my sundress off over my head. The breeze felt gorgeous on my skin. I kept wondering why Josh and I had never done this. What's a mountaintop for if not nakedness and lovemaking in the sun?*

*He held me like a brother. I felt tremendously shy and wished I was drunk, but oh, I wanted that baby. He seemed unaware of me, like he was loving the earth. The sun was in my eyes the whole time as if it had focused in on us for those few minutes. Our love-making was full of feeling, but not for one another. I caught a glimpse of his face and his eyes locked open, like an animal, frightened or in pain. Afterwards, he held me like I like to be held.*

*He left that same afternoon. We ate and walked. He talked about a woman out near Seattle, and asked me how close we were to the border. We haven't heard from him since. I don't worry about him.*

## ABOUT THE AUTHOR

PATRICIA WEAVER FRANCISCO was born in Detroit and was graduated from the University of Michigan. Her fiction and essays have appeared in *Great River Review, Milkwood Chronicle*, and the anthology *Believing Everything*. She is the recipient of awards from the Minnesota State Art Board and The Loft, and is a former Bush Foundation Fellow. She teaches writing in Minneapolis, Minnesota, where she lives with her husband Timothy and their son Andre.